The Passage to Whole

You've heard the story in *People, Rolling Stone,* and the *New York Daily News....* Now read the book!

> *"Author Stephen King is giving back by donating thousands of dollars to ... Farwell Elementary School ... so the students in its Author Studies Program can publish two books. [The students] mapped out character development, plot, and overall story line with the help of another Maine author. The result is two books — an original and a sequel."* — CNN

You are about to read the original book. Be sure to look for the sequel, *Fletcher McKenzie and the Curse of Snow Falls.*

FLETCHER McKENZIE
AND
The Passage to Whole

GARY SAVAGE

**and students in the Farwell Elementary School
Author Studies Program**

KINGSLEY BOOKS
NASHVILLE, TENNESSEE

Fletcher McKenzie
And the Passage to Whole

Copyright © 2021 by Gary Savage

Fletcher McKenzie and the Passage to Whole is the first in a series of books about the adventures of Fletcher McKenzie, a boy living in Maine. The second book is *Fletcher McKenzie and the Curse of Snow Falls*

Contributing authors: Lily Beaulieu, Ella Leo, Hailey Labrecque, Liam Martin, Alex Breton, Jack Caron, and Charlotte Crowley. All these students participated in the Author Studies Program at Farwell Elementary School in Lewiston, Maine.

Published in Nashville, Tennessee, by Kingsley Books, Inc.,
P.O. Box 121584, Nashville, TN 37212

This is a revised edition of an earlier book by the same title published in March, 2016 by WestBow Press.

ISBN: 978-0-9888923-4-7 (paperback)
ISBN: 978-0-9888923-5-4 (ebook)

Cover painting by Frank Victoria

Cover design and typesetting by Bill Kersey, KerseyGraphics, Nashville, Tennessee

Printed in the United States of America

To Mom and Dad—
Love, Brub

Mollyockett was a real person. Her life struggles are not exaggerated. Tomhegan and Pidianiski are not fictional characters. Bethel, Maine, holds a Mollyockett Day celebration and parade every summer. The summer of the Covid19 pandemic was the only time the parade was cancelled.

CHAPTER 1

THREE AUNTS

THE THREE McKENZIE SISTERS WERE VERY COMFORTABLE INDEED. EVER since their brother, Aldous, was stricken with the virus that was sweeping the globe, they were happily busy running Cygnus Foods. Mysteriously, while recovering in the local hospital, Aldous lapsed into a coma and lay in bed at home due to an overwhelming surge with patients at the local hospital. Refinna McKenzie was now the president of the company Winola vice president, and Serena VP of marketing and sales. All three sisters were rotund with long brown hair worn in large buns at the top of their heads. They expressed their individuality through their eyeglasses. Serena preferred black, thin, square frames, which she felt gave her a retro urban look. Refinna always wore bright red glasses with a small row of glittering diamonds set atop each lens, and Winola always wore white bifocals with festive candy cane-striped arms, which served as a reminder of her favorite time of year.

Cygnus Foods had been started many years earlier by their great-grandfather, Thomas Gage McKenzie, a logger turned baker. Thomas named the company after having a vision in his sleep of the northern hemisphere constellation Cygnus on the exact day he baked his first loaf of Birch Bread, a healthy, whole wheat bread with a slight touch of Maine maple syrup. Thomas quickly outgrew his first small bakery in Pinhook and moved the company to nearby Ketchum, Maine. Cygnus quickly grew into one of New England's largest and most profitable food companies thanks to his healthy products, which included New England Oat Cakes, Maine Maple Honey Nut Bars, and Casco Bay Clam Cakes.

The McKenzie sisters had reached the height of success with control of Cygnus during the pandemic. Local people quietly wondered how they could be so different from the rest of the beloved McKenzie family. They spent endless hours reading the daily financial numbers e-mailed to them by the accounting department. They tightly controlled research and development and streamlined the company mandate to serve only one goal: to maximize profits by developing cheap food for the masses regardless of the nutritional content, a major break from tradition for the historically health-conscious company. All three were extremely pleased that Cygnus was considered an "essential" business during the lockdown and was allowed to stay open. Taking advantage of the now horrific unemployment numbers, they slashed wages and increased hours of it's employees knowing full well they had the upper hand.

None of the sisters had ever agreed with Aldous's emphasis on quality products and his generous employee benefits. "All a waste," was the oft-repeated phrase used by Serena, Winola, and Refinna. And for now they were free to do as they pleased and did not care how their decisions impacted others. Few knew, however, that they were not actual descendants of the McKenzie family. You see, when they were very young girls, their parents, both of whom worked for Cygnus, packed their bags in the middle of the night and fled town without telling anyone in their small community. Shockingly, the girls were left in the lobby of the local hospital with a letter that they be placed in the custody of the state of Maine and put up for adoption. The cruel act made headlines around New England and beyond. Horrified by the plight of the three small children, Fletcher's grandparents, quickly petitioned the courts and were granted a quick adoption. Aldous, as an only child, could not have been more thrilled to have three new sisters to play with.

The three sisters had a problem, however, and it was named Fletcher. When their great-grandfather established Cygnus, he established rules of succession in the articles of incorporation.

1. The company was to be placed in trust and always remain a private corporation run exclusively by the McKenzie family.
2. Control of the company would pass from the eldest child of each generation to his or her eldest child. This sole heir would control

100 percent of the company and receive 50 percent of the net profits, with the other 50 percent distributed equally among Thomas's other legal heirs, including the three sisters.

3. In the event that the sole heir was mentally or physically unable to run Cygnus, the duties of running the company would pass to the siblings of this heir equally until the eldest child of the incapacitated sole heir turned eighteen.

Fourteen-year-old Fletcher Gage McKenzie, the only child of Aldous and Muriel McKenzie, was the sole heir to Cygnus. Several months earlier Aldous had lapsed into a coma while recovering from the virus in the Covid ward at Ketchum Hospital. Doctors had yet to find the cause of his baffling condition.

Soon after her husband was struck down by the mysterious Covid ailment, Muriel took charge of Cygnus when the local court granted her temporary power of attorney for Aldous while he was incapacitated. But while visiting the depths of the jungles of South America while on a business trip for Cygnus, Muriel disappeared along with her assistant, Nimsy Cortland. After an extensive manhunt came up empty, they were presumed dead by misadventure. Why they were allowed to travel at all during the pandemic is still the talk of the town and provided regular fodder for gossip. Fletcher's three aunts immediately petitioned the courts for control of Cygnus and guardianship of Fletcher. They were begrudgingly granted both. However, the sisters gladly allowed Fletcher to remain living at his family home with Muriel's parents, Lucille and Edmond, who cared for the unresponsive Aldous. They never gave up hope.

If his father never recovered, Fletcher would take control of the company when he was eighteen, ending his aunts' temporary reign. However, the three sisters knew that if their brother remained incapacitated and Fletcher somehow never reached the age of eighteen, they would retain control of the massively profitable food company. Tensions ran high.

"So where is the little oddball today?" huffed Refinna during the sisters' morning coffee and snack cake break.

"Probably out in Muriel's garden," Serena responded, sitting six feet from her sisters while rolling her eyes.

"A total waste of space that garden is if you ask me," growled Winola. She stuffed a coconut cream muffin in her mouth. "*Mmm*, delicious … this will be a best seller. You ask me, if his mother hadn't insisted on going to the Quetzal during these unique times to inspect the chocolate cocoa beans herself, she would be here today to tend to her garden and that little brat."

"What a waste of time and money that trip was," exclaimed Refinna as she took a slurp of double-sweetened raspberry-flavored tea. "As if the Frizzle Bars needed expensive chocolate from the Quetzal." Picking her teeth, she added, "I always told Aldous that he should switch to a cheaper artificial chocolate. You ask me, once I made that change, the Frizzle Bars tasted the same."

Serena licked the frosting of a double maple chocolate Whoopie pie off her finger. "That was your best decision yet, Refinna. Your switch from Quetzal to artificial chocolate has increased the profits on the Frizzle Bars by a whopping 20 percent. Bravo, sis." Slowly, she slid her blue face mask away from the chocolate dessert.

"What do you think happened to her?" Winola whispered. Her medical mask now hung loosely from her left ear.

"Happened to who?" Serena asked, peering over her black glasses.

"Muriel," replied Winola in a quiet voice, her eyes darting toward the open door.

"For heaven's sake, why are you whispering? It's not like she's here anymore. Besides, the Quetzal is no place for a civilized lady in the first place. Especially during a world-wide pandemic. That retched jungle is crawling with anacondas, and the heat alone is dreadful enough, from what I've heard." Serena delicately picked crumbs off her dark sweater and ate them. "Look here. The past is the past. Don't dwell. I'm just amazed how much that odd-duck child is so much like her," she added with distain. "Just plum amazes me. Wouldn't surprise me if he pretends he has the virus to avoid working at the factory."

"Even has her annoying habit of sneezing whenever a bee comes too close. Whoever heard of such a thing?" Refinna exclaimed. "Aldous always said it was an allergic reaction. Clearly, it's all in his head. Allergic reaction," she said and snorted derisively.

"Only God knows what goes on inside that fourteen-year-old head," Winola chimed in. "Greatgranddaddy McKenzie would roll in his grave if he knew that Fletcher and his odd habits were going to inherit his company. I just can't stand to think about it." She closed her eyes in deep thought. "There must be a way."

Her sisters nodded in agreement.

"Anyway, to answer your question, Riffy," said Winola, "Fletcher said something about a hike up Mount Zircon with Quinn Caxton. Claims he would follow distancing guidelines."

"Are you kidding me?" shouted Refinna, nearly knocking over a pile of double maple chocolate Whoopie pies. "The Hackle Krackle mixing chambers are scheduled to be cleaned today. I clearly told him that. We can barely keep up with that product with all the schools closing early. How dare he! Just wait till I get my hands on that little snit. Did he clear this with either of you?" Refinna glared at her two sisters while restacking the Whoopie pies.

"Never mentioned it," snapped Serena.

Turning red, Winola glanced at Refinna and then looked down and added another heaping teaspoon of sugar to her tea. Silence filled the room

"Ahem," Refinna said and snarled, clearly annoyed by the lack of eye contact. "Did you approve this, Winny?"

"Well ... I, um—" The lenses of Winola's candy striped bifocals were steaming up from the perspiration on her face. "He asked me while I was tasting that new batch of peach-plum pops. My mind was elsewhere." Her eyes pleaded for sympathy from her furious sister.

"Well, the damage is done. The little manipulator clearly took advantage of you, Winny, when you were obviously preoccupied with more important matters. Serena, put up a sticky note to remind me to ground him when he returns," Refinna ordered.

Everyone knew no sticky note was needed to remind Refinna of anything when it came to Fletcher. But they were all distracted by the large plate of creamy cookies that a masked Odella, Aldous's trustworthy secretary, had cautiously delivered during the heated exchange.

"Oh, how glorious," Refinna exclaimed. "Doyle in the bakery just sent these scrumptious little darlings for the *tasting department*. Well, ladies, if I have my employee directory right, that would be us," she said and laughed deliriously. "The masses will be inhaling these scrumptious delights during *and* after the pandemic."

"Are those what I think they are?" squealed Serena, licking her lips. She quickly moved toward the table.

"You bet they are, sis!" snorted Refinna.

"Finally, the Hurly Burly Fudge Supreme Cookies. They look absolutely divine." Serena took a large bite. "I thought they'd never come. Took them four months to perfect the recipe."

"Four months?" Winola yelled in alarm. "That's two months longer than it should have. If it were up to me, I would dock Doyle's pay. His constant delays are costing this company way too much money. I don't buy his excuse that he's lost nearly half his staff to the virus. Plenty of eager people who would gladly work here. Especially now."

"And the way he always goes on about Aldous," Refinna chimed in while licking cream off her upper lip, unaware that she had some on the tip of her nose. "*Aldous would have done this. Aldous would have done that. Aldous would have focused on quality over cost.* Totally makes me sick."

"Why Aldous ever gave him a twenty year contract is beyond me," Serena said and shook her head. "Plenty of good bakers out there who would just die to work for us. Riffy, wipe your nose."

"Maybe Aquidneck Kitchen will convince him to work for them," Winola said. "They're running several ads in the *Food Daily*. One was for a pastry baker." She paused. "Shouldn't be too hard to fill *that* position with everyone losing their jobs."

Aquidneck Kitchen, a health food company based in Newport, Rhode Island, was bidding to buy the company's signature Birch Bread product line. The sisters were eager to sell—for the right price.

Winola moved toward the window. "I'll be glad when that bread is no longer part of this company. It's such a drag on the bottom line. What are it's numbers for this quarter, Serena?"

"Flat as ever. Still the most expensive product to make. But I honestly feel we can hold out for just a little longer. It'll give them a little more time to counter with a higher offer. With every restaurant practicing Covid guidelines, we can take advantage of it's slight surge in demand as more people are eating at home."

"What about that snag with the articles of incorporation stating that Birch Bread, even if sold, still be produced in the Mahoosuc Valley to save local jobs?" asked Refinna. "What did legal say?"

"I've made it clear that if they value their jobs, they'll find a way to make it happen," Winona reported. "I've no doubt they'll get it done. They were shaking in their boots."

"Good job, sis," replied Refinna. "We need to sell Birch Bread and get top dollar to finish building the Woomera chip factory." She held up a cream-filled cookie. "My, my … these are absolutely delicious. Clearly, this is the future of Cygnus." She shouted for Odella, who came running. "Call the Double Moose Coffee House and have them imme-diatley deliver three extra-large chocolate-caramel-mocha lattes with extra cream and extra sugar with whipped cream on top. And tell them not to forget those brown sugar sticks this time."

"Right away, Ms. McKenzie, they're only doing take-away for the next week," Odella said politely through her pink face mask. Walking out, she glanced up at the painted portraits adorning the office walls. Four generations of respected McKenzie men looked down on her, each one depicted in front of the original Birch Bread factory. *Clearly, Cygnus has a new focus*, she thought sadly. And that focus was not on healthy foods.

CHAPTER 2

MAZINGLA

AFTER RETURNING FROM HIS HIKE WITH QUINN, FLETCHER WAS IMME-diately grounded for a week.

"This will teach you to just take off like Columbus searching for America," Refinna yelled. She was so livid her bright red glasses were so steamed she could no longer see her nephew.

Fletcher sat in a chair on the front porch of his aunt's home. "But I was given permission by Aunt Winola," Fletcher explained, though cautiously. "She said I could go."

"Clearly, you took advantage of your poor aunt Winola. You know very well how absorbed she gets when she is doing her work. The tasting of the peach-plum pops is very serious work. Asking her to go on a ridiculous hike just when she is most vulnerable, shame on you, Fletcher. You're a master manipulator, if I must say so myself. Clearly, you get that from your mother. How many times do I have to tell you to always check in with me?"

"But you were participating in a virtual town meeting," he replied, knowing it was a lost battle.

"Clearly, perfect timing on your part. Clean the Hackle Krackle mixing chambers right now, and when you're finished with that, do the taffy-pulling machine after the store closes. That'll teach you to take advantage of us," Refinna said. "Now get going, and remember: Not. A. Spot. You hear me, Fletcher?"

"Yes, ma'am," he said avoiding looking at his aunt as he walked toward the steps.

As Fletcher walked off the porch, he heard, "Just like his mother, that kid. Doesn't deserve the McKenzie name."

━━

When he walked through his front door, Fletcher was greeted by the smell of spiced gingerbread and his maternal grandmother Lucille's famous venison pie recipe. It was good to be home.

Fletcher's father had built the massive house, which he personally designed after proposing to his mother. It was a classic New England colonial with a white exterior and black shutters. The comfortable house had seven bedrooms, five bathrooms, a drawing room, a wine cellar, a billiards room, a large kitchen with a breakfast nook, a formal dining room, an office for Aldous, and a den. (Muriel had always called the den the man cave because Fletcher and his father spent hours there watching sports.)

But Fletcher's favorite room was the root cellar, where his mother preserved the vegetables that she grew in her beloved walled garden. After Muriel disappeared, Fletcher used the root cellar as a meeting place for his secret society with his two best friends: Quinn Caxton and Camway Vincent. It was called Bacchus, named after the Greek and Roman god of wine and revelry, a name discreetly suggested by his Uncle Woodrow. It was a wonderful place to escape restrictive Covid restrictions.

The street where Fletcher lived, Sangar Drive, was located in the exclusive Rugby Hills neighborhood on the slopes of Mount Zircon, a popular ski resort. Quinn's family, who lived most of the year on Block Island, had built a vacation home four doors down from Fletcher. Quinn's father, Jefferson, owned Aquidneck Kitchen, the company trying to buy Birch Bread.

Camway's father, Chamberlain Vincent, was a state senator and owner of the popular Ketchum Ski and Boarding, which was located in an old livery building and heated by an enormous eighteenth-century brick fireplace. In the back room of the shop was an informal coffee room where they roasted their own beans. Chamberlain had left four of the horse stables intact and furnished them with old leather chairs he salvaged when the owners of the elegant Mahoosuc Hotel had renovated the building. A reservation for one of the stables—*the* place for coffee and conversation—was highly prized, especially during the winter months. This past winter, however, was completely different from the others. Due to the pandemic, the popular ski resort closed down three months early. Immediately, the economic pain reverberated throughout the entire community.

Even at her advanced age, Lucille kept the house on Sangar Drive immaculate and humming with activity. The kitchen always smelled of freshly baked pies, breads, and jams. She bathed Aldous every day and did everything possible to keep him comfortable. She did what she could to make Fletcher's life better and offset the terrible treatment he endured from his aunts. Each evening she would quietly retire to Muriel's garden in the backyard and pray that her daughter was somewhere out there alive and well. Muriel was her only child, and her mysterious disappearance had devastated both her and Edmond. They held it together for Fletcher's sake, knowing that if they didn't care for him, the horrible three aunts would have to. The pademic risks were high and they knew it. Without flinching, they both were willing to sacrifice their lives for Fletcher.

Fletcher walked into the kitchen. He was exhausted and filthy from cleaning the Hackle Krackle mixing chambers three times and the taffy-pulling machine twice.

"What happened to you?" Lucille asked when she saw him. "Are you all right?"

Fletcher told her about his day. When he was done, she asked gently, "Have you eaten, dear?"

"I had lunch at work, Grans," he said, avoiding Lucille's concerned stare.

"You must be starved." Her anger bubbled to the surface. "If I had my way, those three beasts would be locked up at the local zoo!" she spat as she started warming up a plate of venison pie.

Fletcher smiled and poured a glass of milk. "It's okay. I should've checked in with Aunt Refinna before I went on that hike."

"Wash your hands and throw your mask away, Fletch."

"Yes, ma'am. I'll check on Dad too."

His grandfather entered the kitchen from the back of the house just as Fletcher walked out. He was a portly, bald man with a handlebar moustache that was not totally gray. When he walked in, he called after his grandson. "Kind of late to be getting home, Fletch," he said.

"Oh, hush, Ed," Lucille whispered. "Those three monsters had him working all sorts of crazy hours. They feel the need to punish him for doing nothing wrong. They even grounded him for a week. Cryin' shame all this," Lucille seethed while blowing her nose with a worn red handkerchief. "I just can't stand it anymore. Isn't there anything we can do?"

"Really wish there was, Lucy. Poor kid. His father upstairs just lying there, and Muriel out there somewhere," he said waving his hand in front of him. "It breaks my heart too. Just be glad they allow him to live with us here. You really think about it, Luce, it could be worse. Much worse."

"I'm starved," Fletcher said with a smile as he joined them in the kitchen. He looked at his grandmother. "What's on the Birch Bread?"

"Your mother's favorite, rhubarb-blueberry jam. Made it the other day." Lucille busied herself clipping a bouquet of daisies she'd picked from the garden. Flowers helped calm her anger. "Apple pie's in the oven when you're done. Now say your prayers and enjoy."

Fetcher lowered his head, quickly said grace, and then dug in. A few minutes later, the phone rang in the foyer.

Edmond answered with a shout. "McKenzie residence!"

"Uhm, is Fletch there?"

"Who's calling?"

"Quinn."

"Fletch!" Edmond yelled. "It's Quinn!"

Fletcher came out and took the receiver from his grandfather. "Hey, Quinn, what's up?"

"Uh, why is your grandfather yelling at the top of his lungs?"

Fletcher laughed. "He lost his hearing aid yesterday while mowing the lawn. Really has no idea how loud he is when talking on the phone."

"Listen, I only have a sec," Quinn said hurriedly. "My parents are driving to Rhode Island tomorrow. I really don't want to go. They said if it's okay with your grandparents, I can stay with you. Let them know we've all quarantined for two weeks."

"I'm grounded for a week, so I think—"

"Grounded? Why?"

"Long story. I'll tell you later. Give me a sec. I'll ask." He went back to the kitchen. "Hey, Grans, can Quinn come over for the day tomorrow? It's okay with his parents and they've quarantined for two weeks."

Lucille was pulling an apple pie from the oven. "Quinn is welcome anytime, Fletch. You know that. Tell him to bring his mask."

Fletcher went back to the phone in the foyer. "It's okay. Grans said bring your mask. What time you coming?"

"First thing in the morning. I'll wake you up. Thanks, Fletch. Later."

"See ya tomorrow, Quinn."

On his way back to the kitchen table, Fletcher tripped on his untied boots and almost knocked the pie off the side of the counter.

"Now that would have been a disaster, Fletch," Lucille said, steadying the hot pie with a blue and white oven glove.

"Sorry, Grans. I'm famished," he said, scooping a piece of venison pie into his mouth.

"Edmond, I have a quilting class in the morning. Can you watch Fletcher and Quinn for a few hours?" Lucille asked, peering over her spectacles. "Relax, there's only three of us and we're staying far apart."

"Would love to," replied Edmond. "Should be a good day to help me weed your mother's garden, Fletch." They both knew that outdoor activities was the best way to avoid contracting the virus.

Fletcher looked up and smiled. "Awesome. Maybe we can find some crawlers for fishing."

"Mazingla for lunch tomorrow," said Lucille, winking at Edmond.

"Awesome! Can Camway join us? He loves Mazingla."

"You can call him in the morning and invite him over," replied Lucille as she wiped off the granite counter.

Mazingla was a dark stew poured over mashed potatoes. It was a concoction created by Aldous when Fletcher was seven years old. He had simply mixed leftovers together, and to make it more appealing to Fletcher, he had named his creation Mazingla.

"What's Mazingla?" Fletcher had asked when his father first mentioned it.

"It's a magical stew created by Mollyockett over one hundred years ago to help the people of Maine grow strong muscles. They were fighting a war and needed them to help win."

"Wow! Did it work?"

"Sure did! Won it a lot quicker than anyone ever expected."

That day Fletcher ate three servings of Mazingla, and after that, it became his favorite meal. He would flex in front of the mirror every time he ate it.

After his father was stricken, the meal became a weekly ritual at 1942 Sangar Drive. It was a reminder of better, happier times.

Lucille picked up his empty plate. "I made sure to follow your father's recipe, so it should be perfect. They'll be plenty for the four of you, and clearly, you all need work in the muscle department. You ready for that pie?"

"Well, mine grew a lot today while working at the factory," Fletcher said as he pulled up his right sleeve and flexed. "Look."

"My, my, lots of growth there. You get the smallest serving of Mazingla tomorrow," Edmond said with a wink.

"You're kidding, right?" Fletcher asked.

"Course he is," Lucille said and laughed. "You can have as much as you like. You'll need every bit to help your grandfather in that garden tomorrow. Land sakes, those weeds grow faster and faster each year."

Edmond looked at his grandson. "You reading to your pop tonight?"

Suddenly Fletcher looked deflated and exhausted. "For a few minutes. I just wish he could hear me."

"I have a feeling that he can hear every word you say," Edmond said.

"You really think so? It's just that he always looks the same."

"Doesn't mean he can't hear you, Fletch. You think God heard the prayers you said just a few minutes ago? And he's all the way up there in heaven."

"You're positive I can't give it to him?"

"Every scientific study says it's an impossibility for him to contract the virus again. I read somewhere that reading also stimulates his brain. A good thing, Fletch, especially for your father. You know how much he loved to read his books."

Lucille sat next to Fletcher. "What are you reading to him now?"

Fletcher smiled. "The biography of Caravaggio."

"Who in the world is Caravalaggio?" Edmond asked, intentionally butchering the name.

Fletcher laughed. "This Italian painter Mom and Dad liked. Mom gave Dad the book as a birthday gift last year." He looked down at the floor, avoiding eye contact with his grandparents, not wanting them to see his despair.

While visiting the National Gallery of Ireland in Dublin they had fallen in love with *The Taking of Christ*, one of Caravaggio's most popular paintings. Muriel secretly purchased the book at the museum store and gave it to Aldous as a birthday gift four months before he tested postive. On the back cover she'd written, "Life without you would be unthinkable. Life with you has been a most precious gift. Love, Muriel."

"You know, he killed a guy," Fletcher said quietly.

"Who killed who?" blurted Edmond.

Laughing, Fletcher said, "Calm down. The painter Caravaggio killed this other man in a fight and had to flee from his home. They wanted to cut his head off."

"Must be all that red wine Italians drink," Edmond declared. He stood and headed toward the back door. "Reminds me of Anthony Biggio while growing up …" He trailed off as he walked out the door.

As Fletcher walked upstairs he could hear his grandmother in the kitchen. "Killed a man, and they still hang his art in a gallery! Land sakes, what on earth is this world coming to?"

Fletcher quietly entered his father's room and looked around. Nothing had changed. The tick-tock of the six-foot, antique, walnut grandfather clock. The large Persian rug on the floor that his mother had purchased while they had been in Egypt. The ornate, four-post, oak bed. The warm and comfortable lighting from the two Tiffany-style table lamps. The numerous portraits of famous Mainers that Aldous had collected, hanging on the walls in well-positioned locations. These Mainers included Margaret Chase Smith, Joshua Chamberlain, Mollyockett, Hannibal Hamlin, and Henry Knox. There were also portraits of Thomas, Rutherford, Jonathan, and Aldous McKenzie. Suspended above a walnut dresser hung the largest painting in the room, a portrait of Muriel sitting in front of a fireplace with a smiling ten-month-old Fletcher Gage McKenzie sitting on her lap.

"Hey, Dad," said Fletcher in a low voice as he approached the bed. Aldous was in the same position he'd been in yesterday and the day before. In fact, every day since Ketchum Hospital was forced to release Aldous due to severe overcrowding caused by the pandemic. The only change was his nightshirt, which Lucille changed on a daily basis after the sponge bath. He was lying on his back, eyes closed. His chest rose slowly with each steady breath. An intravenous IV, his only source of nourishment and his lifeblood, lead from his arm to a clear bag hanging from a metal infusion pole. It was changed by a visiting nurse several times a day.

Fletcher sighed as he sat down in the leather chair. "You ready for a little Caravaggio? Only going to read a few pages tonight. Aunt Refinna worked me to death today. I cleaned the Hackle Krackle mixing chambers and the blueberry taffy-pulling machine. Everything looks good. Everyone misses having you around. Dad, I hope this is over soon. They are changing everything at Cygnus. Everything you worked for. We all hope you get better."

Fletcher picked up the book and started to read. Then he abruptly stopped. He had the odd sense that he wasn't alone. His eyes slowly scanned the room, and the hairs on the back of his neck stood up. Something had changed since he'd last sat in the chair. One side of his mind told him to run out and not look back. The other part, the curious part, told him to investigate. As he searched the room, his eyes settled on the Mollyockett portrait. Something was different. He rose and slowly approached the antique painting. He read the brass plate at its base, which said, "Molly Ockett (Marie Agathe) 1740–1816."

The painting featured a tall, strong-looking woman with long black hair. She had a prominent nose and a square jaw. She was wearing multicolored, beaded moccasins; a tan dress that hung to her calves; and bright red stockings that were decorated with dyed porcupine quills. On her head was a man's black stovepipe hat. Long silver earrings laced with red feathers hung to just above her shoulders.

He studied the portrait. *Hadn't she been facing the other way?* Fletcher thought. *But how can that be? What the—* He stood transfixed. *I'm positive her earrings had blue feathers.*

"Fletch, you almost done reading?" Edmond called from the bottom of the stairs. "Busy day tomorrow. And you need to call Camway early before his parents make other plans. You know how busy those Vincents are."

"Just finishing up, Gramps. Give me a sec."

Fletcher continued to stare at the portrait of Mollyockett. "They must have bought another painting and replaced the old one," he whispered to himself.

As he walked out of the room, Fletcher had a sinking feeling something was not right.

CHAPTER 3

LOBSTER OMELETS

Quinn peeked into Fletcher's bedroom. "Hey, Fletch, you up?"

Not getting any response, he walked over to the dark green, domed tent pitched in the middle of the room. Quinn unzipped the flap and crawled in.

"Fletch, wake up!"

Fletcher yawned and unzipped his thick sleeping bag. "What time is it?"

"Almost seven.

"Quinn, you're crazy." Fletcher lay back down.

"Come on. Get up. Your grandmother's making lobster omelets and blueberry pancakes. Let's *go!*" Quinn tugged on his friend's arm as he backed out of the tent.

"All right, give me a sec." Fletcher rubbed his eyes and removed his ear buds. He'd fallen asleep with them on again and drained the battery to his cell phone.

After crawling out of the tent, he pulled on gray sweatpants and brown leather boots. "Had a crazy dream last night. I kinda wish I'd never fallen asleep."

"Dreaming 'bout Cicely again? Bet you were holding her hand while jumping into Frenchman's Hole like last time," Quinn said while curling a ten-pound kettlebell. Frenchman's Hole was a popular swimming hole at the foot of the Mahoosuc Mountains that featured a twenty-foot drop into a clear, swirling pool of frigid water. Once in, the only way out was a harrowing climb up a steep, fifty-foot incline on the opposite side of the river. Then to make it back across, you had to carefully navigate submerged rocks or cascade back over the falls.

"Please, hold my hand while I jump. Frenchman's is soooo scary. Oh, help me Fletch," Quinn said in a high-pitched voice, mocking how Cicely had flirted with Fletcher when they'd gone to the swimming hole on previous visits.

"Shut up, flatlander."

"Oh, Fletcher, will you be my boyfriend? I love you soooo much. Will you kiss me?"

Fletcher finished lacing his leather boots and approached Quinn. "You're just jealous that none of the girls look at you. Why would they, Rhody Boy?" He abruptly pushed Quinn into a pile of dirty laundry in the corner and then ran out of the room, laughing.

The boys sprinted into the kitchen, still pushing and shoving each other playfully.

"Morning, you two," Edmond said as he banged on the table the hearing aid he'd just found in a planter.

"Lobster omelets and blueberry pancakes coming up," Lucille said and smiled as she poured two large glasses of skim milk.

Edmond held up his coffee mug, his face now buried in the paper. "Top me off, Lucy, will ya?"

She picked up the coffeepot and refilled the mug. "Careful, Ed, or you'll spill. Again." Lucille put the pot down and went back to the stove, which was built into a black slate island in the center of the kitchen. "These are made with almond flour, Fletch, just like your mom always insisted on. Keeps you fit as a fiddle."

She poured out four perfect pancakes on the sizzling griddle located between the burners and then spooned the last of the batter out of the bowl, which landed haphazardly on the griddle. Lucille cocked her head and smiled. "This pancake looks just like a baby seal."

Edmond glanced over, squinted, shook his head, and went back to his paper. "You've done lost your mind. Keep this up, you'll end up at Mayville Acres sooner than you expect."

"Oh, hush, Ed. No difference than you telling me that rock you found yesterday in Muriel's garden looked like Connecticut. Looked more like Florida, you want my opinion."

"Well, be careful. Don't want to burn that baby seal, or PETA will come confiscate the grill. And rightfully so." He chuckled.

Fletcher rolled his eyes at their affectionate bickering.

Lucille looked at her grandson, who looked rested. "By the way, Fletch, don't mention that tent in your room to any of your aunts. You know how they are," she said, flipping the seal pancake.

"I know. Kinda glad they're too big to climb the stairs," Fletcher said and laughed. He kept his eyes fixed on the syrup as it flowed onto the pancakes on his plate.

"Hush! Enough of that talk, Fletch," his grandmother admonished him mildly while serving the rest of the pancakes. "Sounds like you're already in the doghouse."

Edmond peered over the top of the paper and winked at the boys.

Fletcher reached for the antique demijohn that contained warm maple syrup. Aldous had always been particular when it came to maple syrup. "You can always tell Maine syrup from the others. Look at the rich amber color," he'd say with pride.

"These pancakes are awesome, Mrs. Blay. Best I ever had." Quinn illustrated his sentiment by stuffing a large piece of pancake into his mouth, oblivious to the syrup dripping down the front of his Ketchum Katchers shirt.

"Please, call me Grans, Quinn. You know that." She slid the seal pancake onto his plate. "And both of you save some room for the omelets that are warming in the oven."

Edmond turned the page of his paper and read with interest. "That time of year already. The Ketchum Katchers are having their annual fundraiser for the diabetic society. It's mostly virtual this year and once again hosted by Woodrow. *Virtual!* Goodness how times have changed." He lowered the paper and looked at Lucille. "We have any plans for next Friday? Always a good cause. Says here a only small group will be invited to the inn in keeping with state restrictions. It appears everything is last minute as things are constantly changing."

"Honestly, what a question. You know how upset Woodrow would get if we didn't participate. I'll call him later and see if we can do anything to help. I just hope he's more—how should I say?—selective about who he invites this year."

Woodrow McKenzie was Aldous's eighty-year-old uncle. He owned the popular McKenzie's Inn on Mount Zircon. He was an even-tempered, white-haired, frail man, and he always wore a periwinkle blue sweater vest. Woodrow was also one of the most beloved and charitable men in the Mahoosuc Valley. His inn was famous throughout New England for its warm hospitality. When checking in, each guest was greeted with warm cider and homemade Paw-Paw bars, which were made with whole oats, Maine blueberries, nuts, and honey. Woodrow was now busier than ever. Finally, after five long months, the governor of Maine had suddenly announced hotels and inns could reopen. These openings, however, mandated a plan to reopen be submitted to the state and required severe pandemic restrictions. He was unsure if his business could survive.

Just as Lucille expertly slid the omelets off the sheet pan and onto an elaborate serving platter, there was a knock at the front door.

"Must be Camway," Fletcher said. "I'll get it."

"Mornin', Mr. and Mrs. Blay," said Camway, following Fletcher to the table.

"How many times I need to tell you it's *Grans* and *Gramps*?" Lucille said and smiled. "You hungry? Plenty of omelets left. And you can take that mask off. If it's my time, it's my time."

"Enough of that." Edmond quickly chimed in. "You know how I feel about talk like that. Lucille ignored the exchange. She was too busy doing what she loved.

Quinn reminded everyone of a California surfer with his lanky posture, blond hair, and blue eyes. Camway, however, was his opposite. Descended from the first African-American family to settle the valley a century ago, he was tall, muscular, and athletic. His dark complexion, dark eyes, and black hair earned him the title of *best looking* by his fellow students.

Lucille set a plate of food and a glass of milk in front of Camway. The conversation died as the boys concentrated on eating. When the

phone rang, Edmond motioned for Fletcher to stay seated, and then he
went to answer it.

"McKenzie residence. Edmond speaking. How may—"

"Put Fletcher on the phone right now, Edmond. *Right now*, do
you hear?"

"Well, good morning to you too, Refinna."

"Don't you play games with me. You know I can change the arrangement. Just keep talking. *Put Fletcher on right now.*"

Edmond held the receiver away from his ear and shook his head
dismay. He could never get used to the sisters' bad attitude. He regained
his composure and then answered calmly, "No need to yell, Refinna.
Fletcher is not available right now."

"Well, you'd better make him available *immediately*. Unless he's on
Mars, he's available. *Put. Him. On!*"

"Hold on. I'll get him," he responded softly and set the receiver down.

"Mean as a rabid caribou, that woman," he muttered on his way back
to the kitchen.

"Don't know what you did, Fletch. But your aunt Refinna's on the
phone and she's the angriest I've heard her in a long time. And that says
a lot." He looked at his grandson with sad eyes. "You ask me, she just
added a few more rooms to that doghouse you're in."

"I have no idea what I could have done." There was fear and anxiety
in his voice. An uncomfortable silence filled the room as he walked out.

"Hi, Aunt Ref—"

"Don't you *hi* me, you condescending little … where is that belt?"

"What belt?"

"Don't you dare play games with me. You know what I'm talking
about. I know you did it on purpose. How dare you. *Where is that belt!*"
She was too busy screaming to notice the muted *click* as Edmond picked
up the den phone to listen in.

"I really don't know what you're talking about, Aunt Refinna. Honest,
you have to believe me," he pleaded.

"The belt to the taffy-pulling machine, you idiot. The store opens
in thirty minutes. Oberon and Ogden have combined all the ingredients, which is now hardening because you've lost the belt. You

were the last one near that machine."

Fletcher's mind raced back to when he cleaned the machine. "I have no idea where it could be."

"You'd better get an idea. It's quite obvious you did it on purp—" She was interrupted by a voice in the background. "Ogden's found it. Wait till I get my hands on you!" she yelled and slammed down the receiver.

Fletcher stood silent, shocked at his aunt's naked hatred.

"Let it go, Fletch." Edmond said sympathetically into the phone. "Don't let it bother you."

Fletcher hung up and went back to the kitchen.

"Fine way to start a day," Edmond said when he got back to the table

Lucille said nothing and sat down. Refinna always had the last word, and everyone knew it.

"I know I put it on," Fletcher said. "I remember how difficult it was to stretch it."

Edmond ruffled Fletcher's hair. "I believe you."

"So do I, hon," Lucille chimed in.

Edmond smiled warmly at the boys, belying the anger coursing through his body. He had never been this enraged before. His eyes met Lucille's, and they could read each other's minds. They were both well aware of the arrangement, but something had to be done. Their number-one assignment was to protect their grandson, and nothing was going to stop them.

CHAPTER 4

MOLLYOCKETT

THE WEEK PASSED RELATIVELY QUICKLY, EVEN THOUGH FLETCHER HAD to spend three miserable hours each morning working at Cygnus under the watchful and condescending eyes of his aunts. To make matters worse, he was forced to wear a heavy black mask with *Frizzle Bars* stitched in it's center. It was impossible to breathe and every minute felt like an hour. At breakfast on Friday, Edmond read the paper and drank cup after cup of coffee as usual. Grans seemed preoccupied as she filled Fletcher's bowl with two large scoops of homemade granola.

"You ready for Camway and Quinn tonight?" she asked. "I picked up some extra hand sanitizer for the tent. Don't forget to use it."

"I've been looking forward to tonight all week."

"I hope that tent holds," said Edmond, peering over the top of the paper. "I think it's the same one I had when I was your age."

"Lights out at ten p.m., Fletch, you hear." Lucille coated a cast-iron pan with olive oil. "My window's open. I can hear every word out there."

"Who you kidding?" Edmond said and chuckled, setting down the paper. "You can't even hear the television from two feet when it's turned up loud." He looked over at Fletcher. "You almost ready?" he asked.

Fletcher nodded and took his dishes to the sink. Lucille kissed him on the head.

"Try to stay on their good side, honey. I promise it will get better." Without looking at Edmond, she left the room. Silence filled the house.

Edmond drove them to Kemo's Store on Main Street. He ordered a black coffee for himself and a banana smoothie for Fletcher—their daily ritual. As he did every day, after finishing his smoothie, Fletcher walked the short distance to Cygnus while his grandfather stayed and socialized with the other customers. The chatty group was split into two groups. Those with masks and those without. It was a debate that unfortunately now became a political statement nationwide. Edmond wore his mask and kept a safe distance from everyone. He in no way wanted to carry the virus home to his beloved Lucy. He knew her medical history.

As Fletcher walked, he thought about that night's sleepover in the backyard, which lifted his spirits. This was the first time the three boys would be sleeping an entire night in the tent without adult supervision, and he was looking forward to the adventure with anticipation.

When he walked into Refinna's office, she was sitting at her desk, arms folded like a large pretzel over her stomach. "You're two minutes late," she barked.

"I was helping Odella carry packages to the mailroom, Aunt Ref—"

"Clearly, a ploy to avoid work. You just don't get it, do you?" she said angrily, gently stirring a large cup of creamy coffee.

"I guess not," he muttered.

She glared at him, causing her red glasses to tilt down on the left side of her face. "I don't like that tone you're using. Clear as day, you have no respect for your elders. Have you *ever* done anything right in your miserable life, Fletcher?"

Fletcher stood motionless, knowing whatever he said would set her off even more.

"The fact that you're still standing here tells me that you have no intention of working at all today. Get working. *Scram!*" Her masculine voice boomed so loud it caused the items on her shelf to rattle. "And don't forget to wear your *Frizzle Bars* mask. You hear me?"

Fletcher started to leave and then turned timidly toward his aunt. "Can I work with Oberon and Ogden greeting customers at the store today? I can keep the hand sanitizer filled."

"You want to greet customers?" Enraged, she broke open a Tweedle Cake package and popped it into her mouth in a single bite. "We need to entice them, not scare them away," she said sarcastically. "*Get out right now.*"

Fletcher picked up his backpack and ran out the door.

"He's just like Quill," Refinna grumbled, opening a second Tweedle Cake package. "Lazy, good-for-nothing know-it-all."

Quill Foster was Refinna's ex-husband. They'd been married for five miserable years before parting ways. Her sons, Oberon and Ogden, fourteen-year-old twins, were a lasting legacy of the failed marriage. Doted on by their mother, the two overweight teens had bright red, curly hair and freckled faces. They worked as hard as they could to not work at all, but Refinna was blind to their laziness and always made excuses for it.

Winola waddled into the office. "Talking to yourself again, Riffy?"

Refinna crumpled the plastic pastry bag with a deep sigh. "Fletcher was late for work," she said. "And as usual, he was trying to avoid work and mouthing off." She handed Winola a small plate with two cream-filled Tweedle cakes.

"Oh, thank you." Winola quickly stuffed one of the cakes into her mouth. "Spoiled rotten, that kid," she said. "Ed and Lucy just lets him do as he pleases. Can only imagine what goes on at that house."

Refinna poured Winola a cup of coffee. "Any news on the sale of Birch Bread?"

"Serena's with legal right now. They provided the broker with six months of financial statements. Aquidneck Kitchen has two weeks to accept the offer."

"Can't imagine them not. It's a perfect fit," Refinna said. She glanced out the window and saw Fletcher lean his rake against a nearby tree and start to walk off. She heaved herself out of her chair and threw open the window.

"Still lounging around, I see," she called out. "I'm sick of this."

Fletcher stopped and turned toward her voice. "Sorry, I forgot to bring the garbage bags with me, so I was just going to get th—"

"Clearly, another one of your ploys to get out of work. I'm watching you, young man. *Don't you underestimate me!*" She yelled furiously and then slammed down the window. "Let's go, Winny. The pastry depart-ment has a new filling they want us to sample."

—

The weather was ideal that evening as Quinn, Camway, and Fletcher watched Edmond cook burgers on the grill and turn foil-wrapped corn on the cob with large metal tongs.

"Fletch, you got a sec? I need a hand," Lucille yelled from an open window.

"Be right back," he told his friends.

Fletcher sprinted toward the house. The large grandfather clock chimed six times as he ran up the stairs toward his father's room.

"What do you need, Grans?"

"Help hold your father up while I change his bedding, will you?" she asked. "These sheets are so difficult to put on." She grunted, lifting a corner of the mattress.

Familiar with the routine, Fletcher put a new mask on and gently pulled his father into a sitting position as Lucille gently slid a clean sheet under him. Fletcher studied his father's peaceful face and then looked up at his grandmother.

"Thanks for letting us camp out tonight, Grans," he said.

"Couldn't ask for a better night," Lucille replied. "You should be able to see the stars beautifully!" She paused and patted the clean sheet. "Tomorrow's the annual cleanup at Hamlin Park, remember? You boys need to be rested, you hear? Everyone's up at the crack of dawn."

"I know. Lights out at ten. I promise."

"The Vincents and Parkers are meeting us in the parking lot first thing in the morning," Lucille said. She took the soiled sheets and stuffed them into a wicker laundry bin. "It will be a much smaller gathering this year than most. The state of Maine only allows for groups of fifty people or less at any one gathering. Don't want to upset Augusta. They ought to be *helping* us during these times, not *hurting* us. If I had my way, the entire state would be invited today. This is all a bunch of crap."

"Are the Parkers coming?" Fletcher asked. *It's amazing his grandparents were happily married as long as they've been.*

"Everyone's coming. Even Cicely." Lucille smiled and winked at him. "I baked blueberry almond granola bars for the entire group. We'll need them for extra energy. It'll be a long day."

"I remember last year. Wait. What the—" Fletcher gasped, staring at the wall behind the bed.

Lucille looked up from adjusting the homemade afghan at the foot of the bed. "What the what, Fletch?" she asked.

Regaining his composure, he shook his head. "Nothing. I thought I saw a bird almost fly into the window."

Lucille bent over and whispered into Aldous's ear, "I hope you get better, dear." She straightened her mask, felt his forehead, then pressed her hand against her rumbling stomach. "Let's go eat. I'm starved." She turned to see Fletcher staring warily at the portrait of Mollyockett.

"Something wrong?" she asked.

He tore his eyes away from the portrait, "No, I just want to spend a few minutes with dad if that's okay."

"Okay, but hurry up. I heard your grandfather yelling that the food was getting cold. Don't forget to wash your hands for at least twenty seconds when you finish here."

After Lucille left the room, Fletcher edged closer to the large portrait. He traced his fingers lightly over the rough paint. Once again, the portrait had changed. Mollyockett was still wearing the black stovepipe hat. But now she had on a dark brown, cowhide dress decorated with ornamental black-and-white porcupine quills in a zigzag pattern. Her long silver earrings now had bright blue feathers. The beads decorating her moccasins had changed from multicolored to red, and they matched her heavy stockings perfectly. Most startling, she was now facing the front windows, the opposite direction she'd been in the other day. He was sure of it.

"How?" he whispered. Again, Fletcher gently rolled his fingers across the centuries-old paint. He studied the lines in her weathered face. "Are you for real, or am I crazy?"

It was as if her eyes had come alive and were staring directly at him.

"This is just crazy," he exclaimed as he quickly moved toward the door, almost knocking over one of the ornate Tiffany-style lamps.

Later that evening the three boys settled into the tent after spending two hours with Edmond stargazing and searching for various constellations. The highlight of the evening was seven shooting stars. Each time Fletcher wished for his father's recovery and his mother's safe return.

"What you wish for on that last one?" Camway asked as he crawled into a heavy, plaid sleeping bag.

Fletcher zipped the circular door to the tent closed. "None of your business."

"Bet it was about Cicely," Quinn teased. *"Oooooh, Fletcher, I miss you! Do you think of me when you stare at the stars?"* He jokingly threw a pillow at Fletcher.

"Shut up, Quinn. You're not careful a sidehill badger will attack you in your sleep," Fletcher warned.

"A what?"

"A sidehill badger. They eat people only from Massachusetts and Rhode Island."

"Shut up. Are they for real?"

"Only here in Maine, so I'd be careful if I was you."

Quinn tried to laugh it off, but as a native Rhode Islander, he was always a little timid when it came to the great forests and wildlife in Maine. Suddenly and without warning, Fletcher was on him.

Camway backed against the far back wall of the tent, laughing and hitting Quinn with a pillow whenever his head popped up from under Fletcher's hold.

Winded, Quinn struggled for freedom. "Get off me, Fletch. I can't breathe. I give up," he howled.

"Boys, that's enough! One more peep and you'll all be sleeping inside the house, you hear me?" yelled Lucille from her open bedroom window. "Sanitize those hands before you zip up!"

Immediately, the boys settled down.

"Sorry, Grans," Fetcher yelled back. "We'll be quiet. Promise."

Ten minutes later all three boys were zipped inside their sleeping bags.

"You guys want to hear something weird?" Fletcher whispered while adjusting his hooded sweatshirt.

"What? A sidehill badger is inside your sleeping bag, Maine boy?" Quinn joked.

"Shut up, Quinn. You almost wet yourself a few minutes ago, so I wouldn't talk," Camway said and snickered.

"Seriously, it's really weird."

"What is?" Camway asked uneasily.

"My dad has a haunted picture in his bedroom."

Silence filled the tent for a moment before Quinn laughed. "Right!"

"How do you know it's haunted?" Camway whispered, swallowing hard.

"Don't believe him," Quinn said, laughed again, and then he threw a pillow at Fletcher. "You're crazier than your cousins."

"Shut up, Quinn," Fletcher hissed, "or my grandmother will make us sleep inside." A small, battery-powered lantern illuminated Fletcher's serious face. "Cross my heart, hope to die, there is a haunted picture in my father's bedroom." He spent the next several minutes telling them both about Mollyockett's mysterious portrait.

When he was done, Camway was definitely spooked, but Quinn was thoughtful. "My mom paints," he said, "and she told me once something about how lighting in a room can make a painting look different. Maybe it's the light making it seem like the painting is changing."

"This is a lot different than a change in lighting, Quinn. She actually changed her clothes and the direction she was facing. No lighting would do that."

"Is that the same Mollyockett they named Mollyockett Day after?" Camway asked in a hushed voice.

"I assume so. Can't be too many people named Mollyockett," Fletcher reasoned. "Plus my dad only hangs pictures of famous Mainers in his bedroom."

"Let's go see it," Quinn suggested, completely intrigued.

Camway slid farther into his bag. "No way. I'm not going anywhere. If that *painting* doesn't get us, your grandmother will."

"We can't anyway," Fletcher said. "I'm not supposed to let anyone into his room."

"How's he gonna know?" Quinn asked. He crawled out of his sleeping bag and stood up. "No one will hear us this time of night." He unzipped the tent door. "Look, your grandparents' light is out."

Camway's eyes were round pools of terror at the thought of facing a haunted painting or getting caught. "What if she attacks us? Count me out." He zipped his heavy green sleeping bag over his head.

Quinn prodded him with his foot. "Come on, Camway. It's only a painting."

"You're crazy," whispered Camway, now huddled against the tent's far wall.

"Cam, you're an insult to Bacchus. Well, I'm going with or without you guys. I know where his room is." Quinn crouched in front of the tent door and looked back at Fletcher. "You coming or not?"

Fletcher unzipped his bag. "Okay. But if my grandmother hears us, I'll be grounded all summer."

"Wait!" Camway croaked. "I'm not staying here alone." Scrambling from the clutches of his sleeping bag, he ran to catch up with the others.

"You just had to throw Bacchus in, didn't you?" muttered Fletcher.

As they approached the house, Fletcher looked for any sign that his grandmother was still awake.

"Are you sure this is okay?" Camway asked nervously as they entered the house.

"*Shh!*" the other two boys responded.

Following Fletcher, they moved slowly toward the stairs. "Here, put these on," Fletcher commanded, handing them blue masks that sat in a small pile on a side table. The only sound inside the house was the constant *tick-tock, tick-tock* of the grandfather clock from inside Aldous's room. A floor board slightly creaked as Quinn entered the master bedroom.

Fletcher glared at him and put his index finger on his mask. They inched their way toward the back wall. With every step, they nervously glanced at Aldous. They finally stood in front of the painting.

"This is it," whispered Fletcher, who was still looking at his dad.

Camway stood on his toes to get a better look. "Looks normal to me, Fletch."

Fletcher turned to gaze up at the painting and gasped.

"What?" Quinn asked sharply, startled by Fletcher's reaction.

"This is crazy." He pointed at Mollyockett's silver earrings. "When I was in here earlier, those feathers were blue."

"You sure?" asked Camway. He placed his hand on the wall below the painting to help steady his legs.

"Maybe it's one of those reversible paintings," suggested Quinn. He reached out to gently touch Mollyockett's face. "Feels like real paint."

"It looks like she's staring right at me," Camway whispered nervously.

"I know," Fletcher agreed. "I had that same feeling earlier today."

Quinn stared at her eyes and swallowed. "It's like she's alive." He took a step closer. "Let's take it down and see what's on the back. Could be a rotating painting."

"What!" Camway gasped lowly.

Fletcher nodded in agreement while glaring at Camway. "Okay, just be quiet. We're dead if my grandmother finds us here. Quinn, help me take it down. Cam, grab that quilt over there and put it on the floor."

Quietly and carefully they lowered the painting and laid it facedown on the ornate quilt. The portrait's backing was comprised of three old wooden boards. Small, rusted nails held the canvas to the boards. A twisted, crude wire was attached to the back of the spectacular frame by two small hooks that appeared as old as the nails tacked to the painting. All that was expected.

However, they didn't expect the faded envelope hanging from the middle of the center board.

"What is that?" Camway asked.

"*Shh!* You are going to wake my grandparents up," Fletcher whispered.

Camway gently pulled the envelope off the board and held it out. "Let's see what's inside."

Fletcher took the envelope. On the front, visible in the moonlight illuminating the room, they could see the name *Jackson G. McKenzie* written in elaborate cursive.

"Who's he?" whispered Quinn.

Fletcher shrugged. "No idea. Must be related though." He glanced toward his father and then nervously opened the envelope. He carefully pulled out the folded piece of paper inside, which crackled as Fletcher unfolded it, releasing a slight musty scent.

"What's it say?" asked Quinn.

Fletcher scanned the words and then held out the paper for the others to read.

> *Jackson. The time of the Wabanaki is complete. As we prepare to meet one final time, remember that knowledge is power. Use it well, and always protect the passage.*
>
> *—M*

The three boys studied the words, saying nothing. In the background, the clock continued to tick in rhythm with Aldous's slow, steady breathing.

Quinn looked up. "So is she *M*?" he asked.

Fletcher glanced at the painting. "Maybe."

"What's *protect the passage* mean?" Camway wondered. He stood close to Fletcher, still creeped out.

"I've no idea what any of it means?" He turned the paper over. "Wait. There's more. Look at this."

They crowded together and read the cryptic poem.

> *When the moon is full past sun's high*
> *A chief will sing the harvest cry*
> *In Wabanaki north, green leaves blow*
> *In the valley, both rivers flow*
> *Three moons after sowing so soon*
> *The crescent will glow in the moon*
> *A path from the north, one from the west*
> *meet at the spot where eagles nest*
> *A symbol on the grave tells a sign*
> *Said in the light, before dark's time*
> *Patient one soul, it moves the moon*
> *But closes again, ever so soon*
> *For it is here, the stone opens again*
> *Toward the maker of life, the passage bends*
> *Go forth, selected soul*
> *Make your way forward, into Whole*

If you're not there, need not worry
Your blood can be you, but they must hurry
Beware the beast, for if knowledge fails
It is certain Kozart prevails
In the face of danger, look for the squire
For it is he who can guide you through water and fire
When seeking his help, hold tightly the staff
Yell his name to the creator, need not laugh
Be ever aware, even with time
You lose the staff, he'll commit a crime
The first sign of trouble, ergot will double
Even the hole will bubble and bubble
This passage is north, the other south
Keep guard selected soul, build your house

Quinn was awestruck. "Sounds like a code or something."

"Bet it's a magical poem. I read about them somewhere," Camway said.

"Can I hold it? Please?" pleaded Quinn.

"We'll look at it in the tent," Fletcher promised. "We need to get out of here. Quinn, help me put this back on the wall."

Silently, they restored the painting to its original position, refolded the quilt, and quietly returned to the tent. They had no idea that what they'd just discovered would change their lives dramatically and forever.

CHAPTER 5

BLUEBERRIOLA SUGARY
SHAM SHAMS

WHEN THEY ZIPPED OPEN THE DOOR TO THE TENT, THERE WAS A MAD scramble for the three flashlights strewn amid their sleeping bags, backpacks, and clothing.

"Let me see it!" Quinn said eagerly.

"Me too!" Camway cried, shining his plastic blue flashlight directly on the envelope in Fletcher's hand.

"Shut up, you guys! My grandmother's window is still open."

For the next half hour, they studied the ancient document and its mysterious words.

Quinn lowered his flashlight. "You sure the feathers were a different color?"

"I'm positive. It's kinda freaking me out."

"That painting looked completely normal to me, Fletch," said Quinn flatly.

"I don't care how it looked to you, Quinn. I know what I saw. I'm positive."

"Maybe they switched the painting Fletch like they do at museums," Camway suggested.

"Who's *they*?" asked Fletcher.

"Your grandparents."

"Shut up, Cam. Why would they change a painting in my parents' room?"

"Maybe someone else did. Like the doctor."

"Shut up, Cam," Fletcher said again. "You're really an idiot." He looked at Quinn. "What's a squire?"

"No idea, but it sounds British. You sure you never heard of Jackson McKenzie?"

"Positive. We have a family reunion every year. He's never been there."

Camway read the poem yet again. "I wonder who Kozart is. What's the passage? Who's grave are they talking about?"

"Maybe it's on one of the gravestones in Ketchum," Quinn said. He took the letter and placed it on his backpack. "If what Fletcher says about the painting is true—and I'm starting to believe him—I say we take each line and see if relates to anything in Mollyockett's portrait."

Fletcher nodded. "I like that idea of looking for clues in the painting. But it's going to have to wait. We really need to hit the sack. They're going to wake us up in less than six hours."

They agreed to pick up their investigation the next day and crawled into their sleeping bags.

Smoothing out his sleeping bag, Fletcher breathed a sigh of relief. He was positive the painting had changed, and knowing Quinn believed him made him feel less crazy. He took the letter, returned it to the envelope, and tucked it securely in his pack. He'd show it to Uncle Woodrow and see what he had to say after the cleanup at Hamlin Park.

Within minutes both Camway and Quinn were in a dead sleep. But Fletcher was restless and unable to relax. He quietly crawled out of the tent and walked to his mother's garden. Taking a seat on a wooden bench, he contemplated the strange occurrences of the last few days. How long had the letter been tacked to the back of the painting? Why was Mollyockett changing her appearance? Had anyone else—like his dad or mom—seen the mysterious changes or known of the letter?

He looked at the rose garden he'd helped his mother plant five years earlier. Happier times. How things had changed. He stood up and walked toward a large red rose in full bloom. He lovingly touched one of its dewy red blossoms.

Where are you, Mom? Wherever you are, I hope you're safe. I miss you.

He looked up at the moon and wondered if his mother was seeing the same thing. After a few minutes, exhausted and confused, he returned to the tent and zipped in. He succumbed to sheer exhaustion and finally fell asleep … and dreamed.

He was hiking with his parents on a large mountain. As they summited the mountain, a pack of vicious tigers along with some fierce Native warriors attacked them. Running for their lives, Fletcher tripped on a root and rolled off a cliff. As he plunged toward the earth, he heard his mother screaming in horror and anguish.

"Fletcher, wake up!" Quinn shook him roughly.

Soaked with sweat, Fletcher opened his eyes, and for a panicked moment, he had no idea where he was.

"Fletch, are you all right? You were yelling at the top of your lungs," Quinn said in a shaky voice.

Camway scooted over to the tent door, unzipped it, and peered outside. The house was still dark. "You scared me to death. I thought we were being attacked."

Fletcher wiped his eyes and composed himself. "I had a bad dream. Sorry."

Camway zipped the flap back up. "I had a bad dream once—well, more of a nightmare—where I was running toward third base when all of a sudden this flock of huge black birds with vampire fangs attacked me. They pulled out all my hair and bit off my nose. The weird thing was that everyone kept on playing ball like it was a normal thing, and I just laid there on the field. Dakota Thibodeau even stepped over me on his way to home plate."

Fletcher and Quinn laughed.

"Your team win the game?" Quinn asked. He buried his face into his pillow to stifle his uncontrollable laughter.

Camway frowned. "Shut up, Quinn. Bet you wet your pants in your dreams."

"'Night, guys," Fletcher said before they could get into it. "We're up in less than an hour."

He closed his eyes, and the last hour passed in what seemed like five minutes. Lucille roused them, and they slowly shuffled to the kitchen for breakfast. While Lucille served them, the boys exchanged cautious glances. When Edmond innocently asked how their night went, their tension was palpable.

He squinted suspiciously when they all took a huge helping of oatmeal in lieu of answering him. He figured they were guilty of something, but he let the matter pass. No reason to raise the alarm with his wife.

An hour later the three boys were in the back of the open Jeep as Edmond drove slowly toward Hamlin Park for the cleanup. Lucille spent the first minutes complaining about riding in the open vehicle.

"Why we take this ole jalopy when there are two perfectly good cars just sitting there in the garage waiting to be driven is beyond comprehension." Edmond didn't answer. He was always opting for open air as much as possible to protect her. She simmered down once they detoured to Kemo's for coffee, banana smoothies, and bug spray.

The boys loved riding in the open back and spent the entire trip holding their arms up in the cool wind to see who could get hit by the biggest bug. Bonus points were given if you caught one, more points if it was still alive, and even more if you ate it.

They drove through the main gate to the park and found the lot almost half full. Edmond found a spot on the far end. He turned off the Jeep and pulled hard on the hand brake. As Lucille clambered out of the passenger seat, she waved at a trio of elderly masked ladies examining a violet lady slipper flower. Then smoothing her wrinkled kerchief, she turned to Edmond. "Well, *that* was fun, we must do it again sometime."

Edmond laughed at the deep sarcasm in her voice. "Any time you want, Luce."

Fletcher's hope for a fun day was dashed as he stood to jump off the spare tire. Standing on a large stump was Refinna. In her hand, there was a bright white bullhorn. Seated at a plastic table next to her were Serena and Winola shuffling small stacks of cards. Attached to the front of the table was a large registration sign with the Cygnus logo and an image of a blue candy. At the bottom of the sign was the now familiar reminder to mask up and stay six feet apart as much as possible.

Oberon and Ogden sat on a park bench next to the table devouring large chocolate ice cream cones that were melting onto their hands and dripping down their shirts. Oberon's mask hung precipitously off his left ear. They were both oblivious to the crowd's disapproving glances and comments.

"Goodness, what slobs."

"Stop staring Cynthia. Come along."

"Laziest boys on the planet, If I was their parent …"

But people expressed their opinions quietly, fearful that the three ladies who ran the largest employer in town would overhear them.

"Volunteers this way," Refinna pointed, struggling to keep her balance. She was wearing new and freshly polished army-style black boots and a camouflage hunting shirt with the Cygnus logo stitched on the right arm. Her mask matched her shirt.

"Right this way. Lots to do today," she blared into the bullhorn, wiping perspiration from her forehead. "Thanks for volunteering to support this good cause. And don't forget. This event is sponsored by Foods for Fun, the newest Cygnus acquisition. Be sure to sample those delicious Blueberriola Sugary Sham Shams. Gives you an instant jolt of energy for a hard day of work."

"You've got to be kidding me," Fletcher whispered to Quinn while jumping off the Jeep.

"My goodness, of all the places!" Lucille glared directly at Refinna. "Look at her on that stump. She could camouflage the entire armed forces dressed like that. I'd be surprised if there's any material left for the soldiers."

"Luce, let it go. No need to upset things," Edmond responded calmly. He removed two large canvas bags filled with food from the backseat. "I bet they're not going into the woods in this heat. Even if they do, I'll be sure to ask for a square that's farthest from theirs. Everyone have their masks on?"

Fletcher picked up one of the bags, Camway the other, and they walked toward the check-in table.

"About time you've arrived," Refinna barked at Fletcher as he passed her. "Surprised you've even showed, given your propensity to avoid work." She looked at the blue shirt and worn jeans he was wearing. "Clear as daylight you don't give a hoot how you represent what our family has worked so hard for so many generations to build."

He set the bag down, tucked in his shirt, and pushed back his hair, wanting to get the encounter over with.

"Well, you're looking as healthy as ever, Refinna," Lucille said casually. "As a matter of fact, Fletcher's been talking about this day for weeks. He's been looking forward to pitching in just like he does every year." She stood in front of Refinna, looking directly at her.

Refinna mumbled something and averted her eyes.

"Well, well, what do we have here?" Lucille plucked a blueberry treat from a tall metal bin in front of the stump.

Refinna regained her composure and took a step back toward the edge of her platform.

"Well, I see the little snit has got you fooled!' she hissed back. Ogden and Oberon laughed loudly.

Lucille dropped the wrapped candy back into the bin and pursed her lips before she took a step closer to the stump.

"Oh my, here we go," Edmond whispered quietly.

Refinna swallowed hard and looked away.

"You can say what you want about me and Edmond, Ms. McKenzie," Lucille said in a deceptively calm voice. "But when it comes to my grandson, if I ever, *ever* hear you call him a snit or any other derogatory name ever again, I will personally make sure those obnoxious spectacles of yours find a permanent home up those two piggy nostrils of yours. Do I make myself clear, *Riffy*?"

For a moment there was abolute silence. Everyone immediately forgot about six foot distancing and edged closer towards the action. The crowd gaped in amazement as Lucille took another step closer, raised her finger, and wagged it directly in Refinna's face.

"And don't even think about throwing his living arrangements in our faces like you usually do. That tactic is over. You hear me?"

Refinna was so irate she could only sputter, "I ... how dare ... if you think—"

"I'm sure folks 'round here would love to hear about you and

Three-Finger Willy from Aroostook County. I'd say it's about time that story was told."

Refinna froze. *Did she actually mention Willy? And here in front of everyone? Please God, tell me that's not what just happened.*

No one had ever spoken to Refinna like that. She felt dizzy and was confident she was about to pass out.

Lucille smiled and took a step back. "*Do I make myself clear?*" she reiterated loudly.

The shocked crowd was mesmerized. Many of the onlookers watched with deep satisfaction and would have paid to see the public humiliation of the bully Refinna.

"Very clear," Refinna said quietly. *Oh, my goodness, she mentioned Willy.* Nearly, hyperventilating, she stepped off the stump. "It's kind of hot. Humid too. I need some energy." She grabbed a Blueberriola Sugary Sham Sham and sought the comfort of a sugar rush.

Lucille walked to the front of the registration table, ignoring the red six foot circles on the ground. Serena and Winola sat awestruck. They were deeply curious, wondering who on earth Three-Finger Willy from Aroostook County was and why Refinna have never spoken about him.

Lucille stopped in front of them and said pleasantly, "Lucille and Edmond Blay. We're here to register for the cleanup." Her masked smile didn't reach her eyes, but she glared at them with distain. Lucille then turned toward Oberon and Ogden. "You dropped your ice cream cone holders. Pick. Them. Up."

In an instant the twins scrambled off the bench and snatched up every piece of litter within fifty feet.

Edmond smirked quietly. *Well, that was worth all the tea in China,* he thought, never more proud of Lucille.

Behind the registration table, a detailed map of Hamlin Park was nailed to three square posts. The map was divided into four-inch light blue squares, each one named after a local corporate sponsor. The one square surrounding the level parking lot was sponsored by Foods for Fun.

"Not surprising," Edmond whispered to Fletcher. "It's the easiest part of the park to clean."

He found the square listing McKenzie's Inn as the corporate

sponsor—Buck's Ledge and Buck's Hole. Edmond smiled. "Woodrow must have signed us up." He stepped up to the table.

"We'll take the McKenzie Inn square, Winola."

"You sure, Ed?" Serena asked, peering over her thin black glasses as if analyzing him physically. "That's a pretty tough hike."

"Are you implying something, Serena?" Lucille asked. "We've been hiking that trail for more than fifty years."

"Why no, Lucy. All I meant was that with all this heat—" The fury in Lucille's eyes made Serena lean back. *Do not upset this woman. What does she know about me?* She waved away her comment. "Just sign right here." She then turned and drew a large circle on the McKenzie Inn Square.

Lucille thanked her and headed toward a wood picnic table sitting on a large concrete slab.

Buck's Ledge was a five-hundred-foot sheer cliff looming majestically above the entire park. At the base of the cliff was a tiny, landlocked strip of land known as Buck's Beach. The only way to reach the beach was to traverse a narrow footbridge that crossed the swift currents of Sunday River. A short way downriver from the footbridge, the swift-moving water emptied into the deep and treacherous Buck's Hole. Every year the swirling water claimed at least one life despite the numerous warning signs posted on both sides of the river.

Within ten minutes everyone in their group had assembled at the table. Doris Caxton arrived in her new black SUV with Nicole, Joey, and Uno, the family dog. He was a small, muscular pit bull with one blue eye and one brown eye. Camway's family pulled up in a white van towing a black trailer loaded with mountain bikes and inflatable orange rafts. With Chamberlain Vincent and his wife, Jean, were Camway's five older sisters—Elspeth, Siskia, Lux, Paz, and Blanche.

The Parker family was the last of the group to arrive. Cicely Parker went to school with Fletcher and Camway at Balston Prep, an exclusive two-hundred-year-old school well known for producing numerous governors, US senators, one vice president, countless CEOs, and hundreds of doctors, engineers, and scientists. Cicely's father, Ridge, was president of the Mount Zircon Ski Resort. As Ridge pulled his black convertible into one of the last available spaces, Fletcher noticed Cicely had brought Caia Van Ives, who also attended Balston Prep. In the back sat the youngest Parker children, Tulip and Ward.

"Well, that makes eighteen," said Edmond, glancing toward the car. *Gosh, we have the largest group by far.*

Fletcher walked up to their car, and Cicely waved and gestured toward Refinna, who was back on her stump, trying to push Blueberriola Sugary Sham Shams on the volunteers.

"Is she for real?" Cicely asked sarcastically, pulling her long black hair through the back of a Mount Zircon cap.

"I'm afraid so," Fletcher replied. "Dad would be horrified."

"Hello, Ridge," Lucille said as she approached the car. "Lorraine not coming?"

Ridge closed the car door and warmly waived at Lucille. He wanted to hug her but knew he couldn't. It was a new world. "She's getting antibody testing done in Portland so she can donate blood. She sends her regards. You look amazing."

"Has to be the weather. Gorgeous day for a cleanup. Come on, everyone. Let's all gather at the picnic table. Each group stay together and six feet from other groups."

Once everyone was ready, Edmond showed them their assigned area.

"You're kidding me," Jean Vincent said, looking at the map. Everyone laughed as she traced her index finger along the path from the parking lot to the base of the ledge.

"You saying you can't make it, Mom?" Paz asked, laughing.

"I have no problem making it there, Paz, as long as you don't mind carrying your mother back."

Chamberlain hoisted a pack onto Camway's back, and after tightening the straps, he looked at Edmond and asked, "Which trail we taking?"

"I'm thinking the east trail. It's a little longer but less of a climb. With this heat and humidity, I think it's our best option."

"I agree. And it's still early enough where we can take our time."

"I say we take our first break at Talon Rock," Jean chimed in. "My map indicates it's a little after the three-mile marker."

"What's Talon Rock, Mom?" asked Elspeth, leaning over her mother to study the map.

"It's a large rock that looks kind of like an eagle's claw, sweetie," Chamberlain responded. "They say the local Indians used it as a sacrificial altar."

Elspeth wrinkled her eyebrows. "Sacrificing what?"

"Who knows? But they say they did it to please their god."

"Is there blood there? If there is, I don't want to stop."

Chamberlain laughed. "No, honey, that was a long, long time ago. But there is a good story about that rock that I'll tell everyone while we rest there."

"Okay, everyone ready?" Edmond asked. Pointing at the kids he continued, "I want everyone to select a buddy. We should have nine pairs." Smiling, he grabbed Lucille's wrist.

"Fletch, I choose you," Cicely said confidently.

"Um, sure."

Both Camway and Quinn snickered as they moved together as a team.

CHAPTER 6

BUCKS LEDGE

With Edmond and Lucille in the lead and Quinn, Camway, and Uno in the rear, the group walked onto Hamlin Park's East Trail. After thirty minutes of steady walking, they ascended into a small clearing where the trail split in three directions. They forked right and followed the green-and-white *East Trail* signs nailed to trees at random intervals. Everyone took in the sights and sounds of the park, many still masked, so little was said until they reached Talon Rock two hours later. Lucille took out small bags of her granola and passed them around.

While everyone hydrated themselves and refueled on the granola, Chamberlain told the story of Talon Rock. He concluded the tale by saying, "And that's why they had their sacrificial ceremonies at this particular rock."

"Well, that makes the second sacrificial altar we've seen today," Edmond said and laughed.

"What that's mean?" asked Ridge.

Edmond shook his head and continued to chuckle at the memory. "Sorry you missed it, Ridge. Should have seen it. Poor ole Refinna standing helplessly on that stump didn't stand a chance, did she, Lucy?"

"Don't *poor Refinna* me. She deserved everything she got."

"What's that all about?" Cicely asked Fletcher.

"Long story, but you'll love it. I'll tell you as we hike."

Soon, the group finished their break and continued hiking toward their destination, which now loomed in the distance every time they entered a clearing. They could also hear the faint sound of flowing water.

When Fletcher finished the story of his grandmother's confrontation with Refinna, Cicely laughed while holding her stomach. "Are you kidding me?" she asked in disbelief.

He smiled. It felt good to make her laugh so hard.

"And who's Three-Finger Willy?"

"I've no idea. Sounds like a nut."

"Gotta be to go out with *her*," she said, laughing again.

Jean stopped and leaned on the crude walking stick she'd found while at Talon Rock. "Must be right up ahead," she announced. *Please let it be right up ahead,* she thought.

Everyone continued to follow the narrow trail, which was hidden below a thick canopy of tall pine, oak, and maple trees. After crossing over a small stream and descending into a wide valley, they came to an abrupt halt. The beauty before them took their collective breath away. The entire valley was forested with mature pines that blanketed both sides of a blue river, stopping only at the base of a majestic cliff.

"What a sight!" Doris exclaimed, transfixed by the impressive mountain. "Imagine falling off that."

"Buck's Ledge at last." Fletcher pulled his cell phone from his backpack to capture the moment. Almost everyone else did the same thing. The sight was absolutely stunning.

"My God. This quite possibly makes that three-month lockdown worth it." Edmond stated.

"Nothing is worth what everyone went through the last three months," Lucille quickly retorted. "How quickly you forget."

Edmond moved toward Chamberlain. "I say we rest here for thirty minutes or so and then split into two groups," Edmond suggested. "The bridge is right up ahead. One group will clean this side of the river, while the other group will cross the footbridge and clean Buck's Beach." He paused and spoke to the group. "No one—*I mean no one*—is to go anywhere near Buck's Hole. Everyone got that?"

The hikers nodded solemnly. It was clear from their vantage point that Buck's Hole was a place they should not mess with. The snow from the previous winter was still melting off, swelling the river to the very top of its steep banks and turning the rapids into a violent, raging force of nature.

"I say we eat lunch first," Lucille suggested, and everyone eagerly agreed. She walked toward an abandoned campsite in the middle of a small clearing. "Fletcher," she said. "You and your friends gather some old branches so your grandfather can make a fire."

Within minutes, the fire pit was filled with broken branches and old logs.

"While we're eating, let's decide who wants to clean each side of the river," said Ridge, looking out at the river. Jean and Doris stood up and began squeezing hand sanitizer from matching pump bottles into everyone's hands.

"After, can I help clean Buck's Beach, Gramps?" asked Fletcher.

Quinn immediately stood up. "Me too. I want to help clean it."

"I've been cleaning the beach for three years and know where they throw stuff," Paz quickly announced.

"I'm Paz's buddy, so if she cleans it, I have to go too, right?" asked Blanche, moving quickly toward Paz.

Cicely backed up to stand beside Fletcher. "Fletch is my buddy, so if he goes, I go."

Lucille stopped handing out sandwiches and placed both hands on her hips. "Not everyone can help clean the other side of the river. I'll tell you what. The five people who find the biggest pinecones in the next five minutes help clean Buck's Beach."

A mad rush ensued, and after careful measurement, it was decided that Doris would lead Blanche, Ward, Paz, Fletcher, and Cicely over to Buck's Beach.

"You okay with that?" Edmond asked.

Doris glanced at the roaring water and swallowed hard. "As long as they stay away from the edge of the water." Born and raised in Boston, the Maine outdoors experience was foreign to her. "That water really scares me, Ed."

"Everyone stays at least ten yards from the water," Edmond yelled loudly. He threw three of the pinecones into the fire. The flames flared and crackled angrily as they instantly consumed the brittle cones.

Ridge took a quick head count. "Okay, everyone on this side, split into three groups. Group one will go with me. Group two will go with

Mr. Chamberlain, and the rest will go with Mr. Blay."

Lucille took a sip of water and stood. "Ed, I'll go with you."

"Actually, Lucy, I was hoping you would stay here," said Ridge. "This will be the central meeting place. You mind manning base camp?"

"Not at all. I am a little tired. Maybe I should have taken Refinna's advice and eaten one of her energy sticks." Everyone laughed and then moved toward their group leaders.

Ward fell in line behind Fletcher as they walked toward the bridge. "That looks scary. You think there are fish in there?"

"Not this time of year with all the snowmelt," Fletcher replied. "But later this summer, the hole is full of them." He paused to pick up a rusted bottle cap and gazed at the water falling into the swirling hole. "My dad took me fishing there a couple of times," he said quietly.

Doris stopped and turned toward Fletcher. "I'm sure you'll have plenty of opportunities in the future, Fletcher. I'm positive. You okay?" The sympathy in her voice was resolute.

Fletcher nodded, not trusting his voice.

As they approached the narrow footbridge, Doris stopped and blocked access to the span. "Now listen. We all stick together as a group. From what Mr. Blay says, there should not be that much trash this far up the trail. Let's finish as quickly as possible. Then we'll help the others on this side of the river." She had to yell to be heard over the roar of the river directly behind her. "And remember, no closer than ten yards. Everyone understand?"

"What if there's trash near the water?" Ward asked, wide-eyed.

"Leave it. It's not worth the risk."

"*Yuck! Get off!*" shrieked Blanche, flicking a small brown worm off her arm.

"My dad said some worms have five grams of protein," Fletcher said and laughed.

Cicely looked disgusted. "Is that true?"

"Night crawlers do. I know that much. He said that if I was ever lost in the woods, I could survive off water, worms, and berries."

"I'd rather die of starvation," Blanche hissed, stepping delicately onto the bridge.

Doris stopped at the bridge's center, allowing everyone to get a glimpse of the violently churning white water far below them. "Looks freezing," she said.

"I'd say cold is the last thing you need to worry about if you fall in," Fletcher retorted, glancing at Buck's Hole farther down the river.

"Don't fall!" Ward yelled playfully, pretending to push Fletcher over the four-foot rail.

Fletcher quickly grabbed Ward's right leg in an attempt to move him upward. "Oh yeah, big guy?"

Fletcher sent Ward sprawling on the wood walkway with both arms flailing as he attempted to brace himself.

"*That's enough!*" a horrified Doris bellowed. "We're here to pick up trash, *not* to drown each other. Let's go."

When they reached the rocky beach, they immediately started collecting anything that didn't belong on the pristine strip of land, which was illuminated by the early summer sun high above them.

Doris began swatting aimlessly in the air over her head. "These flies are unbearable," she complained. "I've never seen anything like them. There's a cloud of them following me."

"They're called no-see-ems, Mrs. Caxton," Fletcher explained. "It's a Maine thing."

Doris gagged as she swallowed a small fly. "Gross!" She immediately sprayed a tiny amount of bug spray on her mask that was in her pocket and put it on. "I'd rather die of chemicals than chock to death on bugs!"

"I think they have fangs. I'll have no blood left after this day is over," Paz said miserably. She coughed and spit on a rock. "I swallowed one too." She followed Doris' lead and put her mask on.

Doris sprayed a can of repellant directly over her head in a wide arch and then had the others spray themselves. "I'll take the taste of chemicals any day over getting attacked by those things again."

After the no-see-em spraydown, they moved closer toward the base of Buck's Ledge and then moved in a southerly direction. Along the way they collected several tin cans, cigarette butts, a candy wrapper and many other discarded items.

"It's disgusting. Who smokes this much up here?" Cicely said as she threw a large clump of weathered butts into her plastic bag. She spotted a small worn trail to her left. "Where does that go, Fletch?"

"It'll take you to Devil's Leap, which overlooks the entire park. That photo of me with my parents on the fireplace mantle was taken there. Man, these bugs are *horrible*."

"I know. They're vicious," Cicely agreed, but her attention was focused on the trail. "Let's ask Mrs. Caxton if we can go up and clean there."

"You're kidding, right? She was trembling just crossing the bridge."

"Well, do you blame her after that stunt you and Ward pulled?"

Annoyed by the comment, Fletcher called out, "Mrs. Caxton, can we clean this trail?"

Doris walked toward them and continued to swat at the small cloud of flies following her every move. "What?"

"The trail there needs to be cleaned. I know where it goes. Can we clean it?"

"Where does it go?"

"It's takes you to Devil's Leap." He pointed toward a large outcropping high above their heads.

She looked and quickly shook her head. "Up there? Absolutely not."

"Not all the way to the top. Just up there. It's really not dangerous. I've been there lots of times with my parents."

At the mention of Aldous and Muriel, Doris immediately lowered her guard. Her heart panged with hurt for Fletcher and what he must be feeling being back here. She stood silent and studied the entire mountain in front of her. *Well, the trail isn't really that far up.*

"You sure it's not dangerous?" she asked.

"Positive."

"Your grandparents, they won't mind?"

"They climb it all the time. Have been for years. It's where they took that photo for their Christmas card last year."

"Well, just you two and stay in sight. I mean it."

"I want to go too, Mrs. Caxton," Ward yelled from behind her.

Immediately, she regretted the decision she'd just made. "Everyone else stay here on the beach. I said just Fletcher and Cicely."

"Oh, man!"

"Come on, Mrs. Caxton."

"It's not dangerous."

"I went up last year on a school hike."

Doris turned and looked at the others standing on the beach, holding half-full plastic bags in their hands. *I do want them to have some fun,* she thought, watching Fletcher and Cicely moving up the trail at a steady pace.

"Okay, but everyone is to stay behind me and don't wander. The minute anyone—especially you, Ward—starts to fool around, we're turning around."

"We can take a shot with my camera," Paz said happily through her mask.

Breathing loudly, Fletcher and Cicely continued to climb the rugged trail. They moved around two massive granite sections of lichen-covered rock that had broken off from the face of the cliff thousands of years earlier. Tiny flecks of mica glistened in the bright sunlight. Rounding the rocks, they stepped onto Devil's Leap.

"Wow!" Cicely said breathlessly. "It's absolutely beautiful."

"I know. It makes the town look so small."

"It reminds me of Colorado."

Fletcher didn't respond. He was thinking back to the time he'd stood at this exact spot with his parents. So much had changed in such a short time. *I really hate the year 2020,* he thought.

"I wish I'd brought my camera," Cicely said, oblivious to Fletcher's melancholy.

He moved closer to the edge and studied the valley below. "Think it would hurt if you jumped into the river from here?"

"Fletcher, that's not even funny," Cicely said His demeanor scared her. "I'm leaving."

"Relax. I'm only kidding." He stepped back toward her just as the others rounded the huge rocks, *oohing* and *ahhing* at the spectacular view.

"Oh, my stars and stripes, look at that," Doris gasped through her bug spray–covered mask, forgetting about the danger directly in front of her. After a few seconds, she regained her senses.

"Okay, we need to go back down. Everyone, let's go."

"Can't we take one quick photo, Mrs. Caxton, while we're here?" asked Paz. "I can put my camera on that rock over there and set it on auto."

The view was beautiful, and Doris thought it would be nice to have a photo. *I'll never hike this again, I'm sure of that,* she thought.

"Well, okay, but make it quick, Paz. Everyone, stand right beside me and stay away from the edge."

While Doris pulled everyone together for a photo, Fletcher glanced toward the hot sun shining directly overhead. As he did, he noticed a sudden movement at the top of Buck's Ledge. There stood a man with long dark hair. He was beside a stand of tall pine trees that rose precipitously at the very edge of the sheer granite cliff. There was fury in his black eyes, and he was staring directly at Fletcher. *If looks could kill.*

"Fletcher, we really need to hurry if we're going to get a shot." Paz said, clearly perturbed by the small amount of time she'd been given to organize the photo.

"Move closer, Fletcher, if you want to be in it," said Cicely.

He moved next to Cicely and then looked up again at the large stand of pine trees atop the cliff. The man was gone. *It was like he was staring directly at me,* Fletcher thought, unable to shake an eerie feeling that something wasn't right. *He knows who I am.*

"How long does that thing take?" asked a frustrated Mrs. Caxton. She was anxious to get off the ledge and back to safety.

"It's on a thirty-second delay," Paz replied. "Just give it a sec more—"

A thunderous *boom* shook the mountain. The sound was so loud it sent a nearby flock of geese hurling backward in midair. The power of the blast instantly converted the clean Maine air into a tumultuous mix of rock and debris. Less than two seconds later an enormous blast wave enveloped the entire group and knocked them to their feet. The earth shook while releasing enormous amounts of energy.

Fletcher was aghast. The cliff he'd been looking at was now moving towards them at breathtaking speed. The explosion had shaken lose a cascade of smaller rocks from every section of the mountain. That destabilized the cliffs above, causing granite boulders the size of large houses to topple from Buck's Ledge. The rockslide created a violent vibration, and a huge crack appeared on the ledge where they had just posed for the photo.

Doris frantically pushed her charges toward the trail. "*Run, everyone! Run! The rocks are falling! Oh my God, please help us!*"

Everyone scrambled madly away from the ledge as the earth shook, and the sun's rays were suddenly dimmed by the enormous cloud of rock, dust, and falling trees.

"Don't stop!" Fletcher screamed. Bringing up the rear, he helped move the group toward the small opening to the trail. A thin shard of granite pierced his right shoulder, but he was too focused to notice the pain.

"*Help me!*" Blanche screeched. The opening to the path was no longer visible. The others has had simply vanished. She tried to move, but her tiny frame was frozen with fear. Fletcher frantically pulled her back toward the lip of Devil's Leap, and an instant later they were falling through the air amidst a wall of boulders, dirt, and debris, their screams drowned out by the roar of the rockslide and thundering river. When they hit the water, everything went dark.

⸺

"Camway and Quinn, run for help right now!" Ridge yelled loudly as he ran toward the river with Edmond and Chamberlain close behind. "Tell them we have injuries that need immediate medical attention!"

At base camp Lucille cried out, holding onto a small tree for support as a giant dust cloud rolled toward her and behind the blast wave that had almost knocked her over. She could not believe what she was witnessing. When she saw Fletcher fall into the river just ahead with what looked like the entire mountain, her world came to a halt.

⸺

Entangled in a large tree branch, Fletcher and Blanche were viciously pushed down toward the bottom of the river. The pain from the fall was so severe that they didn't register the frigid waves enveloping them. As water entered his lungs, Fletcher felt Blanche's warm hand wrap around his. For the briefest of moments, the contact with another human was oddly comforting as rocks continued to enter the roiling mix and pelt their bodies from every direction. The thick pine branch spun with them and continued to hold them as prisoners in the watery grave. Blanche's white cloth mask floated aimlessly in front of the entangled mess before snagging a pine branch.

Fletcher's last thoughts were of his mother as he slowly lost consciousness and ebbed into nothingness. The last image he had was the white mask directly in front of him.

CHAPTER 7

FLETCHER'S POND

FLETCHER STIRRED SLIGHTLY, AWARE OF FAINT VOICES IN THE DISTANCE. He had no idea where he was or who was talking. His thoughts were blurred and confused. When he tried to move, every bone in his body felt shattered and broken.

"Ed, I think I saw him move," Lucille said in a low voice. "Fletch, can you hear me? It's me, Grans." They both had masks on. Fletcher's current medical condition placed him in the "high risk" category if he contracted the virus.

Edmond leaned forward and placed his hand on Fletcher's forehead. "It's going to be okay," he whispered.

What's wrong with me? He focused on moving his fingers. As he lifted his left index finger, he tried to remember what had happened. There was a bright blast, and then the earth was pushing him down toward the cold water. His heart clutched as though an electrical current was coursing through his body, and a sharp pain pierced his left leg and rib cage. He winced and took a deep, painful breath.

"Stay with me, Fletch. I'm right here," Lucille said softly. "You're going to be okay, honey."

Edmond moved to the other side of the bed and grasped Fletcher's hand. "You're a strong boy, son. We're so proud of you."

Lucille was staring at her grandson's hand. "Look, Ed. He's trying to move. That's right, Fletch. Move your fingers." Small tears rolled down her aged face and onto the white blanket. "We're with you, honey."

The tendons in Fletcher's neck tightened, and he gritted his teeth.

Edmond sniffled loudly. His gaze focused on Fletcher's eyes. He wondered if he heard them speaking.

"Can you move your fingers, son? Do you see anything, Lucy?"

"I thought I saw him move his finger a few seconds ago. He feels hot."

"Well, he should be, going through all that. It's a miracle he's even here."

Fletcher swallowed and bent his index finger toward the palm of his hand.

"Ed! He *is* coming around." She clasped his moving finger.

Slowly, Fletcher opened his eyes and focused on the grainy images of his grandparents in front of him.

"Take your time, honey. We're with you. You're going to be okay," Lucille said as Fletcher closed his tired eyes.

"Can you move your toes, son?"

"Ed, give him time. He hasn't even said a word."

"Well, we need to know if he can walk."

"That'll come."

"I'll call Dr. Dubrielle and tell him he's waking up."

"Tell him to bring a new prescription," Lucille said. "He's getting low."

Fletcher's thoughts slipped back to the river.

He had felt something hard on his back, and he was tangled in what felt like a tree's branch. Cold water swirled in every direction and then rushed into his mouth. He felt the sharp points of someone's fingernails puncturing the side of his hand.

His entire body shook violently, and he opened his eyes again. Surprised by the sudden movement, Lucille flinched.

"Fletch, it's okay. You're going to be fine."

"What ... what happened?" His words were barely audible.

She placed a wet towel on his forehead. "You had an accident. But you're here, and I'm here. And that's all that matters."

"Grans, what happened?" he whispered again.

"There was a rock slide, honey, and you were thrown into the river. It's a miracle you're even here. Clear as daylight that God was on your side."

He relaxed his hand and closed his eyes as the events on Devil's Leap flooded his mind. In the background he heard the ticking of a clock. The sound was familiar. He drifted between sleep and wakeful-ness. Lucille's heart surged in profound relief as she watched him move more and more.

He raised his head and winced in pain. He looked down to see the cast on his leg.

"It's okay, honey. Dr. Dubrielle said it'll take a while, but you'll be okay. Possibly even snowboard this winter."

He turned his head to look at her. "Was anyone hurt? I remember everyone running."

"They're all okay. Just a few scrapes and bruises," she said, her voice a whisper. "I don't think Mrs. Caxton will ever go hiking again. She's been so worried about you, Fletcher." She paused. "You know, you saved Blanche's life. We're so proud of you."

"I remember falling off Devil's Leap with her. And she's okay?" he asked.

"It's hard to believe, but she only suffered a concussion and needed a few stitches in her head. She was here a little while ago to see how you were doing. Those yellow flowers are from her."

The house was quiet. The clock in his father's room ticked rhythmi-cally. He could hear Edmond's footsteps climbing the stairs.

"What about the man on the cliff. What happened to him?" Fletcher's voice was raw. "I saw him right before the rockslide. He did this."

Edmond stopped just outside the door and looked at Lucille. When their eyes met, the anguish they'd felt over the past few days made her eyes fill with tears.

"Why don't you close your eyes and get some rest, Fletcher," he said gently. He thought how strange it was that he and his wife were now caring for Fletcher *and* his father. Given their advanced ages, it should have been the other way around.

"There was a man with long black hair on top of the cliff. He was staring directly at me," Fletcher repeated resolutely. "You believe me don't you, Grans?"

"Yes, I believe you. What I don't believe is how that cliff could have just collapsed on its own. I've been looking at it every day for my entire life. I don't know what to believe anymore—except that it's a miracle nobody was killed."

"The forestry service searched every square inch at the bottom of Buck's Ledge," Edmond reported. He pulled an ornate wood chair next to the bed and sat down. "They're positive everyone made it out alive."

"You don't believe me, do you?"

"About what?"

"The man on top of the cliff. The one with the long black hair."

"Of course I believe you. Given the weather and the fact that it was a cleanup, there were a lot of people in the woods that day."

"But he was different."

"Different how?" Edmond asked slowly.

"He was …" Fletcher began, remembering the image of the cold, dark eyes looking at him right before the explosion. He knew it wasn't a coincidence. "The cause of what happened."

Lucille stood and took Fletcher's hand. "I think you need to get some rest. Your friends are all eager for you to start enjoying the summer with them. The only way that's going to happen is for you to get some sleep."

"I am kind of tired," Fletcher lied.

Edmond stroked his head and leaned forward. "I'm here for you, Fletch. Why don't you tell me everything when you wake back up?"

"How's dad, Gramps?" Fletcher asked.

"The same. But I'm sure he'll come around in due time."

"Any word on Mom?"

The doorbell rang. Lucille was glad for the interruption. "That must be Dr. Dubrielle. I'll go let him in. Edmond, why don't you change the water in the bowl." *I just want this year to end.*

Lucille's muffled footsteps moved down the stairs. Edmond ignored her request and relaxed. "Chamberlain had just commented on what a great day it was for a photograph while we were watching you guys take that picture on Devil's Leap. And then suddenly, everything fell apart. We really thought you were all dead." He paused and stroked Fletcher's head. "The park service told us that slides happen every year. I guess when the ice in the rocks melts, it causes them to break apart. It was just a coincidence that you happened to be where you were at that time. Unfortunately, this slide was the largest ever recorded on that mountain."

Fletcher looked deflated. "It wasn't a coincidence."

Edmond swallowed hard. "That's an understatement. You wouldn't recognize it now. Buck's Ledge looks totally different. Kind of reminds me of Old Man of the Mountain in New Hampshire when it fell."

"That bad, huh?'

"When you're better," Edmond said, "I'll take you to the park for you to see. It's really astonishing. That is if you're up for it." He stood up and paused. "But I do know one thing, Fletcher. You are a genuine hero. Just as those rocks were about to hit you, you pushed everyone to safety. That girl would not be here right now if you hadn't grabbed onto her. We all saw that. You saved poor Blanche from getting crushed. You're both incredibly lucky. Thank God the water was at its highest level of the year because of the snowmelt." Edmond looked out the window and studied a small bird building a nest between two large branches.

Nature can be beautiful yet so deadly, he thought.

"None of us could believe what we were watching," he continued. "It was … absolutely unbelievable. You grabbed onto Blanche and jumped off Devil's Leap in the midst of a hail of boulders." He paused and blew his nose. "The second you both hit the water, a boulder literally the size of this house crashed into the river just behind you. The force created a twenty-foot wave that swept you and Blanche right toward where the rest of us were standing. The campsite where we had lunch was three feet underwater. Once the water receded, we found you both unconscious fifty feet from the river. You were wrapped around a pine tree on top of Blanche. She'll be pleased you're awake."

"Grans mentioned she had stiches."

"Staples, actually. On the top of her head. You, on the other hand, were not so lucky."

Fletcher looked down at the blanket covering his cast. "How bad?"

"You broke your leg in four places. You now have a few new friends in your leg, and they'll set off any metal detector within a three-mile radius. You also have four severely bruised ribs and a couple of nasty scratches on your back."

Edmond pulled the blanket off the cast. "As you can see, you've had lots of visitors. Over my objections, your grandmother has allowed your friends to sign your cast. They all wore masks and only stayed for a few minutes. Everyone's been so worried, Fletch."

Fletcher raised his head and looked down. The cast was completely covered with messages and signatures in various colors. When he spotted a large Bacchus with Quinn and Camway's signatures, he laughed feebly.

"When were they here?"

"Who?"

"Quinn and Camway."

"Yesterday. In fact, they should be here soon. If you don't want any visitors, I can tell them you're sleeping," Edmond said with a chuckle. "That is, if your grandmother will let them in now that you're awake. She won't want you moving around that much because of company. You've really scared her, Fletch. I think she's aged ten years in three days."

Fletcher was taken aback. "You're telling me I've been out for three days?"

"You have. And it's been a long three days. You'd be at Ketchum Hospital if not for the pandemic. They had no rooms for you."

"And no one else was injured?"

"Just a few scrapes. Naturally, everyone's been shaken up. It was a terrible thing."

"Grans mentioned Mrs. Caxton."

"She's a city slicker. You know that. She had to be sedated, and was airlifted off the mountain with you and Blanche."

"Airlifted. You're kidding."

"Totally serious. You've even made the front page of several papers for the past two days." He pointed toward a stack of newspapers on the dresser. "Buck's Beach, that area where you were picking up trash, is totally gone."

"What do you mean *gone*?"

"That huge boulder that crashed right behind you temporarily blocked the flow of Sunday River. As a result, the beach is now fifteen feet underwater. The paper has dubbed it Fletcher's Pond."

Fletcher flashed a smile. "You're kidding."

"As soon as you're better, we'll take a hike and see how it looks."

"I did see a man with dark eyes and long black hair at the top of the cliff. It looked like he was doing something."

"Well, whoever he is, I'm sure he's fine. The park service really did a thorough search."

Edmond turned and watched Dr. Dubrielle enter with Lucille behind him.

"Well, if it isn't our local celebrity. How you feeling, Fletcher?" the doctor asked. "It's good to see your eyes open and your toes moving." He looked at the cast and laughed. "I see you've had a few more visitors."

"None that I can remember."

"Well, you're a very lucky young man. From what I've been told, it's a miracle you weren't crushed." The elderly doctor listened to Fletcher's heart and gave his body a cursory exam.

"When do you think I will be able to walk again?" Fletcher asked. "Gramps said he'd take me hiking to see it all."

"Edmond!" Lucille exclaimed in exasperation. "That's ridiculous, mentioning hiking at a time like this." She yanked down her mask to highlight her full distain.

Fletcher smiled. That day could not come too soon.

"You're right. I'm sorry."

Fletcher looked at him, surprised. He'd never seen his grandfather back down so quickly. "He said only after I'm better," Fletcher said defensively.

"Well, that's not going to be any time soon, Mr. McKenzie," the doctor told him. "Your body's been through a lot. You've got some pretty serious injuries that need time to heal. I've brought you a pair of crutches. You need to be up as soon as possible to prevent blood clots. I want you to use the crutches several times a day. But take it slow. Your leg needs time."

The doctor was making Fletcher anxious. Edmond noticed and smiled encouragingly at him.

"You'll be limping for quite some time," the doctor continued, "but you're young enough. Before you know it, no one will ever know anything even happened. I've given your grandmother some medication.

Make sure you take it whenever you feel any pain."

The doctor stood and glanced toward Aldous's room. "Is Sheila still helping you?"

"She just called from Sandra's. Said she'll be here in a few minutes," Edmond replied. "She's been amazing."

"I can call the Visiting Nurse Association and ask for one more if you want. With the two of them like this, it may be a bit too much."

"I'll hear no such talk," Lucille said. "We're getting along just fine."

"He'll need some rehab for the leg. I'll call the Newry Rehabilitation Clinic and set something up."

Lucille nodded and smiled. "Thank you, Gerald. I wish they were all like you. There's a loaf of fresh banana bread on the table beside the front door for you."

Their eyes locked as if reading each other's minds.

"How's things at the hospital?" she asked. "With no visitors allowed, it's impossible to comprehend what's happening there."

Dr. Dubrielle surveyed Lucielle's eyes as he searched for the right words.

"It's a sight that most people should be able to see," he said. "Then, they would fully comprehend the destruction Covid19 is doing to the country. It's incredible that some people still refuse to wear a mask or to social distance." He knew of her beliefs but pressed on. "We all owe a huge debt of gratitude to those health care workers."

Feeling like a criminal that had just been aprehended, Lucille took a step back and looked down. "How are the patients holding up?"

"As well as can be expected. First comes the shock when we admit them. Most *actually* can't believe they're in the Covid Ward. Then comes the pain of the virus and the feeling of complete isolation. Each one has his or her own room which is a negative pressure room."

"Meaning?"

"They're hospital isolation rooms. They've had to board up one of the windows in each room and install large blue motors to suck the air out of the room which helps keep the virus from spreading."

Lucille flushed but asked, "How do they breathe?"

Gerald's expression softened a little. "There is plenty of oxygen for the patients to breathe. Some are on oxygen. Those are the lucky ones."

She knew where this was going. It was all over the news on a daily basis.

"The unfortunate ones are on ventilators which is basically a machine that breathes for them. Sadly, most in this condition don't make it."

Close to tears, Lucille shook her head. "I'm sorry," she said.

Silently they both looked towards the top of the stairs as the grandfather clock began to chime the top of the hour.

"It's time for me to head back to the hospital and put on my space suit for the patients," Gerald said. "I have the utmost respect for what you and Edmond are doing." He gave her the thumbs up in lieu of hugging her. "You're both saints."

Not long after the doctor left, a car pulled into the driveway. Woodrow had arrived.

CHAPTER 8

UNCLE WOODROW'S STORY

WHEN FLETCHER OPENED HIS EYES THE NEXT MORNING, SUNSHINE WAS streaming into the room. He drained a large glass of water and cautiously sat up against the headboard. He took in the numerous bouquets of flowers, stuffed animals, and get-well cards that littered the room. He slowly lowered his cast-covered leg over the side of the bed and studied the messages from his friends. He laughed out loud when he read the message, "Bacchus would be proud! Cam & Quinn."

"What's so funny!"

He looked up, startled. "Uncle Woodrow. I didn't hear you come in."

"Well, over the years, I've perfected my stealth entries." He was wearing worn jeans, a white shirt, and despite the warm weather, one of his signature periwinkle blue sweater vests. He was holding an old McKenzie Inn cap in his frail hands. His white hair looked like it had recently been trimmed. Woodrow had always been thin, but it was clear he'd lost weight since they'd last seen each other.

Lucille entered the room with a stack of white towels that she placed in the linen closet. She knew that Woodrow's visit would be good for Fletcher's spirits, but she was cautious. She knew he'd push Fletcher for a speedy recovery. Maybe a little too speedily.

"Why don't you make yourself useful Woodrow and water the flowers?" she said. "And thank you for wearing a mask. Keep it on, you hear me?"

Ignoring her, Woodrow walked over to an arrangement of roses, leaned over, and breathed in their scent. "My, these are lovely," he exclaimed. "You say something, Lucy?" he asked teasingly.

"You're as bad as the rest. Fletcher, let me know if you need anything. Woodrow, breakfast will be ready soon. And remember, Gerald says Fletcher needs his rest, so keep your visit short." She walked out and headed toward Aldous's room to give Sheila a hand.

Woodrow approached the bed and saw that Fletcher was grimacing slightly.

"What's wrong?"

"Just a little sore, that's all."

"You taking any medication?"

"Yeah, Grans gave me some a little while ago."

"Well, give it time. It'll kick in." He sat down in the wooden chair Edmond always used and studied Fletcher's face. He didn't know how fast he should go. Even with his worldly travels, he was in unchartered territory. "Care to talk for a while?" he asked.

"Um, sure."

Knowing his time was limited, Woodrow jumped in head first. "I was helping your grandfather take down that tent in the backyard two days ago. When we were moving your belongings out of the tent, this fell out of your backpack," he said as he

pulled an aged white envelope from his shirt pocket. Fletcher immediately recognized it as the envelope they'd found on the back of Mollyockett's portrait. His heart lurched. It felt like that night had happened ages ago.

"Am I in trouble?"

"It's okay, Fletcher," Woodrow said gently. "I just want to know where you found it."

"I, um … I mean, we—"

"We? Who's we?" Woodrow asked, sounding alarmed.

Fletcher didn't know where to begin. He still felt slightly groggy and confused.

Woodrow put the envelope back in his pocket. "We can talk about this at another time if you're not up to it."

Fletcher thought for a moment, grateful for the time with Woodrow. "We as in me, Camway, and Quinn. We found it the night before the cleanup at Hamlin Park."

Woodrow knew Fletcher had no idea what he'd stumbled upon or its importance. It had the potential to change all of their lives dramatically. He sighed slightly and then said, "I've been looking for this for a long time. Well, I think it's what I've been searching for."

Fletcher looked at him intently. "What do you mean?" he asked.

The letter and its contents had shocked Woodrow. Rarely was he at a loss for words, but now he didn't know where to begin.

"You look weird, Uncle Woodrow," Fletcher observed.

"I want you to start from the top, Fletch. From an hour before you and your friends found the letter to how it ended up in your backpack. I want to hear everything. Leave nothing out. Is that okay?"

"What's wrong?" Fletcher asked, completely confused.

"Nothing's wrong, Fletch. In fact, just the opposite. Please tell me everything."

Fletcher explained everything—from seeing the changes in the portrait to the sense that he was being watched to their late-night examination of the painting to finding the letter and trying to decipher it. Fletcher was amazed that Uncle Woodrow never doubted anything he said. In fact, he believed everything.

"Did you know the letter was behind the painting?" Fletcher asked.

"No, I had no idea. But I wish I'd thought to look for it there."

"You've been looking for it, Uncle Woodrow? Why?"

"There are some things that you need to know about. And what I tell you, you mustn't tell a soul. You understand?"

The polite command alarmed Fletcher. He paused and looked toward the window. "I understand. I won't tell anyone."

"Breakfast is ready," Lucille called out as she reached the top of the stairs. "Woodrow, you can help me with this tray if you're going to eat."

Woodrow rose and before heading for the door, he turned back to Fletcher and repeated, "Not a soul."

Fletcher sat back in the bed and pulled the covers up over his legs. A chill went down his sore spine as he contemplated Woodrow's warning.

"You ready to eat?' Lucille asked.

"I'm starving, Grans. What's for breakfast?"

She paused, looking at his cast. "You really should keep that leg on the bed, Fletch."

"It is."

"Well, it wasn't. I can tell by the patterns in the blanket that you've been hanging it over the side."

Woodrow laughed loudly and placed the heavy tray on the small table beside the bed. "You've got to be kidding me, Lucy," he said, winking at Fletcher. "The patterns in the blanket? Give me a break."

Lucille shot him a severe look and then meticulously arranged the plates of whole wheat blueberry pancakes, whipped butter, Maine maple syrup, fresh fruit, sliced pink grapefruits, crisp Canadian bacon, skim milk for Fletcher, and black coffee for Woodrow.

"*Mmm*, looks delicious, Lucy," Woodrow said.

She stared at him. "You move over there by the window," she said, "since you'll be taking your mask off while you eat. Funny how you seem to just show up whenever there's a good meal."

"Take it as a compliment" Woodrow replied. "Oh, by the way, there's a box of Paw-Paw bars for you and Edmond on the kitchen table."

"Well, he'll be pleased. Now if you two are all set, I'll check in on Aldous. Remember, not too long Woodrow. I know how you like to talk."

He laughed, glad that she was here taking care of Fletcher and Aldous.

Fletcher and Woodrow sat quietly in the sun-drenched room and enjoyed their breakfast.

"Morning, Fletch. Woody," Sheila said from the doorway.

"How you doing, Sheila?" Woodrow asked.

"Fine, just fine. Enjoy your breakfast," she said and smiled. Then she walked towards Aldous's room down the wide hallway.

Woodrow stood, stretched, and moved toward the window. "We can talk later if you want, Fletch. You've been through a lot."

"Uncle Woodrow, can I tell you something?"

"Anything, Fletch."

Fletcher relaxed and told his great uncle about the man with the dark eyes and long black hair at the top of Buck's Ledge and how he had a gut feeling he had caused the ledge to crash down on them. After he finished, Woodrow said, "I believe you."

Fletcher closed his eyes. Finally, someone believed him. "Are you all right?" Woodrow asked gently.

He nodded, still not wanting to open his eyes.

"Listen, if you're up to it, I have a long story to tell you. But promise me that you'll tell no one."

"I promise."

Woodrow, now masked, sat down bedside the bed and took a deep breath.

"It's a long story," he began. "And one that would've been told to you one day, just not this soon." He paused. "And it should have come from your father, not me. But here we are. This is what's important. It's actually been part of the McKenzie family for many generations. But, for you to understand why that letter you and your friends found is so important, you need to know the history of Mollyockett and how she became an important part of this family. Her history is uniquely intertwined with McKenzie family history and for that very reason, you need to know all you can about her." He stopped and scratched his chin. "What *do* you know of her, son?"

Fletcher was thoroughly confused. "I know that Bethel has a celebration each summer in her honor."

"Yes, I remember you on that float last year," Woodrow said and laughed.

"And Dad told me about some curse she once put on Snow Falls."

"Yes, that's true. She did put a curse on the inhabitants of Snow Falls. But there's a reason why she's celebrated in Bethel every summer. She helped a lot of people and did many good things during her life."

"Like what?"

"I'll go into that later. But the reason we're having this conversation is because the people of Oxford Country and Bethel had no idea how powerful she actually was. She's far more than a name of a parade or celebration and far more colorful than she's portrayed to be. That picture in your father's room is an accurate depiction of how she actually looked."

"Which outfit? I've seen so many in that painting."

Woodrow laughed loudly and then glanced toward to door. He didn't want the others to hear their conversation.

"I'd have to say all of them. I'm sure she wore them all. But let's start from the beginning. It's very important to understand her history and how it influenced the decisions she made. She was born in the summer of 1740 in what is now Fryeburg. During that time both the English and French were settling the area. But unfortunately for the Pigwackets who lived—"

"The who?"

"Pigwackets, the Wabenaki Indian tribe she was born into," Woodrow explained as he took a sip of coffee. "She was born right around the same time that the French priests, which were called Blackrobes, had established a Catholic mission near the area. It was those French settlers who actually changed her name to Marie Agathe when they baptized her into the Catholic religion."

"So where's Mollyockett come from?" Fletcher asked, sliding his leg over the side of the bed.

"There were English settlers there too, and they couldn't pronounce *Marie Agathe* the way the French pronounced it, so over time, her name changed to Molly Ockett."

"Where'd the name Pigwackets come from?"

"Good question. They were named after their village on the Saco River at the southern end of Wabanaki territory, which encompassed what is now all of northern New England and the Canadian Maritimes. The name Pigwacket means *the cleared place*. They are actually one of many tribes in Wabanaki territory. They would meet up with other Wabanaki tribes in the Androscoggin, Kennebec, and Penobscot River valleys in Maine. They walked as far west as the Connecticut Valley, which is now Vermont and New Hampshire, and as far south as the Merrimac Valley in Massachusetts.

"Unlike the French and English settlers," Woodrow continued, "they had a unique and close attachment to the fertile land. They called spring-time *sowing moon* and would head toward the Atlantic Ocean—where Wells and Ogunquit are today—to spend the summer gathering fish and other foods from the coast. A few tribe members, however, would stay behind and plant corn for the winter months. When fall arrived, they would return to their village for the corn harvest. After they collected the corn, they would then break into smaller family units and hunt farther inland. Many of those hunts took place right here in Ketchum."

"Hunting for what?"

"Deer, moose, bear, fox, rabbits, and coyotes. They actually stayed right in this valley until the moon of the blinding snow forced them to return to Pigwacket. Unfortunately, their way of life and living off the land changed dramatically with the arrival of the European settlers in the late seventeenth century."

"How?"

"It was a time of constant upheaval and war between the British and French. Both wanted to claim the land, and unfortunately these peaceful people were thrust right into the middle of it. They were actually forced to take sides. Quite often they were killed for siding with the enemy." He paused and looked out the window. "Roughly thirty years before the Revolutionary War when Molly Ockett was four years old, her family moved to Plymouth County in Massachusetts to escape the dangerous environment. Less than a year later, her family returned to Pigwacket, but they left her in the care of a strict puritanical judge who lived in Boston. During the nine months she spent there, she learned the ways of the colonists and how to speak English. After returning to Pigwacket, she found balance in both traditions. When she was fifteen, another war broke out between the English and French. The Wabanaki tribe once again attempted to remain neutral. Unfortunately for them, the English expelled anyone who sided with the French or remained neutral."

Fletcher listened intently and waited for the connection to his family.

"Molly Ockett and her family fled to Odanak, a Catholic mission on the banks of the St. Lawrence in Quebec. They remained there for four years until the English crossed the Green Mountains and conquered Quebec. The English raided Odanak and slaughtered most of the Pigwackets living there, including Molly's parents."

Fletcher looked at Woodrow intently. "Why kill them if they did nothing wrong?" There was deep sympathy in his voice.

Woodrow shook his head. "That's the travesty of war Fletch. There was a perception that her family had sided with the French when in fact they were only trying to survive. It's believed that Molly and her brother, Tomhegan, actually witnessed their parents being killed.

After the raid at Odanak, Molly Ockett and Tomhegan returned to Pigwacket—except they arrived to discover the town of Fryeburg was now located right where their village used to be. Drawing on her experience with the English in Boston, she decided to stay and set up camp on the banks of the Saco River. By then, she looked like how she appears in that painting in your father's room. She married a fellow Wabanaki named Piel Susup. Like her, he also had a baptismal name—Peter Joseph. After she became pregnant, they returned to Quebec and helped rebuild the St. Francis mission at Odanak, where her child was baptized."

"How do you know all this stuff, Uncle Woodrow?" Fletcher asked.

Woodrow didn't know how to answer this, so he stood up and walked toward the window. He bent down to smell a red rose and said,

"I've been studying Mollyockett ever since I was a little boy. I wonder what she would *actually* think of the current pandemic. Anyway, Piel died soon after arriving at Odanak. Grief-stricken, Mollyockett took her daughter and returned to Fryeburg. As a single mother, she supported herself as a healer, combining the medical traditions of the Native Americans with what she'd learned from the white settlers. She developed a unique ability to heal the sick. Even though she was considered odd, she was a respected healer. She treated everyone regardless of race, economic station, or religion. That was extremely rare at that time."

"She sounds like a wonderful person. I wish I'd known this."

"It's really amazing how few people today do know this. It's a shame really." Woodrow came over to the bed and sat back down. He continued. "She eventually began a very volatile relationship with a married man named Sabattis, and they had three children together—even though he remained with his wife. It was actually an argument with his wife that prompted Mollyockett to take her children and move to where we are today."

The sound of footsteps on the stairs cut him off.

"Okay, Chatty Cathy, he needs to get some rest," Lucille ordered.

"Can you give us a few minutes, Grans?" Fletcher pleaded. "I'm not tired. Honest."

"Oh, by the way, Lucy, I've been meaning to ask you. Last night I was having dinner outside at Zacarolo's with the Fontaines. Who on earth is Three-Finger Willy?" Woodrow asked, laughing.

Lucille waved him off. "Everyone has their skeletons. And from what I hear, you have quite a few yourself," she said and chuckled. She looked at Fletcher. "You have fifteen minutes," she said. "I mean it." As she headed toward Aldous's room, they could hear her still laughing.

"Quick, finish the story," Fletcher urged his uncle in a low whisper.

"Okay. Mollyockett had set up camp on the banks of the Androscoggin River between Bethel and Ketchum. She lived next to a Pigwacket chief named Swassin and his family. They all lived off the land according to their Indian customs.

"The Wabanakis who lived near here would venture into town for ammunition or supplies. They would trade their beads and jewelry they created for the goods. Many moved on just as their ancestors did. Mollyockett and Swassin came to know the locals well. Mollyockett's oldest child, Molly Susup, was one of the first Natives to attend the local schools. Clearly they respected her mother to allow this to happen."

"What do you mean?"

"It's not like today, Fletcher. Back then, living alongside the Indians was one thing, but to allow them to attend school with their children was another. It was unheard of," he said and then sighed. "Mollyockett was really quite an interesting person. Every year she made the 160-mile journey to Odanak for confession and to take communion. She shot wild animals and sold their pelts. I recently read that in the 1770s, a man named Henry Tufts wandered into her camp critically wounded after getting stabbed in a fight. Without asking any questions, she saved his life and nursed him back to health and became good friends with him and his fellow soldiers who were fighting the British during the Revolutionary War. This is where our family comes into her life."

Fletcher scooted to the edge of the bed in anticipation. "How so?"

"Your ancestor Jackson Gage McKenzie was one of those soldiers who'd traveled to Maine from Boston. His unit was so impressed with Mr. Tufts's recovery that they started consulting her whenever they needed medical services. Back then, most medicines were made from things like roots and the bark from trees."

"Is that what she used?"

"No," Woodrow said and then paused. "You need to promise me that you will never repeat this," he repeated.

"I promise," Fletcher said. His stomach was in knots. He'd been waiting for this part of the story for what seemed like hours.

"Mollyockett had knowledge of a very special place unlike any other. It had been passed down from her ancestors to her when she was a little girl. In time, she came to trust Jackson McKenzie and ultimately shared her secret with him. Do you know where Frenchman's Hole is?"

Fletcher was surprised by the question. "Sure, I swim there all the time … Or at least I used to. Why?" Flether asked.

Woodrow ignored the slight self pity and pressed on.

"In 1943, when I was a young man, not much older than you are today, my older brother, Jonathan—"

"Grandfather?"

"Yes, your grandfather. He was drafted into the army when he was twenty-three. I was considerably younger and looked up to him. I was devastated. Right before he left, our father, Rutherford, your great-grandfather, asked me to join them in the study. Your great-grand-father was a very stern but loving man. He worked seven days a week running Cygnus. I remember hearing him leave before the sun rose to go to work, and he wouldn't return until late in the evening. He made the company what it is today. Anyway, Jonathan's getting drafted altered all of my father's plans. So over the course of several hours, they told me the story of Mollyockett and her secret healing powers."

Woodrow paused and closed his eyes, the memory still vivid.

"They also told me," he continued, "about an incident that took place on August 3, 1781. Six Indians led by Tomhegan came down from Quebec through Newry and plundered the settlers' homes in the valley. In an attempt to disrupt the American settlements, the British were paying the Indians eight dollars per prisoner or scalp. Tomhegan hated both the British and the settlers, but because Molly had sided with the settlers, he took the side of the British. He was intensely distrustful of her close friendship with Jackson McKenzie and feared what ultimately happened. You know, the enemy of my enemy is my friend."

Fletcher winced. "They scalped them?"

"Some of them. It was war, Fletch, and the colonists fighting for independence were considered traitors and even terrorists."

"I learned something like that in history class at school."

"I know. Anyway, that night in August, they took several local men prisoner from Bethel, which at the time was Sudbury, Canada. Even though Tomhegan was Mollyockett's brother, they had taken opposite sides in the war, and he considered her a bitter rival."

"Not many people knew Mollyockett was Tomhegan's sister. If they had, she quite possibly would have been hanged. Because she was siding with the Americans, if they lost the war, she knew she'd be killed by either Tomhegan or the British. She was so shaken by the raid that she decided to share her secret with Jackson and arranged to meet him at Frenchman's Hole."

"Why there?"

"After swearing Jackson to secrecy, Mollyockett led him up a hidden path to a passage."

"A passage to where?"

Woodrow stared intently at Fletcher. "The passage to *Whole.*"

There was complete silence in the room.

Those words would change Fletcher McKenzie's life forever. And deep down he knew it.

"According to my father," Woodrow continued, "*Whole* is a magical place deep below us where you can find the species of flora that provide all the nutrients and medicinal ingredients that gave Mollyockett her unique healing powers. Before sharing the secret with Jackson, her family members—including Tomhegan—were the only ones who knew of its existence. The secret was passed down from generation to generation. But she knew that the time of the Pigwackets and Wabanakis had come to an end.

"Mollyockett spent an entire month with Jackson in *Whole*, where its powers were passed from her to him. Her intentions were to have the McKenzie family pass the power of the passage from generation to generation within our family just as it had with her family. She mysteriously knew how to transfer the power outside of her lineage and knew how important it was to keep this a secret from Tomhegan. He was exceptionally dangerous, especially when it came to any interest in the passage to *Whole*. She had personally witnessed his violence for years and knew that if she were killed, he would kill her children and claim the passage as his own—or at least she thought he would. Her only goal at that point was to protect the passage. What they didn't know at the time was that when the power was transferred to Jackson, it immediately stripped Tomhegan of any possibility to exert power over *Whole*. My father implied this was disputed for generations but didn't tell us why."

"You sure she didn't know that Tomhegan would lose his powers?" Fletcher asked.

"According to my father, she had no idea," Woodrow replied. "But she did know he could use the power of the passage to hurt many people."

"I'm still confused. You say power. What does that mean?"

"Fletcher, that's what I've been looking for all this time. That letter you found is quite possibly the clue to everything. It may even be the key to ending this terrible pandemic."

Fletcher's heart raced. "If Jackson acquired the power and intended to pass it down, who has the power now, you?"

Woodrow pointed toward Aldous's bedroom door. "He does."

CHAPTER 9

THE MALADY OF THE WABANAKI

"Your uncle's here, Fletcher," Sheila called from the bottom of the stairs. "Dinner will be ready in about ten minutes."

Fletcher had spent the previous night and entire day on his iPad researching and compiling questions for his uncle. The moment his grandmother noticed the bags under his eyes that morning, she banned all visitors for the day with the exception of Woodrow. She made him swear that he would limit the visit to two hours around dinnertime. When he entered the room carrying a folder and spiral notebook, he chuckled at Fletcher's blond hair, which was matted against one side of his head.

"What's up, bed head?"

"How many of those blue vests do you have?" Fletcher asked and laughed. He finger-combed his hair and then wet it with a small face cloth.

Woodrow set the folder and notebook on the windowsill and then sniffed a large bouquet of wild flowers. "These are lovely. Mind if I take a few of your arrangements to the inn? I have a few out of state guests staying there. Hopefully they're not behind the increasing numbers in Maine."

"Please, take them all. It smells like a perfume factory in here." He lowered his cast over the side of the bed and scooted so he was sitting on the edge of the mattress.

"Careful, your grandmother might see you."

"It's okay. I need to go to the bathroom," he said, picking up his crutches.

Woodrow watched him propel himself across the room. While waiting for Fletcher to return, he looked out the window and watched a small red fox run across the backyard and into the dense woods. Once his nephew was back in bed, Woodrow settled into a chair and pulled the table between them in anticipation of dinner.

Just then they heard Lucille climbing the stairs. She came in carrying a large tray. "I hope you two are hungry."

Woodrow stood and took the tray from her and set it on the table. "There's enough here to feed an army, Lucy," he teased. "This fish looks divine. What is it?"

"Haddock. Edmond was in Portland this morning, and he bought it at the docks."

"Thanks, Grans. I'm starving."

She gave him a smile and then looked at Woodrow. "Sit over by the window. You know the drill and don't forget, no more than two hours, and I'm not joking. You should have seen the bags under his eyes this morning. He needs his rest."

Once she left, Woodrow got up and closed the door quietly. Before sitting back down, he reached into the right pocket of his trousers. "I saw Quinn and Camway at Kemo's this morning. They sent this over. Apparently, your grandmother wouldn't let them in to see you last night." He paused. "I'm surprised you'd eat something like this. You changing your diet these days?"

Fletcher laughed at the sight of the blue candy. A small white note was attached to it with a blue ribbon. "Fletcher, here's a little something for extra energy. Nutritious too! Get better. Camway & Quinn."

"This is one of the new products we're selling at Cygnus," Fletcher explained.

Woodrow looked stricken. "What on earth for?"

"I know," Fletcher agreed. "Aunt Refinna loves them."

"I'm sure she does. Cryin' shame what they're doing to that company. Wait till your father finds out what is going on."

Fletcher didn't respond. He was too preoccupied with everything Woodrow had told him the day before. As soon as they were done eating, he launched into his questions. "So you have no idea where the passage is?"

"No idea," Woodrow confirmed. "When my father told me about the passage, he said that in the event my brother didn't return from the war, he would pass everything on to me at the appropriate time."

"Then why tell you anything at all right then?"

"I guess he was covering all bases. He wasn't only worried about something happening to my brother. He was worried about something happening to *him*. I've no idea what that could have been. You see, the casualties in the war were dramatically increasing by then. He told me that if this occurred, I was to open the safe behind a portrait of George Washington in his study. I was to get the combination from a safety deposit box he'd rented at Maine National."

"Well, why didn't you open the box?"

"I tried. It was closed the year Jonathan returned safely from the war. Obviously, everything regarding the passage was given to my older brother, who then passed it onto your father." He paused reflectively. "Clearly, their plan had a flaw."

Fletcher nodded solemnly, and as the implication sunk in, his cheeks drained of color. "Does that mean that my father was eventually going to pass everything on to me?"

Woodrow paused, aware how overwhelmed his nephew must have felt. "Yes, one day he will. But if it can end this horrible pandemic, as I fully believe it can, then time is of the essence. From what my father told me, *Whole* holds all the secrets when it comes to our health. I'm not saying that it can. I deeply feel it's worth a try."

Fletcher took a long breath and looked at the envelope Woodrow had taken out of his shirt pocket and set on the table. "Do you think that's what was hidden in the safety deposit box at Maine National?"

"Quite possibly. I've been trying to decipher what it means ever since I found it in the tent. I've actually discovered a few answers online at the Mahoosuc Library and Ketchum Historical Society. Tomorrow I'll hit the Bethel Historical Society. I feel like some sort of spy. It's not like I can just march in and request a historical map that will lead me to a secret passage. You've no idea how nosey that staff is."

"What answers?"

Woodrow shook his head. "Give me a few days to organize everything. I'm not sure the information I have is accurate."

Impatient for some answers, Fletcher was annoyed at being put off, but he let it pass. "So what became of Mollyockett?"

"Well, the Protestants eventually came to greatly outnumber Catholics in the Mahoosuc Valley, and they viewed her with a great deal of suspicion. Just take a close look at the portrait in your father's room, and you'll see why." He chuckled again. "But because of her talent for healing injuries and sick people, they still respected her. As the community continued to grow and prosper, more educated doctors moved in, and people's attitudes changed. In the late fall of 1810, while a major blizzard was raging here in Oxford County, Mollyockett—who was seventy years old by then—was out in whiteout conditions, searching for anyone who might be sick or injured. From what I've read, she hadn't expected the storm. She was just trying to make ends meet. She stopped at every house in the small village of Snow Falls, asking for a place, even a barn to sleep for the night. But every single one of the residents turned her away. Cold and frustrated, she headed south toward Paris Hill but only after placing a curse on the small community."

"What type of curse?"

"According to legend, she cursed the prosperous village with hard times, so much so that no business would be successful there again."

"Did it work?"

Woodrow rubbed the spot between his brows. "Actually, it looks like it did. It may have been a coincidence, but shortly thereafter, the village mill burned down. Many of the residents lost their jobs, which led to stores closing. Within a few years, most of the people had moved to other towns, and their houses fell into disrepair and were eventually demolished."

"That doesn't sound like a coincidence," Fletcher said.

"I know, but the story of the blizzard gets better. This is fact, look it up. When she eventually reached the hamlet of Paris Hill, she knocked on the front door of the largest house, which belonged to Dr. Hamlin, one of the wealthiest men in the state. His family was despondent at the time because his infant son was near death from an unknown illness. Desperate, Dr. Hamlin let this Indian woman into his home without qualm. Somehow, she was able to do for the baby what his father couldn't. After he was healed, she performed a traditional Wabanaki blessing for good health and prosperity for the child and assured his parents that their son would become someone famous."

"Did he?"

"Ever heard of Hannibal Hamlin?"

"Yeah, I have. We studied him in American history. He was the first vice president under Abraham Lincoln, right?"

"Yes, he was. Bravo. Your father actually has his portrait hanging in his room."

Fletcher nodded. "So what happened to Mollyockett after she cured Hannibal Hamlin? And whatever happened to her brother?"

"We know that Tomhegan continued to organize raids into Bethel, Ketchum, Newry, and Mahoosuc every few years. It terrified the local people." He reached over and picked up the folder he had brought. "When I was at the Mahoosuc Historical Society two days ago, I found a sketch of Tomhegan that ran in the local papers the day after one of his attacks." He handed Fletcher the copy he had made of the newspaper drawing. "As you can see, he's a spitting image of his sister."

Fletcher looked at the picture and froze. His leg began to spasm from the adrenaline shooting through his body.

Woodrow jumped up, thinking he was having some kind of seizure. "Fletch, what's wrong? What's happening?"

"It's him!" Fletcher finally blurted out.

Woodrow grabbed his hand. "Calm down," he said.

Fletcher pulled away and pointed at the drawing . "That's the one I told you about yesterday. That's the man I saw on the cliff right before the rock slide." The sudden nightmarish memory of seeing the boulder crashing down made him shudder.

Woodrow slowly sat back down. "Are you positive?"

There wasn't a doubt in Fletcher's mind. He'd never forget those eyes staring directly at him while on Devil's Leap. "I'm 100 percent positive. I'll never forget his face. You have to believe me."

Woodrow looked at Fletcher intently. "I believe you. I just don't understand it."

"Do you think the man on the cliff is a relative?"

Woodrow reread the newspaper clipping. "It says here that Tomhegan disappeared and was never seen again after Mollyockett's funeral."

"What year was that?"

"She died in 1816, six years after that blizzard in 1810. She fell ill while camping with another Wabanaki chief named Metallak in Andover, twenty miles from here. She was also friends with a Captain Bragg from Andover and requested that he build her a wigwam to live out her last days. During the last two months of her life, she shared her life and medical secrets with family members."

"What about the location of the passage?"

"No. From what my father told me, she only told Jackson that secret. According to the cemetery caretaker, the day after her funeral, Tomhegan was spotted sprinkling something on her grave and chanting. To this day, nobody knows what happened to him." Woodrow put the clipping down. "Ever since I started digging, I've discovered things that barely make sense. But if we work together, I'm confident we can get to the bottom of it."

Fletcher glanced at the messages on his cast. "How's that going to happen with me stuck here? There's no way Grans is going to let me do anything."

"Well, you can give me your thoughts on what we should do, and until you've healed, I can do most of the leg work. Your little computer over there should help you look things up."

"What have you discovered that barely makes sense?" Fletcher asked.

"Well, the other day I learned that many believe that both Tomhegan and Mollyockett's spirits are still wandering in this valley. They are also direct descendants of Kozart, the earliest known leader of the Wabanaki people. He ruled more than four hundred years ago, and he was responsible for uniting various tribes together to create what we now know as the Wabanaki Nation. Once unified, his people lived in harmony and prospered tremendously off the bounty of the land. "

"Kozart was mentioned in the letter," Fletcher said.

Woodrow nodded and opened the letter. He found the passage, tracing the words with his finger. "Beware the beast, for if knowledge fails, it is certain Kozart prevails."

"What's that mean?"

"Honestly, I've no idea," Woodrow admitted.

It is like a big puzzle, Fletcher thought. "Where's Mollyockett buried?" he asked.

"Woodlawn Cemetery in Andover. Her grave remained unmarked for nearly fifty years until a group of local women raised the funds to honor her with an appropriate marker. That gravestone identifies her as the last of her kind."

Fletcher was confused. "She was the last one left of the Pigwackets?"

"No, obviously not, but she *was* the last one to understand the balance of nature and its importance to us as humans. She lived on, by, and for the land and used its bounty to heal. In the years following her death, stories about her life and deeds had become legendary. Most admired her knowledge about herbal doctoring, but others suggested that she was a witch with magical powers who inflicted harm on anyone who provoked her wrath. I'm fully convinced she selected Jackson to share her secret with because she knew he would be committed to the importance of the passage and to *Whole*, and she was right. Cygnus is a direct result of everything Jackson learned from Mollyockett during the time he spent with her. That's why Cygnus's focus has always been on healthy foods."

Fletcher pursed his lips. "Not any longer," he chided.

"We all know what they're doing to this company," Woodrow said and sighed. "Every McKenzie who's had anything to do with Cygnus is rolling in their graves right now."

"If I was running the company, I'd continue running it just as Dad did."

"I'm sure you would, Fletch. I'm sure you would."

"Especially Birch Bread. I can't believe they're selling it."

Woodrow gasped. "You're joking."

"No. Quinn's father is buying it for his company."

"Over my dead body," Woodrow muttered, jotting something down in his spiral notebook. "Any idea when this'll happen?"

"Soon, I think. But at least it's Aquidneck that's buying the bread. It could be worse," Fletcher said, trying to put a positive spin on it.

"Oh, it's not them I'm worried about, son. It's that your aunts have decided to sell off the very foundation of the company. Birch Bread is what made Cygnus famous." He paused and then asked, "Have you talked to anyone regarding your legal rights with respect to the company?"

"I think Aunt Refinna's taken care of that."

"Well, isn't that convenient for her," Woodrow said bitterly.

Fletcher had the sudden and distinct feeling his uncle was hiding something. "Uncle Woodrow, what's going on?"

Woodrow glanced toward the room where Aldous lay comatose. "I'm just trying to make sense of everything myself."

Fletcher was getting impatient with his uncle beating around the bush. "My name is Fletcher Gage McKenzie. I carry on two of Jackson's names for a reason. What else haven't you told me?" Then he added, "Don't you trust me?"

Woodrow took a deep breath. "Okay. After your father fell ill, his attorney asked me to take his medical records that weren't online to the hospital. While searching his office at Cygnus for the records, I found a thick folder locked in safe that contained the medical history of every McKenzie dating all the way back to Jackson. I didn't want your aunts to see what I'd found, so I took them to the inn. It's a blessing Odella is still working there."

"You ever find Dad's medical records?"

"Oh, yes. They were in a drawer in his desk. I immediately brought them to the hospital." He paused and said sadly, "Obviously, they didn't help."

"Obviously," Fletcher agreed in a whisper.

"Anyway, I studied what I'd found in the folder, and that's when I realized—"

The anguish in Woodrow's eyes made Fletcher tense. He knew it wasn't good. "You realized what?"

"I traced the McKenzie family tree from Jackson down to your father. And I found that every McKenzie who possessed knowledge of the passage's existence eventually contracted a mysterious medical condition or had an untimely demise." He paused and closed his eyes. "Every single one of them died an early death."

Fletcher looked away and muttered in a pained voice, "Dad." He felt something shift inside, fueled by disbelief.

"Did you share your findings with Mom before she left?"

"Yes, I told her."

"Do you think that she—"

"No!" Woodrow said firmly. "I don't believe that whatever happened to her and Nimsy on that trip is related to what happened to the other McKenzies. She didn't know about the passage."

"But if Mom knew about the passage, it makes all the sense in the world. You just said that something's happened to every McKenzie that had knowledge of Mollyockett's secret."

"You'll have to trust my gut on this one, Fletch," he said calmly.

"Dad and Mom shared everything."

"There's no way he'd do that. He was McKenzie to the core," Woodrow insisted.

Fletcher snorted. "If you were married and you knew that your three horrible sisters were next in line to take over your company if anything happened to you, wouldn't you tell your wife?"

Woodrow smiled. "I see your point. It's hard not to when put it that way. Here," he said handing Fletcher the folder. "I'll leave this with you to read. It's my research—copies of any newspaper clippings, maps, and historical documents. I think you'll find them interesting. If we can find the location of the passage's entrance, all the other pieces of the puzzle will follow. We're in this together. Something good will come of this. You mark my word, son."

"So if every McKenzie died an early death or were *murdered,* how'd the secret to the passage pass on to the next in line?"

"Ah, that's the ten-million-dollar question, Fletch, and why we have lots of work to do and quickly."

"Are those medical records in there?"

"Everything's there. I think you'll be pleasantly surprised with what this helpless old man found at the library and historical society. Why I've even managed to navigate their computers, which in and of itself is amazing. That invention by Mr. Google is mind-boggling."

Fletcher laughed. "When can we talk again?"

"How's Sunday work for you? That'll give you just enough time to read over everything."

Fletcher nodded.

"Good, I'll tell your grandmother to expect me up here for dinner with you on Sunday night." Woodrow patted his head and then left.

Once alone, Fletcher's thoughts kept going back to Tomhegan standing over Mollyockett's grave. As he drifted off to sleep, he imagined him casting a curse over his sister's body for betraying their deeply held family secret—a curse that could one day spell his own demise.

CHAPTER 10

CHIEF TOMHEGAN'S CURSE

DESPITE THE MANY VISITORS WHO SHOWED UP IN THE DAYS AFTER HIS uncle's visit, Fletcher's mind remained preoccupied with everything he'd learned. He spent hours pouring over the material his uncle had meticulously researched and collected. Of particular interest to Fletcher were the medical records and death certificates of all his ancestors, beginning with Jackson.

Jackson McKenzie had lived in the valley when Bethel was known as Sudbury, Canada, a village of three hundred residents. Although not located in Canada, it was so named after the Massachusetts General Court—Maine was Massachusetts territory until 1820—granted the land to several residents of Sudbury, Massachusetts, in appreciation for their service at the Battle of Quebec.

Following the War of Independence, Sudbury, Ketchum, Newry, and Hanover grew rapidly. Settlers were attracted by the fertile soil along the Androscoggin River—land originally cleared by the Pigwacket Indians for growing corn. In 1785, a great flood washed away most of the businesses, houses, and farms of Ketchum and Sudbury.

The name was changed to Bethel in 1796, and soon after that, Jackson McKenzie became the first representative from Bethel to the Massachusetts General Court. Utilizing Mollyockett's knowledge of the area, Jackson developed a detailed flood plan and moved the growing community to higher ground. Jackson's flood plan is still used all these years later.

There was also a copy of the McKenzie family tree in the folder. At the top were Mary Catherine McKenzie and William Gage McKenzie, who in 1749 emigrated from Cork, Ireland, to Boston, where Jackson Gage McKenzie was born soon after. The family tree then followed the McKenzie lineage from Jackson down to Jonathan Gage McKenzie, Woodrow's brother and Fletcher's grandfather.

An oval circle below each date of death contained the cause of death. Fletcher's heart raced as he read each listing—Jackson Gage McKenzie, hunting accident; Joseph G. McKenzie, indeterminate suspicious; Frances Gage McKenzie, possible poisoning; Franklin Gage McKenzie, structure fire; Thomas Gage McKenzie, drowning; Rutherford Gage McKenzie, Jonathan Gage McKenzie, indeterminate—

"Dad, please help me to understand all of this. Please," Fletcher said quietly. He lowered his injured leg over the side of the bed. The pain, which he was oblivious to while reading the documents, was now coursing through his entire body.

Using his crutches, he carefully hobbled down the long hall to his father's room. The only sound was the *tick-tock* of the grandfather clock. Nothing ever changed in this room. Fletcher glanced at his father and then moved to the large portrait of Mollyockett hanging on the back wall. He studied her strong, angular features and royal bearing. With what he now knew, he decided her personality matched her looks.

"Speak to me, Marie Agathe," he whispered. "I need to help my parents. Please help me. I need some direction."

He could imagine Tomhegan standing over her grave, chanting or stalking settlers, waiting for the right moment to strike.

He was startled when his grandmother yelled from the bottom of the stairs. "Fletch, you have a visitor. You decent?"

He made his way to the door. "Who is it?"

He could hear his grandmother climbing the steps. When she saw him, she walked down to Aldous's room. "Cicely is here." She noticed Fletcher looked pale. "You okay?"

"I'm just sitting with Dad. It's good to be out of that bed." He shifted and winced in pain.

"Land sakes, Fletch," Lucille scolded him. "You really shouldn't be up. I'll tell Cicely you're not up for it right now."

"I'll be okay—honest. Please tell her to come up. I'm bored stiff!"

"Well, okay. But just for a few minutes. Her mother is with her, and she seems pressed for time. Honestly, everybody's always on the run. But before I send her up, you may want to change your shirt and sweatpants, young man. I can help you if you want. You've been in them for days now. I'm detecting a distinct Fletcher odor in here. You McKenzie men are all the same," she said with a warm smile. "I ever tell you how much I love you?" She kissed the top of his head and then added, "Time for a haircut too."

"What's wrong with my hair?" he asked, running his hand through his pillow-matted hair.

"And don't forget to brush your teeth. Clear as day what you had for your last meal every time you smile, honestly," she said jovially. As she headed toward the stairs with dirty linens, she called over her shoulder. "Don't forget. Only a few minutes."

Fletcher quickly brushed his teeth and combed his hair. Then with great difficulty, he changed into the clean clothes his grandmother had left on his chest of drawers. He gulped down a warm glass of orange juice leftover from breakfast, and as he settled back on his bed, he heard Cicely climbing the stairs.

"Fletch, it's me," she said quietly as she walked in, mindful that Aldous was down the hall. She was wearing a faded Balston Prep T-shirt, jeans, and stylish leather shoes. She sat down in the chair next to the bed. Her eyes were immediately drawn toward the cast on Fletcher's leg.

"I know. A little inconvenient for summer activities," he joked.

"Fletch, I was so scared," she said, her eyes tearing up at the memory. "I can't get that image of the falling ledge out of my mind. I really thought you both had died."

"I don't really remember too much."

"Maybe that's a good thing."

"I guess I was at the wrong place—"

"At the wrong time," Cicely finished the sentence for him. Then she leaned toward him and lightly kissed his cheek.

Fletcher's face flushed red.

"What? A relieved friend can't give you a little supportive peck?" she asked.

Fletcher smiled. "How's Blanche doing?"

"Honestly, she's a total wreck. We all are. She's decided to spend the summer with her cousins on Cape Cod. Just looking at what's left of Bucks Ledge every day is a painful reminder."

"I know what you mean. Every time I look out those windows, I think how lucky we all were."

"Fletch, I feel so awful. If only I'd have looked up—"

"Cicely, it wasn't anyone's fault. It was just a freak accident. The forestry service told my grandfather that Buck's Ledge has rock slides every year. Lots of them. This one was just a little bit bigger." He was determined to alleviate her guilt etched deep into her face. "I'm just glad to be here. By the way, you remember to bring my trash off the ledge? I suffered many no-see-um bites for that garbage."

"You almost died, and you're worried about that trash?" she exclaimed.

"Almost doesn't count. Plus I hear there's an even better swimming hole at Bucks Beach now."

"You mean *Fletcher's Pond,*" she corrected him with a grin. "Oh, by the way, I brought you these," Cicely said handing him a brown paper bag. "I had to sneak them past your grandmother. Not an easy thing to do. I told her they were Paw-Paw bars from your uncle's inn. I'm sorry, but it was the only way to get them past her."

Opening the bag, he saw a half dozen of the delicious and healthy Paw-Paw bars. Confused, he asked, "Why would you have to sneak these past her? She loves them."

"Dig deeper."

Fletcher gasped with delight. "Whoopie pies!" he said and laughed, pulling out two of the large, chocolate, cream-filled pastries from the bottom of the bag.

"You're right. Grans would have killed you if she saw these. She rolls her eyes in disgust every time she sees them on the counter at Kemo's store."

"My mother made them for you last night. I told her how much you loved them the last time she made them. These have little bits of dark chocolate mixed in with the cream."

"Here, eat one with me."

Cicely shook her head. "Sorry, I'm eating healthy this summer," she said and chuckled, rolling her eyes.

"You sure?"

"I'd rather have one of those Paw-Paw bars. A girl's gotta watch her figure." She smiled and grabbed one of the blueberry-filled squares. "Listen, I've got to run. Mom's waiting downstairs."

"Cicely, we need to get going!" yelled Lorraine Parker from the bottom of the stairs. "We're already behind schedule."

"Coming!" Cicely shouted toward the door and then looked at Fletcher. "Listen, I'll stop in on Tuesday… if that's okay," she said, pecking him on the cheek. "Enjoy your Whoopie pies."

He was still smiling long after she had run out the door.

———

Fletcher was up bright and early Sunday morning for breakfast with his grandparents. He'd spent most of the previous night scouring Uncle Woodrow's documents and surfing the Web for any additional information that might be useful.

Woodrow had called on Saturday with a change of plans. Instead of them having lunch at the house, he wanted to pick Fletcher up and take him out. Of course, Lucille was dead set against it.

"You ask me," Woodrow noted, "a comfortable outside restaurant seat is much better than being in bed all the time. Especially at that age. Shame. You're the one who said he was at risk for blood clots if he didn't move around."

Lucille reluctantly agreed after Woodrow promised to call her every hour with an update on Fletcher's pain and said he would host the first post pandemic Red Hatter's dinner—free of charge—at McKenzie's Inn, a bribe he was all too pleased to offer.

Fletcher was sitting anxiously on the front granite steps when his uncle pulled up in his thirty-year-old, hunter-green Land Rover

Defender 90. Built in England, the steering wheel was on the right side, and the passenger seat was on the left side. Fletcher was excited. The top was off, and it was a spectacular day. What more could he ask for? For a few glorious moments, the world was wonderful again.

Before Woodrow could turn off the ignition, Lucille was out the door and approaching the vehicle with venomous eyes. "Woody, you're taking that? Those shocks are as old are you are. He's in no condition to ride in that jalopy, good heavens."

"Calm down, Lucy. Mr. Trent gave her a complete go-over last month. She's good as new. Look, even these shocks are heavy duty. This thing purrs like a kitten." He kicked the front tire with his worn L.L. Bean duck-hunting boots.

"Well, your kitten roars like a lion. I heard you coming for the last three miles. Property values in Rugby Hills plummet every time you pull onto Sangar Drive," she huffed. "Remember our deal, Woody. And there'd better be lobster salad on the buffet at the Red Hatter's dinner. You know what we like." She bent over to kiss the top of Fletcher's head. "You take it slow today, okay? And remember to keep those masks on."

Woodrow held up a small plastic bottle of hand sanitizer and smiled.

She gave him a final glare before heading inside with a slam of the door.

"Well, that was far easier than I expected," he said, removing a large June bug from the front grill of the truck. "I brought this rig because I know how much you love it, Fletch. I fully expected her to change her mind and stand on the front lawn with your father's old musket. I thought I would need to hightail it over those bushes as an escape." He grinned at Fletcher.

"Thanks for getting me out of the house, Uncle Woodrow," Fletcher said gratefully, sliding into the vehicle with some difficulty. "Where we going?"

Woodrow tossed Fletcher's crutches in the back. "To the Mahoosuc Hotel," he said.

Fletcher was surprised. "I thought we were having lunch."

"We are. I've reserved that small lounge for coffee in the back of the hotel so we can have some privacy before we eat and talk. I've preordered a large platter of seafood linguine—extra lobster, at Zacarolo's afterwards. Don't tell your grandmother though. She thinks we are eating outside. She'll kill me if she finds out that we dined indoors. Social distancing or not, we have an important engagement with Aleksandr Von Piddle."

CHAPTER 11

VON PIDDLE'S MAPS

"MR. VON PIDDLE IS AN OLD FRIEND OF MINE," WOODROW EXPLAINED. "We graduated from Balston the same year and were cocaptains of the ski team our senior year. I was downhill. He was cross-country and jumping. Mt. Zircon only had two trails and a towrope in those days. Nothing like today."

Fletcher immediately relaxed. He was free.

They turned left onto Covered Bridge Road. Fletcher quickly grabbed the support strap hanging from the roll bar and winced in pain as Woodrow rounded the bend a little too quickly.

"Aleksandr obtained a doctorate in both survey engineering and Native American studies. He's considered an expert in locating ancient burial sites and important archeological treasures. He returned home to Ketchum ten years ago when he retired. If there is one person who can help us, it's Aleksandr Von Piddle."

"You told him about the passage?" Fletcher asked, sounding alarmed.

"Relax. I've told him a little white lie. He thinks we're looking for an ancient Indian meeting place for a summer project you've been assigned."

Fletcher grinned. "And he bought it?"

"Hesitantly, yes. He actually thinks I've flipped my lid to have you out of bed this soon, but so do most people. So I guess it doesn't matter, does it?" He winked at Fletcher. "I've only given him the lines from the letter that mention the path from the north and the one with the eagle's nest. Hopefully, he can make some sense of it all."

Fletcher felt happy. He was enjoying riding in his uncle's vintage rig on a sunny day. Uncle Woodrow turned right onto Main Street in downtown

Ketchum and then said, "After lunch I thought we'd go to Mollyockett's grave at Woodlawn Cemetery in Andover. It has to be her grave that's referenced in the riddle. Remember how I told you a group of women had a headstone put on her grave years after her death? According to my research, Mollyockett actually had a marker placed at her grave not long after she died. But it mysteriously disappeared the very next day, never to be found. One of the ladies who spearheaded the drive to replace it, Edna McKenzie—Franklin Gage McKenzie's wife—was adamant that it be an exact copy of the original, right down to the white granite from Odanak. Edna even hired the same monument maker from Rumford," Woodrow said as he pulled into Mahoosuc Hotel's large parking lot off Main Street. "Four years later Edna died in that fire with Franklin."

"Do you think they died in that fire because of that?" Fletcher asked.

They were both silent for a moment. Then Woodrow said,

"I really don't know what to think after everything we've learned these past few days. Let's see if Mr. Von Piddle's made some headway."

"I think *he* killed 'em," Fletcher said, reaching into the backseat for his crutches. Woodrow didn't respond.

Upon entering the hotel lobby, Fletcher was immediately besieged by well-intended "get well soon" wishers and pelted with questions by curious townsfolk. To date, it was by far the biggest story of the decade in the Mahoosuc Valley.

Woodrow quickly steered Fletcher toward the back of the lobby under the guise of proper social distancing. The hotel manager quickly closed ranks and placed a gold-plated "private party" sign behind them to keep people from following.

"Well, that was unexpected," Fletcher said.

"You're quite the attention grabber," Uncle Woodrow said and chuckled, walking toward the man sitting on one of the two leather couches located near the back. "Fletch, the illustrious Aleksandr Von Piddle," he said with pride as he patted the elderly man gently on the back.

Von Piddle stood and nodded at Fletcher. "Pleasure's all mine. Always happy to meet a fellow adventurer," he said warmly through his plaid mask.

"Nice to meet you," Fletcher said.

Aleksandr Von Piddle looks like his name, Fletcher thought. He was slim with thinning white hair, which was tidy and stiff, as was his blue-and-white seersucker suit, which he wore with white leather shoes. Small, wire-framed bifocals were perched tightly on the end of his long, pointed nose. His penetrating dark eyes showed genuineness during the powerful handshake.

Fletcher sat beside his uncle on the couch facing Aleksandr, who looked at him with interest. "I've been keeping up on that dreadful incident at the state park. Reminds me of the time I climbed K-2 with those two Russians. Nasty incident. Lucky to be here today. But that's a story for another time," he said, blinking his eyes rapidly, causing his glasses to bounce on the tip of his nose.

"Splendid affair you hosted, Woody. I was honored to be there given the severe restrictions with crowd size. Quite the impressive crowd. Even Senator Stone was there. He must be up for reelection. Food was absolutely delightful. Especially those plump lobster and clam hors d'oeuvres. You've got a winner there. Almost thought they'd escape me with those three gargantuan women standing at the kitchen door in order to be first to devour every tray the wait staff brought out. Absolute wildebeests the way they gorged on everything. I even saw the one with the red glasses—those diamonds looked fake by the way—stuff a handful of those miniature Whoopie pies in her purse. Reminds me of the time I was on safari in Botswana with the Lithuanian Special Forces. Downright savages. But that's a story for another time," he said with more rapid blinking.

What's that all about? Fletcher thought, amused. He had barely contained himself with how Aleksandr described Aunt Refinna.

"I'm glad you enjoyed yourself, Alek." Woodrow smiled. "That last-minute change to hold the event under a tent at the inn proved to be the right decision. Everyone is anxious to spend more time outside after being locked down for months. It was excruciating, though, to keep the guest list under fifty people to satisfy state law. I have the feeling many uninvited people were offended. Along with online donations, we raised more than forty thousand dollars for the Mahoosuc Valley Diabetic Society."

A waiter approached, and Woodrow ordered drinks. They all pushed apart and removed their masks. "I'll have a triple espresso, and bring two unsweetened ice teas for them, extra mint if possible." When the waiter left, Woodrow got right down to business. "So Alek, how'd you make out with the information I gave you?"

"Well, I've learned a few tasty morsels of information that I'm sure will make your history teacher drool with envy, Fletcher. I always ponder the words before I research. It's always worked for me in the past, and the best way to ponder such things is to paint." He waved his hand back and forth as if making broad brushstrokes in the air. "So I trudged right into my latest work of the covered bridge, quite the handsome structure. Reminds me of the time I was leading that archeological survey of Saint Peter's sarcophagus in Vatican City with the Swiss Guard. Magnificent, simply magnificent. But that's a story for another time."

Is he making all this up? Fletcher wondered. Uncle Woodrow was listening as though nothing was odd, not even the rapid blinking and bouncing glasses.

Aleksandr paused. "Now where was I ... right, your drooling teacher. Highest marks coming your way, young man. What I found after a few hours of painting the small rocks under the bridge was something you mentioned about Wabanaki North, Woody. It suddenly hit me. Mollyockett's tribe, the Pigwackets, roamed this part of Maine following the seasons in search of food and livelihood. Wabanaki North was the area they hunted in during autumn. They hunted moose, black bears, and whitetail deer, which they salted and dried for protein during the long winter. The furs were used as currency with the white settlers or others in New England."

"What's that got to do with all this?" asked Woodrow, attempting to steer the conversation in the direction of the riddle.

"I'm getting there," Alek said, huffing. "The area was ripe with large game and a perfect place to plan for the coming winter. Reminds me of the time I was in Nebraska searching for the grave of Red Cloud, the Oglala Sioux leader. But that's—"

"A story for another time," Woodrow said. "Alek, get on with it. We can do the *National Geographic* world tour when we're not pressed for time, which we are," Woodrow said, gritting his teeth impatiently.

Aleksandr seemed mildly offended but continued. "Right, so they go to Wabanaki North for hunting, which is exactly where Ketchum and the northwest corner of Bethel are located today." He announced this information with a satisfied smile, looking like he had discovered the secret to the universe.

Fletcher and Uncle Woodrow exchanged somber looks.

Alek took a drink of his iced tea and then said, "Those rocks I was painting made me think of a shipwreck off the coast of Maine in 1690. Sir William Phipps was sent by the colony of Massachusetts to reconquer Nova Scotia and Quebec from the French. As he approached the coast of Maine, one of his ships wrecked near Portland. The expedition succeeded in winning back Nova Scotia but failed miserably in Quebec. Forced to retreat, several of Phipps men hightailed it through Maine as they headed home to Boston. Six of these soldiers spent the summer near Frenchman's Hole in Ketchum. One of them, a fellow by the name of Robert Nurse, who was from Marblehead, kept a detailed journal of their stay, which now belongs to the Maine Historical Society in Augusta. That led me to Harvey Knox, an old friend and curator at the society. I rang his office and kindly asked if he would take a gander at Mr. Nurse's journal, which he did and called me back less than an hour later."

"And?" Woodrow prompted.

After another sip of tea, Aleksandr continued, "Mr. Nurse had written about a small path created by whitetail deer on their way to the river for water. There was also another well-worn path leading from Frenchman's Hole toward the direction of Quebec that was a direct route for the Indians who traveled from the coast to the Mahoosuc Mountains and beyond. According to the journal, there was an ancient elm tree at the intersection of the two paths. It was the highest in the valley, where a pair of eagles nested for years."

"But that tree would not be there today, Alek," Woodrow noted.

"No, it's long gone. Killed off likely by the elm disease that swept the North American continent last century. But according to Mr. Nurse, that trail was called Passamaquoddy Road by the local Indians, which was dominated by the Pigwackets. If you followed the larger trail due east, it lead directly to the Passamaquoddy tribe in Downeast, Maine, thus the name. So using that juicy bit of information, I set to work and archived the historical maps of Ketchum and Mahoosuc as well as Sudbury, Canada ... and *voilà*," he said victoriously, clapping his hands in delight.

Woodrow looked confused. "But there's no Passamaquoddy Road anywhere in the valley."

"Have patience, Woody. Let me get there." Alek reached for a blue folder. He removed copies of several old maps and spread them on the coffee table. "The map with the faded stamp in the upper right hand corner is of Ketchum when it was first incorporated in 1713. Right here," he said and pointed, "is Frenchman's Hole, and that little line is Passamaquoddy Road."

Fletcher leaned in closer to see what Aleksandr had pointed out.

"Now see those little dots? That is the deer trail Mr. Nurse referenced in his journal."

"What's there today?" Woodrow asked.

"Well, in 1880, the name was changed from Passamaquoddy to Clark's Run after Benjamin Clark, a most unfortunate fellow. You see, he was actually kidnapped for a brief time by Chief Tomhegan, Mollyockett's brutal brother."

Woodrow again glanced at Fletcher and then said to Aleksandr. "There's no Clark's Run now either."

"Right you are again, Woody," Alek confirmed gleefully. "Take a look at the next map. It's shows a more recent Ketchum. Start at Frenchman's Hole and follow that same trail. In 1961, Clark's Run was renamed Sangar Drive in honor of Governor Sangar, who—"

"That's the street I live on," Fletcher blurted out, stunned. The small hairs on the back of his neck stood up. He glanced at his uncle, who was holding the map with shaking hands.

"What a unique coincidence. Stranger things have happened. Reminds me of the time—"

"Alek, please, *please* get on with it," Woodrow begged.

"Your impatience is going to kill you, ol' boy," Alek said and smiled.

"Anyway, I went straight to the Ketchum town hall where they keep the deeds. I was determined to pinpoint the exact location of the intersection of those two old trails—you know, where the eagles nested." He pulled a piece of paper from the folder. "Whoever lives at 1942 Sangar Drive is the proud owner of an ancient eagle's nesting spot."

"*That's where I live*," Fletcher practically shouted.

"Well, slap me sideways," Aleksandr said, blinking wildly. "You'll shock the pants off that history teacher of yours when you turn in your summer project. Heavens to Betsy, I can only imagine what's waiting to be unearthed in your backyard. Reminds me of the time I was in Central Mexico on that Aztec dig. Poor family never even knew that their comfortable house was actually sitting on a ancient mass grave. Simply terrified them. But that's a story for another day."

Woodrow and Fletcher barely heard him. They were too stunned by what they'd learned.

"What do you mean we don't have a reservation!"

They all looked toward the café to pinpoint the source of the commotion. Fletchers three aunts, along with Ogden and Oberon, were impatiently standing at the hostess stand. Aunt Refinna was bright red and screaming at a terrified teenage girl who was furiously scanning the reservation book. The hotel was famous for its Sunday brunch buffet and was always sold out in advance. Reservations were even harder to secure during the pandemic with fifty percent seating in all restaurants mandated by the state. It was *the* place to meet and be seen with your Sunday best by the residents of Mahoosuc Valley.

"You'll call the Kragly Moose for us? *Are you out of your mind?* You actually think I would eat there? We came for a decent Sunday brunch, not donkey meat served by clowns in a roach-infested henhouse. How dare you," Refinna exclaimed. "My secretary made our reservations two days ago," she spat into her mask.

"I understand, Miss—"

"It's *Mizz* McKenzie to you," Refinna boomed, her flabby arms flailing wildly at the panic-stricken hostess. Serena and Winola stood behind her with both hands on their hips, scowling with unified hostility.

"But Ms. McKenzie, we've been sold out for three weeks," the flushed hostess squeaked.

"Where's Claus? Get him out here *right this instant.*"

As the hostess picked up the phone, Aleksandr pointed with genuine surprise. "There they are again, those three rhinos from your fundraiser. Just look at her ranting and raving at that poor girl. What an utterly vulgar walrus. Reminds me of the time I was in Uzbekistan on that government-sponsored dig, unearthing a—"

"*Uncle Woodrow!*" Refinna screeched in a piercing voice. She brushed aside the cowering hostess and strode toward the closed-off lounge, knocking over the private party sign with her oversized hunter-green crocodile skin purse.

Fletcher immediately stuffed the documents back into the folder and slid it under the table.

"You're their uncle, Woody?" Aleksandr's face turned bright red and beads of sweat formed on his wrinkled forehead. "Never in a million years," he whispered behind his mask, cringing as he watched Refinna approach them. *Looks like a bull in a Dresden china shop*, he thought.

"Can you have a word with Claus?" she demanded. "The twins are absolutely famished."

"Now Refinna, calm down," he said gently to his disheveled niece. "Obviously, there was a small miscommunication somewhere. I'll speak to Claus. Give me a sec." Woodrow headed toward the hostess stand.

Refinna looked at Fletcher. "Look who's up and about. I take it you'll be back to work sooner than we expected," she said sharply. "That's what you get for all your horseplay. Why on earth—"

"I don't believe we've met, *Madame*," Aleksandr interrupted while graciously nodding toward the frazzled woman.

Refinna quickly took a step back, glaring cautiously at Von Piddle. "Refinna McKenzie. Woodrow is my uncle," she said, taking in his blue-and-white-striped suit.

"Aleksandr Von Piddle, old chap of your eccentric uncle," he said and gently shook her hand for a brief moment. "We grew up together.

Those glasses … anyone ever tell you how much they accentuate those lovely eyes?"

"Um, well, on a few occasions. Actually, um, people compliment me on my features quite often," a totally disarmed Refinna blurted, blushing a deep red.

"I can see how you're related to Woodrow. You're clearly a woman of class."

It had been decades since anyone had spoken to Refinna like that. Her heart skipped a beat as she focused on Von Piddle in a new light. *Hmm, he's a little older, but maybe,* she thought nervously.

"Well, birds of a feather, you know," she said and giggled like a schoolgirl, batting her eyes playfully.

Fletcher pressed on his bruised rib cage, causing instant pain, which kept him from breaking into uncontrollable laughter at the sight unfolding before him.

"I noticed you at the fundraiser Woodrow hosted, you and your two lovely sisters enjoying the wide array of foods," he continued playfully. "Clearly, you're a connoisseur of the better things in life. Why don't you give us the privilege of joining us." Aleksandr gestured toward the empty side of his couch, ignoring social distancing guidelines.

"I'd be delighted," said Refinna, awestruck. She quickly sat down, which caused Von Piddle to rise up because of her immense weight.

"So tell me, those handsome boys at the front … your brothers?" Alek said coyly, nodding at Ogden and Oberon, who were inhaling the licorice-filled mints intended for departing guests.

"My, no." Refinna said, attempting to suck in her massive stomach, causing a suction so powerful that she practically inhaled her mask. "They're actually my sons," She said, exhaling a torrent of air so swift it actually blew her mask off and lifted Aleksandr's stiff hair an inch off his scalp while slightly fogging his glasses.

"*Impossible!*" he said with disbelief, wiping his glasses with a cloth napkin. "I never would have guessed. You remind me of that Norwegian actress. The one who played Cleopatra, but that's a story for another time," he said, gazing directly at Refinna's melting eyes.

Fletcher sat transfixed, waiting for the impending finale. *Three. Two. One.*

Aleksandr blinked rapidly at the dazed Refinna, his newly cleaned glasses bouncing on the tip of his pointed nose.

Refinna raised one of her bushy eyebrows. "You've got something in your eye, you poor man. Let me." She violently grasped his head and shoved it onto her wide lap. The movement happened so quickly that Alek banged his temple on the huge metal clasp attached to the side of her purse. The impact almost knocked him out cold. Unable to comprehend what was going on, he struggled unsuccessfully beneath her two large arms as Refinna yanked the glasses off his nose and stuck a spit-covered finger in his eye. Clearly, all Covid restrictions were thrown out the window.

"What on earth? *Refinna!*" Woodrow screamed as he ran toward the lounge. "*Let him up.*"

Bewildered, Refinna abruptly let loose of the flailing Aleksandr, who fell to the floor, looking like he had just been asphyxiated.

He got to his feet and adjusted his wrinkled suit. Still dazed, he squinted at the couch, attempting to locate his glasses. "Woody, I believe she thought that there was something in my eye."

Woodrow immediately passed his small bottle of hand sanitizer to a befuddled Von Piddle.

Fletcher looked around the floor to help locate the glasses. He was careful to keep his cast away from his aunt, who was having difficulty getting out of the sunken couch. After a few minutes of nervous glances and irrelevant chatter, Claus restored order in the lounge by offering Refinna's party an immediate table in the exclusive Goose Eye Room, which was usually reserved for VIP corporate gatherings. While booked solid during the busy ski season at nearby Mount Zircon, the room was used for weddings during the summer months.

The busy restaurant was reminiscent of a rowdy European soccer match, with dozens of patrons standing on chairs to get a better view of the action taking place in the lounge. Refinna stood motionless beside the couch as Woodrow attempted unsuccessfully to tape Aleksandr's glasses, which had been crushed when Refinna put her hand down to push her hefty body off the cushion.

"I'm so very sorry, Mr. Von Piddle," Refinna apologized. "It looked like something was causing your eye to … I thought you were having a seizure. Please take my card and send me a bill for your glasses."

"No harm done Madame. I have several other pairs at home," he said, blindly looking toward Winola, whom he thought was Refinna. All he saw was the blurred outline of a large person wearing glasses.

"Alek, Fletcher and I are heading to Zacarolo's for lunch. I'll drop you off at your house first. I know you're blind as a bat without these," Woodrow said, glancing toward the mangled frames in his hand.

"I'd rather be dropped off at Ye Old Boot if you don't mind. I really could use a good aperitif right now, and they have the strongest ones, even better when it's served outside," he said, reaching in front of him randomly to avoid hitting others as he walked towards Woodrow's voice. He was still clutching the plastic bottle of sanitizer, unable to determine what had been handed to him. "Dr. Stanilov can drive me home from there. He's always there on Sundays."

"Woodrow, thanks for those Paw-Paw bars. Monica will love them," an exhausted Claus said, extending his elbow towards Woodrow.

"It's my pleasure, Claus. Thanks for all you do," Woodrow said as he tapped his old friend's elbow. "Ladies, Ogden, Oberson, enjoy your lunch. I must say it's been a unique experience … as always."

"Oh, that reminds me," Winola said, looking at her uncle. "Your square was drawn on cleanup day, but we had to disqualify you because of your relationship with Cygnus. And the prize was the Sugars of the Universe basket by Foods for Fun," she said with a masked frown.

"What on earth are you talking about? What square?" Woodrow asked, confused.

"That square you sponsored at the state park. You know, Buck's Ledge? Your note said you wanted to sponsor the Buck's Ledge and Buck's Beach areas for the annual cleanup," Serena chimed in. "That's actually why Edmond chose that area to clean."

Woodrow took a step toward her so fast that Aleksandr stumbled forwarded and landed in a large potted plant. "Oh, dear. I really need those glasses," he muttered, pulling several large leaves from his stiff hair.

Woodrow was too intent on what he was hearing to even notice his friend had fallen. "I never sponsored a square or left a note. I was too busy planning the fundraiser."

"Well, looks like someone gifted you," Winola said excitedly. "You do have lots of friends."

"Do you still have that note?" he asked.

"Heavens no. What on earth for? I threw everything away right after the drawing."

"And you said Edmond actually selected that area because—"

"It had McKenzie's Inn written on them," Winola said, finishing his sentence.

The full impact of the conversation hit Fletcher like a ton of bricks. Someone had paid for that square and left specific instructions for it to be placed on the grid that included the dangerous Buck's Ledge area. *Someone wanted him to be at Buck's Ledge at that particular time. It's him. I knew it was him.*

Chief Tomhegan's deadly eyes flashed in Fletcher's mind. *He's alive. He knows who I am.*

"Fletcher, let's go," Woodrow said firmly, gently herding his nephew out of the lounge while holding onto Aleksandr's hand. They slowly made their way to the Defender '90 parked out front.

"Refinna mentioned something about flirting," Woodrow said to Alek as he helped Fletcher crawl in the back.

"Rubbish. I was only helping Claus defuse a messy situation. You saw how busy he was. I was attempting to apply my gorilla-taming techniques I learned on that expedition in Malawi. That woman was acting like a fool at the hostess station. I just didn't expect to be savagely mauled. Real jungle woman she turned out to be. That reminds me of the time …"

Fletcher was oblivious to Aleksandr's ramblings. His brain was branded by what he had just learned in the lounge. Someone was definitely trying to kill him.

CHAPTER 12

CRYPTIC PAST

THE SMALL PRIVATE DINING ROOM AT ZACAROLO'S WAS WARM AND comfortable. The smell of garlic and Italian spices permeated every nook and cranny. Impressively large framed paintings of various Italian vineyards covered the walls in well-positioned places. A corked bottle of red wine sat in the center of all five tables. Beside the wine sat a slim bottle of herbed olive oil and two clay dishes for sea salt and hand-ground pepper. Items on the table were Covid *no-nos* but Mr. Zacarolo didn't care. He firmly felt he was offsetting this by spacing his tables a minimum of six feet apart. A sort of silent peace offering with Maine's governor.

Woodrow ordered a second cup of coffee, watching his nephew absently twirling long strands of linguine with his fork.

"You haven't even touched those chunks of lobster. Cryin' shame. You okay?"

"No, not really," said Fletcher quietly. "I just don't know what's really happening. Who do you think paid for that square on cleanup day?" Fletcher asked.

"And sent the note," Woodrow added. He stared at his nephew with deep concern and sympathy. *What more does this boy have to endure? First, his father and then his mother, the rock slide, the injuries. And now all this*, he thought.

"Fletch, let's talk about everything," he said gently. "I know things don't add up. I wish I could magically make everything better, but I can't. No one can. I'm just as confused as you are. But you know what? We can do this. We *have* to. Let's go over all that we've learned so far. I think we both know where that passage is."

"What good's that gonna do if I'm dead?" said Fletcher coldly.

Woodrow sat calmly, sipping the coffee their waiter had just delivered. He moved his eyes from painted vineyard to vineyard on the wall then turned his attention back to Fletcher. After a few minutes of watching him pick out large clumps of lobster meat, he plucked one of the three mussels from Fletcher's plate.

"I've noticed you just staring at these. Smells good. *Mmm*, tastes even better," he said jovially, making Fletcher grin slightly. "Fletch, we can beat him or join them."

"Who's *him* and *them*?" Fletcher said, looking confused and exhausted.

"Whoever was at the top of the cliff that day—that's *him*. *Them* are our ancestors and their untimely deaths."

Fletcher studied the expression on his uncle's face. "So you do believe me."

Woodrow nodded slowly. "I've always believed you. I've told you that," he said, his bright blue eyes brimming with pride.

Fletcher set his fork down and leaned back against the seat. "So what's next?" he asked with renewed energy.

"First, we don't insult Mr. Zacarolo by not eating this delicious meal. You know how he is about his food," Woodrow said with a smile.

"You too." Fletcher smiled back, glancing at his uncle's unfinished pasta.

"Good, so we're in agreement. It's ours to figure out."

After eating, they began picking everything apart. Woodrow read the first line of the letter from the back of Mollyockett's portrait. He told Fletcher that he had come to the conclusion that it referenced a date.

"*When the moon is full past sun's high.* That has to be the full moon after the summer solstice, the longest day of the year. So the full moon in question would be the one appearing on July 25 of this year. You following me?"

Fletcher nodded.

"Now we know where Wabanaki meets the other path."

"1942 Sangar Drive," Fletcher murmured.

"Right. Now look here. It talks about a stone that opens again.

Hmm … there any large rocks in your backyard, Fletch?"

"A few, but none that are larger than a baseball. Dad cleared all of them away when mom built her garden."

"Okay. Let's highlight that line, put it in the unknown column. We can—"

"What about the root cellar?" Fletcher suddenly asked, his eyes fiery with excitement. "The far back wall of Mom's root cellar is made of huge boulders that are stacked on top of each other."

"Well, well, well … we'll definitely have to take a gander at that unique masonry. Good thinking, Fletch," Woodrow said proudly. He picked up his notes and drew an arrow from the opening stone line in the riddle toward the solved column. Beside the arrow, he drew a big question mark.

"Now let's see. That line about your blood can be you. I've really been thinking about this. I suspect it refers to all your ancestors. I'm quite positive the blood it is referring to is your blood, the McKenzie lineage. Let's put it beside the stone wall in the cellar with another question mark."

Woodrow studied the letter. "We know who Kozart is and what he did, unifying the Wabanaki people for the first time as their own nation."

"Weren't Chief Tomhegan and Mollyockett direct descendants of Kozart?" Fletcher asked. Just saying Tomhegan's name made Fletcher shudder. His hatred was resolute.

"Indeed, they are. We'll just check off Kozart. Okay, now. Here's what it says:

> *In the face of danger, look for the squire.*
> *For it is he who can guide you through water and fire.*
> *When seeking his help, hold tightly the staff.*
> *Yell his name to the creator—*"

Woodrow stopped and looked up.

"No need to laugh," Fletcher whispered, finishing the line.

"Who on earth is the squire and that staff?" mused Woodrow, jokingly blinking his eyes like Aleksandr. "That reminds me of the time I was in the jungles of Peru with that group of headhunters. But that's a story for another time," he said, laughing.

"The blinks come after the story," Fletcher said and laughed, correcting his uncle

"Whatever. I'll put the squire and the staff in the unsolved column. It's quite obvious who the creator is."

"God?"

"Hopefully. We'll definitely need him on our side. Now look at these lines: *The first sign of trouble, ergot will double. Even the hole will bubble and bubble.*"

"I've referenced the dictionary, and ergot is a fungus that infects rye and other cereal plants like corn and wheat. It invades the plant and kills it within weeks."

"What's that got to do with anything?"

"I'm getting there. Ergot has mysteriously reappeared in Maine after a sixty-five-year hiatus. More importantly, it's only being reported in one location in the state—Mahoosuc Valley."

Fletcher read the article about ergot his uncle had printed. "Where's Bragg's Farm?"

"Andover. It's that big farm with those two red barns right after crossing the East Andover covered bridge. It's one of only two farms to have their crops killed off by the fungal invasion."

"Where's the other?"

"Seton Farm in Bethel. It's on the Androscoggin River in the Mayville section of town." Woodrow put down his cup and looked at his nephew thoughtfully. After blowing his nose and clearing his throat, he pulled out a newspaper clipping. "Fletcher, the name Bragg stood out. I knew I'd heard it before, so I did a little more digging. The Bragg farm was built by Captain Bragg, US Army, at Beaver Brook in Andover in 1807. His family has been living in that exact location for the past two hundred years."

"So?"

"*So,* if you recall our conversation when I told you the life story of Mollyockett, you will recall the soldier who built that wigwam beside the brook for her was . . . Captain Bragg."

Fletcher softly gasped in astonishment.

"And it gets even more interesting. Once I found the history of Bragg's farm and the ergot invasion, I went to the Bethel Historical Society. Seton Farm is located at the exact location where she cared for Henry Tufts, the man who should have died from that nasty knife wound. He's the one who wrote this article for the local papers after she died." He handed Fletcher a copy of the original newspaper article. "Those two farms are located on the main campsites for Mollyockett during her time in the valley, and they have both been devastated by the ergot invasion. The State of Maine Agricultural Bureau has issued a crop quarantine for the five miles surrounding them."

"Some year 2020 is. Even the crops are quarantined. Do you think it's related to what we've discovered?" Fletcher asked.

"*It* as in the ergot?" Woodrow asked.

Fletcher nodded.

"Too much of a coincidence if you ask me," said Woodrow.

Fletcher read the article and then turned toward his uncle while sliding his cast outwards to get more comfortable. "You said earlier that we're visiting Mollyockett's grave."

Woodrow nodded. "We need to look for the symbol on the headstone that's mentioned in the riddle. It has to be her grave. I'm positive. I really think it's a major piece of the puzzle. I hope it will link—"

"Um, excuse me, Mr. McKenzie?" The hostess stuck her head into the private dining room.

"Diane. How are you?" Woodrow smiled

"Fine, thank you. I really hate to bother you while you're eating, but you have an urgent phone call at the front. A Mrs. Blay seems quite intent on speaking with you immediately."

Woodrow looked at his watch. "My goodness, I forgot to call her," he said nervously. "She's going to spit me out like a three-day-old piece of chewing gum." Forgetting his mask, he rushed toward the door. His cloth napkin still tucked into his shirt collar.

Fletcher watched in amusement as his uncle exited the room. He selected the strawberry pastry from the dessert tray Mario had sent out to them and then picked up the copy of the letter in Woodrow's pile of papers. He took a close second look at the riddle and Woodrow's messy notes. He reread the section about the squire. The day before he had looked up the meaning of squire. "A man who attends or escorts a woman; an English country gentleman; a judge or other dignitary; a young nobleman attendant ranked next below a knight."

A disheveled and slighty sweaty Woodrow came back to the table and sat down wearily. "Well, I'd rather have been massaged with barbed-wire than taken that call. We need to head to Mollyockett's grave now. I failed to call your charming grandmother as promised, and she wants you back home within two hours," he said gruffly, reaching for a small éclair. "That woman won't budge an inch." He huffed, inhaling the small treat in one bite.

"Will Mario be upset if we don't eat all these," Fletcher asked, nodding toward the tray.

"Ten people couldn't make a dent in that tray. I promised your grand-mother I would bring the rest home in a doggie bag. You know how she loves leftovers. I suggested bringing it to her as some sort of peace offering. I couldn't get her to shut up." He grabbed a small hazelnut-fla-vored Italian cookie. "If Marion Flickers is next door to your home, she'll love these. I believe she's back from the University of Maine now that they've gone virtual for all summer classes."

"What do you think that line about the hole bubbling means?" Fletcher asked inquisitively.

"I'm at a dead end with that one," admitted Woodrow. "As you can see, I Googled everything—bubble, Maine; bubble, Frenchman's Hole; bubble, Wabanaki; bubble, bubble. Interestingly, one hit led to a story about the rock slide at Buck's Ledge."

"What d'you mean?"

"Let's see. Should be somewhere here. It's the one with the blue paper clip. *Aha*, here it is," he said victoriously.

Fletcher read the article from the *Newry Tribune*, moving his fingers along each line of the article. Woodrow chuckled to himself when Fletcher raised his eyebrows and grinned at how the article referred to him as heroic in the face of nature's fury. When he got to the pertinent part, he read it aloud. "The fifteen-ton granite boulder that catapulted

Fletcher and his friend Blanche the distance of a football field, caused the entire area known as Buck's Beach to be permanently submerged under twenty feet of newly created, class-one, raging rapids. In addition, a thirty foot, awe-inspiring waterfall now cascaded over the mountainous slab of granite, causing treacherous Buck's Hole to bubble like a witches' cauldron from Salem."

Fletcher sat quietly.

"I know. It's a bit over the edge," Woodrow agreed. "Stanley Mull wrote it. Quite a flowery fellow. Always embellishes to the extreme. He thinks *National Geographic* will one day discover his talents and take him to the far fetches of the globe as the chief draftsman of its latest hit show. More like *National Enquirer* with it's own flowery writing will notice his, um ... *talents*—and I use that word with caution. Fletch, we need to get going. Your grandmother will personally throw me off Stanley Mull's awe-inspiring waterfall if we're one second late. We can discuss it on the way to Andover."

CHAPTER 13

MOON ON THE MARKER

ON THE DRIVE TO MOLLYOCKETT'S FINAL RESTING PLACE, WOODROW mused, "I really think it's a bit of a stretch to think that the bubbling of Buck's Hole is remotely connected to the riddle. Tomhegan would have to be the world's most brilliant engineer in history to pull off that feat. Even the illustrious A. G. Eiffel couldn't make that happen. No matter how hard he tried."

"Who?"

"A. G. Eiffel, probably the greatest engineer to ever live. He designed the Eiffel Tower in Paris along with hundreds of other significant structures. He ranks right up there with good ol' Thomas Edison. You know, the lightbulb guy," Uncle Woodrow said sarcastically, turning onto Rumford Road towards Andover.

"Yeah, I know," Fletcher said. He was preoccupied reading an article he'd taken from the folder. He had to use both hands to keep the paper from flying out of the open rig. He was particularly intrigued by one section, which he shared with his uncle.

"According to this, Timothy Buck and Nathaniel Segar were also kidnapped along with Benjamin Clark. Tomhegan handed them over to the British, who were fighting the American colonists. He was paid an eight-dollar bounty for each man. The three men were held prisoner in an old jail in Quebec for almost a year before being released. It took them almost another full year to find their way home to Ketchum and Bethel. From what it says here, Buck's Hole and Buck's Ledge was named after Mr. Buck ten years after he died. He was instrumental in the planning of Ketchum State Park, which was eventually changed to Hamlin State Park after Hannibal Hamlin." Fletcher turned and looked inquisitively at his uncle. "How come he never became President after John Wilkes Booth assinated President Lincoln?"

"The North was winning the Civil War, so in a conciliatory gesture, President Lincoln chose Andrew Johnson, a Southerner, to join him on his reelection ticket instead of Hamlin. It's actually the closest Maine's ever come to having a US president."

"You said earlier he was from here?"

"From Paris Hill, not too far from here. I'll take you to the Hamlin Library-Museum on Paris Hill later this summer. It's located in the old county jail next to the Hamlin mansion. The same house where Mollyockett saved his life right after he was born."

Turning his thoughts back to their current issue, Fletcher said, "I still think that the bubbling of Buck's Hole has something to do with her riddle. How can it not?" he said with firm conviction.

Woodrow was not convinced. "You need to go work with the flamboyant Mr. Mull at the *Newry Tribune*. He could use your wildly creative imagination." As they approached Hanover Village, Woodrow pointed as he said, "Fletch, see that white house over there?"

Fletcher looked at the ordinary, two-story, white house located at the edge of the wide Androscoggin River and next to a lush green potato field. A modest *Hanover Town Hall* sign stood in front and was surrounded by a well-kept flower garden. A small library was located next to the structure.

"An old friend of mine lived in that house for many years a long time ago. Way before the town purchased it for their town hall. His name was Mr. Jean. Quite a magnanimous fellow. He owned the Hanover ferry, which crossed the river behind his house. With his newfound wealth in his pockets and his deep distrust of banks, he decided to be his own banker. Whenever anyone he knew wanted a loan, he would sit with them in his kitchen and ask a few questions. If he approved the loan, he would head to his cellar. A few minutes later, he would be back with the requested sum regardless of the size. No one ever knew how much Mr. Jean had or where he kept his gold coins and cash. His family searched every square inch of that basement after he died and never found a penny. It's still down there somewhere. It has to be."

"How much you think is down there?" Fletcher asked, excited at the thought of undiscovered treasure chests full of gold and gems hidden behind a loose stone waiting to be turned the right way. He imagined sneaking into the basement with Quinn and Camway to search for the treasure.

"Don't even think of it," Woodrow said, squinting his knowing eyes at the boy.

Fletcher laughed at being busted. His amusement turned somber when Woodrow said, "Here we are." They drove under an ancient wrought-iron arch that said *Woodlawn Cemetery*. It looked as if it had been skillfully created by a meticulous craftsman more than a century ago.

Woodrow turned left onto a narrow pebble lane, that had a newly mowed strip of grass in it's center. Fletcher looked curiously at the hundreds of headstones—many weathered beyond recognition—memorializing more than three centuries of local citizens, their names forgotten for the most part.

Woodrow pointed to his left. "She's buried over there in the middle of that section."

Fletcher was silent, lost in thought as they slowly approached the grave of the Indian woman who had somehow become a central figure in his young life. It was a perfect summer day in Maine—blue sky, fluffy clouds, a slight breeze, and the barely audible flow of the Swift River off in the distance behind the burial ground.

"It's right there," Uncle Woodrow said pointing out a simple weathered marker.

> *Marie Agathe*
> *Molly Ockett*
> *Born 1740–Died 1816*
> *Last of the Pigwackets*

Fletcher stared at the granite marker, envisioning Mollyockett with her stovepipe hat, long black hair, and ornate beads and jewels buried six feet below him. Then he shuddered, thinking how Tomhegan had stood on the exact spot over a freshly dug grave and placed some type of curse on his sister. He closed his eyes in the bright sunlight and recalled her portrait. He thought about Jackson McKenzie, his brave ancestor, fighting the British Army for the freedom of a cluster of colonies. He recalled the story of him meeting Mollyockett at Frenchman's Hole, a place where he innocently swam. Never again would he think of the swimming hole with such a carefree attitude. Fletcher opened his eyes and focused on the headstone etched with her French baptismal name.

Woodrow left Fletcher to his thoughts and walked toward the cemetery caretaker, who was spreading fertilizer on a large family plot in an adjacent section of the tranquil graveyard. Only the sound of an occasional passing car on Swift Road interrupted the melancholy scene.

When he returned from talking to the caretaker, Woodrow asked Fletcher, "You find anything that looks like a symbol, anything that looks out of place?"

"I'll look." Fletcher slowly lowered himself onto the freshly cut grass, using his crutches for leverage. "You'd think there'd be flowers on her grave," he said with sad conviction.

"Mr. Walton over there, the caretaker, said there are trinkets, hand-crafted items, coins and a few bundles of flowers that were left. He moved them to mow her grave. I told him we'd return them." He gestured toward a small wooden crate located at the edge of the forested side of the cemetery. "Now let's see if we can find a symbol." Woodrow bent over and rubbed the edge of the white marker. "I hope acid rain hasn't destroyed it."

Fletcher crawled to the back of the marker, ignoring the green grass stains on his jeans. They spent the next ten minutes meticulously examining every square inch of the solid marker, looking for the smallest clue.

"I guess this isn't the one," Fletcher said with disappointment in his voice. He crawled back to the front of the grave and glanced around at the various headstones.

"Ya lookin' fah something in particulah?" the caretaker asked with a thick Downeast accent. He approached them cautiously. After twenty years of working at the cemetery, he made it a point not to disturb those who came to pay their respects. Rarely, however, did someone rub the front and back of a marker.

"Well, we were just looking to see if any of the words had faded over time," Woodrow said convincingly, stealing a quick wink at Fletcher.

"Ah, just like that fellah the othah day," Walton said.

Woodrow stepped closer. "What man?"

"Weird fellah, mean as a Maine cooncat. He was heyah two days ago doin' the same thing yah doin'—rubbin' and lookin'. Even turned thah grave ovah. Disrespectful son of a—" he muttered, not finishing his thought in deference to Fletcher.

"What did he look like?" asked Woodrow.

"Long black hayah, brown, tanned skin, fit as a fiddle, but those eyes … real dangah in those eyes. Scaahed the dickens outtah me. Aftah he turned ovah the stone he left that black rock ovah in that box with jibberish on it." He said, pointing toward the box.

"Mind if I take a look?" Woodrow requested calmly, belying the fact that his heart was racing.

"Not at all. Glad if yah took it with yah. Spooks the daylight outtah me."

After exchanging glances with Fletcher, Woodrow strolled quickly toward the crate and found the rock. It was about four inches thick and roughly the size of a pancake.

When he returned to the grave, Fletcher asked impatiently. "What's it say?"

Woodrow turned the stone over. "It's Gaelic."

"Hah. I knew it was some sort of city slickah language," Walton huffed, spitting on the grass.

"Gaelic is the language of many of our ancestors, Mr. Walton. It's a Celtic language from Ireland, Scotland, and the Isle of Man," Woodrow explained.

"My ancestors aah from Bah Hahbah and Bangah. Bin in Maine fah nearly two hundred yeeahs," Walton said, oblivious to his possible heritage.

"Uncle Woodrow, what's it say?" Fletcher asked again, growing slightly agitated. He hobbled over to his uncle and stared at the black rock in his wrinkled hand.

"*Coimheaʹd fearg fhear Na foighde,*" he said slowly.

"What's that mean?"

"No idea. I'll look it up when I get home." He glanced toward Mr. Walton. "Thank you for letting me take this."

"Yah a wicked brave mahn. Yah house will probably burn down. Glad it's outta heeah," he said with relief.

"And you said this man with dangerous eyes actually turned the head-stone over?"

"Yessah. Staared at the bottom and then left."

"Mind if we take a look?"

"Help yahself. Just be surah to put it back. Nevah want to angah the dead," he said and then headed back to the family plot he had been working on.

When he was out of earshot, Woodrow said, "I never thought of the bottom of the grave. It makes all the sense in the world. Mollyocket would want to preserve any symbol from the elements. Remember, she was one with the earth and understood how the natural world worked."

"But who was here before us?" Fletcher asked.

Woodrow looked at Fletcher. "I'm positive we both know who was here the other day."

Fletcher gasped. He held his hand over his mouth. "How's that even possible? He's been dead for over a century." His uncle ignored him.

Standing beside the gravestone, they pushed it to see how heavy it was.

"Looks like he loosened it," Fletcher said.

"I'll get it. Stand back."

Woodrow placed both hands on the marker, and without much effort, the weathered stone fell softly on the grass. They both fell to their knees to look at the dirt-covered bottom, which had become stained by the rich soil over the years. Woodrow rubbed the dirt off to reveal a small indentation. He pulled out his handkerchief and cleaned the small section, revealing a crescent moon surrounded by six stars.

"The symbol," Fletcher whispered in awe.

"That's it," Woodrow agreed, with delight.

For several moments they stared in silence, contemplating its meaning. "I'll take a small rubbing," Woodrow finally said. He removed a small white piece of paper and pencil from his shirt pocket and created a rubbing that left a detailed replica on the paper. He quickly glanced at his watch. "We need to get going. Your grandmother is going to kill me."

Fletcher painfully helped upright the headstone to its original position then patted the dirt back in place while his uncle retrieved the items from the wooden box. They respectfully arranged them on the grave.

"Before we leave, we should say a prayer for her," Woodrow said, producing a small tin can and paper from his pants pocket. "On the Mahoosuc Historical Society's website I stumbled across a two-person chant the Native Americans would say to honor the departed. Most likely, it's what Mollyokett and the Wananaki people chanted when they lived in this area."

Fletcher looked fascinated. "Okay."

Woodrow read from the paper. "You say, *Heey, heyha.* Then I will say, *Ay hey ha ya hey yo* sixteen times. You'll actually chant every fourth line. I will tap this can, which represents the beat of a drum. From what I've learned, the Native Americans would also beat drums for the departed to guide them in their final journey to the afterlife."

"What do I say again?"

"Heey, heyha."

"Heeey, heyha," Fletcher repeated softly.

"Okay." Woodrow started tapping his fingers on the empty soup can. "Ready? You start."

They started chanting to the beat of the improvised drum, honoring Mollyockett, unaware that Mr. Walton had stopped raking and was staring in amazement. Unsure if he should run for his life or alert the local police.

CHAPTER 14

RUSSIAN SAUCE

FLETCHER STAYED IN BED THAT EVENING PRETENDING TO READ. HE WAS sore from his first outing since the accident but hid it from his grandmother, knowing she would ban all future trips with Woodrow if she knew. It was enough that his grass stained jeans had set off alarm bells with the matriarch. Stretching his arms in front of him, he fixed a steady gaze at the open windows. The long day's sun was setting quickly, spilling its last rays on the grandiose Buck's Ledge. He barely recognized its new shape. His thoughts wandered from Mollyockett to Tomhegan to his father and mother and finally settled on the two discoveries at Woodlawn Cemetery. Watching the sun's rays turn blood red on the granite face of the majestic mountain in the last seconds before setting, he wondered how everything was connected.

Why hadn't his dad thought ahead and left him some type of clue just in case something happened? For a quick second, he allowed himself the faintest hope that his father would somehow hear his thoughts and respond with the fatherly direction he had always provided before he fell silent.

"Fletch, pick up the phone," Lucille yelled from the bottom of the stairs. "It's your uncle Woody."

"Hey. I was just—"

"It means, *Beware the anger of a patient man*," Woodrow said excitedly, cutting Fletcher off.

"What does?"

"The words on that black rock we found today. *Comhead fearg fhear*

Na foighde means *Beware the anger of a patient man,*" Woodrow said. "When I got back to the inn, I did a quick typed the words on the rock into Mr. Google's search engine. Several dozen sites popped up immediately with the translation."

"Beware the anger of a patient man," Fletcher repeated. "What do you think it means?"

"You want my opinion, it's pretty obvious, Fletch," Woodrow said. "*Someone* is definitely out for revenge after waiting for a long time."

In the background Fletcher could hear the sounds of a laughing crowd. "Where are you?"

"I'm at Ye ol' Boot. Believe it or not, Mr. Von Piddle's still here."

Surprised, Fletcher looked at the clock above his chest of drawers. "We dropped him off more than eight hours ago."

"I was just as surprised when I walked in and saw him sitting here. He's still frazzled from Refinna's atrocious attempt at doctoring him. He's actually in the middle of several dozen people, telling his wild stories," Woodrow yelled over a sudden roar of laughter in the background.

Fletcher laughed. "But what about his broken glasses?"

"To be quite frank with you, Fletch, I really don't think he'd be able to see *with* his glasses," Woodrow said humorously only to be drowned out by a mountainous wave of laughter behind him.

"Listen, it's hard to hear in here. I just called to give you the info on that rock and to let you know that Mr. Caxton's coming to see you about some business tomorrow morning at nine. I saw him at the Cygnus Company Store after I dropped you off."

"Why'd you go there?" Fletcher asked suspiciously. He immediaely thought of his scheming aunts.

"To pick up some Birch Bread for the inn. The inn is booked for the next five days. It'll be a challenge enforcing the mask rule as well as all the extra cleaning that's now required. Mr. Caxton was coming out of the Double Moose Coffee House when I ran into him."

Fletcher smiled when he heard Aleksandr's slurred voice in the background saying, "That reminds me of the time I was in Peru, climbing the extinct Huascaran Volcano."

"That man's totally out of his mind," Woodrow said and chuckled.

Alek slammed down a pink, fizzy concoction a newfound admirer has just handed him. "Listen, Fletch. I've gotta get him home. I'll stop in to see you in the next few days. Remember, we need to scout out that rock wall in your basement. I'll do what I can to get your grandparents out of the house for a few hours," he said, and then he quickly hung up.

Fletcher put the phone in its cradle, laid his head on the pillow, and stared at the white ceiling. "Beware the anger of a patient man," he whispered lightly as a cold chill ran down his spine. *Tomhegan*, he thought as he drifted off.

———

The next morning Fletcher sat with Edmond in the kitchen and listened to Mr. Caxton talk about his current business ventures. Lucille had insisted that everyone wear masks given that Mr. Caxton had just returned from Rhode Island. She'd prepared enormous Spanish-style, egg-white omelets filled with Russian Sauce, locally produced cheddar cheese, jalapeno peppers, and lean turkey sausage. She left them in the warmer an hour earlier. She had rushed off to work on the Red Hatter's float for the upcoming Mollyockett Day celebrations. Always on the third Saturday of July, the celebrations included concerts, crafts on the common, a five-mile road race, a Miss Mollyockett contest, a popular Adirondack chair contest—in which local artists painted scenes on locally constructed chairs that were raffled off at noon on the common to benefit the Mahoosuc Arts Council—and a huge parade up Bethel's Main Street. Each year the Mollyockett Day Committee selected a theme and gave out first, second, and third place trophies for the best floats. It was highly competitive if only for bragging rights. The grand finale of the day was an enormous fireworks display in the evening.

This year, the theme of the parade was children's storybook characters. The Red Hatters chose the dim-witted maid Amelia Bedelia as the central figure in their float. Each lady on the float was to be dressed in a maid's uniform with a large white apron. They would all have frilly white cleaning caps on their heads, and they would all hold black feather dusters.

Edmond, along with the other husbands of the Red Hatters, had borrowed a race car trailer as the base of the float. They had painstakingly recreated Amelia's living room on the large trailer. They wired it for electricity to power the antique Victorian lamps, which stood beside comfortable, overstuffed chairs and couches. They carefully bolted the large antique highboy to the floor to prevent it from falling off the float. On one side of the float, they constructed a wall with a door and several windows. Outside the wall the put up a replica of an old clothesline with dozens of lightbulbs attached to it. In the book, Amelia's employer had instructed her to "put out the lights." So she literally put the lights out by stringing them on the clothesline.

This year, the celebrations would be different. At first the planning committee had announced the entire event would be cancelled. Due to enormous uproar, they decided to scale back the event. After heated debate, the parade would still be held but each float could have no more than eight participants and everyone would be required to wear masks and social distance at all times. No exceptions, regardless of your beliefs. Additionally, all spectators for the parade would be required to stay in their cars. The same applied for the fireworks display. All booths on the common would be spaced thirty feet apart and all vendors were required to enforce the six-foot rule at all times. Everyone who participated was required to sign a promissory contract agreeing to follow the stipulations. Still, a large percentage of New Englanders viewed this as a super-spreader event for the virus and began to voice their concerns on social media and various news channels.

"She's quite confident the Red Hatter's will win this year," Edmond said, spreading fresh jam on his toasted Birch Bread. "There's not a lightbulb left in the house" he said, smiling. He took a bite and raised his eyebrows at Jefferson Caxton. "*Mmm*, this jam's delicious!" he exclaimed. "What's it called again?"

"It's called Block Island Blissful Berries," Jefferson said. "It's a mixture of wild blueberries, raspberries, and huckleberries. We can't make it fast enough with more people eating at home nowadays. I've added a second shift at the Newport site to help speed up production. Luckily, we've had no infections there."

"Well, it's just scrumptious." Edmond said.

"So how you doin', Fletch?" Jefferson asked. "Quinn's been beside himself since the accident. Doris just sits on the front deck and stares out at the ocean for hours at a time. After they airlifted her off the mountain, she had a slight nervous breakdown. She'll never hike again, I'm sure of that. But like they say, time heals everything—at least I hope," Jefferson said with a heavy sigh while looking directly at Edmond.

"When's Quinn coming up again?" Fletcher said.

"He'll be here for Mollyockett weekend. He mentioned that you asked him to be on the Cygnus float."

"I was hoping we could camp out in the backyard again," Fletcher said pleadingly, looking at Edmond.

"Let's cross that shaky bridge when we get there. You know how your grandmother is with that leg," Edmond said.

"Fletcher, I saw your uncle Woodrow yesterday," Jefferson said. "He suggested I fill you in on why I was meeting with your grandfather this morning."

Fletcher watched with curiosity as Quinn's father opened his large leather briefcase.

"What do you think of this?" Jefferson said, removing a jar and setting it in front of Fletcher. It was a large container of bright red sauce with an image of a man standing beside a lighthouse on the side. The words "Russian Sauce" were above the picture. Fletcher picked up the jar and looked closely at the label. "What's Russian Sauce?"

"It's a healthy sauce made with tomatoes, carrots, garlic, sweet peppers, hot peppers, and vinegar," Mr. Caxton said and pointed to the nutrition label on the back. "There's mild and spicy. Apparently, there was a large community of Russian immigarants living in Newport at the same time as Joseph McKenzie, one of your descendants who was fighting against the British during the American Revolutionary War while stationed on Rose Island in Newport Harbor. He's the man on the label. According to his letters, he befriended many of them and some were actually aiding him quite heavily. He mentions a man named Oleg, in particular, who was quite instrumental in disrupting British plans for victory. We learned all of this in a very unique way, which I'll fill you in on in a few minutes. Russian Sauce has been passed down from Russian generation to generation for many centuries. It's absolutely delicious. Your grandmother has added it to these omelets.'

Fletcher nodded. "It looks like the painting in my dad's room," he said, turning the jar over. "This one of your new products, Mr. Caxton?"

"It's actually one of *your* new products, Fletcher."

"What do you mean mine? I don't—"

"Fletch," Edmond cut in gently, "there's something we need to tell you. We've just been waiting for the right moment while we work everything out discreetly. Your father knew that if anything ever happened to him or your mother before you turned eighteen, his sisters would take over the daily operations of Cygnus. He really covered every base when it came to the company. He was convinced they would immediately steer the direction of the company away from healthy products toward mass-produced, cheaply made foods. Exactly like they're doing now. That means selling off the healthy products, such as Birch Bread, New England Oak Cakes, Maine Maple Honey Nut Bars, Casco Bay Whole Grain Clam Cakes, and Goose Eye Granola Mix."

"But why would they sell those products? People love them."

"Yes, they do. But they're more expensive to produce and make less of a profit than items such as Tweedly Cakes and those ridiculous Blueberriola Sugary Sham Shams," Edmond said, butchering the names of the sisters' heart-clogging, fat-filled snacks. "Unbelievable that high fructose corn syrup is the first ingredient. Those ladies, I ought to—"

"But what's that got to do with me?" Fletcher interrupted.

"He wanted to prevent these products, the historical backbone of Cygnus, from being sold off to the highest bidder. Your father wanted you to inherit a health food company not a company associated with obesity, diabetes, and the like," Edmond said as he looked at Mr. Caxton. "He also knew that if Refinna, Serena, or Winola found out that these transactions benefited you, they would double if not triple the price. They genuinely despise you Fletch and we all know that. We're using funds your father set aside to buy these product lines."

"That's' where I come in, Fletch," Jefferson said. "I'm not actually the competition or adversary of Cygnus, regardless of what your aunts may think or say. I'm currently in the process of buying Birch Bread and a few other healthy food items from Cygnus. They don't think they're the future of your family's company. The name of the company that's actually purchasing the products is called Fifth Ward Whole & Healthy not Aquidneck Kitchen. Fifth Ward Whole & Healthy is *your* company, Fletcher." Jefferson pushed a folder in front of Fletcher.

"What do you mean *my* company?" he asked, confused. He looked at the folder and opened it slowly.

"If you notice the first paragraph," Jefferson said, pointing at the first page. "The company is to be held in trust until you reach the age of eighteen. Until that time, Aquidneck Kitchen would serve as guardian of your company."

Fletcher scanned the pages, unable to comprehend the legal jargon spelled out in long, rambling sentences. His eyes stopped on a familiar name. Slowly, he looked up.

"Nimsy Cortland, the woman who disappeared with Mom?" He looked at his grandfather.

"That's right, Fletch," Edmond said. "Nimsy was named as the overseer of your company because she was close to your mother."

Jefferson added, "They were actually roommates in college. She was a trusted friend and thought the world of you. Additionally, she was also named your trustee should anything happen to your parents. I was named as the backup trustee should anything happen to Ms. Cortland. Unbelievable it's gotten to this point to say the least." He turned the jar of jam and gave it a slight push toward Fletcher.

The same man from the Russian Sauce jar was on the jam label standing in front of the same lighthouse. He wore a funky sailor's hat on his head and what appeared to be overalls made of heavy canvas. Behind him stood a traditional white New England lighthouse, its curved roof covered with dull red slate shingles. Inside, an octagonal black lantern stood firm to guide ships as they entered the harbor. A small brick structure sat on the large rocks below the dignified beacon.

"Can you tell me about him?" Fletcher asked quietly, gazing at the smiling man in front of the lighthouse. His mind wandered to his mother.

"His name is Joseph Gage McKenzie. As mentioned, you are a direct descendent of him," Edmond said. "He grew up in Ketchum and eventually took over as head of the household when his father, Jackson Gage McKenzie, was killed in a suspicious hunting accident. Jackson actually was the first McKenzie to settle here," Edmond explained, unaware that Fletcher already knew very well who Jackson McKenzie was. "Before his father was killed, Joseph spent many years in Rhode Island as the caretaker of the Rose Island Lighthouse, which overlooks the busy Newport harbor. He returned to Ketchum when his father was killed."

"The lighthouse in the picture is Rose Island," Jefferson said, smiling at Fletcher. "Your father personally selected it as the logo should something happen. You see, while in Newport, Joseph made quite a name for himself. He would take his boat from Rose Island, which was a short distance from downtown Newport, and pick up, uh … what he called *visitors* each evening. These visitors would actually spend the night on the small island plotting against the British, who were based in Newport at the time. As mentioned, many of these were Russians who had settled in Rhode Island. These meeting on Rose Island actually caused tremendous chaos amongst the well-organized English soldiers."

"How'd he die?" Fletcher asked. "Uncle Woodrow's research had said *indeterminate.*"

Jefferson and Aldous Edmond were immediately confused by his announcement but let it pass. It was now obvious to them that additional events were transpiring.

"He died of unknown causes in 1821. He really should be remembered as one of the Mahoosuc Valley's leading citizens, but he's been forgotten over time," Edmond said, taking a sip of coffee.

"Even though he lived in Rhode Island for a part of his life?" Fletcher asked, flaking off a mushroom inside the omelet with his fork.

"He made up for lost time when he returned. Back then students went to school only when there was no work to be done on their farms. Many spent weeks-on-end in the forests and fields working with their parents to help make ends meet. It was nothing like it is today. Joseph worked diligently with other leaders of the community to build a better school in Ketchum, enabling the local children to be educated beyond grammar school, which was usually the highest level of education attained at the time. That school eventually became Balston Prep after Captain Balston, a Revolutionary War hero, donated one hundred thousand dollars towards a new building. The next time you're in the library, take a look at all the portraits on the wall at the resource center. Joseph McKenzie's portrait is amongst them," Edmond said with pride. "Balston's portrait is beside Joseph's. He's the one on the horse."

Jefferson watched Fletcher sift through the papers. "If you have any questions, Fletch, fire away."

"You know, Fletch, Joseph McKenzie is the reason you and Quinn are friends," Edmond said in a serious tone. "How we all know each other is really a stroke of luck, which is a wonderful blessing given your close friendship with Quinn."

Fletcher looked up at his grandfather with a confused look.

"That's true," Jefferson said and smiled. "Quinn's mother has volunteered for the Rose Island Preservation Society ever since she was a teenager. One day Doris was working with local volunteers who were replacing rotted floor beams inside the caretaker's living quarters at the bottom of the lighthouse. Under old wooden planks, they found Joseph McKenzie's letters and journals hidden inside a tin box. It was a treasure trove of information for the Newport Historical Society, including detailed information on the struggle Newporters experienced during the Revolutionary War. It also contained many letters from Joseph's father, Jackson McKenzie."

"And his mother, Virginia," Edmond added.

"Those papers were entrusted to Quinn's mother while they decided what to do with them," Jefferson continued. "Doris and the historical society made the decision to return the letters and journals to the descendants of Joseph, if there were any alive. After reading the letters, she located McKenzie's Inn online and contacted your Uncle Woodrow to see if there was a family connection. Woodrow was thrilled when he learned of the lighthouse discovery and invited us up for a weekend of skiing. Quinn was two at the time. We all fell in love with Maine that weekend, and we've been coming up to Mount Zircon ever since."

Jefferson looked out the window toward the Mahoosuc Mountain Range from inside the cozy kitchen.

"For the first few years," he said, "we stayed at McKenzie's Inn. That's how I came to know your parents. It was actually at the suggestion of your father that we built our ski house here in Rugby Hills."

Fletcher listened as he focused on the Russian Sauce jar. "Does Quinn know about Fifth Ward Whole & Healthy?" he asked.

"Not yet. I figured it would be better for you to tell him. He'll be thrilled that you now have a Rhode Island connection. Give's you another reason to visit."

Fletcher took a bite of omelet. "Why Fifth Ward?"

"It was actually your mother's idea," Quinn's dad explained. "She loved to visit the little nooks and crannies in that Newport neighborhood, which was where the people who worked in the huge mansions lived. I think the name's perfect, but I may be a little biased." He smiled, winking at Fletcher.

"The name *is* ideal, especially for a health food company," Edmond agreed, picking up the jar of jam. "I'm sure ol' Joseph McKenzie would agree, given his love for the sea. I've read a few of his letters. He was quite reluctant to leave the coast."

"Well, maybe Quinn can help me run the company when I'm old enough," Fletcher joked.

"You can do anything you want once you've reached eighteen. In the meantime, most of the proceeds from Fifth Ward Whole & Healthy will be put into a trust held at Mahoosuc National Bank. Ten percent of the net proceeds, as per the instruction of your parents, is to be donated to Ketchum Hospital, which is absolutely astounding given the pandemic and all."

"Your grandparents and your uncle Woodrow have worked hard to make all this happen," Jefferson told Fletcher. "They know it's what your parents would've wanted for you. It's just that nobody ever expected your aunts to move so quickly. They seem quite driven to slice off the healthy parts of Cygnus in your parent's absence." Jefferson was confident Aldous would be deeply distraught when the day came that he found out about his sisters' shameful actions. "Your company has nearly a dozen foods at the moment. I'll drop off a box for you before I head back to Block Island. All the products will be inside. Let me know what you think."

"Can you have Quinn look at them too?" He suggested, moving his cast out from under the table so he could stretch his tingling limb. "I'd like his input as well as Camways."

"They'd be thrilled to help you," Jefferson said, laughing at Fletcher's beaming face. "You should know that your aunt Refinna accepted the latest bid. She almost tripped over herself to sign the terms of the sale yesterday," he joked, glancing toward a laughing Edmond.

Fletcher grinned at the thought at getting one over on his three greedy aunts. He envisioned the looks on their plump faces staring at him with distain as he broke the news to them. But his thoughts then drifted to Nimsy Cortland. He pictured her warm smile and long blond hair. He remembered her sitting in this very kitchen, talking and laughing with his mother before their morning walk. His mother had been adamant about taking the ill-fated business trip quickly. At that time, most European countries and Canada had banned American visitors due to the horrific Coronavirus numbers in the U.S. Fearful that South American countries would soon follow suit, Muriel decided it was now or never. The products were too important for Cygnus and its focus on quality.

Fletcher shuddered as an image of his mother and Nimsy flashed in his mind. He sensed they were in trouble and needed help. Immediate help. Every part of his body flinched at the thought of his weeping mother giving up in desperation, knowing that they had been given up for dead, lost forever in the wild depths of the jungles of South America."

CHAPTER 15

MURIEL'S ROOT CELLAR

THREE DAYS AFTER LEARNING ABOUT FIFTH WARD WHOLE & HEALTHY, Fletcher sat on the front steps, waiting for his uncle. In a ploy to rid the house of Edmond and Lucille, Woodrow had conveniently secured two VIP tickets to Lisbon's Moxie Festival near the city of Lewiston. After reconsidering the decision to cancel the event due to Coronavirus, its planning committee instituted the same restrictions as the Molloyockett Day celebration. Edmond was a lifelong fan of Maine's official drink, which was among the first mass-produced carbonated soft drinks in the United States and had been produced in Lisbon for more than one hundred years. Much to Lucille's dismay, Edmond feverously collected Moxie memorabilia. His most cherished possession was a framed poster of legendary Red Sox player Ted Williams holding a bottle of the unique drink. A quote at the bottom stated, "I get my moxie from Moxie." Edmond proudly submitted it for the program's cover at last year's well-attended festival.

"Remember, we're only stayin' for two hours, Ed," Lucille said as she walked out the door. "And remember, if it doesn't fit in a bread box, you ain't buying it. The house only holds so much, land sakes." She pulled out a plastic rain bonnet decorated with small black doodlebugs after noticing dark clouds on the horizon. "Looks like rain. We can skip the parade. Who wants to watch a bunch of fools march up a street dressed like an orange bottle? I can think of a million better things to do on a Saturday," she said jovially, kissing Fletcher on the head.

Edmond said nothing. He was just glad to have the much-sought-after

VIP tickets in his pocket. With the pandemic and all, the number of invi-
tees was greatly reduced, and these tickets were at a premium this year.

Lucille glanced at Fletcher's dirt-stained cast. There were long grass
stains on the bottom half. "That thing must have a million germs by now.
Surprised we haven't all contracted the virus from it. Good gracious. I'll
be glad when Norman takes it off."

Fletcher's heart raced at the sight of his uncle pulling into the drive.
Lucille raised a disapproving eyebrow at the open roof.

"Man thinks he's still in college, running around town like he's
pledging a fraternity," she grumbled to Edmond, who was double
checking that the tickets were in his pants pocket.

Lucille and Edmond exchanged brief pleasantries with Woodrow.
Lucille explained that Edmond was in a hurry to get on the road for fear
of not being able to find a parking space.

"For some reason, he thinks we'll have no place to park like we're
attending an ABBA concert or something," she said sarcastically, opening
the car door. Her eyes looked disapprovingly at the open truck. "Woody,
make sure he stays off that leg and nowhere near that dilapidated Tonka
toy of yours." She spied three large wood-carved black bears sticking out
of the backseat. "Where'd you—"

"Lucy, *let's go*," Edmond growled. "Ralph Dummers is reserving us a
table beside the Moxie fountain." He fumbled with the radio to find the
Red Sox game. This year he'd rather listen to them instead of watching
them on television. With fans banned from all ballparks, the empty
seats were a constant reminder of the new way of life.

"Those are awesome," Fletcher said enthusiastically. "Are you putting
them at the inn?"

"I bought them this morning on the way here. G. R. Lancaster had
them on his front lawn."

"Doesn't he live all the way out in Bryant Pond?"

"Long story. I had to drop a box of supplies off for Alek Von Piddle.
He's a little laid up right now and recovering at his cabin on Lake
Christopher." Woodrow looked at the darkening sky with growing
concern.

"What happened to him?" Fletcher asked. The thought of Alek's blinking eyes and his bouncing glasses made Fletcher smile.

"A most unfortunate incident. Remember when I called you the other day from Ye ol' Boot? Well, after I hung up and moved to take him home, he totally ignored me and continued to dance on a table with his shirt off."

"You're joking," said Fletcher. "Why?"

"From what he says, he was showing everybody some tribal dance he'd learned from a Peruvian tribe while hiking an extinct volcano."

Fletcher roared with laughter. "That's hysterical. What a doofus."

"I know. Hard to believe. Before I could reach him, he fell and landed on Harriet Zonka. You know how boney she is. He suffered a severely sprained back and has a black bruise the size of a coconut in the center of his spine. It could have been much worse. Landing on Harriet prevented him from landing in that huge fireplace. Mr. Trent had just stoked it too. Blazin' like the dickens," Woodrow said as he sat down beside Fletcher on the granite steps.

"How's Mrs. Zonka?"

"A little embarrassed, but okay. You know how those librarians are. Tough as nails. Fletch, you look exhausted. You okay?" Woodrow asked with a concerned look.

"Yeah, I was up late the last two nights. I wanted to finish that book on Caravaggio with Dad. It's a huge book," he said wearily.

"Anything else keeping you up?"

"Um, just a lot on my mind right now, Uncle Woodrow," Fletcher said, looking down at the brick walk.

"You sure? I mean, I'd have thought that what you learned from Mr. Caxton may have been a lot to take in."

"How come you never mentioned anything about Nimsy Cortland?"

"Because, Fletch, you may not want to hear this, but like it or not, you're still a kid. You've had a lot thrown at you the past few months. That was just another huge stressor."

"But she may be connected. I had a right to know," Fletcher snapped. He was dismayed that his uncle of all people would keep it from him. "How long have you known?"

Woodrow rubbed Fletcher's back. "From the day we received the news that your mother had gone missing. From day one I've done what I could to help with the situation. I've actually hired two private investigators to work on the case. They've been to the South American jungles three times."

"And?" Fletcher asked with urgency.

Woodrow looked deflated. "Nothing. But it's obvious that your parents knew more than we'd originally thought."

"What do you mean?"

"Look at what they did. They established a contractual agreement that would set up a new company for you in the event that something happened to both of them. I had honestly forgotten about Jackson's letters until Jefferson reminded me of your father's instructions regarding Fifth Ward. It was then that I decided to revisit them."

"When was this?"

"A little while ago. We both agreed that it would be better to hold off telling you until we had more information. Unfortunately, your aunts are moving at the speed of light to unload the healthy division of Cygnus, *and* some startling things are happening right before our eyes."

"Like the rock slide?"

"Like the rock slide and Mollyockett's portrait in your father's room. Look at what we've learned so far. Don't you agree that all of this is extremely mysterious and shockingly bizarre?"

"That's an understatement," conceded Fletcher. "I just feel like it's getting more and more confusing every day with no end. I can hardly sleep anymore." He couldn't hide the deep frustration in his voice.

"Fletch, let's take a step back," Woodrow said. "We've mastered most of that riddle you found on the back of her portrait. If we focus on the squire—whoever or whatever that means—I'm positive it will lead us in the right direction. We'll also take a look around your basement today, *where the two paths meet, where the eagles nest.*"

"Well, I hope the squire turns out to be an ally and not a foe," Fletcher said uncomfortably. "We have enough enemies."

"I'm with you on that one. We also need to determine what the staff is referring to, so we can hold it tightly," Woodrow joked, blowing a small ant off his pants. "But it's quite obvious who is holding on to a grudge so tightly that it's literally destroying many others."

He glanced at Fletcher, who was watching a large black cloud approach on the horizon just behind the Mahoosuc Mountains. He slowly turned his head to look at his uncle. They always thought alike.

"Woodrow reached for an envelope in his leather satchel. Fletcher noticed the name and address of Quinn's father's company in the upper left-hand corner. *McKenzie's Inn* was written in elegant cursive in the center of the envelope. Uncle Woodrow looked at Fletcher and leaned against the granite rise to the front step he was sitting on. "In your conversation with Mr. Caxton the other day, did he mention Joseph McKenzie?"

"The lighthouse keeper, the one who's on the labels on those jars of food."

"Exactly! Did he mention that Joseph's papers were found beneath the floor boards of the lighthouse?"

Fletcher nodded.

"Well, here are his letters and daily journal." Woodrow slid the envelope across the rock step. "They are very detailed and historically quite significant. Jackson, Joseph's father, wrote quite frequently from Ketchum while Joseph was stationed on Rose Island. It was the only source of communication in those days."

"Primitive texting, huh?" Fletcher said with a laugh.

"Uh, not even close. Anyway, the letters in that envelope have been locked away in my safe at the inn since they were handed over to me by the Caxtons during their first visit to Mount Zircon."

"And they're all in there?" Fletcher asked, eagerly reaching for the envelope.

"All of 'em. What they say is quite revealing and a little unsettling, especially given your recent turn of misfortune. Here, I'll show you."

As he reached for the envelope, a loud boom of thunder jolted them as the wind increased in intensity, blowing several pieces of paper out of Woodrow's truck. Lucille's wind chimes clanged wildly from a nearby tree limb.

"Looks like we're in for a soaker," Woodrow said, studying the menacing clouds. A lightning bolt shot across the horizon. Three seconds later a loud thunderclap reverberated over them. "I need to put my top up. Rain will short-circuit the electrical system. Don't want that to happen again. We can finish our conversation inside." Woodrow bolted toward the open truck.

"Wait up. I'll help you," Fletcher said, grabbing his crutches.

In the rush to help cover the exposed truck, Fletcher almost tripped over his crutches while stepping off the granite landing. He laughed loudly as he approached the three wooden bears protruding from the back of the rig. Each one had a different expression ranging from rage to delight.

"Where are you putting 'em?" he asked, feeling the rough wood on the largest one.

"Probably near that rock path in front of that large red maple. I can use one of the holes I've dug for those bean-hole bean dinners," Woodrow said, unfolding the black canvas roof.

He took a step back to locate the front seam with a thick band to insert into the tube located over the windshield. "Here, grab this, Fletch."

He grunted as he raised the top over the bars, which Fletcher had snapped into place. "Here, grab the other end. I'll tie it down," he said, studying the lower flaps of the black weathered material.

Fletcher quickly reached out in compliance after watching three quick and successive lightning bolts in the distance.

Woodrow held out his hand. "We'd better head inside. It's starting to rain."

Fletcher did his best to stay in step with his uncle, who had quickened his pace as the rain increased in intensity. As they opened the front door, a wall of rain descended on the house.

"Phew, that was close," Woodrow exclaimed, looking out the window. The drenching rain was now falling sideways as the wind ratcheted up the violent storm. "Looks like your grandmother left us a note."

Fletcher studied the trees, which were now whipping wildly in the side yard while Woodrow laughed at the note. "Woman's got a sixth sense."

"What'd you mean?" Fletcher asked as he propped his crutches against the table and sat down. He extended his cast-covered leg under the table in the center of the room.

"*Fletcher and Woody,*" Woodrow read. "*Lunch is in the warmer. Baked beans with those red hot dogs you love. Whole grain buns are on the counter. Make sure you steam them. Tastes much better. Whoopie pies are made of almond flour, so eat up. These should sustain you two for whatever activity you've got planned. It's quite obvious those Moxie tickets are a ploy to get rid of us. Hope it works. Love, Grans.*"

Fletcher howled as his uncle folded the note.

"That woman should work for the CIA," Woodrow muttered, lifting the cover of the large pan on the stove. "Let's eat and discuss Jackson McKenzie's letters. Then we'll venture down to that basement and see what awaits us," he suggested, breathing deelply the aroma of beans. "Here, you can read them while I get things ready."

Fletcher opened the envelope and studied the ornamental writing on the faded paper.

"Why'd they write like this? It's just like the kind on the riddle," he grumbled, annoyed at the script writing. He squinted at what appeared to be the word *dearest* at the top of the letter.

"It's written by a quill pen dipped in a bottle of ink," Woodrow explained, opening the bag of whole-wheat buns and placing them in the small steamer on the counter.

"You see, they didn't have pens or pencils back then. So they dipped a bird feather in a small bottle of ink to write their letters."

"Ingenious." Fletcher said, analyzing the loopy scrolls and oddly shaped letters.

He took his time reconstructing Jackson McKenzie's words into recognizable sentences, raising his eyebrows at various, jarring words.

"You do understand what you're reading, right?" Woodrow asked, placing two white plates in the center of the table. "Lunch is almost ready. Why don't you wash up?"

"It's obvious he's worried about something," Fletcher said, heading to the sink. He watched in delight as his uncle placed the pan of beans, brown bread, hot dogs, and a plate of steamed brown buns on the table alongside various condiments.

"Here, let me," Woodrow said, shuffling the papers, looking for specific entries. "Okay, here Jackson is writing about his past conversations with Mollyockett, who shared her deep fear of a revengeful and angry brother."

"Because she shared the secret of the passage with Jackson?" Fletcher asked.

"Actually, it's worse than that," Woodrow said gravely, tracing the words in the letter with his finger. "Listen to this. She's telling Jackson as they sat beside Frenchman's Hole about the time when she was only fifteen years old. The French and English were involved in another war, which was one of many wars in North America. The Pigwackets, who were camped along the Androscoggin River, were drawn into the conflict as we discussed. Mollyockett's father literally begged for peace but to no avail. The English issued bounties for Wabanaki prisoners, and scalps. Soldiers were paid handsomely for each Indian scalp. That along with a vicious smallpox epidemic that decimated the Wabanaki people. They had no immunity from this European disease when it arrived on the shores of America. It literally killed hundreds of thousands of Native Americans."

"What's smallpox?" Fletcher asked.

Woodrow explained to Fletcher the virus that caused flu-like symptoms and a terrible rash that left scars and often led to death.

"That's awful," Fletcher said sadly, shaking his head in disgust. "A little bit like the current pandemic."

"I know. Unbelievable, isn't it? But it gets worse. Indian villages were burned to the ground by soldiers just to prevent them from assisting the French. Mollyockett's entire family, including Tomhegan, fled to Canada. Eventually, the English made their way north and invaded Quebec. On their way they pillaged and burned the Wabanaki village at Odnak. At the time Mollyockett was only nineteen years old. She escaped the soldiers by hiding behind a bush with Tomhegan. Mollyockett recounted the brutal violence she witnessed on that day. She described the piercing screams of Wabanaki women and children being slaughtered by the masses. That day was a turning point for Mollyockett, Tomhegan, and the French infantry, whose footing soon after began to slip in the northeast. This is far worse than what we talked about earlier when you read *her* very words." Woodrow set the letter down. "She tells Jackson that her brother vowed revenge on the white man for the rest of eternity."

Fletcher had heard this story before from his uncle. "Well, yeah, I'd be more than peeved too," Fletcher said. "How come they killed the women and children? And how come Mollyockett didn't think like her brother? I mean, they both lost their parents." Fletcher fidgeted in his seat. For a fleeting moment, he had a tinge of sympathy for Tomhegan. He'd have done the same thing.

"Fletcher, think about what happened a few years later."

"I don't get what you're asking."

"The American Revolution, which took place right here in New England. Suddenly, the remaining Wabanakis who had returned to the banks of the Androscoggin River, not too far from here, had an ally against the people who had killed most of their tribe. Remember, what was Joseph McKenzie doing at that lighthouse off Newport?"

"Fighting the British soldiers," Fletcher said proudly, smiling at the thought of Joseph standing in front of the lighthouse on the jar of Russian Sauce.

"Exactly. Remember how Mollyockett met Jackson?"

"Um, didn't you say he was in Maine to fight the British?"

"That he was. I'm quite positive Mollyockett welcomed the American troops with open arms after what she'd experienced in Quebec." Woodrow pointed to Jackson's artistic writing on the page. "According to this letter, she told him of her deep disappointment in and concern about Tomhegan. He was wild with rage and considered the American colonists fighting the British as evil as the soldiers who had killed most of his family. He openly murdered and tortured any white man he encountered."

As Fletcher listened to his uncle, he envisioned Mollyockett sitting next to Jackson McKenzie on the large rock that overlooked Frenchman's Hole many, many years ago. He imagined her wearing her black hat, earrings jangling in the wind while she shared her personal story with a man her brother was out to kill.

"Why didn't she want revenge like Tomhegan?" Fletcher asked, thinking of his own parents. Never in a million years would he have expected to have something in common with Tomhegan.

"Take these with you and read them. It's quite clear that she was a deeply religious person, a rather colorful one at that," Woodrow said with a smile. "She sure made a name for herself, even during a time when the native Indians were persecuted and ill-treated."

"How come they never tell you that during the Mollyockett celebrations in Bethel?" Fletcher asked.

"It's a very good story to tell," Woodrow said and sighed. "Over the course of time, people tend to forget. History teaches us lessons if we really take the time to look. A good example would be this pandemic. There are pararell lessons to be learned from the deadly influenza pandemic of 1918, which, by the way, claimed the life of the grandfather of our current president. It's true, google it."

Fletcher nodded. "Maybe one day we can put up a monument to her," he said, smiling at the thought of him, Cam, and Quinn standing in the front row of thousands of people as a majestic statue of Mollyockett is unveiled for the first time.

"I don't think you'd have a difficult time selling it to the public," Woodrow told him.

"But if everyone knew what we knew—"

"Let's cross that bridge when we get there. First, we need to figure all this out." He started reading the letter again. "Right here she's telling Jackson of her innate fear that Tomhegan has somehow cursed her."

Fletcher sat back and looked toward the window behind his uncle as a small pine limb bounced off the glass with a low thud.

"I hope we don't lose power. Storm's really brewing," Woodrow said with concern as he watched the rain cascade down the blurred windowpanes.

"What kind of curse?" Fletcher asked, turning his attention back toward his uncle.

"According to this, it's the same type of curse she put on the residents of Snow Falls after she was turned away in that blizzard." It was apparent he had the same powers as her.

Fletcher had temporarily forgotten about her curse and its negative long-term impact on the tiny community.

"I know this is a bit of a stretch, but you did say you're absolutely positive you saw Tomhegan on the edge of Buck's Ledge ... or someone who resembled him."

"It was him," Fletcher exclaimed with certainty. "I'd bet my life."

"Well then, maybe that explains the sudden and unexplained appearance of ergot after a long hiatus. Remember, the Bragg and Seton farms in Andover and Bethel were Mollyockett's two favorite places to set up her wigwam." Woodrow raised the letter closer to his face. "According to what she told Jackson, she actually felt, and I quote, *I've felt the poison of his curse in both spots. No longer are they the tranquil and serene places God created. I fear that I will die in an unfamiliar land.*"

"I thought she died at the farm in Andover?"

"She did. Chief Metallak brought her there when she became too weak. From what the Andover Historical Society says, she was very ill and afflicted with dementia."

"What's that mean?"

"It means she was losing her mind, so to speak. She may have been unaware where she was or who she was during her final days."

"I feel so bad for her."

Suddenly, Mollyockett took on a whole new person for Fletcher. *How could they have taken her to a place to die that may have been cursed by her brother?* he thought as he looked at the words Mollyockett had spoken to Jackson.

"Who was Metallak?" he asked Woodrow.

"Metallak was a chief who had taken kindly to the American colonists fighting the British. He was also accepted as a friend and lived freely amongst the local citizens."

"Where's he buried?"

"That's a good question. I never thought to look." Woodrow took out his pen from the leather satchel. "I'll make a note to check it out."

"How did Mollyockett know that ergot would be a sign? You know, like it says in the riddle."

"Another good question, Fletch." Woodrow put his pen down and studied his nephew gazing intently at his notes. He hoped he hadn't made a huge mistake sharing the letters with this fragile fourteen-year-old boy.

"So you think the rock given to us at her grave refers to Tomhegan's revenge for the killing of his parents and Mollyockett's decision to share her secret with Jackson?" Fletcher asked, looking into his uncle's bright blue eyes.

"I'm somewhat positive of it. Unless you have another explanation."

"I have a strong feeling we're about to find out," he whispered in a low voice. His eyes blazed with determination as he took a deep breath. They sat in silence as a huge thunderclap shook the house. After about thirty seconds, Fletcher leaned back in his chair and looked at his uncle. "The riddle speaks about a symbol on the grave," he said. "If it's the thing we found on her grave, then it needs to be said in the light 'before dark's time.' Does that mean it needs to be said at her grave or at another place?"

"Beats me. We'll have to take a stab in the dark, so to speak, unless your basement gives us a clue. Who knows? We may find nothing down there, but I'm really hoping that the stone in the riddle is part of that rock wall you've mentioned or is part of some entrance or at least part of some clue." Woodrow bit into a steamed bun filled with a bright red hot dog, spurting two large drops of yellow mustard onto Lucille's favorite crocheted tablecloth.

"She's gonna have a fit," Fletcher said and laughed as Woodrow quickly wet his napkin and scrambled to remove the stain.

"I know. I spilled coffee on it once. She actually sent a dry-cleaning invoice to the inn for almost fifty bucks."

Fletcher chuckled as he watched Woodrow make an ill-fated attempt to clean the immaculate tablecloth. He stopped and looked at Fletcher with a smile. "Wouldn't life be wonderful if this was our only problem?"

They quickly finished lunch, deciding to leave the decadent, almond-flour Whoopie pies for a treat after they explored the basement.

"I've died and gone to heaven," Woodrow cried out in jubilation, stepping off the bottom landing. In the far corner of the well-furnished recreation room, there stood dozens of wooden wine boxes stacked from floor to ceiling. He approached the crates inscribed with various French vineyards. "There's a little Bordeaux down here. Well, I'll be. Even some Rothschild," he said, shaking his head in wonder.

"A little what?" Fletcher asked. He secured the crutches under his arms after hopping down the stairs while firmly holding the rail for support.

"Bordeaux. It's this wonderful wine country located in the heart of France. Rothschild is the ultimate in Bordeaux experience. The family has been making wine for European kings for hundreds of years. It's absolutely my favorite place on earth."

Fletcher looked at the crates as his uncle jotted down various names and dates on his small pad.

"Looks like another immediate visit is in order. Your basement is a treasure trove of secrets already," Woodrow said eagerly. "I've no idea how I missed knowing about this. But let's get on with why we're here." He led Fletcher toward the dark brown door in the back. "If I remember correctly, your mother's root cellar is located behind this door, right?"

"It's actually called the Bacchus den now," Fletcher said proudly, grinning at his uncle.

"Ahh, I stand corrected. The Bacchus den."

He was well aware of Fletcher's little fraternity with Camway and Quinn. "Quite the appropriate name too. What with all that delectable red wine guarding the entrance."

Fletcher looked around the cool, dark room, focusing on the stone wall supporting the north end of the huge house.

"Has anyone used this room since your mother … went missing?"

"Grans comes down every now and then to dig up some of mom's vegetables or grab a canning jar," Fletcher said. "She doesn't bury any vegetables like mom did though." He turned the overhead light on as they moved into the center of the dank, musty room. Woodrow scanned the peripheral of the room, looking for any immediate clue that might help them. He then focused on three comfortable, well-worn leather chairs sitting atop a frayed oriental rug.

"I take it that's where Bacchus is honored." Woodrow smiled, winking at Fletcher.

"Pretty neat, huh?" Fletcher said, walking toward the setting. For a moment, time reversed itself and he was happy.

"What do you three do during these meetings, Fletch?"

"We just talk, you know … stuff," Fletcher responded hesitantly.

Woodrow eyed him disbelievingly. "Ahh, of course … stuff," he repeated. He chuckled a little as he sat down on the stuffed leather chair closest to the stone wall. "Comfy. I could have a nice little siesta down here with all that glorious celebration just sitting over there in those lonely boxes patiently waiting for a friend to come along and spring it free." He sighed as he closed his eyes and leaned back in the leather chair.

Fletcher ignored his uncle and hobbled to the back wall. He leaned his crutches against it and focused on the different sizes of boulders and rocks pressed tightly together to form the base for dozens of wooden beams supporting the first floor.

"I really hope this is the spot," he said, looking at a small crevice at the bottom of a large rock. "But it doesn't really look like an entrance anywhere here." He inserted his finger into a small crack at the base of the wall.

Woodrow reluctantly rose from the comfortable chair and walked toward Fletcher, looking intently at the sturdy wall. "Let's look for that symbol. Lots of history in that wall, Fletch. It's obvious it was here long before your father had this place built."

"What'd you mean?" asked Fletcher, intently studying the intricate stone patterns in the corner. He crouched on his knees, carefully extending his cast behind him. The clay dirt would be an instant clue for Lucille when she returned.

"Well, look at these marks," Woodrow said, pointing to two long chiseled lines in the center of the largest boulder. "This was obviously moved here by a team of oxen. Those lines were put there to prevent the thick rope from slipping when it was moved into place. That plus the fact that they stopped using rocks to build cellar walls long before this place was put here."

Woodrow removed the paper rubbing he'd made at Mollyocket's grave from his back pocket. He unfolded it and held it up to the light. "See anything that resembles this? We really need to …" His voice trailed away as he studied a square-shaped boulder supporting three smaller rocks near the top of the wall.

After fifteen minutes of meticulously scouring every stone, Fletcher announced, "Man, I don't see anything." His cast was now dark gray from the clay floor.

"Me neither," Woodrow said in disappointment. "I was absolutely positive we'd find something down here." He slowly stood and took a small step backward. "Absolutely amazing what detailed planning and engineering went into building these ... and so long ago. Today they just line up square cement blocks. Any nitwit could figure that out." He huffed in protest.

"So what's next?" Fletcher asked, sounding defeated as he moved slowly toward the Bacchus chairs.

"I guess it's plan B," Woodrow said jovially as he sat beside him, removing a cobweb that had become entangled in his thin hair.

"Which is?"

"That's the million-dollar question, Fletch. But I'll be sure to tell you first when I've thought of it. We need to remain positive though. The last thing we need to do is give up."

Fletcher's dampened spirit rose at his uncle's positive attitude. "I guess you're right."

"Anything you can think of in your backyard or nearby woods that may help us?" Woodrow asked. "Aleksandr was 100 percent sure this is the spot where the two paths meet. He's never been wrong in all his years of locating historical landmarks."

Fletcher sat back and closed his eyes. He carefully reconstructed the entire property of 1942 Sangar Drive in his mind. His eyes snapped open, and he looked intently at his uncle with newfound hope. "There is a rock wall in my mother's garden. Dad had it built for her," he said with a glimmer of hope.

"*Hmm*, sounds a little too new, but it's worth taking a gander at," Woodrow said. He studied the back wall, rolling his fingers on the double leather padding covering the thick arm of his chair. "Maybe one of those rocks will—"

"Hello. Hello. Anyone here?" someone shouted from upstairs.

"Refinna," Woodrow said, annoyed. He glanced at Fletcher. "Of all times. Why on earth is she here?"

"Probably to check on me," Fletcher responded dryly. "You know that arrangement she's always holding over my grandparents' heads."

"Well, it's poor timing. Clear as day you're in good hands. I mean, my truck's parked right out front," Woodrow said angrily. "We might as well go up and see what she wants." He stood and shouted, "*We're down here. Give us a sec.*"

They could hear the floor creaking above them, caused by the immense weight moving from room to room. Quickly, Fletcher followed his uncle up the stairs. Woodrow carried the crutches while Fletcher gripped both rails for support, his dirty cast extended behind him for balance.

Uncle Woodrow opened the cellar door and faced Refinna, who was now sitting at the kitchen table, her plump arms resting in front of her.

"These things are scrumptiously divine," she squealed in delight as she plucked a mound of white creamy filling from the center of one of the Whoopie pies. She took a large bite of the overstuffed pastry while picking up Lucille's note with her other hand. She glanced at the plate of Whoopie pies with lust while scanning the contents of the letter. A small dribble of cream rested precipitously on the edge of her upper lip, covering a small unplucked black hair. Her pink mask was hanging from her right wrist.

"Refinna, you have this innate ability to sniff out junk food no matter how far it is from you. Why on earth are you out and about in a storm like this?" Woodrow questioned, annoyed at the interruption. As he approached the table, he set the grave rubbing beside the plate of Whoopie pies.

"I came over to check on *him*," she replied glancing at Fletcher and hardly hiding her distain..

"For goodness sake, didn't you see my truck parked right out front? You think I'm in here teaching him secrets of the dark world? Get a grip on reality," Woodrow retorted with increasing anger.

Refinna lowered her head slightly in response to her uncle's berating tone. "It's just all the stress. You know running Cygnus is such a demanding task," she said, looking for any sympathy she could muster. She glanced at the note and blurted out, "*Humph,* almond flour. I knew there was something wrong with these," she exclaimed with disgust, setting the uneaten portion on the table.

Fletcher watched quietly as his uncle's face turned from annoyance to anger at the haughty woman sitting in front of him. He'd had enough. Slowly, Woodrow approached Reffina and poked his boney finger in front of her face.

"Did I hear you right? You actually have the nerve to come here and criticize the cooking of one of the finest culinary masters in the entire valley?" he boomed.

"But I … um," she stammered nervously. "I was only referring to the price of the almond flour. You know it's—"

Woodrow cut her off. "Serena said the same thing about quinoa when Clyde Pickers suggested Cygnus start adding it to those prepared meals you're so freely and deceptively marketing as healthy. Healthy for who? Godzilla? You'd better be listening to me young lady," Woodrow continued. Refinna cowered in her chair as beads of sweat formed on her red forehead.

"Have you even noticed how immence your two sons are? Look at them. They arrogantly traipse all over town, poking fun at others when they're actually the poster boys for both the diabetic association and the obesity epidemic that's hit our country. It's amazing they can still walk. And don't try to act naïve to the situation."

Fletcher remained utterly silent. He was careful not to interfere. Any confrontation he'd ever had with his aunt was always a losing battle. He may not lose in front of his uncle, but she would find a way to seek revenge. He so wanted to put his two cents in regarding the sale of Birch Bread, his father's pride and joy.

"Uncle Woodrow," Refinna gasped in shame. "I was just saying that almond flour would send our prices through the stratosphere. All we're trying to do is make our products more readily available for hardworking Americans. Especially during the Coronavirus pandemic. You know, sell, sell, sell to the masses," she said with a hint of arrogance.

Woodrow exploded with shame and disgust. "*Enough!* You and your sisters have clearly taken advantage of Aldous's most unfortunate situation *solely* in the name of profit. I am honestly ashamed to even be associated with the Cygnus brand these days. You've single-handedly moved every company-branded item from the healthy section to the fat-laden snack food section in every grocery store in New England. I'm actually surprised the Society for Prevention of Obesity hasn't slapped a class-action lawsuit on you and those two other profit-seeking scoundrels of yours. Absolute travesty of grotesque proportions. Have you even—"

Woodrow lowered his shaking finger when he saw Lucille and Edmond standing in the open door, the rain now coming down in a low drizzle. Edmond's mouth was wide open as he watched the scene before him. Fletcher immediately noticed a look of deep pleasure on his grandmother's face from witnessing Refinna's whiplashing by such a gentle man.

"We disturbing anything?" she asked casually, glancing at Refinna with a gleam in her eyes. "I mean, we can come back at a later time," she added sarcastically while removing her rain bonnet. Edmond slowly walked toward the pantry with a wet cardboard box filled with items he'd proudly purchased at the Moxie memorabilia auction. He sidestepped the table like it was a land mine ready to blow 1942 Sangar Drive to smithereens at any second.

Woodrow glanced at the wooden clock above Lucille's butcher-block table. "You're back early," he said.

"Absolute disaster. Never again," Lucille announced. "The wind practically blew the tent over. Rain was pouring down on us from a million leaks. And get this—some Moxie-filled lunatic actually spiked the Moxie fountain. You should have seen the chaos. Animals, the entire lot. And talk about following COVID restrictions. Ha! You had to actually search for people wearing masks. You're on your own next year, Ed. And you can go with him, Woody. You and your convenient VIP tickets." She huffed as she filled the metal coffee kettle with water. "The best part of the entire charade was the slogan they chose this year. You ready for this? *Moxie, it's Maine in a bottle.*" She rolled her eyes at Fletcher. "Makes me want to pack up and move 'cross the border to New Hampshire. I see you found my Whoopie pies, Refinna," she said without missing a beat.

"Delicious. Beyond words. I applaud your use of almond flour to make them healthier," Refinna squeaked with delight, clapping her plump hands. Her eyes darted toward her uncle for support, vividly remembering her Three-Finger Willy encounter with Lucille at Hamlin State Park.

Lucille studied Refinna's face and her eyes. She noticed a slight smile on Woodrow's face. "Mmm, I'm sure you do," she said sarcastically, irritated that Refinna would even think she could fool her. She was surprised that Refinna even knew how to pronounce almond flour.

Lucille sat a metal jar of coffee on the table, noticing Woodrow's drawing he'd made at Mollyockett's grave.

"I see you've discovered that carrot rock," she said casually.

"The carrot what?" Woodrow asked, confused.

"Carrot rock. I accidentally broke this nail on it the other day when I was digging up the last of Muriel's carrots in the middle of the root cellar," she said, raising her affected finger. "It has the exact design on it as that drawing. "I tried to pull it up, wouldn't budge. Kinda spooked me. Something you'd see on one of those weird vampire shows, so I reburied it. Gave me the heebie-jeebies." She shuddered at the thought.

Fletcher glanced at his uncle but said nothing. He knew they were both thinking the same thing. This *was* the right spot. Mr. Von Piddle was still 100 percent correct.

Refinna, taking advantage of the shift in the conversation, slowly rose from the table. The last thing in the world she wanted was to have Woodrow pay attention to her again. "You mind if I take two of these home in a doggie bag?" she asked with feigned politeness while looking at Lucille.

"I'd be honored. You want the recipe?" Lucille responded, knowing Refinna had no intention of ever making a healthy version of anything.

"Uh, that's so thoughtful of you. You sure you have time?" Refinna asked, doing her best to sound genuine.

"Anything for you, Riffy. Here, sit back down. I'll recopy it for you," Lucille said, enjoying the defeated look on Refinna's face as she hesitantly sat back down at the table.

Edmond chuckled with Woodrow at the sight of Refinna's hopeless situation.

"Lucy, you mind if I take a look at your wine collection before I leave? I want see what that wine club is still sending Aldous," he said, glancing toward Fletcher.

"Help yourself. It's all Greek to me," Lucille said as she poured hot water in the two cups.

"Fletch, why don't you show me where your Bacchus fraternity meets. You promised you'd show me."

Fletcher smiled at his ingenuous uncle. He knew they were both thinking the same thing. They'd found the passage at last.

CHAPTER 16

THE SQUIRE AND ONION

It had been two weeks since Fletcher and his uncle had located the large circular stone beneath eight inches of cool soil in the center of Muriel's root cellar. Lucille was right on the money. The drawing Woodrow had rubbed from Mollyockett's grave was an exact replica of the symbol expertly engraved in the center of the flat granite stone. Additionally, the stone in the root cellar appeared to have been cut from the same quarry in Quebec as the gravestone. They both quickly gave up on any attempt to move the stone after several minutes of pushing and prying with two large crowbars. After uncovering the entire stone, Uncle Woodrow estimated its weight at more than half a ton. It was not moving. They both now wondered how much Muriel *actually* knew with this discovery hidden in plain sight.

Fletcher lay in his warm bed. He was excited by the bright sunshine outside his windows. It was July 18, Mollyockett Day in Bethel. Fletcher had circled both July 18 and July 25 on his daily planner, which sat on his nightstand. After returning from the root cellar, he'd circled both dates after his uncle informed him that the date of the full moon in the riddle, which indicated the full moon *after sowing so soon,* definitely pointed to the full moon occurring on the Saturday after Mollyockett Day. Just to be sure, Woodrow consulted with the chief astrolonomer at the Weston Observatory located outside Boston, who confirmed that the referenced full moon was indeed on July 25.

"Fletch, breakfast is ready. It's a busy day. Let's get going, honey!" Lucille yelled from the bottom of the stairs.

Fletcher looked at the clock sitting beside his bed. In little more than three hours, he'd be meeting Cicely and Quinn in the parking lot of the Brew Pub on the outskirts of Bethel. They were all riding on Cygnus's Mollyockett Day float, much to the chagrin of Refinna, Winola, and Serena. Camway would be joining his family on the Ketchum Ski and Snowboarding float.

With the assistance of Edmond and Zack Domino, the facilities manager for Cygnus, Woodrow had taken complete control of planning, designing, and building the eccentric float. Woodrow firmly and quickly nixed Serena and Winola's idea of a Moby Dick theme. It was the first time he had ever taken control of anything at the giant food company. He did it for Fletcher and the McKenzie reputation and didn't care what his three nieces thought.

"The whale's mouth can be wide open, and everyone can be dressed as sailors or fishermen standing inside the mouth, chucking Cygnus treats at all the spectators," Refinna had offered. "They'll love it!" she had exclaimed.

"Are you all absolutely off your rockers?" Woodrow had retorted, pointing out that the image of a massive whale didn't help to promote their fat-laden snack foods. Additionally, the last thing the town needed was for people to leave the socially distant safety of their cars for an artificial blueberry treat. Reluctantly, they accepted his strong suggestion of a Jiminy Cricket theme.

"Well, I hope it's a winner," Refinna had said negatively, after learning of the theme over creamy cakes and coffee at their morning meeting. "But I doubt it.

"Ketchum Ski and Snowboarding has Peter Pan and Mount Zircon Ski Resort selected Charlotte's Web," she had huffed while licking the outer edge of a newly created cream cake filled with red speckles of cherry-flavored candies. "Who's gonna vote for a cricket over Peter Pan?"

Fletcher showered and dressed as quickly as his cast would let him. Mentally, he was checking off his to-do list as he approached the kitchen.

"I really think we'll nab first place this year, Ed. We've even wired the strings of lightbulbs hanging from the clothesline. They'll be glowing as we pass the judge's stand," Lucille said, kissing Fletcher on the head.

"Lovely day for a parade," she said, looking out the window for the hundredth time. "I've finished that blade of grass costume for you. I had to widen the bottom to accommodate that filthy cast of yours," she huffed, glowering at his leg. "Your green mask is on your dresser."

"Jefferson called a few minutes ago," Edmond said to Fletcher. "I'll be dropping you off at the Brew Pub. Seems Quinn's costume isn't finished yet."

"You two can wash your dishes when you're done," Lucille said as she quickly removed her apron. "I've promised Martha and Alberta I'd meet them at the Double Moose for a pre-parade coffee. Fletch, you be careful with that leg. I'm a little leery about the design of your costume. It's a little too tight for your cast," she said, kissing his head again. Smiling, she approached her husband and gave him a light peck on his cheek. "I'll meet you on the common for the Adirondack chair auction. Remember, no more than two hundred for the one with the Nubble lighthouse scene. Don't forget your masks. They're being super strict today."

———

Because of the large number of entries and social distancing, the Mollyockett Day Parade route was extended from the Brew Pub to the Chamberlain Hotel at the end of Main Street. The entire length of the parade was a little more than two miles. The floats weren't allowed to move if everyone wasn't wearing masks.

Fletcher, Quinn, and Cicely all laughed at the sight of Fletcher's portly cousins. Ogden and Oberon were both dressed as extremely large lime green crickets. Refinna had demanded in Woodrow's absence that two green thrones be built at the front of the float to seat Ogden and Oberon, and they were painted lime green to blend in with the overall theme.

Both spoiled boys had thrown wild tantrums when it was announced that there was only one Jiminy planned for the float.

"We absolutely can have two Jiminy Crickets seated at the front of the float. Just angle them in opposite directions. Who owns this company anyway?" Refinna had boomed to make her point. "My two precious dumplings will just touch the hearts of the judges."

"I can see it now," Serena said proudly. "Ogden and Oberon as Jiminy Cricket. They'll make the front page of every newspaper in New England."

Refinna closed her eyes, smiling at the vision of her two boys being displayed on the front of *The Boston Ledger*. "Just warms my heart," she said quietly, sighing.

Many of the volunteers threatened to leave because of Refinna's ridiculous demands. When Woodrow showed up he was able to calm everyone down. He had to promise free all-day passes at his inn's spa when the pandemic was over if they stayed on the job. Then he cornered Refinna and made her promise she'd personally reimburse him for the entire cost of the expensive gesture. The volunteers had enough on their hands with social distancing and wearing masks in the heat.

Woodrow and Edmond worked tirelessly with Mr. Domino to construct the float. They built a large hill covered with plastic grass on the front end of the trailer in the hopes of partially hiding the two obese crickets from the spectators and the hard-to-please judges. They reworked their plans to include six people dressed as blades of grass who were to sit on the hill and act as a barrier. Fletcher, Quinn, and Cicely were chosen to be three of the blades of grass.

As Ogden and Oberon approached the float, Fletcher and Quinn laughed at the sight of the two enormous crickets.

The Cygnus float was eleventh in line, directly behind the Mahoosuc Hotel's "Paul Bunyan and Babe the blue ox" float. Fletcher looked at the long line of floats behind them. Marcus Rapple, a member of his lacrosse and ski teams, was waving wildly from a totally green float. A huge rainbow ran from the front of the long trailer to the back, high above seven leprechauns. Beside each small Irish leprechaun sat a gleaming pot of gold.

"That must be Rowdy Rick's Taco Hut's float," Quinn shouted. "That's hysterical."

Behind the leprechaun float, Fletcher studied several other ensembles. Each was a serious contender for first place. There was a Don

Coyote float; an Anansi the Spider float that showed a huge spider in a woven web slowly moving toward the clay pot of wisdom and a little girl dressed as a firefly trying to decide which one to attack; and a King Arthur-themed float that included a huge castle, a royal family waving from a second-floor balcony, two iron-clad knights, and a lanky court jester who was jumping between the still knights.

As Fletcher scanned other floats, he noticed the oddest character he'd ever seen standing in front of the Brew Pub sign. At first glance he thought the man was waiting for a lift on one of the floats. He had piercing brown eyes and long, jet-black hair woven into an intricate braid that hung well below the bottom of his muscular back. He was tall with wide shoulderes and looked like a natural athlete. Fletcher guessed his age to be roughly fifty. An Abraham Lincoln-style stove-pipe hat rested comfortably on his head. Three large blue feathers had been poked into the hat's center, increasing his height by another foot. Large loopy silver earrings with smaller blue feathers hung low from his tanned ears.

The man was mumbling to himself, causing nearby onlookers to subtly move away from him. He was wearing an immaculate long-tail black tuxedo with well-polished boots. A bright yellow sweater vest covered a smart white dress shirt. The top two corners of a black bow tie were poking out from behind the vest. He leaned on an impressive gold-tipped mahogany cane. Fletcher did a double-take when he noticed that his well-manicured fingernails were painted black. Beside the man sat a short-haired white dog patiently panting in the mild summer heat.

As the Jiminy Cricket float approached where the man was standing, the dog suddenly stopped panting and stood at attention. The bizarre man turned in Fletcher's direction, his large white teeth gleaming in the sunlight as he smiled, raised his hand, and waved.

"Splendid day, wouldn't you say, Fletch?" he shouted with an air of authority. He then raised the cane and twirled it effortlessly.

Completely shocked, Fletcher was fixated on the strange man's warm eyes.

"Quite the costume," he yelled, gracefully catching a small blue candy thrown from the Cygnus float at the cars filled with spectators over Woodrow's previous objection regarding the sweet treat.

"Here, Onion," the man said to the dog. "But just one. Don't want you getting the shakes." The dog accepted the sugary snack.

"Who's that freak?" Quinn asked Fletcher casually.

"Dunno. Considering how he's dressed, he's probably just waiting to jump on one of the floats behind us," Fletcher responded, unnerved by the unknown man's presence and the fact that somehow this eccentric character knew his name. He continued to stare at the man.

"Another one of your friends, Fletcher? Looks like he'd be the type you'd hang out with," Ogden said and snickered with contempt.

Fletcher ignored the comment and quickly glanced back toward the man, who was gingerly patting the dog on his head.

As the parade proceeded over the Androscoggin River's bridge and onto Main Street, the parked cars swelled to capacity, leaving a narrow strip for the floats to pass. Everyone was enjoying a brief return to *normalcy*.

"It's boiling in here," Quinn complained, wiping his sweaty forehead. The thick green mascara on his face immediately turned to smeared streaks of thick green goo. His green mask was hanging off his left ear.

"I think I'm about to pass out," Cicely whined. "Why's it taking so long to reach the common?"

Fletcher opened a small blue cooler his grandmother had prepared for him and handed out bottles of water. "Here. I really don't care how it looks to the judges. Blades of grass *do* need water. Drink then put your masks back on quickly."

Judging by the reaction of the spectators, Fletcher firmly believed their float was a contender for one of the three prized trophies. He laughed at one of the comments he heard from those standing on the edge the parade route.

"I love that book, but I didn't think there were two Jiminy Crickets. And look how large they are. Are they that husky in the book?"

As they stopped to allow a socially distanced high school band to perform for the judges, Fletcher and Quinn chatted with Quinn's mother, Doris. It was the first time she had been back to Maine since the Hamlin State Park incident. She had dark circles under her eyes and was even thinner than usual. She was sitting in a yellow convertible.

"I owe you my life, Fletch, no matter what you say. You're a very special person to me and always will be," she said. "I've spoken with your grandparents. They've agreed to let you spend a week on Block Island at the end of August. Cicely, you and Camway are invited too. Nicole's been talking nonstop since we've redone the cottage. You can enjoy the beach right from the front porch."

Cicely, Fletcher, and Quinn all cheered at the thought of spending an entire week on sandy white beaches. School was still in limbo as the governor hadn't decided what to do yet. Every school administrator and teacher carefully tracked the daily virus numbers for Maine in hopes of making the right call.

"And this thing will be off," Fletcher said joyously, knocking on his cast.

Just then the float jerked forward.

"We're coming up on the judge's stand," Mr. Domino yelled from the driver's side of the Cygnus truck hauling the float. "Everyone, let's put on a good show. It's all or nothing. Places."

"What's that supposed to mean?" Quinn asked, smiling at Cicely.

"You're blades of grass," Ogden glared at Quinn, standing up from his green throne. "It means act like a stupid plant. Shouldn't be too hard for you."

Before Quinn or Fletcher could respond, they heard a boisterous woman in a blue minivan laugh hysterically while pointing towards the front of their float.

"You've got to be kidding me. Look at that hefty cricket. His costume has split wide open," she shouted, shielding her small daughter's eyes from the sight.

Not only had Ogden's costume split open in the back, but his bright orange smiley-face boxer shorts were riding up his entire back-side. Suddenly, the entire crowd focused on the single heavyset cricket standing on the left-hand side of the Jiminy Cricket float.

Immediately, Ogden reached behind, snagging his orange undergarment with the pointed tip of the clawlike pincer he had on his hand. As he pulled it free, he tore a large section of the smiling face off the well-worn pair of boxer shorts, exposing his pale white skin beneath.

"Ogden, you've torn your costume. Sit down!" Fletcher yelled.

Dozens of people were snapping their cameras furiously at the Cygnus float. Others quickly looked away or shielded their children's eyes.

"You've got to be kidding me—and right in front of the judge's stand," Cicely said. She was standing right next to Ogden and immediately hid her eyes with her green glove as not to be recognized in any pictures. "Sit down … *right now!*" she growled angrily, peeking at Ogden through her glove.

Fletcher and Quinn howled loudly at the sight of Ogden desperately trying to sit down, but his large cricket wings were entangled in his throne, preventing him from sitting. Finally, Ogden ripped the right wing off his costume and sat down. A wave of applause rippled from every car within eyesight. Many honked their horns.

Fletcher stopped laughing as he watched the judges furiously scribble notes on their score cards while whispering loudly in deep consultation. Since they were dutifully following the rules, each was seated six feet apart. Fletcher shook his head and glared at his cousin, who was attempting to reattach the severed cricket wing. "Thanks, Ogden. I'm sure you've just earned us enough points for first place."

Fletcher glanced toward the cars parked in front of the grocery store which was adjacent to the judge's stand. Directly beneath a large blinking *Humpty Dumpty Barbecue Chips* sign, the man in the tuxedo and stovetop hat stood, his dog remained seated comfortably beside him. Fletcher was startled when the man raised his right hand and waved directly at him with a pleasant smile on his face.

"Mother would be laughing right now, Fletcher. Trust me on that," he yelled.

Fletcher quickly glanced toward Cicely and Quinn. Both were arguing with Ogden and Oberon, oblivious to the man's comment. When Fletcher turned back towards the Humpty Dumpty sign, the man and his dog were gone. Somehow, they had managed to slip through the tightly parked cars. He scanned the other side of Main Street, hoping to catch another glimpse of the odd character and his dog.

Maybe he went inside the store, Fletcher thought. He stared intently through the large window behind the potato chip sign. The man had simply disappeared. Fletcher grasped a fake cornstalk as the float made a wide turn onto Broad Street.

Huge applause erupted from the spectators scattered around the park to Fletcher's right. Dozens of tents were set up on the busy common, most were filled with artwork and crafts created by local artisans. An elderly man with a white bullhorn was constantly reminding everyone to wear their masks and to keep six feet apart whenever possible.

"We're almost at the Chamberlain Hotel," Cicely cheered. She waved her hand at a group of friends who were sitting on the back of a truck and staring daggers at Ogden.

After passing Bethel's library and historical society, their float slowly crept into the huge parking lot beside the Chamberlain Hotel, Bethel's only five-star resort. Fletcher looked at Ogden and Oberon with contempt as they waited for the high school band to pack their equipment in the parking lot. Both boys were greedily slurping giant chocolate ice cream cones that Refinna had quickly bought once she spied them turning into the parking lot. Their green masks were nowhere to be seen.

She totally ignored her nephew sitting smack dab between the two portly crickets as she handed them the giant cones. "I'm so, *sooo* proud of you both. Hiram Mead promised me you'll both be on the cover of next month's *Mahoosuc Magazine*. Imagine that," she blurted proudly as she stepped back to take a photo of her two boys dressed as crickets.

"I really, really hope it's a picture of Ogden in front of the judge's stand. I'd pay a million bucks for *that* to be on the cover," Fletcher whispered to Cicely and Quinn as they moved toward the back of the float. They quickly removed their sweaty costumes, leaving them in a single pile as earlier instructed.

"Me too. As long as I'm cropped out. I want nothing to do with that moron," Cicely said, rolling her eyes as she stepped off the trailer. "Don't forget your masks."

"You should have seen your face. You were absolutely horrified,"

Quinn said, doubling over with laughter.

"I'll never in a million years understand how you're related to them," Cicely told Fletcher.

"I know," Quinn agreed. "Did you see those boxer shorts. What was *that* all about?" Quinn said, looking at the twins heading toward the common with their mother. Both were still wearing their cricket costumes.

Fletcher chuckled when he noticed a large gray sweatshirt wrapped around Ogden's ginormous waistline. He stepped aside as the large float with the leprechauns pulled into the parking lot.

"Hey, Fletch, how'd it go?" Marcus Rapple yelled from the center of the Irish green trailer.

"There's *no* way we won, thanks to Ogden."

"Why? What he do?"

"He tore the back of his cricket costume *and* his britches right in front of all the judges," Fletcher said, laughing despite his annoyance as he replayed the scene in his mind.

"What a complete idiot. But maybe he helped us win first place," he said and smiled. "The judges just might be sympathetic toward that idiot."

"Fletch, we're heading to Zacarolo's pizza tent for a slice. Wanna come?" Quinn asked.

"I can't. I promised my grandmother I'd wait for her to arrive. She's on the Red Hatter's float, which should be here soon," he said, sitting down on the granite base of a Civil War statue in front of the hotel driveway. "Save me a slice of buffalo chicken."

Fletcher put on a beat-up Red Sox cap to help cover his cracked green face. He opened his small cooler for another bottle of spring water and a small protein bar. As he took a bite, he watched six burly loggers scramble up greased fifty-foot poles as part of a loggers competition taking place off to his right. Each wore blue masks that where fastened by a black elastic headband to prevent them from slipping off. *They've thought of everything.*

"You know, he actually saved the North from losing the war," boomed a voice from behind him.

Startled, Fletcher quickly turned his head to see who it was. Standing beside a large decorated water fountain was the man in the tuxedo and top hat. His dog was next to him, lapping water from the fountain's large basin.

"Um, who saved the North?" Fletcher asked, taken aback. Quickly, he put his mask on.

The tall man pointed his cane toward the huge statue looking down on Fletcher. "Joshua Chamberlain, the man this hotel is named after. He led the Twentieth Maine at the Battle of Gettysburg during the Civil War. Chamberlain's men actually ran out of ammunition while fighting an overwhelming Southern army. Had they been flanked, the war would have ended immediately with disastrous consequences for the North. So you know what he did?"

As the man approached him, Fletcher stared at the three blue feathers poking out the top of his black hat.

"He ordered his men to fix bayonets. They actually charged the enemy with their bayonets. Stopped the horrified Confederate soldiers in their tracks, causing them to swiftly retreat. Now that's what I call bravery." He stopped in front of Fletcher, his masked face shaded by the long shadow of the Chamberlain statue. He extended his right hand and introduced himself. "Squire Susup, longtime friend of the McKenzie clan."

Fletcher's eyes jerked up. "Did you say *squire*?" he stammered, firmly shaking the stranger's hand, staring at his polished black fingernails.

"I certainly did. I presume you've been expecting me," he said jovially as his dog slowly walked toward them.

"Onion, say hello to Fletcher McKenzie." He stooped down to pat the dog's head. Onion looked up at Fletcher as he sat down in the grassy shade.

"I saw you on the parade route. How'd you know my name?"

"I'm terribly sorry if I came off as rude. Sometimes I forget what age I'm in. But I actually know quite a lot about you," he said, smiling warmly at Fletcher. "So does Mother." He saw Fletcher taking in his tuxedo. "It's made of mohair from Angoran goats. It's deceivingly comfortable, even in this weather." He picked a small piece of white lint from his shoulder.

Fletcher looked at Squire Susup and studied the loopy earrings, which turned every time he moved his head. The small blue feathers in the loops quivered slightly in the wind.

"You mentioned your mother. What's her name?" Fletcher asked, wondering if she was a friend of his grandmother.

"Would you actually believe it if I said Mollyockett." He glanced toward the action on the common, smiling with excitement and hidden adventure. "This *is* her day."

Fletcher removed his cap and ran this hand through his wet hair, trying to determine if Mr. Susup was insane, joking with him, or totally serious. He gave a small laugh. "Given what I've learned with my uncle this past month, nothing really surprises me."

"Well, good, because it's true. She is quite the unique person. One of a kind. She's looking forward to meeting you. She wanted me to tell you—"

"Fletcher, there you are!" Cam yelled from the entrance to the hotel's parking lot, which was now filling to capacity as more and more floats arrived. Dressed as Peter Pan, Cam jumped off the side of the float and ran toward his friend. Onion happily wagged his tail at the sight of the green boy. Cam came to an abrupt halt after noticing the man wearing a top hat with three large blue feathers sticking out its top.

The squire walked toward Cam. "Name's Squire Susup. And you are?"

"Camway Vincent—Cam. I'm a friend of Fletcher's," he responded cautiously, taking in the uniquely dressed man.

"Pleasure's all mine, Mr. Vincent."

"So you win?" Fletcher asked.

"Dunno. They're announcing it in a few minutes over at the white gazebo," he replied, lowering his guard.

The squire was about to respond, but he was interrupted by Lucille yelling from atop the Amelia Bedelia float. "Fletch, how's your leg?"

The squire looked toward them, humored by the eight elderly women all dressed in maid's uniforms standing under a string of lit lightbulbs swinging from a clothesline. She stepped off the float with Martha and Alberta and headed for Fletcher.

"I heard there was an incident on the Cygnus float. I was worried sick that it was your leg," Lucille said, still wearing her fluffy white cleaning cap. Her black feather duster was blowing in the warm breeze. Fletcher watched in amusement as Lucille spied the squire. She stopped midstride and stared at him, focusing on his loopy silver earrings and blue feathers on top of his head.

"*Who* are *you?*" she asked bluntly, her long apron blowing sideways.

Martha and Alberta stood behind Lucille, using her as a protective barrier from the interesting stranger. All three were deeply suspicious. He was obviously not a local.

The squire smiled warmly and held out his hand. "Mr. Susup. Joseph Susup."

Camway scowled as if he'd caught him in a lie. "You just said your name was squire something."

The squire gave Lucille a reassuring smile. "Squire Susup is my nickname. Legally, my Christian name is Joseph Susup."

Lucille and her two friends relaxed at the Christian reference. "What on earth are those three feathers sticking out of your hat for?" she asked. "You on a float?"

"Actually, I always dress this way on Mollyockett's Day in honor of her creative and one-with-nature spirit. She's quite the character. I mean, I've read that she *was* quite the eccentric soul," he said quickly, correcting his mistake.

In her mind Lucille immediately placed the tall man in the weirdo category. *Must be from Boston*, she thought.

"Well, Mr. Susup, nice to meet you. I'll be sure to look for you again next year," Lucille said. "Fletch, we need to head to the gazebo to hear the results. Your grandfather is waiting for us."

Fletcher looked at the squire, sensing they had unfinished business. "I'll catch up with you in a sec. Mr. Susup's been telling me a story about Joshua Chamberlain," he said, giving his grandmother a reassuring look that everything was okay.

Lucille glanced toward the lobster roll tent. "Come to think of it. I'll just grab us three one of those lobster rolls. I'm sure Ed's starved. Be ready to head to the gazebo once I've purchased them," she said with finality. "Should only take me about five minutes, judging from that line."

"Fletch, Elspeth just texted me from Zacarolo's Pizza tent. Everyone's with Quinn and Cicely. Quinn's got two slices waiting for you," Camway said as he motioned toward the crowd. "You coming?"

"Tell them I'll meet them at the gazebo. Looks like everyone's heading that way," Fletcher said, watching the steady stream of pedestrian traffic heading in that direction. Each group at six foot intervals.

Cam nodded and left. Fletcher pulled out his protein bar and took a bite.

"That protein bar looks healthy," said Squire Susup, "but it's loaded with high-fructose corn syrup."

"My grandmother's always said how bad that stuff is for you," Fletcher said, glancing at the ingredients list.

"Sends your cells into a tizzy. Not a healthy way to feed what you're actually made of, is it?" Squire Susup said to Fletcher, tipping his hat toward Lucille and her two friends who were watching them as they slowly advanced toward the front of the line after carefully moving forward on socially spaced red circles.

"Criminal what they're doing to foods these days," he said with disgust, glancing toward Refinna. She was sampling a large square of white fudge with nuts she'd just plucked from an oversized sampler box purchased by Serena and Winola. The squire shook his head and frowned.

"Are you the squire that's mentioned in the riddle on the back of your mother's portrait in my dad's room?" Fletcher confronted him directly.

"The one and only. Guess it kind of makes me famous in these parts, huh?"

Filled with anticipation, Fletcher looked over to see that his grandmother had reached the front of the line. "So what's next?" He knew his time with the man was about to be cut short.

"You ready for the adventure of a lifetime?" Squire Susup asked. The squire saw the excitement lighting Fletcher's eyes and felt the positive energy emanating from him. "You're definitely a McKenzie. I'll meet you at the entrance to the passage exactly two hours after sunset during the next full moon. I've left you something there. You may want to study it. This year's different young man. Many people will be depending on you. You see, I've been assisting relatives of many unfortunate Mckenzies reach Whole for centuries." He paused. This year, however, is completely different and of utmost urgency. You'll be working with mother to help deliver a vaccine that is badly needed right now. I'm not going to lie to you. The danger is most extreme, and I do hope you make it back." Fletcher opened his mouth to reply, but Susup cut him off. "I believe you know where it is. Don't worry 'bout me. I'll have no problem getting there." He bowed once while tipping his hat toward Fletcher. "Good day to you. The pleasure's been all mine."

As he walked away, Fletcher heard the man say, "Onion, you ready to catch some trout?" Squire Susup turned back toward Fletcher and yelled, "Please tell Woodrow he's more than welcome to come with you. He'll need to wait though." He then continued walking away, twirling his gold-tipped cane with the expertise of a drum major.

Lucille walked up carrying a large cardboard tray with three lobster rolls and three bottles of spring water. "Fletch, I just called your grandfather. He's waiting for us."

Fletcher's heart beat wildly as he leaned on his crutches, his mask shielding his expression of jubilant delight. He needed to find his uncle to tell him what had just happened. His thoughts were interrupted by a loud commotion taking place in front of the packed gazebo. Dozens of agitated people were yelling and screaming at one another and at the five cowering judges who'd just arrived at the gazebo with the results of the parade. Masks were strewn everywhere and social distancing was immediately thrown out the window. The man with the bullhorn screamed at the top of his lungs for everyone to calm down, which served only to attract more attention.

The seriousness of the Mollyockett Day Parade was never more evident than in the minutes before the judge's announced the results. There was guaranteed to be drama and controversy. There was no monetary prize, but the opportunity to proudly display the coveted plastic and marble statue of the Indian woman in the front window of your business mattered more than anything else.

This year there were three controversies being argued in front of the judges. The first was over whether the giant Snoopy balloon-style float, the first ever in the storied history of the parade, constituted a float. It did. The second involved a challenge against a float with the *Beverly Hillbillies* theme because it was based on a TV show, not a children's book. But when the float manager proudly produced a *Beverly Hillbillies* book on his phone, the judges dismissed the challenge.

The last and most boisterous controversy involved the *Curious George* float and the Davy Crockett float. The man dressed as Davy Crockett kept firing his shotgun, which caused the monkey from the *Curious George* float to jump in horror every time the gun boomed. Finally, the agitated monkey had had enough and escaped. Horrified spectators quickly rolled up their windows as the small animal, which was eventually captured, randomly jumped from car to car. The judges agreed not to deduct any points for having a monkey-themed float without the monkey. Order had been restored.

Finally, the chairman of the Mahoosuc Arts Council rang a large bell hanging from the center of the gazebo, and everyone settled down to hear the much-anticipated results.

Fletcher was about to sit down on the wool blanket his grandfather had placed near the microphone when he noticed his obnoxious neighbor, Brick Clements, sitting beside his grandfather. Fletcher decided he'd rather not listen to Brick, so he looked for a better place to sit.

"Hey, Fletch, over here!" he heard his uncle yell from behind the crowd that was now sitting on blankets placed in the center of spray-painted circles spaced six feet apart on all sides.

Fletcher quickly spied Woodrow standing at the entrance of Ye ol' Boot's tent. He was wearing a bright red uniform with an extremely tall, black-feathered hat. Fletcher laughed, realizing that he was dressed as one of the guards that stood in front of Buckingham Palace in London.

"I'll be right back. I need to talk with Uncle Woodrow," Fletcher told Edmond while gesturing toward the pub.

"What? You'll miss the results," Lucille said and huffed.

"I'm sure I can hear them from over there. Uncle Woodrow's waving for me," he replied and then made his way over to his uncle, carefully navigating around the crowded blankets with his crutches.

"How come you're over here?" Fletcher said when he got to the temporary pub. "I thought you had to work at the inn. Isn't it booked?"

Woodrow was examining the licenses of two men at the pub's wide entrance. He let them pass and then said to Fletcher, "Remember Mr. Von Piddle? This was supposed to be his job today, but he's unable to put on the uniform." A bead of sweat rolled down his face as he glanced at a woman's license before giving her the okay to enter. A roar of laughter filtered out of the pub.

"But it didn't stop him from coming," Woodrow said angrily. "Just take a look."

Aleksandr was sitting in the center of six large tables, wearing a bright red mask and plastic neck brace that prevented him from moving his head. He was surrounded by a small group of revelers listening intently to him tell a story while excitedly waving his arms. Fletcher laughed as the onlookers exploded in delight, clapping at the end of the tale, totally oblivious to the action happening at the giant white gazebo or the busy common.

Fletcher looked at his uncle and smiled. "A million guesses who I met today," he said excitedly, and then he spent the next several minutes— in between Woodrow checking IDs—telling his awed uncle the events that had unfolded under the Joshua Chamberlain statue. They agreed to meet at 1942 Sangar Drive the next morning for breakfast. Woodrow wanted to formulate a plan for next Friday and desperately needed to see what Squire Susup had left for Fletcher at the entrance to the passage.

Fletcher said good-bye to his uncle and rejoined his grandparents just in time for the awards presentation. The Double Moose took third prize with its well-executed Johnny Appleseed theme. The Red Hatters, much to the surprise of many, came in second place. Lucille accepted the award gleefully on behalf of her ladies' group. A huge roar erupted when it was announced that the *Beverly Hillbillies* had won. Granny was given a standing ovation as she proudly strode to the stage still carrying her musket, her dingy apron blowing in the wind. Sticking to it's theme, her mask was sewn with pieces of old and faded quilts.

After the trophy presentation, everyone settled in for the one-hour Adirondack chair auction. Timing had to be perfect as the afternoon's activities ended at 3:00 p.m. sharp to allow for the dismantling of the tents and vendor booths. By 4:00 p.m., any animosity that still lingered from the results of the parade were quickly forgotten.

"I knew we'd come in second," Lucille said as she helped Edmond load the Nubble Lighthouse Adirondack chair onto the back of his truck. "It's impossible to beat anything that has the *Beverly Hillbillies* in it. I wished we'd have thought of that. I'd have voted them first too. Oh, well, there's always next year," she said happily, glancing toward Fletcher to hurry him along. Edmond silently rolled his sarcastic eyes at his grandson.

Fletcher was quiet as they pulled out of the parking lot behind the local newspaper. The paint on his face had peeled and was now covering most of his mask. He silently watched the small clusters of people heading in every direction. But the only place he wanted to go was the root cellar to see what awaited him.

CHAPTER 17

THE PASSAGE

Fletcher spent that night reading the old book, *Whole Abounds*. Squire Susup had left it for him in a wooden box on the floor of the root cellar directly above the rock marked with the crescent moon and stars. Attached to the book was a note that said,

> *Fletcher,*
> *It was wonderful to finally meet you.*
> *This is Mother's favorite book. She'd like you to read it. Your father thoroughly enjoyed it, as did his father, and his father before him. It was written in 1707 by Marie Mathilde, a member of the Wabanaki Tribe from Downeast Maine. We all know her as Pidianiski, which is her tribal name.*
> *Henry Tufts translated it while recovering from a horrific knife wound. I look forward to our meeting. Please bring the book. I'll be sure to bring the staff.*
> *Warmest*
> *Regards,*
> *Squire Susup*

When Woodrow showed up early Sunday morning, Fletcher retold the entire conversation he'd had with Squire Susup after the parade. They were both still stunned and shocked. Fletcher intentionally withheld the part about extreme danger. *It did no good to worry his uncle.* Woodrow quickly came to the conclusion that the old book was clearly an original. Its leather cover was cracked and worn thin by extreme usage. The entire book had been written by hand with a crude quill pen with thick black ink. Every one of the 170 brittle pages was filled with diagrams of various plants, animals, and unrecognizable symbols, followed by a brief description of the item, where to find it in the world, and its importance in relation to the human body. Additionally, it detailed the close relationship the Wabanaki people had with nature as well as the deep and profound respect they had for the bountiful foods and healing nutrients she provided.

Woodrow borrowed the note, box, and book to study, promising Fletcher he'd return them the next day. On Monday morning he secured permission from Lucille to take Fletcher for breakfast at the Double Moose. They sat down in a corner booth, and Woodrow set the box and its contents on the table. They ordered, and after their food arrived, he pulled out a large white envelope and laid it in front of Fletcher's plate.

"Joseph Susup is a real person, although I didn't find any mention of the name Squire," he said in hushed tones as Fletcher slowly opened the envelope and pulled out several documents and a copy of a magazine article. "Little is known of him. But I did manage to locate an interesting article published by *Mahoosuc Magazine*. It was written by Pierre Fontaine, the Paris Hill historian, to commemorate the 250th anniversary of Mollyockett's birth." He paused. "It makes all sense in the world that he would be assisting the next-in-line McKenzie, so to speak, into Whole. With everything that's happened to our relatives who have possessed the power of the passage and their sudden demise, who else would assist descendants like you into Whole?" "And that part about the vaccine ," Woodrow said. "My God, Fletch, did he actually say that? Not that I'm doubting you. It *has* to be the vaccine for coronavirus, and you're the key!" Woodrow stared down at the papers and then up at Fletcher.

"What else does the article say?" Fletcher asked while chewing on a piece of toast and ketchup-laden egg. He didn't know where to begin.

"Don't eat and talk at the same time," Woodrow gently chided, sipping his black coffee. "It was printed in 1975. It references several incidents where Mollyockett miraculously healed individuals who had what appeared to be fatal injuries. Here, look."

Fletcher browsed the article, stopping to read the section toward the end that mentioned Tufts and his near fatal knife wound. *He then translated Whole Abounds with Mollyockett. How was that possible?*

"Who stabbed him?" he asked.

"One guess," Woodrow said with a deadly serious expression.

Fletcher's eyes widened. He quickly read the rest of the article, which concluded by recounting the bitter animosity Mollyockett had toward her brother, and he for her. "So he killed some settlers, and she saved some."

Woodrow took the article back from his nephew. "She also healed her son after he'd been beaten and shot by a settler up in Carritunk. Apparently, Joseph fought back when he was insulted by the white settler. Unfortunately, Native Americans had no rights in those days. They often bore the brunt of abuse by Indian-hating settlers. Terrible, just terrible, if you ask me."

"The settler beat and shot the squire?" Fletcher asked, feeling both anger and sympathy.

"Would you like a refill, Mr. McKenzie?" asked a petite waitress wearing a white T-shirt and matching mask, both with the two-headed moose logo painted on the front. Her face reddened when she realized she'd interrupted a sensitive conversation.

"Thanks, Kelly. That'll be great." He swallowed the remainder of his coffee before handing her the heavy white mug. When she left, he said, "How Joseph Susup was able to survive his serious injuries was nothing less than a miracle. According to what I found, even the local doctors refused to treat him, giving him only hours to live. Mollyockett, however, didn't give up hope for her son. She used her natural medicines and herbs to heal him."

"Do they have a picture of him?" Fletcher asked eagerly.

"Unfortunately, no. I've searched every library and historical society's online archives in the county. It's pretty obvious that your new friend wasn't well known. Now you're absolutely positive he said *this* full moon and that I could go?"

"One hundred percent. He just said you'd have to wait."

I wonder what that means? Woodrow thought as he watched Fletcher finish his scrambled eggs. What his nephew didn't know was that Woodrow had worked out a plan with Jefferson Caxton the night before. Without questioning Woodrow's intentions, Jefferson agreed to invite Edmond and Lucille to Block Island later in the week. The excuse was that he needed to spend time with them to discuss Fletcher's involvement in Fifth Ward Whole & Healthy. It would be a sensitive topic with Winola, Refinna, and Serena when they found out everything. The next call was to Dr. Dubrielle, who consented, again without asking why, to call Lucille and schedule a mandatory doctor's appointment for Fletcher at a prearranged time so that Woodrow would conveniently be there to volunteer. It would be a miracle if Lucille didn't catch on.

Uncle Woodrow leaned forward and looked intently at Fletcher. "What are you thinking right now?"

Fletcher set his fork down. "I just don't know what to expect, Uncle Woodrow. What do you think will happen? And how are we going to do this with everyone in the house?"

"Sheila and the other nurses will be taking care of your father at the other end of the house. As for your grandparents, I've got it all worked out. Just have faith in your ol' uncle."

"I'm not nervous if that's what your thinking. I need to do this for dad and everyone else."

Woodrow beamed proudly. *He is truly a McKenzie.*

"Fletch, I've been waiting for this day to arrive ever since my father had that talk with me and my brother many, many years ago. It's been a long wait."

Fletcher laughed. "So what *do* you think will happen?"

"Well, young man, if what Squire Susup says is true, I think you're in for quite the adventure."

—

Fletcher sat at the kitchen table, watching the clock on the wall. They had less than an hour before they'd head down into the basement. The plan to get rid of his grandparents had gone off without a hitch. Much to the pleasant surprise of Woodrow, Lucille didn't suspect a thing. The forecast for picture-perfect weather in Rhode Island was too enticing for the hardworking couple. They were tired and needed a vacation. Lucille spent two days in preparation for the trip, and they departed at noon on Thursday.

For Fletcher, the minutes had dragged on, but finally it was time.

"I say we go down," Woodrow said, ten minutes before they were to meet. "Let's bring our masks just in case they're required."

Fletcher grabbed his crutches, and they headed toward the basement door. His mind raced with anticipation as he slowly followed his uncle down the wooden stairs. Woodrow flicked on the overhead light, and they both jumped when a voice boomed from the back of the rec room.

"A little early, but not to worry. We've got plenty to discuss." Squire Susup was standing in the open doorway to the root cellar.

He was wearing the same clothes he'd had on at the parade, except for his shirt. It was now a light blue, which accentuated the black bow tie and the yellow sweater vest. Fletcher noticed that his cane with the gold tip was leaning against a stack of wooden wine crates. Woodrow stood on the bottom landing, saying nothing as he took in the strange man standing before him.

His eyes were immediately drawn to the loopy earrings and blue feathers on the hat, which were bent slightly as they touched the wooden ceiling. He stepped off the landing and slowly approached the squire.

"You must be Uncle Woodrow," Susup said. You're the spitting image of your brother and father."

Woodrow stopped momentarily at the mention of the two people he so dearly missed and then stepped forward to shake the squire's hand. "It's an extreme pleasure to finally meet you. You knew my father and Jonathan?"

"Indeed, I did. Two of the most honest and affable men I've ever had the privilege of knowing," he said, firmly shaking Woodrow's thin hand. "I'm very sorry to hear what happened to them," he said sincerely.

"They were both great men. I take it they've been here in this exact situation," Woodrow said.

The squire's relaxed gaze was still fixed on Woodrow. "Yes, they had a little different scenario, but yes … and with that book." He nodded toward the wooden box.

"Well, it's certainly an original," Woodrow said with easy humor.

"That it is. It's actually quite a unique book as you'll soon find out," the squire said confidentially as Fletcher and Woodrow sat in two of the three Bacchus chairs.

"How'd you like it Fletcher?" Susup asked, joining them.

"Loved it. It's amazing what plants can do. Most I've never even heard of," he said uneasily, wondering if he'd given the correct response.

"It takes time, Fletcher. There's a lot to learn," the squire said and smiled. "Just remember what Walter De La Mare said,

> *It's a very odd thing*
> *As odd as can be*
> *That whatever Miss T. eats*
> *Turns into Miss T.*

"That, my boy, is what the book's all about."

Woodrow laughed loudly and nodded. "Well said."

Sensing that Fletcher was confused, Squire Susup said, "In due time, Fletcher. In due time."

When he turned his head, Woodrow noticed a large scar hidden behind the pointed tip of his black bow tie.

"Gunshot wound," Susup said without missing a beat.

"Carritunk?" Woodrow inquired.

Susup paused and then said, "What that article doesn't tell you is that I was completely paralyzed from the neck down. Thank God for my mother and that little book over there in that box."

"I'm so sorry to hear that," Woodrow said.

"That's all in the past, and he's long gone," Susup said cheerily. He looked directly at Fletcher. "We really need to ready ourselves for our journey. Don't want to be like a swarm of bees in July."

A swarm of bees? Fletcher's mind raced furiously. *Is that important?* he thought.

"The passage, Fletcher. Timing needs to be perfect … and on this day. The bees refer to that old saying, 'A swarm of bees in May is worth a load of hay. A swarm of bees in June is worth a silver spoon. A swarm of bees in July is not worth a fly.' "

Fletcher gave his uncle a totally lost look. Woodrow explained, "Bees pollinate these parts in June. It's when they're most useful." He rose and moved toward the mahogany cane. "This is absolutely beautiful. I take it it's the staff you mentioned to Fletcher the other day."

"Indeed. It actually was made for Kozart."

Woodrow's mouth opened in surprise. "I never would have thought it was that old."

Squire Susup approached and handed the staff to Woodrow. "Here. You'll soon see what it does."

Uncle Woodrow inspected the gold tip. "It looks like a seed of some kind."

"Actually, it's a whole grain of wheat," Susup said. "Kozart insisted on it when it was designed."

"My goodness," Woodrow said, awed by the gleaming gold tip. He carefully set it down and went back to his seat.

The squire nodded toward the wine. "By the way, I've noticed a 2010 Chateau Lafite Rothschild in those boxes. You've got quite the impressive collection."

"Would you like to take one with you?" Woodrow offered.

"Mind if I take a raincheck? I assure you I'll be back for it. Right now time is very precious." He glanced toward the window through the root cellar door. "That full moon should be visible and in the right spot soon."

Woodrow looked at Susup thoughtfully. "I'm still confused and deeply concerned for Fletcher's well-being."

"I'd be deeply concerned too."

"Do you mind if I ask a few questions, or is that not permitted?"

"Ask anything you want," the squire said. "You've got every right."

"Where are you taking him, and why is timing so important?"

"I'm taking him where every McKenzie who's held the power of the passage has been since Jackson. That is, with your permission. This year is especially important."

When Susup was done, Woodrow began with the questions. "Exactly what does that mean?"

"We're going to Whole. More people than you can imagine are depending on this—most with their lives."

"I'm really having second thoughts about this.

Susup ignored him. "We need you to guard the entrance. It won't be that long, I promise."

"Why me?" Woodrow asked. "Who's guarded it in the past?"

"Actually, we're in new territory, Mr. McKenzie," Susup admitted.

"Woodrow … please call me Woodrow."

"Woodrow, it's a dangerous time. As the riddle indicates, while Fletcher's in Whole, the entrance is quite vulnerable." The squire recited from memory, "If you lose the staff, he'll commit a crime. The first sign of trouble, ergot will double. Even the hole will bubble and bubble."

Fletcher sat forward. "Those lines are right before *This passage is North, the other South.*"

Woodrow closed his tired eyes. "You're saying we're in troubled times?" he asked, looking deeply concerned.

Susup said, "Look around. Do I have to remind you what's going on?" Plus, Muriel could use his help."

Fletcher gasped loudly. "Mom!"

Woodrow's heart sank. "What are you implying?"

Susup pressed on. It was almost time. "The other passage, the southern one, it's in the Quetzal. There's a reason for two passages—one for northern temperate foods and one for southern temperate foods."

"Like cocoa to make chocolate," Woodrow said, referring to Muriel's trip, the one that led to her mysterious disappearance.

The squire nodded.

"What's happened to her?" Woodrow asked, feeling curious, surprised, and frustrated all at once.

"You know about the others, everyone since Jackson. It's not hard to figure out that they all fell prey to Tomhegan's revenge. Had it not been for sheer luck, Fletcher would have joined his ancestors. But you've already figured that out."

Fletcher nodded, his emotions a roiling mix of fear, anger, and determination to do what he could. *Did he really just mention mom?*

Susup continued, "He's getting bolder and more determined in his efforts to regain control of the passage. Once he found out that Fletcher was going to be cleaning the park . . . I tried to watch over the cleanup, knowing that he was desperate," the squire recounted. "I lost him at Talon's Rock."

Woodrow turned to his nephew. "Fletch, you were absolutely right that it was Tomhegan you saw on the cliff."

"You actually *saw* Tomhegan?" Susup asked, surprised.

"I did ... right before a flash of light," Fletcher responded, a faraway look in his eyes as he remembered. "I'd never forget those dark eyes. I've had many nightmares ever since."

"If it's any consolation, he was badly injured in that blast."

Uncle Woodrow stood up and moved behind Fletcher, his mind filled with thoughts of his father and brother. "I wish it had killed him."

Squire Susup looked at Woodrow sympathetically and said nothing.

"How can he *still* be alive?" Fletcher asked flatly.

"Descendents of our family who have held or *could* have held the power of the passage have possessed unique powers once Mollyockett transferred the power of the passage to Jackson. No one ever expected that. Both in this world and in Whole. Remember, Tomhegan *could* have held the power if some in his family were no longer there. The same goes for me."

Fletcher and Woodrow knew who he was talking about.

"Does this mean that *he* also travels to Whole?" Woodrow asked.

Susup ignored the question.

Fletcher leaned forward, completely spellbound.

Woodrow looked at Squire Susup askance. He held out his hands, palms up. "Forgive my naiveté, but Mollyockett and Tomhegan have been dead for over two hundred years. I know you said—"

"In *your* time, Woodrow. Not the passage's time," Susup replied, cutting him off. I understand how confusing—" He stopped talking when he saw the rising full moon through the small window in the root cellar. "You need to make a decision *right* now," Susup said urgently.

"If it will help Mom and others, I'm ready!" Fletcher announced boldly and reached for his crutches.

"Fletcher," Woodrow groaned, consumed by fear and worry for his nephew.

"Woodrow, I know it's hard to understand what's happening right now, but trust me. It has to be *now*. You need to trust me," Susup repeated. "Failure exists only for those who fail to take action. I'm not one of those people. And if I've read you correctly—and I think I have—neither are you."

Woodrow took a deep breath and said, "I'll guard the entrance to the passage, and you guard my nephew." He looked at Fletcher and clasped his shoulders. "Make me proud. I'll be right here waiting."

Fletcher quickly hugged his uncle and whispered, "Remember what you said. I'm a McKenzie."

"It's time! We've only got seconds," the squire exclaimed. He grabbed the book from its box and the gold-tipped staff and then rushed toward the middle of the root cellar.

Fletcher and Woodrow followed him without hesitating, where the squire stood directly in the middle of the circular stone. He waved Fletcher over.

"Quickly, stand beside me!"

Fletcher took huge strides with his crutches and joined him.

Susup grabbed the crutches and tossed them aside. "You'll not need them anymore."

Fletcher stood next to the squire, eyes blazing with nervous excitement as the moon's bright rays, through a small window, illuminated the center star above the crescent moon chiseled in the cold stone.

"Now!" the squire said, giving Woodrow a thumbs-up as he inserted the tip of the gold staff into a round indentation located in the center of the crescent moon. He tucked the book under his arm, closed his eyes, and chanted, "O our Mother, the Earth, O our Father, the sky, your children are we, and with tired backs, we bring you gifts."

The room suddenly began to shift, causing Woodrow to grab onto the doorway. His mouth dropped as he watched the huge stone turn into a thick gray gas. Fletcher was thrown off balance by an overwhelming whirling sensation. He reached for Susup, but his hand moved through the squire's body as if it was made of air. Suddenly, he tumbled into total darkness, spiraling downward. His arms flailed as he desperately tried to grab onto something, anything.

Then there was nothing.

CHAPTER 18

WHOLE

WHEN FLETCHER OPENED HIS EYES, HE WAS ALONE. SQUIRE SUSUP WAS nowhere to be seen. The book and intricate staff lay at his feet. He was standing in a huge hall with brick walls at least two hundred feet tall that extended as far as Fletcher could see. In front of him an arch constructed of thousands of honeycomb-shaped stained glass windows soared to the ceiling. Each colorful pane—illuminated by an unknown light source—depicted a different plant, fruit, vegetable, and animal.

The three brick walls contained numerous arched windows, each perfectly spaced between a pair of pink marble pillars shaped like giant Sequoia trees and adorned with tendrils, giving them a garden look. The windows contained stained glass pieces in the shape of leaves depicted in the vibrant colors associated with a northern New England autumn. Every window looked like a masterpiece that belonged in the world's finest museums.

Fletcher reached down and picked up the book and staff. He carefully tucked *Whole Abounds* in his waistband behind his back and leaned on the staff as he stepped forward tentatively as if testing thin ice on a pond. The entire floor was a deep mossy green that looked soft as silk. He was shocked to find it was as hard as granite when he took his first cautious step.

Off in the distance, he heard what sounded like an enormous waterfall. Nearby all he heard was the harmonious chirping of birds. He looked up and noticed a dark dome ceiling completely covered with a lush canopy of magnolia leaves. Intermingled among the shiny leaves were countless flocks of birds in every shape and color. Miraculously, the floor was devoid of any droppings.

Hanging from the ceiling were massive gold chandeliers in the shape of upside-down weeping willow trees. Their bright, pear-shaped lights illuminated the structure with what looked like natural light from the sun. Each golden pear light was attached to the branches by strings of red rubies that cast a reddish hue.

Hesitantly, Fletcher reached out to one of the Sequoia columns and placed his palm on the polished stone. Looking up, he noticed each column's marble branches reached up into the dome.

"Where am I?" he whispered.

Unsure if he should continue walking, he reached out and touched a small stone dragonfly adorning the column. Glancing at the next column, he saw it was covered with decorative marble lizards. The one after that was festooned with small crabs.

Suddenly, two crystalline stones rose from the green floor directly in front of him. Startled, he jerked backward and dropped the staff. His heart raced as he cautiously moved forward to study them.

"It's okay," a woman's voice said behind him. "It's only calcium and vitamin D."

Fletcher spun around. In the center of the back brick wall, a tall, athletic woman stood still on a spiral stairway that looked like a giant snail shell and rose into the canopy of magnolia leaves.

Fletcher froze. He recognized Mollyockett immediately, but all he could do was gape at her.

"Fletcher Gage McKenzie, it's a distinct pleasure." She stepped off the staircase and walked toward him. "You certainly do look like your father and grandfather, the spitting image. Just as cautious too." She reached out to shake his hand. "A warm welcome."

He reached out and shook Mollyockett's hand. Her inviting gaze and sincere smile put him more at ease.

She looked down at the staff on the floor. "You may want to pick that up. It' extremely important that you not lose it. If you do, the consequences could be tragic."

Fletcher quickly bent down, extending his cast behind him, and retrieved the staff. Without thinking, he brushed its gold tip on the front of his shirt.

Mollyockett pointed at the crystals jutting out of the ground in front of him. "Calcium and vitamin D will heal that nasty injury of yours. Rub them. You'll see."

She looks just like that portrait in my dad's room, Fletcher thought. She was wearing a brown dress that hung to her knees and thick, bright red and black knitted socks that came to the hem of her dress, which was detailed with small acorns dangling from delicate beads. Tiny white shells adorned the entire garment. Her soft leather moccasins were decorated with miniature red, black, and white stones. She wore the same silver looped earrings as in the portrait. When she walked, they swayed with the rhythm of her stride.

Her shiny black hair hung below her waist in a thick single braid. The crude hat she wore was adorned with penny-sized red and blue gems and three lines of porcupine quills that were dyed red. Her well-manicured nails were painted black just like Squire Susup's. For a brief second, Fletcher caught a glimpse of a red Maine tourmaline stone hanging from a small gold chain around her neck and held securely by a curling gold tendril.

Seeing Fletcher's reluctance to touch the two protruding stones, Mollyockett said, "Suit yourself, but if I had a bone that was as broken as yours, I'd be quick to fix it. Who wants to traipse around with that troublesome thing on?" she asked, glancing at the filthy cast.

Fletcher hesitantly reached for the rough stones. As he cautiously touched them, a surge of energy flowed into his body—starting with his palms, through his arms, and down into his injured leg. He jerked his hands back, unnerved by the tingling sensation in the part of his leg underneath the cast. Fletcher looked from the giant crystals to his hands and then up to Mollyockett.

"What just happened?"

"A pretty good way to fix a broken bone, huh?" Mollyockett smiled.

"You're kidding me."

"It certainly is," she boomed in delight. "That's the miracle of calcium and vitamin D. It just works a little quicker here in Whole."

He looked around. "Whole?"

"Yes, Fletcher, you're in the glorious land of Whole. Isn't it wonderful?" she exclaimed as the gems on her triangle-shaped hat glimmered in the warm light. "You'll soon see it's like no other place in the universe. So tell me. How was the trip?"

"Trip?"

"The passage you just went through." She inspected his ears and fingers. "Well, at least you didn't get hung up at the Double S like your grandfather did. Completely unnerved him."

"The swimming hole?"

"That's right. The passage actually follows the exact contour of Sunday River. That bend you no doubt felt was the Double S swimming hole."

"No way."

She reached out her right hand and playfully wagged her index finger at him. "Never in a million years would I kid about such a thing. Believe it or not, we're right below Frenchman's Hole at this very moment. Actually, deep below it." She glanced up at the leaf-covered ceiling. "Your grandfather somehow got hung up at the bend. Almost took his left ear off. Of course, a little vitamin E and quality protein healed it immediately after his arrival. Shook him to the core though," she recounted casually. "So let's head to my garden. I'll take that cast off. I'm sure it has to be hindering your walking."

He reached for his mask in his right pocket.

"Don't be silly. The virus will never rear it's ugly head in Whole. In fact, its at the top of our agenda during your visit. You see, *Whole Abounds* holds the very secret to fighting the current pandemic. That, and your actions while you're here," she said while looking directly at him.

Fletcher nodded and followed Mollyockett to the stairway. Given what he'd been through, he was willing to do anything to help the cause. At that moment he realized he wasn't limping anymore. In fact, the protective cast now impeded his ability to walk.

"I studied what I could decipher in *Whole Abounds*," he told her. "Some of it was way over my head."

"How did you like the plot?"

"Um ... plot?"

When she laughed, he realized that she'd been joking with him, and he blushed. As they walked, Mollyockett casually pointed out unique features he would have missed in the spectacular landscape.

"If you look closely, Fletcher, you'll notice the pinnacles at the top of those windows are shaped like leaves from the ginseng plant, a forked root with tremendously useful medicinal properties. And the arch in the front wall is a large mosaic of a human cell."

Fletcher squinted, taking in the totality of the monolithic glass arch.

"It's what we're all made of. Look at the upper right corner. That squiggly black circle made up of those five black birds is the nucleus of the cell. And those little pieces of red glass are the mitochondria. The alternating white minks and doves along the border represent the cell membrane," she said. A shadow swept over her face. "Coronavirus quickly attacks these very cells and destroys them. Absolute travesty what is happening."

Fletcher nodded then thought back to biology class as he listened to Mollyockett. "How is all this possible? It's beautiful." He gasped in astonishment. "And this is all below Frenchman's Hole?" Never in his wildest dreams would he have ever expected to be experiencing this.

"Directly under the waterfall. Hard to imagine, I know," she said and smiled.

He followed her up the staircase, holding on to the gleaming gold banister. The cast made climbing difficult. Midway up—after what seemed like an eternity—they reached a bridge made of amethyst, a vivid purple gemstone. At the end of the bridge, there was an enormous entryway made of pink marble carved into the shape of a Venus flytrap. For a brief moment, he half-expected the massive needle-sharp leaves of the stone plant to snap shut the moment he stepped in.

When he followed Mollyockett through the entrance, Fletcher stopped and stared in awe. Before them was a lush garden that stretched as far as the eye could see. There were thousands of fruit trees. Their flawless branches hung low with apples, oranges, pears, tangerines, plums, and hundreds of other fruits he didn't recognize. In the distance was a huge waterfall, whose mist created a slight fog.

Fletcher stared delightedly at the gigantic swarms of fireflies hovering over the spectacular orchard. Their bodies glowed like sunlight, and their vibrating wings creating a gentle hum.

Fletcher stepped onto the soft grassy ground. "This is my favorite place to sit and relax," Mollyockett said, walking into the garden. She pointed toward the waterfall. "Watch."

He looked on as small fluffy clouds, formed from the mist created by the aqua blue water cascading over the cliff, drifted over the fruit trees. They stopped directly above a pomegranate tree and then released a steady sprinkle of water. Back at the waterfall, more clouds were forming, each responsible for watering a specific tree. Fletcher wondered if this was all a wild dream.

"They only rain for about three minutes," she explained. "If you look in the distance, you'll see a few other clouds that have finished watering their trees. Once they're done, they'll head to the valley of the ferns to provide shade." She plucked a newly emerged fiddlehead, bit into the tightly curled plant, and closed her eyes.

"*Mmm*, I absolutely love fiddleheads, don't you? Go ahead. Try one. Just pick the curl though. It's the best part."

Fletcher stepped forward to the curled plants poking from the fertile soil. Not wanting to offend her, he bent down and broke off a small green curl from the top of the edible fern. He took a tentative bite. His face brightened in surprise. "You're right. They *are* good. Kinda like a nutty Brussels sprout."

As he ate, he glanced around and noticed one of the most beautiful objects he'd ever seen. A stunning gold pyramid stood in the center of the orchard.

Following his gaze, Mollyockett told him, "It's the symbol of equilibrium. Fantastic, wouldn't you say?"

"Is that gold?"

"Solid," she replied, plucking two more newly sprouted fiddleheads and savoring every bite. "How about you let me take that cast off. It has to be uncomfortable."

Fletcher nodded. "It'll be good to get this thing off."

Without warning, a cluster of clean brown roots suddenly rose out of the grass-covered ground behind Mollyockett.

Fletcher jumped back and watched in absolute amazement as the roots expertly wove themselves into an egg-shaped chair.

"We need to sit, don't we?" Mollyockett lowered herself into the chair and let out a satisfied sigh as the roots finished conforming to her body. "Now that's what I call comfort." She closed her eyes and inhaled in relaxation.

"That's awesome," Fletcher said and laughed in delight.

"So where's yours?"

He looked around, confused. She chuckled and told him to think about sitting in the most comfortable chair he'd ever sat in. While Fletcher shut his eyes and thought of the chair he'd sat in while reading to his father, Mollyockett closed her eyes and began to hum.

Fletcher suddenly felt the ground below him vibrate. When he opened his eyes, he saw a tangle of roots behind him. In a matter of seconds, they had formed a chair in the exact shape of the one in his father's room.

"You've got to be kidding me!" Without hesitating, he sat down, and the roots moved and tightened to the contour of his body.

"How's that possible?" he asked, grinning as he lightly bounced on the seat to test its support.

"Fletcher, this is Whole. You'll soon learn not to ask such questions." She laughed and gave him a quick wink before standing. "Just help me for a sec and extend that foot of yours."

As he lifted his cast-covered leg, a thick root suddenly emerged from the ground and wove itself into a small foot rest.

Mollyockett pulled out a pink shell from a pocket in her skirt. Its white outer edge looked as sharp as a medical scalpel. "This should only take a sec."

Preferring not to watch, he concentrated on a fluffy cloud forming at the base of the waterfall. *Quinn and Cam will never believe me*, he thought as the cloud drifted toward a fig tree in the distance. Fletcher closed his eyes and imagined the next Bacchus meeting. *How can I even describe this to them?* The constant hum of the fireflies was oddly soothing, and he felt himself relax, almost to the point of dozing. He was roused by Mollyockett prying open the cast.

She set the cast pieces aside and handed Fletcher a coffee bean. He breathed in its wonderful smell and rubbed it gently between his thumb and index finger. His eyes widened, and his pupils expanded as a sudden surge of energy ignited his body and caused the hairs on his arms to bristle.

"There, that'll keep you awake for the next day or so," she said. "Nothing like a quick jolt of caffeine to get the juices flowing." She patted him on the back. "How are you feeling now?"

"It's the strangest sensation I've ever had," he said and smiled at her. Extending his arms over his head, he exclaimed, "This place is awesome!" Then he noticed she held a soft tablet. What's that?" Fletcher asked.

"Vitamin E." She used her shell scalpel to cut the soft tablet in two. "Put it on your scars."

He rubbed the thick gel along the scars on his leg. He was fascinated as the thick red scar quickly faded, leaving behind completely healthy skin. He gasped as the scar vanished.

"If there was ever an antiaging elixir, Fletcher, it's vitamin E. How do you think I keep this stunning face so perfect?" she joked.

He looked at her tanned, leathery skin and laughed. He stood and tested his newly healed leg, which felt stronger than ever. He smiled. "Thank you."

"*Shhh.*" She placed an index finger in front of her lips. Her loopy earrings bounced from side to side on her cheeks as she turned toward the valley, watching a large herd of animals with long pointed horns approach a cluster of jacaranda trees.

"What are those?" he whispered.

"Oryx. They're indigenous to North Africa."

Fletcher watched with excitement as they stopped to eat. "What are they doing here if they're from Africa?" he asked quietly.

Mollyockett didn't respond right away, watching the large animals nibble on the trees' flowers. After a few moments, she said, "If you look closely, you'll see that a new flower grows right back after it's been eaten."

Fletcher leaned forward to see better, bracing himself on a sturdy hydrangea bush teeming with blue flowers in front of him. He watched in wonder as an oryx casually nibbled on one of the purple flowers. It regrew immediately once the beast had consumed it.

"What do you say we head to the Valley of the Ferns?" she suggested. "Seems like you have lots of questions I need to answer."

Fletcher turned toward Mollyockett. "Is that near here?"

"Everything is close in Whole."

She headed toward the entrance, and he followed her after taking one last look at the swarm of fireflies obscuring the tip of the gold pyramid. They passed back through the Venus flytrap to the bridge where Mollyockett stopped before a large vertical beam of bluish matter.

"This is how we travel in Whole," she explained.

"What is it?" Fletcher asked, warily eyeing the beam that extended up through the leaf canopy and down to the floor far below.

"Hyper-metabo-flow plume. We call it *Flow* for short. You'll see why. It's actually sodium and potassium, the electrolytes that enable your muscles to work properly," she explained, and then she stepped into the beam.

"Wait!" Fletcher shouted but she had already disappeared into the blue beam that glowed and hummed. Knowing he had to move quickly, he instinctively stepped forward into the glowing beam and immediately felt his body painlessly disassemble into billions of individual cells, which then cascaded down the pulsating flume.

CHAPTER 19

VALLEY OF THE FERNS

FLETCHER COULD HEAR WATER FALLING AND SMELLED THE SWEET SCENT of lilac bushes just like those in his mother's garden. When he opened his eyes, he was sitting in a similar root chair surrounded by lush green ferns with billowing fronds in a variety of shapes and sizes. In front of him blazed a large fire inside a pit made of smooth river rocks. To his right was the foot of a waterfall, emptying into a clear pool of blue water before continuing to free fall into an enormous gorge. The sky was filled with small puffy clouds, which he watched form into larger rain clouds in the mist that hung over the pool of water.

Fletcher stood up and turned around to see Mollyockett sitting in her root chair, casually puffing on a foot-long corncob pipe, a wisp of light gray smoke curling above her head. Instead of her triangular hat, she was now wearing a stovepipe hat, much like Squire Susup's hat, absent the three blue feathers. To their right sat a perfectly constructed wigwam. Its arched framework was overlaid with birch bark and animal hides. Its entrance faced the swift currents of a stream flowing from the pool of water just before it leaped over the gorge.

Mollyockett took a small drag on her pipe and beckoned him over to where she was sitting. "It transports your individual cells to their destination after disassembling them. Once you've arrived, *voila*—your cells are reassembled." She took a long puff on her pipe and held the smoke in her mouth for a few seconds before blowing out intermittent puffs of smoke. "Flow travel is something, isn't it?"

"How does it work?"

"It literally reads your thoughts and wishes. I stepped into the beam, wanting to come here. You stepped in the beam, hoping to find where I'd gone. Following me was rather brave. You're definitely proving to be a McKenzie."

Fletcher didn't answer. He was fixated on an unusual-looking pair of light brown animals standing at the edge of the water and casually drinking as if they'd didn't have a care in the world. They had heavy bodies, mouse-like ears, short legs, and long fleshy lips at the end of a curved snout.

"Those are tapirs," she told him. "You'll find them in tropical America or Asia. The darker one's named Madockawando. The other one's Ogbomosho." Both animals lifted their heads and briefly glanced toward Mollyockett at the mention of their names. "I call them Mado and Ogbo for short. They're harmless, and they love to be petted." She smiled as they resumed drinking.

Mollyockett motioned for Fletcher to come closer. She picked up a clay pot sitting on a tree stump beside her root chair, its contents releasing a trail of steam through a tiny hole in its lid. As she poured hot tea into two stone mugs, a root chair immediately formed behind him. Without hesitation, he sat and let the roots conform to his body. He noticed *Whole Abounds* and the staff on the ground next to her chair.

"You forgot those," she said. "Mado went back and retrieved them for you. Didn't you?" She asked as though baby-talking him.

The animal raised his head and gave her a look of deep loyalty before resuming his casual drinking.

Mollyockett handed Fletcher one of the mugs, which smelled of orange and mint. He inhaled deeply. *"Mmm,* what's this?"

"It's green tea with a little natural flavoring."

Mollyockett gently blew on the tea, savored a small sip, and then sighed in contentment. Again, he was struck by the unimaginableness of the moment. His mind replayed all he'd seen since stepping on the stone in the root cellar. His thoughts were suddenly interrupted by a large parrot that swooped in and perched itself on Mollyockett's right shoulder.

"Well, hello, Merrimack. Where have you been?" She lightly ran her hand over its brightly colored feathers. His head was green, and his neck was ruby red.

"He's beautiful," Fletcher said.

"He's an Australian Outback parrot. He's incredibly shy and can mimic human speech like a pro." She nuzzled the bird's large beak and then nudged him off her shoulder. Merrimack flew upwards and perched on a nearby pointed rock. Mollyockett settled into her chair and looked at Fletcher. "It's time we talk. Tell me what you know, and I'll fill in the gaps. Why don't you start at Buck's Ledge?"

Fletcher carefully went through all the events he'd experienced from the day of the landslide to the time he met Squire Susup. He also recounted all the research his uncle had done on the McKenzie family tree and on Mollyockett and Tomhegan's history. Finally, he told her about his father's sudden setback from Coronavirus and the disappearance of his mother and Nimsy Cortland in the vast jungles of South America.

Mollyockett closed her eyes and slowly rocked back and forth in her root chair, humming a tune unknown to Fletcher. While waiting for her to respond, he studied her angular profile, wondering what she was thinking. She opened her eyes and looked directly at him.

"Well done young man. Please tell Woodrow he's an absolutely wonderful man. With respect to your immediate family, that's one of the reasons why you're here. You'll soon find out that it all comes down to control of the passage."

The increasing suspense was killing him. Even though she had only confirmed his suspicions, hearing it made it real and made the danger more imminent. Images of his parents flashed in his mind. "Why's the passage so important that everyone has to die?" he asked. His anguish was etched on his face. "My grandfather's been murdered. My father's practically dead, and my mother has just vanished from the face of the earth."

Mollyockett searched for the right words. "I've known your wonderful family for as long as your country has existed. For every second of every day for the past two hundred plus years, I've been haunted by the unfortunate death of every McKenzie since Jackson. They have all been the most genuine people you'd ever want to meet."

She placed her hand on his shoulder. "Look at me."

His teary eyes met her determined, sympathetic gaze.

"This needs to end, and *you* can help me do it. I'm so very sorry for all that has happened to your family, but we can make it right for both your parents before it's too late. You need to trust me."

Fletcher leaned back. He was emotionally exhausted. He knew he had no choice. "Okay. I'll do whatever you tell me to."

"Thank you. I'll never violate your trust," she promised.

His gaze moved over her face with its deep wrinkles and then down to her weathered arms, bony fingers, and the occasional strand of white hair interspersed among the shiny black braid. He looked at her quizzically. "How can you and the squire still be alive if you both lived so long ago?"

"Because of *this* world. Whole is *the* place where everything that's good in the universe lives. When in Whole, nutrients function here exactly like they function on earth. But as you've observed for yourself, their power is magnified exponentially when you're in Whole, which is why your leg was able to heal so fast. On earth, foods such as fish, fruits, whole grains, and olive oil give you the ability to live well into advanced age. In Whole, those foods extend one's life indefinitely, which is how I'm still alive. As is Susup. But, that doesn't mean there aren't any dangers. Life can still be snuffed out down here." She picked up her pipe and gave him a wry smile. "Thank God the antioxidants down here undo the horrible damage caused by this thing."

Fletcher still didn't understand how everything was connected. "So the passage is how plants and nutritious foods get to earth from Whole?"

"Not just the nutrients in their intended form, but the knowledge as well. Do you remember that line in the riddle *Beware the beast for if knowledge fails, it is certain—*"

"Kozart prevails," he finished the line for her. "Uncle Woodrow tried but was unable to find out what it meant."

"Fletcher, whoever takes control of the passage—the keeper of the keys, so to speak—is entrusted with not only retaining the location to the entrance to Whole but must also swear to apply its importance to others. Birch Bread and other recipes Cygnus produces came straight from *Whole Abounds*. They're all made from the healthiest ingredients and represent what's best. Exactly how the creator intended. It's a wonderful way to pass on the knowledge of Whole to others. Trust me. It's a lot easier to share a slice of Birch Bread with someone than a lesson on proper nutrition." She took a dainty sip from her steaming tea. "But if this duty is violated, control of the passage will revert back to Kozart's bloodline."

"If control reverted back to Kozart's bloodline, wouldn't that be you?"

"No." She stated flatly. "In your world, I died many years ago. It would have had to follow my bloodline, which unfortunately, died out decades ago. If your bloodline does the same thing, so does knowledge and control of the passage. And with it, access to Whole for my family and yours. And if what happened to the southern passage is an example, the end game could be absolutely devasting."

Fletcher glanced at the ornate cane by his feet. "Now I'm really confused?"

"If it wasn't for Squire Susup, knowledge of the passage would be long gone. He's been the only one who's been able keep in touch with each successive generation of McKenzie, especially after the unexpected deaths of so many. He's a little eccentric, but he gets the job done. I'm content at the moment to act as the unofficial caretaker of Whole. But I must tell you—things may take a drastic change for the worse if we don't act soon."

"What's that supposed to mean?" he asked with concern.

"You know there are two passages, right?" Merrimack squawked, mimicking Mollyockett, who brushed him off. "Well, the northern passage is very well protected in your root cellar. The southern passage, for the time being, is hidden deep inside the jungles of South America, far away from any civilization. Unfortunately, because of unchecked clear-cutting of the ancient forest and rampant, uncontrolled industrialization in that part of the world, the entire existence of Whole is in dire jeopardy. Once that passage is discovered ..." she sighed. Her expression turned grave. "No one knows what will actually happen."

"Does that have anything to do with my mother?"

"I fear so."

Fletcher fought back the fear and anxiety churning his stomach. "You said I can help my parents, How?"

Mollyockett reached inside the top half of her dress and pulled out a green stone attached to a gold chain. She stood up and walked toward the waterfall. "You ready for another ride in Flow?"

Without responding, he stood and followed her. The roots from the two chairs uncoiled and disappeared into the damp soil. Mado meandered over to where they'd been sitting. Grunting slightly, he picked up the staff and book with his fleshy lips, turned, then followed them.

CHAPTER 20

UMBEGOG GULCH

FLETCHER OPENED HIS EYES AND LOOKED AROUND. HE WAS SEATED IN A perfectly carved granite chair that didn't feel at all like it was made of stone. Its soft surface felt more like an expensive body glove. As with the root chair, the seat altered its shape to conform to his movements. Its cool surface felt like it was part of his body.

Looking around, he realized the chair had been sculpted within an enormous gray boulder that jutted out over a large pool of swirling rapids. The savage whitecaps lapped fiercely at both sides of the bubbling stream. Upstream, the torrent of water was turbulently surging over a small cliff, and then moved at breakneck pace through a narrow fissure in the rock walls of a small canyon before descending into a deep crevasse.

Panic surged through him as he imagined losing his balance and falling into the raging water. Turning his head, he saw Mollyockett sitting calmly in a smoothly carved chaise lounge made of the same material. He looked nervously down at the water and then back at her. "Where are we?" he shouted so that she could hear him over the rapids.

She cupped her hand around her mouth and yelled, "Umbegog Gulch. Kinda reminds me of Frenchman's Hole."

Fletcher watched a large tree limb swirling hazardously in the pounding waves cresting with white foam. He looked up to see Mollyockett impatiently rolling her fingers while muttering to herself.

"Okay, let's go see if he's at Sixth Day," she shouted and then stood up on the edge of her seat.

Fletcher gasped as she stepped off the chair toward the water. But instead of falling to certain death, the stone instantly morphed into a narrow set of stairs that extended into the lapping waves below.

She looked over and mouthed, *You coming?* As she walked down the steps, fireflies flew over and arranged themselves with military precision along the sides and base of each stone step. Remembering his promise to trust her, Fletcher stood and watched in awe as a similar set of stairs formed from the stone that had been his comfortable chair.

"This is absolutely bonkers," he whispered, moving slowly down the newly formed stairs toward the roiling water below as a small cloud of fireflies positioned themselves to illuminate his path. His heart raced wildly with each step. He glanced up just in time to see Mollyockett walk off the last step onto a large flat stone that magically rose from the depths of the churning water followed by another ... and then another.

Fletcher watched as she gracefully walked across a growing bridge of boulders that created a direct route to the other side of the river. Each stone was quickly encircled with strings of glowing fireflies for much-needed lighting in the misty conditions. Stepping onto dry land, she turned back and waved him on.

"Here goes nothing," he said nervously, taking a careful step toward the water.

Mollyockett watched proudly as he navigated the stairs and the stones and then stepped onto dry land with a wide smile.

"That was awesome," he yelled jubilantly, watching the rocks that had formed the bridge disappear into the water. "Quinn and Cam will never in a zillion years believe I just did that."

When he looked back around, Mollyockett had already disappeared over a slight ridge and toward a dense forest of ancient elm trees. Fletcher sprinted to catch up, running along a foot path that was flanked by enormous beds of vibrantly colored lady's slippers. As he ran, the roar of the river faded into a low droning sound that blended harmoniously with the earthy environment.

When he ascended the low ridge, he looked up and grinned at the swarm of fireflies hovering a foot above his head and following his every movement. Hanging from the high domed ceiling were shafts of silvery mica and silicate minerals. As he rounded a huge granite boulder, he slowed to a jog. Mollyockett was standing in the center of a large clearing. Beside her was another root chair in front of a roaring fire inside a circle of stones. He spotted the staff and the book on a crudely cut stump beside her. He was expecting an immediate lecture for forgetting them again.

Following his gaze, Mollyockett said, "Mado. He's mastered Flow quite well, considering his size. Tea?" she asked. She then moved to another stump on which sat a clay pot and two stone mugs.

He smiled as the familiar root chair formed behind him. He took one of the mugs, which smelled of mint, and sat facing Mollyockett. She sipped some tea and then looked at Fletcher, her demeanor turning somber.

"I'm sure you remember the line *The first sign of trouble, ergot will double. Even the hole will bubble and bubble*? Well, the river we just crossed is the exact center of Whole, its heart and soul. As you know by now, everything works in harmony here. Everything has a purpose, a place, a meaning. We've discovered over the years that whenever there's impending trouble, Umbegog Gulch has always given us notice—like an early warning bell, so to speak—by turning into a raging river. Had you been there six months ago, you would have found it to be the most peaceful and placid place you'd ever experienced. It's where you can find true serenity. I'd go there to contemplate Whole or just to relax. But now ..." Her sense of pending loss was palpable.

"Uncle Woodrow and I thought the bubble and bubble line was referring to Buck's Hole."

She smiled at his obvious disappointment. "We've all been wrong at one time or another. *On ne saurait faire une omelette sans casser des oeufs.*"

"Um, what?"

"It's French. It means, 'You can't make an omelet without breaking eggs.' Father Gionet at the Saint Francis Mission at Odanak would say that every time I was wrong."

"So why is the gulch so angry?"

She paused to look at a large gathering of bright blue and red butterflies rise over the lush flowers. "While Whole is a wondrous and spectacular place, as you've seen for yourself, the danger's actually grave right now. It must be protected. Its very existence must be kept a secret. Imagine what would happen if the knowledge of what's here got out?"

"I'll never tell anyone," Fletcher promised.

"It's *never* been you or anyone in your family I've been concerned with," she said and sighed heavily. "It's the southern passage. I'll reiterate, the northern passage, the one in your root cellar, is protected quite well—at least for the immediate future. I've always known that. The southern passage, however, is right on the extreme fringes of massive deforestation with clear-cutting of the ancient forest taking place at an unprecedented pace. I'm telling you this again to drive home the point that all is not well."

"Who guards that one?" he asked, moving forward to the edge of his chair, the roots adjusting to accommodate his new position.

"No one is guarding it. It's a horrible story, one that has been going on for hundreds of years."

Fletcher looked around at the majestic world he was now part of and felt a strong desire to protect it. "How come?" he asked.

"A Quechuan tribe that was once located deep within the Quetzal for thousands of years was tragically wiped out after European settlers discovered the many riches their land offered."

"Wiped out? How?"

"Battles with the Europeans, starvation, but mostly diseases brought by the conquerors. The tribe slowly recognized the inevitable truth but made the decision to transfer power to those they trusted too late. The Quechuan's demise happened too quickly. All that remained were their stone houses and temples within fortified walls on the side of a huge mountain. Soon the forest overtook these monuments, and they've been lost to time."

As he listened, Fletcher thought back to the ritual he had to perform with the squire to access Whole. "How can someone just enter Whole? I needed Squire Susup and that staff plus the words he recited."

"You'll find out that Whole closely guards her secrets. I wish I could answer that. Squire Susup's only task was to bring you here, Fletcher. It's my responsibility to transfer the power of the passage to you.

Remember, Whole is like the universe itself, always changing. There are no rules other than the one rule: that there will always be change. Quite often, I've had to *wing it* so to speak. And time's definitely a precious commodity right now."

"Isn't the power with my father right now?" Fletcher asked.

"It is, and I know what you're thinking. But no, I haven't given up on Aldous. I want you to listen to me. What I have to tell you can save not only your life but the lives of both your parents and many many others. Very soon, you'll meet someone who will show you the power of that book. It'll become not only your best friend but the one thing that can help you accomplish everything you need to do—that is, if you apply it properly. Used wrongly, and it will kill you," she warned with grave finality. Once the power is transferred, in addition to helping your family, you can help create an immediate coronavirus vaccine. Obviously, I've been watching what's going on."

Fletcher was stunned. "But . . . but how?" He asked.

Mollyockett glanced up as if she were expecting someone. "Machias will fill you in."

"Who's Machias?" he asked, apprehensive at the prospect of meeting someone else and anxious at the thought of the power of the passage being transferred to him. It was all too much to comprehend.

She ignored the question. She was preoccupied scanning a small path that cut through the center of the large clearing and into the dense woods. "He should be here any minute. Surprisingly, he's late. You need to listen and learn everything you can from him. Remember, knowledge is power. You only have two days before you head back to your basement. Whole's only accessible once a year and it has to happen this year." She turned and looked at him. "*When the moon is full past sun's high. A chief will sing the harvest cry. In Wabanaki North, green leaves blow. In the valley—*

"*Both rivers flow. Three moons after sowing so soon. The crescent will glow in the moon,*" Fletcher recited. "So those words Squire Susup said in the basement are the harvest cry?"

"Yes. And the rivers are in Andover and Bethel, where I camped when

I was in your world. That river you saw in the Valley of the Ferns actually flows out through the cracks in the earth. It's the water source for
both places."

"*The ergot will double,*" he whispered, feeling a chill go through
his body.

"That's right," she said and nodded. "It's the second sign of trouble."

Everything was coming together for him.

She held out a red tourmaline stone hanging securely around her
neck on a gold chain. "Look closely. I think you'll find a few words you
recognize."

He stood and approached her. On the stone he could see the inscription *Coimhead fearg fhear Na foighde.*" He ran his hand over his face,
trying to absorb the barrage of information she was giving him. "That
was at your grave."

She winced. "Exactly. This was given to me by Jackson McKenzie. I
came to know him well when I was camped in Bethel and Andover. I
shared with him many secrets of the water at both places along with the
proper medicinal plants and animals to help heal people. Over time we
developed a bond of trust. He could have taken the knowledge I shared
with him and made a fortune, but he never violated his pledge to me and
what I told him. Just as important to me, he had tremendous sympathy
for the plight of my people and the horrors they suffered at the hands of
both the French and English. He did what he could to allow us to roam
the lands that had belonged to us for thousands of years. It became
obvious to me that I could no longer pass power of the passage to my
blood." With an edge of bitterness, she continued, "Every year civilization—if that's what you call it—was encroaching closer and closer on
the entrance to the passage. Because of Jackson's trustworthiness and his
deep sense of commitment to my people, I made the decision to transfer
power to someone outside the Wabanaki Nation for the first time ever.
We really didn't know what to expect. We spent several days together at
Frenchman's Hole. I told him the stories of my people going back to
the earliest generations. I shared with him the power of various plants
and the vital importance of nutrients. Once he'd read the exact book
you've been reading, I took him to the passage and into Whole, where I,

along with Machias, successfully transferred the power. After returning to the Mahoosuc Valley, he gave me this stone. *Coimhead fearg fhear Na foighde … Beware the anger of an patient man.* Jackson was furious at the treatment of my people. He chose those words in the native language of your ancestors as a constant reminder of his deep anger and solid determination to always protect Whole. In his twisted way, Tomhegan desecrates that commitment by leaving reminders with those exact words. He likes to think it now applies to his personal anger and determination to gain control—at least temporarily—to further his plan."

"How'd he find out about that?" Fletcher asked, pointing to the stone on her neck.

"I have no idea."

"So he's never had access to Whole?"

"Never with respect to your basement. But, unfortunately he did somehow obtain knowledge of the southern passage and it's exact location. Obviously, he been exploiting it. Again, another mystery known only to Whole. Clearly, that's how he's been able to live as long as he has. Unfortunately for him, there are very few who can travel from the northern passage's area in Whole to the southern passage's area and visa versa. Fletch, it's the southern passage he's using, and he thinks that by destroying you and Aldous, he can obtain control of the northern passage.

Fletcher's face paled. "How?"

"Our best guess is once the power is transferred to you, he will use your mother to try to lure you to the southern passage. He's been planning this for a long time." She turned toward the forest just as her expected visitor emerged.

He immediately had a hundred questions but what Fletcher saw walking from the woods made his jaw drop.

CHAPTER 21

SIXTH DAY

THE TALL PERSON EXITING THE DARK WOODS WAS COMPLETELY COVERED with black-and-white animal pelts that swayed as he walked toward them with long, steady strides. An animal mask with two curved horns covered the top half of his face; the lower half was covered with a long white beard that hung down to his furry vest. A large gathering of fireflies hovered above him, their light reflecting off the gold bracelets jangling on his tanned, leathery wrists. In the same manner as Mollyockett and Squire Susup, his fingernails were painted a shiny black. A wicker basket hung off his back by two thick leather straps.

Directly behind the man were four small lemurs—a type of monkey that looked half cat and half bat with a long raccoon-like tail—that bounded forward in springy leaps, twisting and turning with each jump. When they noticed Mollyockett and Fletcher standing in the large clearing, their pointy ears quivered in warning as their bright red eyes fixated on the strangers.

"Finally," Mollyockett said, obviously relieved.

"*That's* Machias?" Fletcher asked, looking at her for guidance.

"He's not how he looks," she said and smiled. "But he does travel with interesting company."

"You can say that again. Why's he dressed like that? It's not even cold."

The smallest cat-bat, a mischievous expression on its face, sprinted directly at Fletcher, who instinctively stepped back, startled.

"*Hooey, stop!*" Machias boomed.

The small primate jerked to a sudden stop and then bolted back to the pack, avoiding Machias's admonishing glare.

"We waited for you at Umbegog," Mollyockett said with a hint of impatience as Machias reached them.

"I apologize, Molly." His deep, melodious voice sounded sincere. He took off the wicker basket, set it on the ground, and then removed the mask, revealing a zigzagged tattoo etched across his forehead. His thick white hair was pulled back into a long ponytail. "Hooey wouldn't have anything to do with the river. We had to detour around Three Suns. I still can't figure out why the lemurs can't travel through Flow. It's frustrating." He looked at Fletcher and held out his hand. "It's a pleasure to finally meet you."

"Nice to meet you, Mr.—"

"Machias. Always been just Machias. Ah, I must say, you're the spitting image of your father. It's uncanny," he clucked with delight.

Hooey playfully jumped on the animal head mask lying at his feet and immediately let out a screech as one of the pointed horns jabbed into its hind leg, causing it to spring onto Machias's fur-covered boot. He bent down and picked the animal up. Gently he rubbed a white substance he'd removed from a fur covered pocket. Fletcher shook his head as the bloody opening on the animals leg immediately healed with only a trace of the injury.

"With these four, you've always got to be prepared. This is Hooey, and those three are Sebago, Casco, and Monhegan," he said, gesturing toward the other lemurs chewing on white cactus flowers. None of them looked up at the mention of their names. "They're actually pollinators like the honeybee, but they do it by carrying pollen on their muzzles and hands. Our creator is quite ingenious." He set Hooey down and nudged him to go join the others.

"I've never seen Umbegog that high or that violent," Mollyockett said, bringing everyone back to the business at hand.

"It's not a good sign," Machias said. "But I think you know that."

"I hate to rush, but we're short on time. And I've got to get back to the valley," Mollyockett said.

"Then let's get down to business," Machais said as he sat on a root chair in the shape of a modest throne that had just materialized behind him.

As Fletcher and Mollyockett settled into their own root chairs,

Machias reached into the wicker basket and pulled out a folded, multi-colored silk scarf and gently tossed it toward her. Fletcher noticed it was decorated with scenes featuring various animals and plants and realized they all looked familiar.

"My dad has one similar to that," he said in surprise.

But Mollyockett didn't respond. She was engrossed in examining the different scenes and counting with her index finger. She stopped and glanced at Machias. "Why three?"

He shrugged. "No idea."

Mollyockett muttered something to herself and then looked at Fletcher. "Now's better than never. You ready?"

Fletcher felt anxious and asked, "Ready for what?"

"The transfer. It has always taken place at Sixth Day. Didn't Squire Susup mention it?" Seeing his nervousness, she teased him. "Oh, for heaven sakes, it's not like you're going to the dentist."

Machias laughed and winked at Fletcher. "If it helps, your father was just as reluctant, maybe a little more so."

The mention of his father ignited Fletcher's determination to help his parents. "Let's go," he announced.

With pride in her eyes, Mollyockett picked up the staff and the book and wrapped them carefully in the colorful embroidered cloth. She got up and walked toward the center of the large pasture where lay an enormous flat, circular stone that was larger than a football field. Fletcher and Machias dutifully following. In the center a deep bowl had been carved out. In the middle was a perfect circle of darker stone. Mollyockett stepped up onto the enormous stone and quickly led them to the edge of the crater.

Machias overtook Mollyockett and led them down the short slope to the bottom and stood in its center.

"What kind of rock is that?" Fletcher asked, gesturing toward the dark circle.

"Lodestone," Machias said, scraping the rock with the bottom of his hairy boot. "The whole thing is a giant natural magnet."

Mollyockett unfolded the embroidered cloth and handed Fletcher the staff. "Now if you'll kneel, we can begin," she commanded confidently.

Fletcher quickly knelt and grasped the staff tightly, his body quivering in apprehension and excitement.

"Good luck," Machias whispered and then took *Whole Abounds* from Mollyockett and silently held the book high over his head.

Fletcher closed his eyes and thought of his father in this same situation years ago. Slowly, he began to relax.

Mollyockett carefully draped the ornate scarf over Fletcher's head, laid her hands over it, and began to chant in an unrecognizable language.

Fletcher had a feeling it was the native language of the Wabanaki people. His attention was drawn to the dark stone circle, and he watched in amazement as it turned lighter and lighter as Mollyockett chanted. It was as though the stone was responding to her words.

During the ritual, small clusters of jittery fireflies spontaneously drifted together directly over their heads. They formed a giant ball resembling a small glowing sun. Mollyockett's low chants were barely audible over the growing hum of the fluttering firefly swarm.

It was over as quickly as it had begun. The fireflies dispersed, and the stone turned dark again. Machias handed *Whole Abounds* to Mollyockett, who removed the scarf from Fletcher's head and folded it around the leather book. "Congratulations, Fletcher," she said and smiled.

"It's over?"

Mollyockett handed him the scarf-covered book. "It's a little souvenir. When you've got some time, study the scarf. It tells a story ... your story. It's like no other before or after you."

Fletcher stared thoughtfully at the cloth-covered book in his hands, not sure he understood. *My story? What story?* he thought.

"Jackson would be immensely thrilled right now," she added glowingly, hugging him tightly for a few seconds.

When she let him go, Machias shook his hand heartily. "Congratulations, young man."

Fletcher was still unsure what exactly had happened because it felt like nothing had. Looking past Machias, he spotted Mollyockett walking up the slope and out of the crater.

"Where are you going?" he called out.

"I'm off. Merrimack's waiting, and I'm *way* behind schedule." She reached the top and paused. "Fletcher, it's been an absolute pleasure. You're in good hands. I'll see you soon. Make sure you study hard. And good luck." Mollyockett looked at Machias and tipped her stovepipe hat. "As always, thank you. You've always come through. It's in your hands now."

She left in the direction of Umbegog Gulch, leaving Fletcher feeling slightly abandoned. He turned to Machias, a lost expression on his face.

Machias smiled. "Things happening a little bit faster than you expected?" he asked.

"I guess—except I just didn't *feel* anything."

Machias put a hand on Fletcher's shoulder. "Well, I'm quite positive you've changed. It's always worked. Now, let's take a little hike. There's something I think you need to see. I've also got quite a lot to share with you. Some of it is vital, a matter of life or death," he said as he stopped walking and turned to face Fletcher.

Fletcher swallowed hard but said nothing. *Death for whom?* he thought.

Machias reached into his basket before slinging it back over his shoulders. He held out a small twig with fan-shaped leaves that had several yellowish seeds attached. "Here, rub this while we walk."

Fletcher took the plant and made a face at its pungent odor. "What is this?"

Machias chuckled at Fletcher's reaction. "Ginkgo. It's native to Asia. It's a surefire way to greatly enhance your memory while you're in Whole. It does the exact same thing where you're from, but it doesn't pack quite the same punch. The only way it'll help you is if you rub the leaves."

Fletcher put the twig's oily leaves and yellow berries between his thumb and index finger, and as soon as he started rubbing, his mind exploded in vivid flashes of bright blues and whites. A small electrical current pulsated and energized every part his brain, giving him unimaginable clarity. "What just happened?" Fletcher gasped.

"You've tapped into the inner sanctum of your memory," Machias explained. "It's something, ain't it? Now you'll have no difficulty retaining everything you learn as you prepare for your journey."

Fletcher again thought of the next Bacchus meeting with Quinn and

Cam. *They'll totally think I'm nuts.* He barely believed it himself.

"Remember, what you experience in Whole can never be divulged. Not even with your two friends. Let's go," Machias said, turning around so the basket faced Fletcher. "Put your things in the side pocket. They'll be safe there."

Fletcher swallowed hard then quickly slid the bundle containing his possessions into a large pocket and latched it. With a nod, Machias walked out of the crater and into the woods, following his previous path. Fletcher stayed on his tail, not wanting to get lost. Machias pointed out hundreds of plants and flowers, explaining their various uses. A low hum filled the air as bumblebees and large brown moths by the thousands flitted among multitudes of blossoming flowers.

Machias pointed to a group of large brown moths with yellow spots lining their bodies and long antenna-like pointers protruding from their heads. "Those are Manduca hawk moths. Like lemurs, they're pollinators. To reproduce, every one of these plants, especially those with flowers, requires that a pollinator—bees, certain moths, ring-tailed lemurs, or some types of beetles—transfer pollen between the plants male and female parts. There's literally hundreds of thousands of different types of pollinators on earth, and all of them originate here at Sixth Day. Should you decide to eat any honey while you're here, Fletch, you'll be awake for months."

Fletcher laughed at the thought. "Why?"

"Because it's a sugar. Where you're from, it gives you immediate energy. Here, it'll give you enough energy to sustain you until you've quite literally worn out your body."

While Fletcher was taking it all in, he lightly brushed up against a thick bush with light blue flowers, disturbing a small cluster of bees. He quickly sidestepped the bush to avoid being stung, making Machias chuckle.

A short time later, they approached an enormous pine tree that was twice the height of the other trees in the forest. The top of the tree almost brushed up against the bottom of a long pointed stone jutting downwards. Machias carefully took off the wicker basket.

"Follow me."

Knowingly, he stooped down to enter a small opening in the bottom of the huge tree, and he carefully stepped over a small brown snake slithering nonchalantly under one of the pine's large roots. Once inside the tree, he reached out and grabbed his basket.

Fletcher saw the familiar bluish glow of Flow travel. He quickly went through the opening, and when he stepped into the pulsating beam, he wished to be where Machias went. The blue ray hummed, and he felt the familiar suctioning sensation pull at his body. Then he felt nothing.

When Fletcher opened his eyes, he was sitting in a stone chair similar to those at Umbegog Gulch. Next to him sat Machias, who was stretched out in a throne-shaped stone. They were looking out onto an enormous flower-filled pasture. A large crescent moon with six massive stars along its curve has been erected in the center of the field.

"Where are we?" Fletcher asked.

"High above Sixth Day. Impressive, isn't it?" He pointed to the crescent. "You recognize that symbol?"

"It's the same as the one in my basement."

"Look closely at the center of the crescent moon. You see that little indentation in its center?"

Fletcher leaned forward and squinted. He sat back in awe when he realized the small bowl shape was where they had just performed the ritual to transfer the power of the passage. "It's in the exact same spot where Squire Susup inserted the tip of the staff in the crescent in my root cellar."

"That's absolutely correct. It's the very center of Sixth Day." Machias glanced up at the stone ceiling. "We're in one of those long spikes you saw hanging down. This one's called Entreat Point. It's a great place to be if you're trying to get somewhere special."

Fletcher looked around and saw he was eye level with the the bottom tips of the stone spikes suspended from the hard ceiling. He studied the etched symbol and the vibrantly colored field below him.

"Much like the marker in your root cellar, there's also an identical one located at the entrance to the southern passage," Machias told him, a hint of pensiveness creeping into his voice. "The two bottom stars are made of sandstone. The two green ones are serpentine, and the top two yellow stars are agate. The moon is made of cumberlandite, except for the bottom of the bowl, which, as you know, is lodestone. The symbol in your basement and the one in the Quetzal are made of the same types of rocks." Machias sat forward and retrieved the copy of *Whole Abounds* and then turned in his chair to face Fletcher. "We only have a short time to do what has to be done. We needed to transfer the power to you for several reasons, each one of them important in its own right. First, you should know, now that the power of the passage is with you, it cannot be transferred back to your father. That's the way it's always been—forward, never backward," he said with finality.

Fletcher nodded slightly to show he understood.

"As you surely know, Tomhegan has attempted numerous times to infiltrate the passage and subsequently Whole. Unfortunately, his despicable and loathsome actions have had grave consequences for many innocent people."

"Like my entire family," Fletcher said bitterly.

"Yes," Machias agreed wearily, "like your family. Tomhegan's always tried to make it look like an accident—mysterious poisonings, bizarre and unwitnessed accidents, unexplained fires. Each taken alone might not raise suspicions, but lumped together, everything points to one conclusion. No doubt about that."

"So what happens next?" Fletcher asked. "You mentioned a journey. What's that all about?" he asked.

Machias handed him *Whole Abounds*. "That book can be your best friend, or it can kill you. What's inside must be taken seriously now that you've obtained the power of the passage. Those pages can magically enable you to do things otherwise deemed impossible."

Fletcher caressed the book. "Like what?"

"Like creating a vaccine for a virus that's the cause of a pandemic. Flip to page sixty-two." Fletcher complied and opened to the page depicting dozens of plants. "Each one of those plants has unique abilities—to heal, to feed, and in some cases, to hurt," Machias continued. "Most of them are beneficial—carrots for your eyes, spinach to help build muscles, even bananas to ease a cough. These are the easy ones. But look at pokeweed. Its roots are poisonous. If they don't kill you, they'll put you into a perpetual sleep. And it's undetectable in the body unless someone knows exactly what to test for."

The realization made Fletcher turn ghostly pale. "Is that what Tomhegan gave my father?" he asked feeling immediate anger.

Machias nodded. "Mollyockett confirmed it. He's lucky to be alive."

"You know, he would give my mother a single red rose every Friday. Mom said he'd done it every week since they first met." Fletcher wanted to personalize his father with Machias.

"Well, you can help him send those roses again," Machias replied quietly. "Don't forget, I'm familiar with him too."

Fletcher's head snapped up. "Tell me how."

"Turn to page 131." Fletcher rapidly thumbed his way to the correct page. "That's Saint John's Wort, which has wonderful medicinal properties. It's the one plant that can reverse the poisonous properties of pokeweed. If you rub your father's hand on some that I'll be giving you to take back from Whole, he'll be just fine. And that is a promise."

"Are you serious?" Fletcher shouted jubilantly, a radiant smile appearing on his face.

"Scout's honor," Machias promised. "In your world, whoever has *Whole Abounds* and the power of the passage can access the intended purpose of every plant and animal found in Whole, greatly magnified of course. The dilemma we've been faced with is that even though Aldous had the power of the passage, he couldn't access the power of *Whole Abounds* because he was in a poison-induced coma. So after much deliberation, we made the decision to have Squire Susup bring you to Whole and transfer the power to you. It was our only option to heal your father and save countless others. From this point on, *Whole Abounds* and the special powers contained within are yours. As is Kozart's staff, which will grant you temporary access to Whole once a year. I highly suggest you let Squire Susup safeguard that."

I can heal my father. Fletcher was almost deliriously gleeful. Then he grew somber. "How do you know for sure the power has transferred. I mean, I felt nothing."

"Look at the back of your right hand. See that brown marking?"

Fletcher lifted his hand and noticed a tiny brown circle in the center of his hand that hadn't been there before. He smiled slightly. His father had the exact same mark on his hand.

"That's how we know."

Fletcher almost laughed. "Thank you."

"So," Machias said, running his fingers through his long beard, "to the business at hand. You should know that I'm Kozart's eldest son. Mollyockett is directly descended from me."

Fletcher's jaw dropped. He studied the strong angular features on Machias's face. He could see the resemblance to the portrait of Mollyockett in his father's room.

"Tomhegan is playing a dangerous game in a last ditch attempt to control the passage. First, it's always been his goal to weaken the passage's power held by your family by chipping away at the very bloodline itself. Remember, knowledge is power."

"*Beware the beast, for if knowledge fails, it is certain Kozart prevails,*" Fletcher recited.

"If knowledge of the importance of Whole—especially the importance of Sixth Day—fails, Kozart's line or the line holding the power of the passage must relinquish control to the person with the knowledge. You see, Kozart was unyielding in his determination to keep Whole's purpose alive with those in your world. Never in a million years would he have envisioned someone pursuing the power of Whole for such evil purposes."

"Can't something be done?" asked Fletcher.

"As far as changing what Kozart had instructed? We've no idea. When he brought the Wabanaki people together, he was granted access to Whole by someone whose identity is still a mystery. When I was only a boy, much younger than you, he took me to Frenchman's Hole and then up the path to where your house sits today. I watched him insert the staff into the center of the crescent moon before we entered Whole. I vividly remember him performing the exact same ritual you've just experienced."

"Who held *Whole Abounds* if there was only the two of you?" Fletcher asked.

"When I exited the passage the next day, my mother was waiting for me at the passage's entrance. I was holding a series of lengthy scrolls of birch bark wrapped in tanned animal hides that my father had placed on my head during the ceremony. Each one had very specific and detailed information regarding Whole, the passage, and the importance of each plant found within, specifically those found at Sixth Day. My father gave very explicit instructions that these scrolls be preserved in written form."

"What happened to Kozart?" Fletcher asked.

"He stayed at Whole."

"How'd you know?"

"Each year I'd spend three wonderful days with my father. I'll always cherish those memories. Then he took me down to the stone bowl for the second time and told me about the importance of recording what was here. Before we departed, he taught me how to transfer the power of the passage to subsequent generations within my bloodline."

"Why'd he give that up?"

"I'm really not sure why he did that. But it was the last time I would ever see him," Machias said quietly as his eyes began to water slightly. "I spent almost a year working with Pidianiski, transcribing those birch scrolls into a crude book. Later, Mollyockett wrote the book that you now safeguard."

Fletcher looked at the book in his lap. "Pidianiski?"

"She's my eldest sister. She created that beautiful scarf Mollyockett placed on your head during the ritual."

"Did she create the one for my dad too?"

"She did. Now back to the vital matter at hand. Tomhegan has spent years and years whittling away at both the knowledge of Whole and the McKenzie bloodline. Then like the coward that he is, he discards people without the slightest bit of remorse.

"But why take my mother?" Fletcher said.

"He knows that the southern passage is too important for us to ignore. According to Kozart's writing, if a passage stays unguarded for long enough, it can be accessed by anyone. I've recently learned this. From what we can ascertain, that time is almost here. This will have disastrous consequences for Whole. Its discovery would doom the very existence of everything you're looking at. Once Tomhegan found out that the southern passage was in imminent danger of being exploited, he set his trap. Machias looked gravely at Fletcher. So we need to send the only person who has access to the southern passage to close off that entrance before it's too late. The very existence of Whole depends on it."

Fletcher nervously looked at Machias. "And that person is me?"

"Yes, you're the only one who's permitted near the southern passage because of the unique powers you now possess."

Fletcher did not flinch. "Will this help my mother?"

Machias nodded.

"How do I close the passage?" he asked resolutely.

Machias's eyes softened. "Clearly, Mollyockett and I made the right decision. I've no doubt you'll succeed. Flow travel will take you to the most southern part of Whole. The Quechuan entrance sits deep inside one of their ancient temples, which fortunately is still lost to the ages. But those days are numbered if what Squire Susup tells us is correct. So you have only two days to prepare and travel to Quechuan."

Fletcher thought of his parents. "I'm ready. Tell me what I need to do to prepare."

Machias put his hand on Fletcher's shoulder. "You'll also be taught how to use *Whole Abounds* to create an vaccine for the virus. It's a tall task to learn in just two days, but I'm positive you'll succeed. Discovering it will be one thing, getting it home will be another." Machias lowered his head so that he was looking Fletcher in the eye. "First, it's vital you master the powers you now possess. You can use them to your advantage when you encounter Tomhegan. You should always expect the unexpected. He's savagely cunning and shrewdly deceptive. The ginkgo plant your rubbed between your fingers will improve your odds substantially."

Machias pulled out a piece of parchment from a side pocket of his fur vest. He unfolded it and smoothed it out on the stone floor. He pointed to an X on the map. "You'll exit Flow here deep inside the Quechuan temple. After you've accomplished your goal and are ready to leave, Flow will be located directly behind this large pillar. According to Merrimack, it's decorated with a large flower with three leaves. The symbol with the moon and five stars should be located directly above the passage's entrance."

"So I won't exit Flow at the passage?"

"No, you'll have to make your way to the symbol. To permanently close the passage, you'll need to insert your staff into the moon's indentation while removing the top star engraved with a sun. From what my notes say, this shouldn't be that difficult. Mollyockett made a small knapsack for you to protect these important artifacts."

"Where will my mother and Nimsy be?"

Machias placed his finger on the map. "Our best guess is here ... in this little room. If you look closely, it's the only room with one entrance and exit. Where Tomhegan will be is anyone's guess. Trust me, he will be there because he knows our sole window of opportunity."

Fletcher stood up to walk off his nerves. He was careful not to get too close to the precipitous edge of Entreat Point. "Squire Susup said Tomhegan's been injured. What's that all about?"

"That's what we learned from Merrimack, who is originally from the area around the southern passage. However, once you've showed yourself inside the temple, Tomhegan will quickly be on your heels. You need to act fast before he can gain the upper hand. Never underestimate him."

Fletcher swallowed hard. "How'd he find the temple if it's still undiscovered?"

"I don't know. But I'm convinced a few unlucky souls have paid a heavy price to accommodate him," Machias said.

Fletcher shook his head with dismay while clearing his throat

"What now?" he asked.

"I want you to think of the one place you wish you could be right now ... other than here."

"Like anywhere in my world or this one?"

"Anywhere," Machias said and smiled.

Fletcher thought of the weathered cottage that belonged to his family on the rocky Maine coast. He looked at Machias and nodded.

"Okay, close your eyes and wish to be there and then count back from ten."

After one last look at the vibrant field below him, Fletcher closed his eyes and whispered, "Ten, nine, eight, seven ..."

CHAPTER 22

CHRISTMAS COVE

FLETCHER IMMEDIATELY SMELLED SALTY SEA AIR. ITS MOIST, DANK AROMA reminded him of clamming with his father during low tide in the mud flats. When he opened his eyes, he found himself on the front porch of the rustic McKenzie family cottage at Christmas Cove. He looked out at the familiar rocky and majestic coastline that had been protecting the cottage for more than a century.

"I'd say it's a perfect place, especially on such a glorious day," announced Mollyockett.

Turning toward her voice, Fletcher saw Machias and Mollyockett sitting on a long wooden bench his grandfather had built by hand years ago. Next to them in his mother's favorite rocking chair, there was an Indian woman he'd never seen before.

"Hello, Fletcher, I'm Pidianiski. I've heard a lot of good things about you." She stood and moved toward him, extending her right hand to properly greet him. "I'd have chosen this place too."

He shook her hand. "You wrote *Whole Abounds.*"

"I did. That was many, many years ago. But it seems like yesterday. I hope you liked it," she said warmly, returning to the rocking chair.

Fletcher sat in his grandfather's old rocking chair beside her. She had warm, delicate brown eyes and long jet-black hair braided into two large strands elaborately woven into a bun. "I think it's a wonderful book." His thoughts were on the book's ability to help heal his father.

"Well, I can assure you it would've been a lot more enjoyable to transcribe had I known this place existed." Pidianiski watched a large blue wave crest over the water-soaked rocks jutting toward the open ocean in front of the cabin. "It took me most of a summer. The black flies were murderous in Maine that year—"

"My, my, how soon we forget." Mollyockett said with enjoyment. "Had you not abandoned everything to go on that sudden Passamaquoddy fishing trip, you'd have finished it a lot sooner. What was that all about? Set us back four months."

Pidianiski didn't respond.

"I believe we're pressed for time," Machias reminded them. "Besides, if I remember correctly, *you* are the one who has the habit of taking off at a moment's notice," he said to Mollyockett. "Like the time you were out on that Penobscot island in the driving rain. You scared the Helms family half to death when they stumbled on you sleeping in their wood shed. Thankfully, Constable Ratta was there to vouch for you."

Mollyockett studied the floor. "Well, that was years ago."

"As you can see," Pidianski said to Fletcher, "some things in Whole aren't perfect." There was playfulness in her voice.

Rocking slightly in the chair, Fletcher looked toward the open ocean. A white seagull was darting up and down over a clump of algae and seaweed drifting toward a small crevasse between two large granite rocks.

He looked at Machias. "Can I ask how we got here from Whole?"

Mollyockett stood and stretched her arms. Above her was the hand-crafted McKenzie sign Uncle Woodrow had made the last time he'd been there with both his parents.

"Actually, you're in Mortaise Realm, Fletcher," she told him.

"What's that supposed to mean? It looks like we're at my parents' cottage at Christmas Cove."

Machias cleared his throat. "Well, you are, and you aren't. Mortaise Realm is the reason why I took you to Entreat Point. It enables you to visit any place you desire without actually leaving Sixth Day. It can recreate any place. You wished for Christmas Cove, Maine, so this is an exact replica right down to that silly little orange bottle opener," Machias said, pointing at a small Moxie opener sitting on a glass-covered lobster trap. Fletcher smiled slightly. He recognized it as the one his grandfather had given to his father many years ago.

"It feels like we're *really* at my parents' cottage. I mean, even Cicely's flamingos are here." Fletcher pointed toward three sun-faded, plastic pink flamingos. Their thin metal legs were stuck deep into the middle of his mother's small herb garden at the base of an ancient pine tree standing at the very edge of the small yard that sloped gently toward the open ocean.

"Mortaise Realm's quite impressive," said Mollyockett. "It was the deciding factor in my decision to transfer power to Jackson. I knew the Mahoosuc Valley was changing and would never be the same again. The only saving grace for me was knowing that I could revisit Frenchman's Hole, the Androsgoggin River, Odanak, Ogunquit, Swift River, and many other places simply by going to Sixth Day. The best part, however, is that it takes you to your desired location you've wished for. Unfortunately, never to the future. Again, one of Whole's closely guarded secrets.

Fletcher immediately stood and looked around.

Machias said gently, "Unfortunately, it only takes *you* to that location, Fletcher. I'm sorry. But trust me. If they could be here, they'd be sitting right beside you."

Fletcher nodded and tried to hide his crushing disappointment by focusing on a framed poster of Olympia, the world's largest snowman ever built by the people of Bethel.

"I'm quite positive they're here in spirit though," Mollyockett added. "Now if you don't mind, I think I'll check and see if there are any lobsters in those traps. Fletch, I'll make sure to put your name on the biggest one." She smiled as she headed toward the rocky shore.

After Mollyockett left, Pidianiski stood and walked toward Machias. "The reason why I'm here is to show you the special powers you've inherited while at Sixth Day. I've spent more time there than anyone. The summer I translated *Whole Abounds*, I learned a great deal from Kozart's writings, most of which had never been read before, which is unfortunate, given how much we've learned from them. Even more important, considering the current state of affairs, I luckily became very familiar with the southern passage that summer."

"You mean where I'll be going," Fletcher confirmed. "Then wouldn't it make sense for you to take me there using Mortaise Realm? Don't you think it would be to my advantage to at least see what it looks like? I mean, all I've seen of it was on a crude map."

"You think fast. It'll serve you well," Pidianiski said approvingly. "If that were possible, we'd be there right now, but it's not. Let me explain. It was the summer of 1707. I was the one who held the power of the passage at that time. I was studying Kozart's notes, readying them for translation. Midway through the project, he began to reference a small town called Ollantaytambo and a people on the verge of extinction. According to him, these peaceful and hardworking people located deep within a tropical rain forest also possessed the ability to access Whole with their own passage, which was marked with a symbol exactly like the one in your root cellar."

"The Quechuan people?"

Pidianiski nodded. "I'd have done anything to help them if I could. So that summer when I traveled through the passage into Whole, I applied what I leaned in those notes and visited the temple at Ollantaytambo. That temple is truly one of the wonders of the world. I'll never forget a moment of it. It was a special time when anyone who was in Whole could travel between the north and south. But, given the grave status of the southern entrance, Whole mysteriously created an inpenetrable barrier preventing everyone from visiting the other side. Now, the only person who can move between the two sections is the individual who holds the power of the passage."

Time slowed for Fletcher. Nothing seemed real anymore. "So the only way I can travel to Ollantaytambo is for me to go alone," he concluded.

"Exactly."

"When I held the power of the passage, I never knew the place existed," Machias explained. "And as you know, Mollyockett had more pressing concerns to deal with while she controlled the passage's power."

"What happened while you were there? What were they like?" Fletcher asked. "Didn't you have only three days?"

"I have no idea what they were like, and I had less than a day left. When I entered the temple, it was abandoned. But I think they were expecting someone from the other side of the passage to visit their temple."

"Why?"

Pidianiski pulled out an ancient oval stone from a pocket in her leather dress. It was covered with dozens of small symbols. She handed him the disk-shaped stone. Fletcher could instantly feel a strange aura surround him the moment the dark stone touched his skin.

"What is it?" he asked, immediately studying the drawings on the stone's cool surface.

"Vilcanota's patera," she said and smiled. "Just like the book *Whole Abounds,* it holds the power of the six nutrients necessary for human life, both good and bad. It's named after the river that flowed near Ollantaytambo."

Fletcher turned the patera in his hand. "How'd you know that if no one was in the temple?"

"Because the patera along with detailed stone tablets inscribed with native symbols and short stories was sitting next to the symbol that marked the entrance to their passage. Not knowing what they were at the time, I took them with me when I returned north. It was only later that I learned the tablets contained specific instructions regarding the use of Vilcanota's patera."

"What kind of instructions?"

"After we were finally able to interpret the markings, we discovered that any person holding the patera has the ability to literally transfer the wonders of the six nutrients of life onto physical objects. In other words, it has the same powers as *Whole Abounds.* And more importantly, it can be gifted from one person to another, providing they hold the passage's power. It's even transferrable from one bloodline to another."

"Machias said that *Whole Abounds* has the power to heal my father? Is that what you're talking about?" Fletcher asked.

"That's exactly the power I'm talking about. Don't be startled Fletcher, but it can also teach you how to make a vaccine for the virus," Pidianiski confirmed. "Yes, coronavirus. But it's vital for you to know how to access the special powers of these nutrients and how they interact with the human body. This is one of the reasons why you've been brought here. First, we all felt you needed to experience Mortaise Realm on your first visit to Whole. Second, and more urgently, I'm here to teach you exactly what that patera you're holding as well as what *Whole Abounds* can do for you."

For the next several minutes, Pidianiski explained the six nutrients of the body and their functions. She drew in a long deep breath and aimed both hands at the patera. Everyone fell silent. A small tornado was now hovering above *Whole Abounds*. Slowly, it dropped down into the crevasse of the open book. Everyone watched in a daze as the pages sprung alive and wildly turned from one page to another as the tornado remained on each one for roughly five seconds. While looking random, it was clear certain pages were being selected for a reason. Hypnotized, Fletcher absorbed the information on every page the tornado hovered over. This went on for several minutes. Finally, the tornado dissipated as it moved towards the Atlantic Ocean.

Pidianiski lowered her hands. "Congratulations Fletcher.

Everyone clapped and yelled in celebration.

Fletcher knew he had no choice but to bow. It was a well-earned respite from what lay ahead for him. "You don't even need to tell me because I know." He was beaming from ear to ear.

Pidianiski glanced back at the book and patera trying to see if was over. "Now that you have the vaccine, make sure you move quickly with it when you arrive home."

"Uncle Woodrow will know what to do with it. Give it to him in the root cellar quickly after you arrive," said Mollyockett.

"Thank you," replied Fletcher.

For the next several hours, Pidianiski taught in great detail the six nutrients of the body and their functions. She repeated the purpose of the twenty amino acids in proteins and their specific functions. Fletcher immediately saw the correlation between the acids and muscular strength. She also pointed out where they were located on the patera. His newly altered mind absorbed everything right down to the smallest detail.

Knowing time was running short, Machias cleared his throat and stood up. "While you're inside that Quechuan temple, you'll be tested. Knowing the purpose of each nutrient could mean the difference between life and death during your inevitable encounter with Tomhegan."

Pidianiski added, "You can access the powers of the patera and

Whole Abounds while in north and south Whole or in your root cellar," she continued with urgency, "The nutritional effects are magnified to the millionth degree once you unleash them, both the healthy ones and the deadly ones. So be careful. And just so you know, you'll need to use only the patera while in the temple because it's far quicker to access."

Machias checked on Mollyockett's progress. She was holding her wicker basket over a steaming pot hanging above a blazing fire. She opened the basket, and several plump lobsters fell angrily into the large cast-iron pot. Sweating and soaked, Mollyockett pushed back her long black hair as she jostled the lobsters with a long wooden stick. Pidianski looked back at Fletcher.

"Remember, it's vital that you seal the southern passage. The very existence of Whole depends on it. Once sealed, no one will be able to get in or get out—unless they have the star you are to remove. Remember, if Tomhegan gets his hands on the patera, he may be able to heal himself. None of us know what the rules are anymore in the south. Use it wisely and for your benefit only. We don't know if he is even aware of it, but we can't take any chances."

Pidianiski shrugged. "Squire Susup's been diligently guarding the passage where you live. It's probably frustrating for Tomhegan that the squire's always been one step ahead of him. He and Onion make one serious team."

"He wasn't one step ahead of him when it came to my parents," Fletcher said.

"I know," she said gently.

Machias stepped in, stressing the importance of focusing on the future instead of dwelling on the past. "Fletcher, Tomhegan's definitely setting a trap for you. He selected the southern passage for two reasons. First, he knew we'd have to rescue your mother and her friend. Second, he's well aware of the impending discovery of the temple. To have a fighting chance, you need to retain everything you've been taught."

"Lunch is ready!" called Mollyockett loudly from the front yard. She was holding up four mesh bags filled with steaming red lobsters, Maine potatoes, corn on the cob, shrimp, clams, and dark mussels.

"Fletcher, the best part of Mortaise Realm is that you can enjoy foods that are native to where you're visiting," said Machias, smiling toward Mollyockett. "Your final lesson with Pidianiski can start after we eat."

Realizing how hungry he was, Fletcher eagerly agreed and raced outside. He pushed all worries about Tomhegan and his parents aside for now.

Fletcher watched the large waves crashing rhythmically over the rocks on the shoreline. The dank smell of the cool sea hung thickly in the air. He'd spent the last six hours or so listening to Pidianiski instruct him on the power of each of the six nutrients and how to use them to his advantage with Vilcanota's patera. Surprisingly, he'd had no problem retaining the mountain of information, thanks to the ginkgo Machias had given him. He kept whispering the usefulness of the twenty-one amino acids that made up proteins, and he now knew how to amp them up and build massive strength just by rubbing the right etching on the stone in his pocket. There was, however, one caveat. He had to rub the right symbol on the Quechuan stone while simultaneously thinking of the appropriate nutrient and what it was designed for. Any mistake could easily cost him his life. And he had no idea what Tomhegan knew.

"We need to get going, Fletcher," Mollyockett said. She was standing on the front steps of the cabin. Perched happily on her shoulder was Merrimack, who'd arrived just as Pidianiski had presented them with a homemade blueberry-rhubarb pie. It tasted exactly like his grandmother's award-winning pie.

"Get going," Merrimack squawked loudly, bobbing up and down slightly.

Fletcher smiled and waved. "I'm coming. Just give me a sec." In just a few minutes, he'd be heading back to Sixth Day with Machias and then onto the Quechuan temple through Flow. Listening to the soothing sound of waves crashing, he closed his eyes and pondered what lay ahead. The fate of his parents and that of countless others depended on his actions alone. Reaching into his pocket to hold the patera, he felt the Paw-Paw bar he'd been given moments before they'd met Squire Susup in the root cellar. It felt like a lifetime ago.

"We need to get going," said Machias. He was standing on the rocky shore, holding his beastly mask. "I want to thank you for showing us this beautiful place. It's truly one of the most memorable we've ever been to," he said sincerely, watching a baby seal sun itself on a flat stretch of rocks.

Fletcher walked toward him. "The first thing I'm gonna do when I return to Ketchum is plan a trip back here … with *both* my parents."

Relishing in his confidence, Machias gave him a thumbs-up. "I've no doubt. I wish I could join you." He placed his hand on Fletcher's shoulder as they walked toward the cabin. "You represent the McKenzie name well, Fletcher. Thank you."

Mollyockett was standing next to Pidianiski on the porch. She told Fletcher, "Pidianiski and I are heading back to Whole. We made this for you." She held out a necklace made of small shells and smooth sea glass.

"Kind of a good luck charm, Christmas Cove-style," Pidianiski explained.

Fletcher bent forward with a big smile and let Mollyockett place the charm around his neck.

"Will I see you again?" he asked pensively, looking at them both.

"Every year," replied Mollyockett. "Just promise me one thing."

"Anything," he said immediately.

"Promise me you'll represent a more respectable character in next year's Mollyockett Day parade," she said and laughed. "A blade of grass? What was that all about?" she teased, ruffling his hair.

Fletcher laughed, absently thumbing a small piece of red sea glass on the necklace.

Pidianiski handed him the small knapsack Mollyockett had sewn for the star in the Quechuan temple. "Make us proud. We're with you in spirit," she said.

Both women had a somber look on their faces. They knew the extreme danger that awaited him.

Eager to get moving, he looked at Machias. "How do we get back to Sixth Day?"

"Exactly like you got here."

Understanding, Fletcher took one last look at the open ocean and then closed his eyes and thought of the pinnacle overlooking Sixth Day. He began to silently count backward. Just as before, he felt a slight tingly sensation and then numbing blackness. Even before he opened his eyes, he recognized the faint sound of dancing fireflies illuminating the opening of Entreat Point.

"Flow is just inside that opening. It'll take you to the temple," Machias announced. Fletcher's eyes widened, thrown off at how fast it was happening. "No need to delay," Machias explained. "It'll only rack your brain. I don't doubt your abilities. Remember, the quicker you act, the more you'll throw Tomhegan off. From what Pidianiski's calculated, Tomhegan will immediately be healed if he can wrestle the patera from you, but there will be a delay, however, between his physical self and mental state."

Fletcher looked confused. "Meaning what?"

"His body will be fully recovered, but it'll take a little time for his mind to realize it. It'll give you a small window of opportunity. I'm hopeful it won't pan out like this. Remember, *coimhead fearg fhear na foighde.*"

Fletcher repeated, "*Coimhead fearg fear na foighde,*" and then he quickly turned, closed his eyes, and stepped into the brilliant blue rays.

CHAPTER 23

TEN-SECOND DRIP

FLETCHER JERKED HIS EYES OPEN, KNOWING HE HAD TO ACT QUICKLY. He was deep inside a massive stone building. He hadn't expected the temple to be so big. Enormous blocks jutted out at an angle from four directions, giving him the impression he was inside a huge pyramid. Pillars rose from the floor to the top of the pyramid at exact intervals. The thick stone blocks on the floor were engraved with dozens of snakes, scorpions, deer, and elongated goats.

"Those are their guardian spirits," he whispered, thinking back to his lesson with Pidianiski. In his mind he recalled the map Machias had shown him. A shiver of fear ran through him as he slowly looked around for any movement. A small stream flowed gently through a winding canal set in the center of the stone floor, creating a quiet gurgle in the dimly lit arena. Looking up, Fletcher noticed slender rays of dusty sunlight poking through small openings throughout the stacked stone blocks. Leafy green vines covered the walls and traveled upwards as they extended their reach toward the ceiling. Water dripped constantly at exactly ten seconds intervals. Seeking assurance, he rubbed the stone patera in his pocket.

"*Fleur de lis*," he whispered quietly. Swallowing hard, he started to walk in the direction Machias had pointed out on the map. Running down his mental list, he extended his arm behind him and felt for the staff located in the knapsack. Satisfied it was there, he looked in the direction he'd been told his mother and Nimsy Cortland were possibly being held.

He spied a small opening carved within a tall flat wall far off in the distance. His heart raced, and he had to restrain himself from running toward the room. He'd given Machias his solemn word he'd remove the stone star first and permanently seal the passage from the outside world. He came to an abrupt halt in front of what looked like a sacrificial altar set within an enormous square stone. At its base someone had etched several images into the stone—carved heads laying several feet from their headless bodies. Moving on, he continually scanned the temple's periphery for any movement. The methodical dripping of water eerily counted down the time he had.

He swiftly rounded a large stone column.

"There it is," he whispered excitedly.

Set within the small rocks was the same crescent on Mollyockett's grave stone, in the root cellar of his basement, and in the center of Sixth Day. He quietly shrugged off the knapsack and pulled out the ornate staff. In an attempt to save time, he stooped directly over the top star, placed his fingers on it's edges, and yanked with all his might. He screamed loudly in pain as the points of the star ripped into his fingers, pulling back the tops of two fingernails and tearing off the skin from the tips of three others. Instinctively, he gently slid the injured fingers into his mouth, the echo of his shout reverberated off the sides of the stone temple. Sweat dripped from his soaked hair as he nervously scanned the immediate area for Tomhegan. His injured hand throbbed as he held on firmly to the staff. Anxiously, he moved toward the moon and inserted the staff while cautiously pulling the top star with his uninjured hand. The stone star pulled free effortlessly. With fumbling fingers, he opened the knapsack and carefully placed it inside. He pressed his mangled fingers against his stomach as he contemplated what to do next. He looked down to see streaks of blood on his shirt. Heading toward the room where his mother was possibly being held, his eyes darted to the numerous corners, searching for any sign of danger. Suddenly he stopped and looked back to where he'd just removed the star. He was positive he'd heard something. He listened intently, but only heard the methodical dripping of the water.

To his left, behind a square block consisting of six large stones, he noticed an intricate etching of a set of stairs with three elaborately dressed tribesmen ascending them. At the top of the stairs the sun illuminated a multitude of various fruits, vegetables, large stalks of grass with plump whole grains, exotic fish, and various other animals. Fletcher thought of Noah's ark and the story of the great flood.

He turned to continue on and abruptly stopped. "Idiot," he scolded himself. It just occurred to him that he had the power to heal his injured hand. Stealing a quick glance in every direction, he quickly pulled the warm stone out of his pocket. He closed his eyes and thought back to Pidianiski's lessons and what he could do to heal his fingers. He gingerly rubbed the symbols representing vitamin B-2, tuna oil, olive oil, and vitamin E, and his injured fingers instantly healed before his eyes. He gasped with delight as a deep sense of accomplishment enveloped him. Elated, he strode forward. *I can do this.*

Every sound was amplified in the dimly lit vastness. A slender ray of sunlight illuminated a small stone shelf. Handsomely carved vines scrolled around and under the two supporting blocks. Below them someone had etched three words: *Gaudium et Spes.*

Fletcher said to himself, "Joy and hope." He wondered if Pidianiski had noticed the inscription.

Moving forward slowly, he looked around at the towering walls of the temple. To his right in the distance was an arch leading to a chamber of sorts. Moving quickly, he made his way toward the opening. Along the way he spotted a small crude pipe. Thinking of Mollyockett, he pocketed it then continued on his way. As he reached the opening to the room, he stopped and listened for signs of Tomhegan. Still nothing.

He slowly entered the dim room through a small opening. It took a few seconds for his eyes to adjust to the dark chamber. The room was musty with a low ceiling, two elongated walls, and two smaller walls. He took a few steps and then abruptly stopped and gasped. Lying motionless on a large flat rock was his mother. He raced toward her and dropped the knapsack to the ground as he fell to his knees. He lowered his ear over her nose and could feel her faint breath.

"Mom, it's me, Fletcher," he whispered, tears rolling down his cheeks. She didn't stir. He reached out and held her hands. "Mom, please." He rested his head on her stomach.

Glancing up, he spotted a grotesque depiction of a person being beheaded by an executioner in ceremonial dress. His large ax was only inches from the neck of the man soon to be sacrificed. In the background of the painting, hundreds of human skulls were stacked in an orderly fashion. Every one of them faced the gruesome scene as though they were watching.

He remembered what Pidianiski and Machias had said. *Tomhegan's become increasingly lazy and careless. More than likely he's done to your mother and Miss Cortland the exact same thing he did to your father.*

Fletcher held up Vilcanota's patera in the low light and intently focused on the tiny designs. His hand shook as he reached for his mother's right hand and gently rubbed her forefinger over a small twig-like symbol near the lower center of the stone. Closing his eyes, he silently whispered meditative words correlating to that nutrient. If Pidianiski was correct—and he prayed she was—the symbol he'd selected would show results quickly.

Not knowing exactly what to do next, he leaned against the cool rock and held her hand while taking in the cold room. From outside the opening, he could still hear the methodical dripping of water. He reached forward and pulled the knapsack toward him, mindful of the stone star's importance and Machias's instructions regarding its return.

"Well, well, well … I guess he was right with his timing. Some things can be predictably foretold."

The chillingly monotone voice came from behind him. Instantly recognizing the voice as Nimsy's, Fletcher jumped up happily and turned to greet her.

"Nimsy!" he said, his voice thick with relief. "Thank God you're—"

"*Shut up!*" she rasped. She had a venomous expression on her face. She stood in front of a small alcove he hadn't noticed.

Taken completely off guard by her demeanor, Fletcher stepped back, almost falling onto his mother. Nimsy continued to glare hatefully at him and then glanced greedily at the knapsack. She knew the treasures it held.

"Push it here … *now!*" she commanded.

Fletcher didn't move. His mind raced as he attempted to fully grasp exactly what was happening. Nimsy continued to stare at the knapsack, her mouth curled into a sneer. The hatred in her face made her appear to have aged ten years. Fletcher swallowed hard and gently kicked the knapsack toward Nimsy in an attempt to lure her closer to him. He discretely turned Vilcanota's patera over in his hand trying to keep it hidden. He wondered if she even knew of its existence.

"You traitor," he whispered, rage roiling through his veins.

Nimsy smiled smugly. From behind her Fletcher heard the distant sound of footsteps approaching.

"My parents trusted you. They even named you trustee. How could you?"

"How could *I*?" she asked. She smiled sinisterly as she brushed her long blond hair back over her shoulders. "I'll tell you why. I've been waiting my entire life to get back at your family after what they've done to mine."

Fletcher looked deeply confused. "What are you talking about?"

"That story your uncle Woodrow likes to tell at his cozy little inn," Nimsy said. "You know, the one that you and everyone else tell while sitting around their campfires and toasting marshmallows. The little tidbit about the curse Mollyockett put on the people of Snow Falls? Well, there's a real family behind that charming and entertaining little tale. What your uncle Woodrow failed to tell you was that Mollyockett was turned away during the blizzard because she'd *mistakenly* stumbled into the very home that was protecting the one person she most wanted to encounter —Tomhegan. We all knew what she was *actually* doing on that fateful day."

Fletcher didn't know what to say to placate Nimsy. His attention was drawn to a slight movement in the shadows behind her. He realized he no longer heard footsteps approaching. He tuned his eyes back toward Nimsy.

"Not everyone coddled the American colonists fighting the British soldiers for independence during the revolution. In fact, there were many loyal colonists who supported the crown. After the British lost, those people were treated like second-class citizens, most with outright savage hostility. Many had their homes and businesses confiscated after being labeled traitors." She had worked herself up into a fury. "My ancestors are *the* Snow family! My grandfather is Chesley Snow, who is directly descended from John Snow. You remember him. The poor man on that plaque at Snow Falls that was massacred by the Saint Francis Indians in 1755."

Fletcher's mind raced back to Uncle Woodrow's story. With the help of the ginkgo, he recalled every detail, "I thought John Snow was scalped by the Native Americans 150 years before Mollyockett cursed Snow Falls," he said, glancing toward the shadowy opening behind her.

"They did, but that's our business," she snapped. "My family fully supported Tomhegan's efforts to rid the Mahoosuc Valley of your land-greedy ancestors."

"But you're not—"

"Not what? Not Native American?" Her words were heavy with sarcasm. "Remember that old adage, *The enemy of your enemy is your friend?* Our family's main interests found commonality with Tomhegan. Especially those who took the power of the passage from him. He helped us, we helped him."

My God. She knows about the passage to Whole.

"I know what your thinking, Fletcher. Yes, the family that took the passage away from Tomhegan's people. The exact same one who degraded my entire family and took everything we ever worked for away from us," she seethed.

He's using her. He thought.

Behind Fletcher, his mother let out a barely audible groan. Instinctively, he turned.

"Leave her alone, and look at me!" Nimsy roared, annoyed by the interruption. "All we had left was our modest farm at Snow Falls. The same one Mollyockett cursed during the blizzard. Who gave her the right to destroy what little we had left? Do you have any idea how many generations of Snows have suffered while your family has prospered? And why? Because an arrogant and pompous Indian doctress decided so?"

"You're crazy," Fletcher whispered.

Nimsy glared at him. "For generations we've given protective cover to Tomhegan as he attempted to regain control of what your family stole from him. He's known of this very place for a long, long time. It's why he's still here. Slowly, at his behest, we've managed to infiltrate your family. Do you really think that rooming with your mother in college was happenstance? I think not," she said with a shrill laugh. "The Snows have also been the silent driving force behind Tomhegan's actions every time a McKenzie has suddenly died. I'd say we've done an excellent job. Wouldn't you?"

Fletcher felt his body go cold. "Why?"

"Because we've been promised what your family has had for so many years—respect, a good name, money, and authority. All those things were taken away from us many years ago. And in return, Tomhegan gets the one thing he so craves. You have no idea how many years we've waited for this very moment. Even those private detectives your uncle Woodrow hired to find your mother. That was my brother's suggestion. Little did your precious uncle realize they were my cousins, both intent on exacting revenge for the years and years my family has spent suffering. They never left the state of Maine. Ha! Took the money though. How do you think we paid for those explosives at Buck's Ledge?" Her eyes swept up and down the length of the room.

Her voice was raspy, her face flushed red, and the veins in her temple were pulsing so hard he thought they might explode and allow the devil himself to jump out. Nimsy wasn't finished. She had a lifetime of resentment to vent.

"It was me, Fletcher, who suggested that your mother replace your father on his scheduled trip to the Quetzal. The one he was planning before he got sick. Poor, poor Muriel," she said in mock sympathy, looking over at Fletcher's mother. "Of course, being her *best* friend, I insisted that I accompany her—you know, for protection. What else are best friends for?" she sneered. "Oh, by the way, I was also the one who did that nutritional assessment on Quetzal beans for Cygnus. In my final recommendations, I urged Muriel to quickly take the trip south before the borders closed due to the pandemic. That pandemic, though unexpected, worked well for us."

Fletcher bit down on his lip to help contain his growing rage. He gripped the patera firmly to keep himself from lunging at her. Behind him, his mother moved slightly and let out another moan.

"You stupid McKenzies are so pathetically predictable," Nimsy said with distain. "I'll still be poor Muriel's best friend when this is all said and done. But don't worry. I'll play the role well. I've even selected a proper memorial for her at Saint John's Cemetery. As her best friend, everyone will agree with me in their deep grief. And of course, I'll make sure your name is right beside hers. What a tragedy! Lost forever as well as her only son. I'll be so traumatized," she said, placing her hand over her forhead, simulating one who's deeply grief-stricken. "I may even have to take a few months to pull myself together. Paid for, of course, by the generosity of Aldous McKenzie. Stupid fool.

"Nantucket—that's where I'll go. A few months of island retreat should start my recovery from deep depression after having lost my best friend. Thank God everyone in Ketchum will be there to support me." She sighed happily as if living a dream.

Fletcher turned and softly rubbed his mother's temple. Nimsy seemed oblivious and continued to rant.

"Tomhegan, he's the brilliant one. It was his idea to lure you to Buck's Ledge. He knew the rockslide would pull the attention away from this Quechuan Temple and the southern passage, giving everyone the impression he was still in Ketchum. That way there'd be no concern allowing you to travel to Whole. Squire Susup missed that one, didn't he? He and his smelly mongrel. And just like Mollyockett, he's a traitor to his people." There was deep venom in her words.

Everyone was well aware of the danger of me traveling to Whole, he thought. *She's an absolute lunatic.*

Muriel slowly opened her eyes. Fletcher knelt beside her. "Mom, it's okay. It's me, Fletch."

"Stand up!" a deep voice commanded. "Now!"

Fletcher jumped up and spun around to confront the one person who terrified him the most. He was standing beside Nimsy, his large hand on her shoulder.

"Having fun?" he asked her lightly, seemingly amused.

"Oh, I was just getting started," she said and laughed shrewdly.

Tomhegan turned his attention back to Fletcher. "Don't tell me you didn't expect me?" He asked, glancing at the knapsack and smiling victoriously. "Good job, Nimsy. Looks like our little venture will pay off handsomely for both of us."

Muriel lifted her head, trying to focus on who was talking.

"You obviously now know that we've been waging a campaign of misinformation," Tomhegan continued. "I was never injured at Buck's Ledge. Do you really think Machias, Mollyockett, and Pidianiski would let you travel here if they knew I was healthy? I'm sure they're back in Whole envisioning a sort of David versus Goliath scenario right now. Amazing how gullible Squire Susup is. Even Merrimack had it wrong. Fell right into our hands."

Fletcher tried to control his nerves, which weren't helped by the large knife tucked into the side of Tomhegan's gem-encrusted belt.

"After I'm in control of everything, I'll be a god. Oh, you people can attempt to invent your foods, but we all know that Whole is the only place to find the foods that sustain life. Forever. And I'll decide who's worthy and every decision will be mine to make."

"Fletcher?" Muriel murmured in a low voice, rubbing her eyes.

"I'd like to stay and continue this chat," Tomhegan said matter-of-factly. "But as you know, time's a-ticking."

Fletcher wondered if either one of them knew that the southern passage was now sealed.

Nimsy laughed loudly in anticipation as Tomhegan bent down and picked up the knapsack.

"Let's go," he said with urgency as a sudden roar filled the room.

Fletcher watched in horror as Nimsy and Tomhegan crawled out of the room. He could hear them both pushing a large round bolder into the hole to block their escape.

"Fletcher," Muriel cried.

"Mom—"

He was drowned out by a torrent of water cascading from the opening Tomhegan and Nimsy had come through in the back of the chamber. The swirling water lifted him in an instant off the floor and onto his mother. Too weak to fight for her life, Muriel closed her eyes and succumbed to the rising water, disappearing below its surface.

Fletcher screamed for his mother, trying to reach her as the water pinned him against the wall. Unable to feel her, he took a quick, deep breath and plunged under the surge. A large sharp rock smashed into his temple, propelling him toward the back of the narrow room. He gulped a large amount of water. Flailing and thrashing in the swirling current, he managed to reach the surface. He touched his head and felt the warm blood.

He furiously paddled in the rising water. Quickly, he dove back under the murky water, swimming toward where he thought his mother was. But he was no match against the fierce current, and once again he was swept by the water and slammed against a jutting rock that impaled his back. He slid under the water, paralyzed by the searing pain. His lungs filled with water as every cell in his tattered body screamed for air. His body shook violently as his brain protested.

Everything became blurry. Just as darkness set in and he felt his soul ebbing from his damaged body, he felt a weight against his thigh. Through the haze he realized it was the patera in his pocket. He summoned all the strength he could muster to reach for it. Rolling in the churning water, he rubbed four symbols—the same three he'd rubbed to heal his injured fingers plus one representing honey for immediate energy. Fletcher gloriously felt the hole in his back and the gash in his head instantly heal. The intense pain was miraculously gone. Simultaneously, his body was electrified with an enormous amount of energy from the honey surging throughout his body. He surfaced and was able to cough out the water in his lungs and take deep breaths of air.

He focused on the stone and rubbed the etching representing protein a second time for additional strength and then moved his finger over the tiny circular etching representing omega-3 oil, prompting his muscles to dramatically grow. He watched in astonishment as his biceps ballooned and leg muscles bulged.

Totally invigorated, Fletcher dove under the water and swam forward powerfully, desperately searching for his mother, terrified of finding her dead. His left foot became entangled in something, and reaching down, he realized it was his mother's long hair. He swam deeper and grabbed her arm. Then he effortlessly glided toward the sealed exit. When he reached the stone blocking the hole, he kicked it viciously, and it exploded outward, sucking them out of the temple and thrusting them onto the hard ground.

Fletcher gently picked up his mother and ran to a large flat rock beside a massive stone column. He laid her down, pinched her nose, and blew several breaths of air into her lungs. But she remained unresponsive. He turned her on her side and gave her back two sharp blows. Muriel's body jerked then almost fell off the rock. He'd totally misjudged his new strength. A stream of water flew from her mouth and landed several feet from her. Muriel jerked up and immediately gasped for air.

Fletcher hugged his mother tightly. His magnified strength caused her to wince in pain.

"What's happening," she cried, struggling to get her bearings.

Before he could answer, he saw Tomhegan and Nimsy running toward them, fury blazing in their eyes. They couldn't find an escape.

"Stay right here mom," Fletcher told his mother. Then he ran to confront them.

With explosive power, he jumped forward and furiously kicked the circular base of a towering pillar. The earth rumbled under their feet. A massive stone structure next to them split in two. The enormous top half slowly teetered to one side and gained speed as it crashed right where Tomhegan and Nimsy had been standing seconds earlier, enveloping them in debris. The dust stung Fletcher's eyes as he cautiously scanned the area searching for his rivals. He focused on the massive pile of stone and then glanced over to see if his mother had been hit by any of the flying rocks. Satisfied that she was safe, he slowly crouched behind a large circular section of the destroyed pillar. Then he noticed the knapsack that had been on Tomhehan's back moments earlier. It had become wedged between two sections of the stone structure. He wiped the sweat streaking down his forehead. Suddenly, the knapsack moved. Quickly, he backed himself behind the stone again.

"Fletcher," his mother called out weakly. Every word strained her vocal chords. "Where am I? What's happening?"

He kept his eyes fixed on the knapsack and avoided the temptation to look toward his mother. He still had no idea where Tomhegan or Nimsy were.

"It's okay, Mom," he whispered back, knowing he might be giving up the possibility of a surprise attack.

As the dust continued to settle, he noticed a portion of Nimsy's body beside the wiggling knapsack. One of them must be trying to free themselves from the rocky grave.

"So now it's just the two of us."

Fletcher turned to see Tomhegan casually leaning against the wall.

"What? But ... how?"

"What? You continue to doubt me, Fletcher. You honestly think you can defeat me?" Tomhegan's snakelike gaze pierced Fletcher's eyes. Slowly, he turned toward the knapsack while Nimsy continued to cry.

"Tomhegan, help me. I'm really hurt," she cried out. Her words were muffled by the rocks holding her hostage. Tomhegan casually ignored her cries.

"You really think you'll win this one, Fletch?" he asked. "I've always been one step ahead of you ... always."

Fletcher's eyes stayed fixed on Tomhegan as a slight shadow suddenly moved near the top of the temple toward them. He hoped Tomhegan didn't notice.

"You see, the thing I'm enjoying most is that they'll never find either you or your mother." He laughed devilishly. "Your people and their rituals. It's only a matter of time."

His leathery hands slowly rubbeda white stone in his right hand. Fletcher ignored him. His heart raced as he noticed his mother attempting to stand.

"Fletch, help me ... please," she begged.

"Mom, sit down!" Fletcher barked. The fierceness of his command frightened him. He'd never disrespected his mother.

Muriel's jaw dropped as she fell to the floor. She barely recognized her son's voice. Confused, she closed her eyes and began to sob. Just then a loud screech pierced the temple. Tomhegan's head jerked up, confused.

Merrimack glided forward, and with pinpoint accuracy, he dropped a massive white glob directly into Tomhegan's black eyes. He screamed out in excruciating pain as the white acid temporarily blinded him. "Arggghhhh! You little!"

Aimlessly, he moved forward and then right, unaware of the large ravine next to him. His arms flailed as he stepped into the newly formed crevasse. His desperate scream followed him as he fell downward. Even though he could no longer see Tomhegan, Fletcher heard the immediate thud of a body hitting the bottom. Several seconds later, it echoed throughout the the temple.

"Not that deep," he whispered to himself. His first thought was to peek over the edge to see what the result was. Taking advantage of the opportunity, he jumped toward the knapsack. He grabbed a small jagged rock and effortlessly cut it free from Nimsy's body. Proteins were still coursing through his body. He stopped and looked at her body. She was no longer moving or talking.

"What happened to you, Nimsy? How could you? My mother and all of us trusted you," he whispered. Quickly, he abandoned her and raced back to comfort his shocked mother.

She stared at her son emptily as if he was a complete stranger. Looking up, he spotted the pillar with the fleur-de-lis marking their exit. He grabbed her hand an quickly scanned the contents of the knapsack.

"Come on. We have to go right now."

They sloshed through the waist-deep water and reached the bluish rays. Fletcher grasped his mother's hand tightly, closed his eyes, and jumped into Flow and then their world went black.

———

"Fletcher, it's okay. I'm right here."

Fletcher opened his eyes and looked at Uncle Woodrow's shell-shocked face. He bolted upright and looked around. He was in the root cellar. His mother was propped against the wall and covered with a blanket. She smiled at Fletcher, who ran over and hugged her. Both of them were soaked to the bone.

Woodrow stood in the middle of the room, sputtering in confusion, trying to get answers. "Fletcher, what happened? You found her!

242   FLETCHER MCKENZIE AND THE PASSAGE TO WHOLE

Where's your cast? And what's in that backpack?"

"Uncle Woodrow, you'll never believe what happened," Fletcher said.

"Just how much could've happened in fifteen minutes?" he demanded.

Fletcher's jaw dropped. "Wait. I've only been gone for fifteen minutes?"

Just then Squire Susup entered the root cellar and smiled at Fletcher. "Whole is really something, ain't it?" There was jubilation in his words. "Don't forget that vaccine for coronavirus you helped discover. Remember, you need to move quickly. There are many people out there who are depending on you with their lives."

Woodrow's eyes widened at what he had just heard.

Fletcher took a deep breath and looked at his uncle and mother. "You ready for the story of your life?"

Woodrow backed into one of the leather chairs, dazed. What he was told next shocked him to his very core.

CHAPTER 24

ONE YEAR LATER:
MOLLYOCKETT DAY

"How dare you insinuate that Foods for Fun's products are unhealthy," Refinna boomed angrily. "They're an excellent source of immediate energy for active people."

At issue was Foods for Fun's Mollyockett Day float in the just concluded parade. The theme of this year's parade was healthy living. Uncle Woodrow and Weller Zefran, who'd been elected to the Mollyockett Day executive committee, decided on the new campaign. Foods for Fun's professionally built float was a dazzling display of whirling lollipops in every color, spinning Blueberriola Sugary Sham Shams, and a gigantic taffy machine that pulled and stretched massive globs of brown taffy. On the side of the long float, a huge blinking sign read, "Post-workout snacks. Feed those muscles."

Aldous and Fletcher watched the heated exchange taking place in front of the judge's stand, and they were waiting for the judge's decisions.

Once Fletcher healed him, Aldous paid his three sisters handsomely to depart Cygnus, taking with them their beloved Tweedle Cakes, Honey Hum Hums, and all the other sugar- and fat-laden snacks.

"I'm just glad they're not part of Cygnus anymore," Fletcher said, idly thumbing the Christmas Cove charm around his neck. I'm really glad the pandemic is over too."

"Well, I wish them all well with their new company," Aldous said, brushing his hand through Fletcher's dark hair.

"Did you see how happy Mom and Mr. Von Piddle looked riding in Uncle Woodrow's Defender 90?" asked Fletcher.

Aldous nodded and smiled. "They made the perfect Grand Marshalls for this Mollyockett Day Parade, all things considered. It's nice to have things back to normal."

The parade was a family affair. Cygnus and Fifth Ward Whole & Healthy had combined forces and produced a float that awed the bulging crowds that lined the long parade route. It was an enormous stained-glass human cell that mimicked the one Fletcher had seen while in Whole. Masterfully constructed by Italian glass artisans, friends of Mr. Zacarolo, the float bedazzled everyone. At the front of the trailer, Fletcher had recruited a large contingency of Balston Prep classmates to wear elaborately sewn costumes depicting fruits and vegetables, bottles of olive and flax seed oil, fish, and lean cuts of meat. Thankfully, the eight person limit per float was over.

In the days after Fletcher returned from Whole, they'd learned from Muriel that Nimsy had actually hired Von Piddle before any of this had transpired. She told him she had been secretly hired by the Peruvian government to locate a lost temple located in the Quechuan Valley. It was Tomhegan's idea, and it had worked diabolically well. Von Piddle had unwittingly contributed to Tomhegan's devilish plan by successfully locating the lost temple. And as a trusted professional, he kept his word to the "Peruvian government" that he would keep the find confidential. Just like many others, he'd been used.

Once Muriel had recovered at home, she and Von Piddle were spirited back to the Quechuan Valley, where they both *discovered* the lost temple. Within weeks, they were international celebrities, appearing on talk shows and gracing magazine covers around the globe. The official story was that Nimsy Cortland had become lost in the vast jungles of South America, never to be found. To maintain the ruse, Muriel begrudgingly agreed to give Nimsy's eulogy at the packed memorial service, and everyone in town mourned her loss.

Fletcher immediately gave Uncle Woodrow the coronavirus vaccine ingredients when he returned from Whole. That day, Woodrow quickly shared it with Adam Blanton, chief scientist at Jewell Island labs in Portland. Blanton was a close confidant of both Woodrow and Alek and promised not to share with anyone where it came from even though he was awestruck and totally confused. For the sake of the world, he left the many questions unanswered. The vaccine quickly passed all three stages of the trials without a hitch and was immediately put into production. Blanton was now a worldwide celebrity. Within two months, it was shared with the entire world and the horrific 2020 pandemic was over.

"I'm really excited about Sixth Day Foods, Dad," said Fletcher, watching Refinna shouting at another judge.

"Organically grown and local foods are the way to go. They'll totally compliment Fifth Ward's other line of healthy foods."

Fletcher sat up when he caught sight of Squire Susup dressed in his annual Mollyockett Day tuxedo. He lifted his stovepipe hat in greeting. Beside him, Onion was drinking from a small bowl of water. Susup bent over and said something to Onion before heading toward them. Beside them stood a girl with long dark hair. She was petting a totally black cat in her arms.

They both wondered who she was.

Aldous smiled as he saw the squire approach.

"It's good to see you, Aldous," Susup said, shaking his hand. He turned to Fletcher. "Fantastic job last year. Everyone is still talking about it. You ready for next week?"

"I am. I've been studying *Whole Abounds* and Vilcanota's patera for the past two weeks.

" Pardon me and sorry for being so rude. I'd like you both to meet Lalia and her cat, Humeante." Squire Susup took off his hat and wiped his forehead. "You'll be seeing more of them in the very near future, Fletch."

Lalia nodded at Fletcher and Aldous. "Very nice to meet you both. I've heard so much."

Is she from Whole? Fletcher wondered.

"Very nice to meet you Lalia. Your cat is beautiful," said Aldous.

"Mollyockett's looking forward to receiving that pipe you found in the southern temple. Don't forget to pack it." Susup looked glowingly at Fletcher.

Fletcher nodded. It felt like years ago when he'd picked it up in the Quechuan temple.

"Do you think Tomhegan is … gone for good?" Fletcher asked.

Susup's expression was thoughtful. "Considering how you used the patera, I don't think you need to worry about him anymore. But Nimsy's relatives are another matter."

Aldous stiffened. "What do you mean?"

"Haven't you seen the Snow family float?" he asked with surprise.

"No, we were busy with our own."

Just then Fletcher heard his grandmother shout his name. He turned and saw Lucille and three of her friends strutting toward them. Lucille was dressed as an elongated blue iron tablet, and her friends were various vitamins.

Lucille stopped abruptly when she saw the squire. "You again. Seems like this is getting to be a yearly habit."

Aldous and Fletcher chuckled as Susup took off his top hat and bowed. Lucille gave the young girl and her cat a quick look-over before returning her attention to Susup. His greeting was interrupted by the judge's announcement blaring from the loudspeakers.

"And in first place … the Snow Family from Snow Falls with their float, 'The Magical World of Whole.' "

The huge gathering cheered as Fletcher and Aldous stared in stunned silence at the float, which featured swarms of handcrafted fireflies, a waterfall, and a line of fluffy clouds watering rows of small fruit trees.

"I think," Susup said quietly, "this is their way of showing you that *they* know what actually happened to Nimsy. Tomhegan might be gone, but his spirit lives on in the Snows, and their thirst for revenge has only gotten stronger."

Chesley Snow, who they now knew was Nimsy's grandfather, raised the first-place trophy in triumph. Then he turned and looked directly at Fletcher and Aldous with eyes full of revenge.

Fletcher stared back, unblinking and unconcerned. After all, he had Mollyockett and the power of *Whole Abounds* on his side, and that was an unbeatable combination.

Fletcher closed his eyes and smiled. Both of his parents were back, the tragic pandemic was over, his three aunts were no longer part of Cygnus, and he now had the power of the passage. Life was good.

ABOUT THE BOOK

THIS BOOK IS ONE OF MAGIC. IN 2015, GARY SAVAGE STARTED VOLUN-teering weekly as Resident Author at Farwell Elementary School in Lewiston, Maine as part of the library's new Author Studies Program. The central topic of the weekly elective for grades third through sixth was his book *Fletcher McKenzie and the Passage to Whole*. Roughly eighty students participated every Thursday. In addition to reading the book as a class, participants competed in essay writing, skits and plays involving characters in the book, artwork competition based on characters and locations central to the book's theme, field trips, and a year-end presentation during an all-school assembly with parents and press invited. Every year, four students were selected to win the prestigious Barbara Bush Author Studies Award for excellence in the program. In 2018 and 2019, United States Senator Susan Collins announced the winners of this award in front of an all-school assembly as well as hundreds of

onlookers. Throughout the year, dozens of residents and local business leaders volunteered to judge the competitions and mentor students for the popular program.

In 2018, as part of the year-end competition, sixteen small groups of students vied for L.L. Bean certificates by creating a major character for *Fletcher McKenzie and the Curse of Snow Falls*, the book's sequel. As a result, Lalia and her cat, Humeante, were born. You'll find a brief appearance of both in this very book. In the sequel, they become pivotal characters in the quest to protect Whole and the McKenzie family. Both books have been published at the same time.

In the photo above, the students are traveling throughout Western Maine as they retrace the lives of nonfictional characters and locations that are an important part of both books. Characters and locations that include: Mollyockett, Hannibal Hamlin's residence and museum (Abraham Lincoln's first Vice President), Snow Falls, Mollyockett's grave in Andover, Maine and the Bethel Historical Society.

Unfortunately, everything changed in March of 2020. As a result of the Covid19 pandemic, the school was forced to close and all classes went virtual. The year-end competition and annual field trip were cancelled as well as all weekly meetings in the school's library.

Fortunately, after short deliberation, Kathy Martin, the school's popular librarian, turned on a dime and made the decision to continue Author Studies through Zoom meetings with a few volunteers. The Students were thrilled.

The original manuscript for *Fletcher McKenzie and the Passage to Whole*, which was first published in 2016, became the new assignment for the many students who continued to participate during the school's closure. The task was to convert the original manuscript into the year 2020 and make the Covid19 pandemic a central theme in the book. Manuscript changes were made simultaneously with *Fletcher McKenzie and the Curse of Snow Falls*.

Each week, students were assigned two chapters in the book and vied for L.L. Bean gift certificates and monetary awards by rewriting entire sections of the manuscript with Covid19 and the pandemic in mind. Quite often, they incorporated their own experiences in their writings.

It was a gargantuan task and took seven months to ready the re-edited manuscripts for both books for the publisher, BookBaby. While imperfect, this student-inspired book, *Fletcher McKenzie and the Passage to Whole,* is a journey throughout Maine and the wildly fantastic world of Whole. These major edits, written by elementary school students, gives readers exactly what they crave — excitement, vividly funny characters, healthy eating, proper nutrition, Covid19 fatigue and exhaustion, nonfictional historical lessons, magical journeys, confusing and strange ventures, deadly danger, and closure.

Everyone will be thrilled when that day comes when they can rejoin each other as a group in the school's library.

We all hope you enjoyed this special book.

Gary Savage is the author of several health and fitness books. He is a graduate of Dean College and Boston College. He holds a doctorate from Suffolk University. In 2019, Gary was voted *Best Artist* in Portland. He resides in Portland, Maine. This book was first published in 2016.

Kathy Martin, Librarian. Ms. Martin has worked as the Librarian at Farwell Elementary School for over fifteen years. She, with the assistance of Gary Savage, has lead the Author Study Program since 2015. At Farwell, Ms. Martin is well-known for her wacky story-telling, silly voices, and fun-filled library. Most students consider the library program their favorite subject. She is very proud of every student who has participated in the Author Study Program and is elated with the lessons and experiences they are gaining as they participate with Gary Savage every week. She is an avid reader and definitely the captain of our ship.

Carol A. "Grammie" Christopoulos, lead volunteer and mentor. Carol is a retired elementary school teacher. In June, 2013, she joined the Senior Corps "Penquis Foster Grandparent Program," and became a volunteer at Farwell Elemetary School. During her time as a volunteer, she met Gary Savage and has been a vital part of the Author Studies Program. She is thrilled by the growth she has witnessed with every student in the program. Grammie has added recipes for food dishes found in *Fletcher McKenzie and the Passage to Whole* at the end of this book.

Hailey Labrecque is an eleven-year old sixth grade student at Farwell Elementary. She has been working with Gary Savage as part of the Author Study Program for two years. She enjoys reading his books and being involved in the creation of a new manuscript. She is a past recipient of the Barbara Bush Scholarship Award and has put her heart and soul into this competition. She is an avid soccer player and downhill skier.

Liam Martin is in the 5th grade at Farwell Elementary School. He has been an active participant in the Author Study Program for three years. He has designed a unique *Fletcher McKenzie* treasure map, created a new character for the book, edited numerous chapters, and participated in all writing assignments. He was selected as a recipient of the prestigious Barbara Bush Scholarship Award last year. He enjoys Author Studies, sports and video games.

Alex Breton is a typical active kid from Maine. He enjoys school, movies, video games, and playing with his friends. Alex has always been drawn to reading and writing, making him a perfect fit for the Author Studies Progam. Working on this book has been a particular pleasure for Alex and a wonderful opportunity. His dream is to write a novel of his own.

Before graduating in 2020 from Farwell Elementay, Ella was a dedicated member of the Author Studies Program for three years. She loved having the opportunity to participate in this program. She has read *Fletcher McKenzie and the Passage to Whole* many times which has enabled her make numerous alterations to the new manuscript. Ella and her group took first place in the end of year competition with their Mollyockett and Hannibal Hamlin presentation. She has set high goals and expectations for herself. She will forever cherish the memories and opportunities the program has provided her.

Jack Caron is an eleven-year-old sixth grader. He has two dogs and a seven-year-old brother at Farwell Elementary. Jack is very active. His loves sports, hockey, hiking, and downhill skiing. Jack has been participating in Author Study for three years and believes it has played a huge part in his success at school. The Author Study Program has taught him to listen, pay attention to his fellow peers, work hard, and put in the effort to succeed in life. He his excited about the future of Author Study at Farwell.

Charlotte Crowley is in the sixth grade and a veteran of the Author Studies Program. She has been a leader in group projects for three years. With her hard work and dedicated participation, she has won numerous awards and certificates. Outside of Author Study, Charlotte's interests are well-rounded. She loves skateboarding, biking, lacrosse, playing video games, and hanging out with her friends.

Lily Beaulieu is twelve years old and loves Maine. She has an older sister and a cat named Gizmo. She enjoys playing soccer, basketball, and camping with family and friends. Her favorite places are Acadia National Park, Baxter State Park, Pennsylvania, and cruising in the Caribbean. She fondly remembers hiking Mount Katahdin with her family in 2019. She has been participating in Author Study for four years and has won many drawing contests in the program. She has stood out in the program as someone who always asks thoughtful questions. Lily is so thankful for the Author Study opportunity because "it has been so wonderful and lots of fun."

GRAN'S RECIPES

Apple Pie

Pastry for two crust pie

1¾ cups flour
½ teaspoon salt
⅓ cup canola oil
2 Tablespoons cold water

Combine flour and salt in a bowl. Blend in oil thoroughly with a fork.

Sprinkle all the water over mixture and mix very well.

Press dough firmly into a ball. If too dry, add 1 or 2 Tablespoons more oil.

8 cups of apples
¾ cup granulated sugar
¼ cup light brown sugar
¼ teaspoon salt
¼ teaspoon nutmeg
½ teaspoon cinnamon
1 tablespoon butter

Pare washed apples, core and slice thin. Lay slices on bottom pastry to make a layer. Turn rest of apples into pastry so you have a well-filled pie.

Sprinkle white sugar over apples, then light brown sugar. Next sprinkle nutmeg, cinnamon and salt over sugar. Dot top of filling with butter pieces.

Lay top pastry over filling. Bring edge of lower pastry up over top edge and fold together. Flute edge.

Bake at 425 degrees for about 40 minutes.

Reduce heat to 325 degrees, 20 minutes longer.

Bakewell Biscuits

4 cups flour
4 teaspoons Bakewell Cream
2 teaspoons baking soda
1 teaspoon salt
½ cup shortening
1½ cups milk (I use 2 cups milk for fluffier biscuits.)

Mix first 4 ingredients.

Add shortening and cut in, using pastry blender or 2 knives. Add milk all at once, stir quickly using a fork to make a soft dough.

Turn onto a floured board, knead 5 or 6 times. Roll out ½ inch or more thick.

Cut with biscuit cutter, place on ungreased cookie sheet.

Bake at 475 degrees for 5 minutes turn off heat and continue to bake on stored heat until golden brown.

If you prefer, bake at 450 degrees for 12 to 15 minutes.

Blueberry Pancakes

2½ cups flour
6 teaspoons baking powder
2 Tablespoons sugar
1 teaspoon salt
2 beaten eggs
2 cups milk
4 Tablespoons canola oil
Combine dry ingredients.

Combine egg, milk, canola oil. Add to dry ingredients and stir just until moistened. Mixture will be lumpy.

Add as many Maine Blueberries as you think you would like, preferably low bush berries.

Cook on greased heated skillet.

Casco Bay Clam Cakes

2 stacks of Saltine Crackers
2 cans of Snow's chopped clams (6 ounce cans)
½ sweet onion or Vadalia onion
2 teaspoon grated horseradish
2 Tablespoons Old Bay seasoning
1 Tablespoon Italian seasoning
1 teaspoon paprika
1 teaspoon each of salt and pepper
4 large eggs (divided)
1 cup Panko bread crumbs
Olive oil for pan frying

Crush the Saltines into very fine pieces.

Add the Old Bay seasoning, salt, pepper, Italian seasoning, and paprika. Set aside.

Finely mince the onion.

Beat 2 of the 4 eggs. Add the onion and the 2 eggs to the Panko bread crumbs.

Open the clams, do not drain completely. Keep a little of the juice to make the mixture more moist. Add the horseradish to the clams and mix and finely chop.

Add about 1 inch of olive oil to a Dutch oven or deep cast iron frying pan. Heat oil to no more that 350 degrees, which takes about 3 minutes.

While the oil is heating combine all of the ingredients plus the 2 remaining eggs.

Form into 4-inch patties then press into some dry Panko crumbs on both sides. Place in oil and cook on each side for about 3 minutes. Remove from oil and place on paper towel lined plate. Pat off excess oil.

Serve with your favorite Tartar sauce.

Rhubarb Blueberry Jam

1½ pounds of fresh chopped rhubarb
1 pound of fresh Maine blueberries (low bush)
3¼ cups baker's sugar
2 teaspoons grated orange zest
⅓ cup orange juice
½ cup water

In a sauce pan, combine the rhubarb, blueberries, sugar, orange zest, orange juice, and water.

Bring to a boil and then cook over a medium-low heat for 45 minutes, stirring occasionally or until thick. It will thicken more as it cools.

Ladle into hot sterile jars and seal with lids and rings.

Store in refrigerator.

Ironed Grilled Cheese Sandwich

Make a cheese sandwich. Do not butter the outside. Wrap a piece of aluminum foil around the sandwich, using one thickness of foil; do not overlap the foil.

Using the highest heat on your iron, iron your sandwich. Keep checking under the foil to see if the bread is toasted brown.

Turn over the sandwich and iron the other side. The cheese melts and you have an ironed grilled cheese sandwich.

This is great if you live in a dorm and cannot have a stove or hot plate.

Cornbread

1½ cups flour
1 cup stone-ground cornmeal
¼ cup granulated sugar
2 teaspoons baking powder
1 teaspoon salt
3 Tablespoons unsalted butter, melted and cooled
2 large eggs
2 Tablespoons olive oil
1½ cups whole milk

Preheat oven to 425 degrees.

Grease a 9" square baking pan with extra butter.

Whisk together the flour, cornmeal, sugar, baking powder, and salt. Set aside.

In a smaller bowl, whisk together the butter, eggs, olive oil and milk. Pour over dry ingredients and fold together until just combined. It is important to not overmix.

Pour the batter into prepared pan and bake until the top is lightly golden brown.(25-30 minutes) When you insert a toothpick into the center, it should come out clean.

Transfer to a wire rack to cool.

Corn Chowder

6 strips of thick cut bacon, diced
5 medium potatoes, peeled and cubed
1 medium sweet onion, chopped
1 Tablespoon minced garlic
1 teaspoon garlic powder
3 cups low sodium chicken broth (I use sodium-free
chicken broth)
2 cans cream-style corn
2 cans whole kernel corn (drain only one can)
2 teaspoons salt
Ground black pepper to taste
3 cups half-and-half (some people prefer evaporated milk)
4 Tablespoons butter
¼ teaspoon red pepper flakes (optional)

Place bacon in a large pot over medium heat and cook until crisp. Drain and crumble.

Reserve all of the drippings in the pot making sure all of the bacon is removed.

Mix potatoes, minced garlic and onion into the pot with bacon drippings. Cook and stir 5 minutes. Pour in the chicken stock. Season with salt and pepper and garlic powder.

Bring to a boil, reduce heat to low, and cover pot. Simmer 20 minutes stirring often until potatoes are tender. Stir in both kinds of corn.

Add optional spice, if using.

Slowly add the half-and-half (or evaporated milk), crumbled bacon and butter, and mix into the chowder just before serving.

This chowder goes well with the cornbread or biscuits.

Lobster Mac and Cheese

1 stick butter
¼ cup minced onion
½ cup chopped green pepper
1 teaspoon salt
¼ teaspoon pepper
¼ teaspoon dry mustard
¼ teaspoon oregano
One 8-ounce package of elbow macaroni
2 cups water
1 Tablespoon flour
One 13-ounce can evaporated milk
2 Tablespoons chopped pimiento
2 cups cheddar cheese, finely chopped
1 pound lobster meat (more if you prefer)

Melt butter in electric frying pan or skillet on stove. Add onion and green pepper; cook until tender, using low heat.

Stir in salt, pepper, mustard and oregano. Add macaroni and water, turn up heat.

Bring to a boil and stir so it is well mixed. Cover and simmer in electric frying pan at 220 degrees or on low heat in skillet on top of stove. Check to see that macaroni is cooked the way you like it before you add the rest of the ingredients.

Sprinkle flour over all, blend well. Stir in evaporated milk. Cook another 5 minutes on low heat.

Add pimiento and cut-up cheese; heat, stirring once in a while until the cheese has melted.

Add Lobster meat at end and heat for an additional 5 minutes.

Lobster Omelet

3 eggs
3 teaspoons water
¼ teaspoon salt
1 Tablespoon butter
2 asparagus spears diced (precooked)
Shredded cheddar cheese
Shake of onion powder
Cooked lobster meat to taste

Mix eggs water and salt with a fork until whites and yolks are blended.

Heat butter in a pan or heavy skillet (preferably one with low sloping sides). When pan is hot enough to sizzle a drop of water, it is ready.

Pour egg mixture into pan; it should start to bubble and cook at the edges. With a pancake turner move the egg away from the edges and swirl in pan until eggs reach exposed spaces of the pan.

When the mixture no longer flows and is moist and creamy on top, add the fillings (cheese, asparagus, a sprinkle of onion powder and the lobster meat) to one side of the egg in the pan. Holding the handle of the pan and using the turner, flip the other side of the omelet over the fillings. When heated through, remove from pan and enjoy.

Maine Maple Honey Nut Bars

2 cups flour
1 cup sugar
1 teaspoon baking soda
1 teaspoon cinnamon
¾ cup canola oil
¼ cup honey
1 large egg
1 cup walnuts, chopped
Glaze
1 cup confectioners sugar
1 Tablespoon warm water
3 Tablespoons Maine maple syrup

Preheat oven to 350 degrees.

Mix first 4 ingredients. Stir in canola oil, honey and slightly beaten egg. Add nuts and blend in.

Pour batter into an ungreased 9 by 13 pan. Bake 20-22 minutes or until an inserted toothpick comes out clean.

In small bowl mix the confectioners sugar, water and Maine Maple syrup. Spread on bars while they are still warm.

Mazingla #1

Leftover chicken breast, diced
Leftover broccoli
Leftover cauliflower
2 cans of cream of chicken soup

Enough water to make it gravy consistency.

Cook it all in one pan.

Serve over cooked brown rice.

Mazingla #2

Leftover ground beef
Leftover carrots
Leftover peas
Leftover green beans
½ diced onion

Saute all of the above in butter. Add a premade beef gravy.

Serve over mashed potatoes.

Mazingla #3

Leftover pork tenderloin
Leftover peas
Leftover carrots
Szechuan sauce
Soy sauce

Spray pan with Pam, heat all of the above in pan and add a premade brown gravy.

Serve over cooked white rice.

New England Oatcakes

3 cups quick-cooking oatmeal
3 cups flour
1 cup sugar
1 pound shortening
¼ teaspoon salt
¼ to ½ cup cold water

Mix flour and oatmeal together, add salt and sugar, mix well. Cut in shortening using a pastry blender. Add water, mixing with a fork. If you prefer, use your hands to mix.

Roll out to desired thickness, about ¼ inch thick. Cut in any shape

Place cut outs on ungreased cookie sheet. Bake at 375 degrees for as long as necessary or about 20 to 25 minutes. These are not sweet cakes.

Pumpkin Bread

4 eggs
⅔ cups water
1 cup canola oil
1 can pumpkin
3⅓ cups flour
3 cups granulated sugar
2 teaspoons baking soda
1½ teaspoons salt
1 teaspoon cinnamon
1 teaspoon nutmeg

Using a wire whisk and a medium sized bowl, combine all of the wet ingredients (the first four listed). Mix thoroughly.

In a large bowl combine all of the remaining ingredients. Mix thoroughly.

Pour wet ingredients into center of dry ingredients and blend thoroughly with a wire whisk.

Turn into 3 well-oiled loaf pans. Bake at 350 degrees for 1 hour. Remove pans from oven, set on rack so that bread may cool in tins. Remove, wrap in foil and store.

I have never made this using 3 loaf tins. I always use miniature pans and bake for 30 minutes. It usually makes 16 mini loaves (depending on size of pans) and 12 mini muffins. Muffins need less time to bake. Always check your oven while baking.

Spiced Gingerbread Loaf

2 cups flour
1 teaspoon baking soda
1½ teaspoons ground ginger
1½ ground cinnamon
¼ teaspoon salt
⅛ teaspoon fresh ground pepper
¾ cup dark molasses
¾ cup hot water
½ cup unsalted butter, softened to room temperature
⅓ cup packed light or dark brown sugar
1 large egg, room temperature
1 teaspoon pure vanilla extract

Adjust the oven rack to the lower third position and preheat oven to 350 degrees. Grease a 9 by 5 loaf pan. Set aside.

In a medium bowl whisk the first six listed ingredients together until combined. In a separate bowl whisk the molasses and hot water together.

In a large bowl using an electric mixer beat the butter on high until smooth and creamy, add the brown sugar and beat on high until creamy. Always scrape the sides and bottom of bowl so that all ingredients are mixed.

On medium-high, beat in the egg and vanilla extract until combined. Again, scraping sides and bottom of bowl.

With the mixer on low speed, add the dry ingredients in three additions alternating with the hot molasses mixture until incorporated. Avoid over mixing. Batter will be thin. Whisk out any big lumps.

Pour batter into prepared pan. Bake for around 50-60 minutes or until it is baked through. All ovens are different so check throughout baking process. Check for doneness with toothpick inserted in center of loaf. Allow to cool completely before removing from pan.

Orange Icing

1 cup confectioners sugar
2-3 Tablespoons orange juice

Combine until smooth and pour over loaf.

Vegetable Casserole

6 or 8 large carrots
2 packages frozen cut string beans
2 Tablespoons butter
2 Tablespoons flour
Salt
Pepper
1 can cream of mushroom soup
1 cup medium white sauce
Grated parmesan cheese

Pare carrots. Slice thin. Cook in small amount of water until tender.

Cook frozen string beans by directions on package.

Make 1 cup of medium white sauce using 2 tablespoons butter, 2 tablespoons of flour, salt and pepper. Melt butter, add flour and seasoning.

Add milk slowly and cook over low heat until thickened. Mix with 1 can of cream of mushroom soup. If needed, add a little milk to make a creamy consistency. Taste for seasoning.

Place drained carrots and string beans in a shallow baking dish and combine.

Pour cream sauce over vegetables. Stir gently with a fork to blend. Sprinkle top with grated parmesan cheese.

Bake 30 minutes at 350 degrees.

Venison Pie

1½ pounds venison
2 onions
2 garlic cloves
3 Tablespoons of canola oil
2 Tablespoons flour
1 bay leaf
½ pound button mushrooms
1 pound frozen puff pastry dough
1 egg yolk
Grease for baking dish
Rinse the meat, pat dry and chop.
Peel onions and garlic and finely chop.

Heat the oil in a Dutch oven and sear the meat over high heat in portions. Add the onions and garlic and season with salt and pepper. Sprinkle over the meat and stir while sauteing. Then pour 1 cup of water over mixture, add bay leaf, cover and cook over low heat for 1 hour.

Trim mushrooms, cut into slices and add to the pot 5 minutes before end of cooking.

Grease a 9-inch pie dish.

Place thawed pastry sheets on top of each other so you have two sets to roll out. Cut one set into a 9-inch circle for the bottom of baking dish. Pour the meat mixture into lined pie dish. Cut the second so that it will cover the filling and form an edge for the pie. Cut a hole in the middle of top crust to allow steam to escape. Brush the surface with beaten egg yolk and bake in preheated oven at 350 degrees for about 40 minutes, until golden brown. Remove and serve immediately.

Whoopie Pies

Cookie

½ cup shortening (Crisco)
1 cup sugar
2 egg yolks
1 cup milk
5 Tablespoons cocoa
1 teaspoon baking soda
½ teaspoon salt
1 teaspoon baking powder
2 cups flour
1 teaspoon vanilla

Cream shortening and sugar. Add egg yolks, milk and vanilla. Combine cocoa, baking soda, salt, baking powder and flour. Add wet ingredients to dry ingredients and mix well.

Drop by spoonfuls onto ungreased cookie sheet.

Bake at 375 degrees for 12-13 minutes. Since all ovens are different. check before done time.

Filling

½ cup shortening (Crisco)
1 teaspoon vanilla
2 cups confectioners sugar
2 egg whites

Beat and fill cooled cookies

It's a lot easier to just buy a "Wicked Whoopie".